W9-BHX-719

MAGNUS CHASE

and the GODS of ASGARD

III

THE SHIP OF THE DEAD

Also by Rick Riordan

RICK RIORDAN

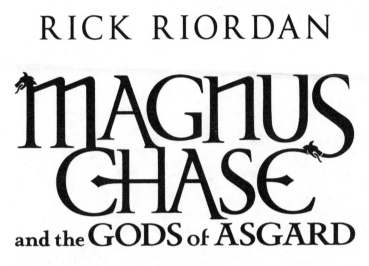

MAGNUS CHASE
and the GODS of ASGARD

III

THE SHIP OF THE DEAD

Disney • HYPERION

Los Angeles   New York

Copyright © 2017 by Rick Riordan

All rights reserved. Published by Disney • Hyperion, an imprint of
Disney Book Group. No part of this book may be reproduced or transmitted
in any form or by any means, electronic or mechanical, including
photocopying, recording, or by any information storage and retrieval system,
without written permission from the publisher. For information address
Disney • Hyperion, 125 West End Avenue, New York, New York 10023.

First Edition, October 2017
1 3 5 7 9 10 8 6 4 2

FAC-020093-17249

Printed in the United States of America

This book is set in Adobe Caslon Pro, Goudy Trajan Pro Medium,
New Baskerville, Gauthier FY Regular/Fontspring; Janson Text LT Pro,
Zapf Chancery Pro, Zapf Dingbat Std, Sabon LT Pro Roman/Monotype
Designed by SJI Associates, Inc.
Rune and symbol art by Michelle Gengaro-Kokmen

Library of Congress Cataloging in Publication Control Number: 2017029354
ISBN 978-1-4231-6093-9

Reinforced binding

Visit www.DisneyBooks.com

SUSTAINABLE FORESTRY INITIATIVE   Certified Sourcing
www.sfiprogram.org
SFI-00993

THIS LABEL APPLIES TO TEXT STOCK

To Philip José Farmer,
whose Riverworld books kick-started my love of history

CONTENTS

MAGNUS CHASE

and the GODS of ASGARD

III

THE SHIP OF THE DEAD

ONE

Percy Jackson Does His Level Best to Kill Me

"TRY IT AGAIN," Percy told me. "This time with less dying."

Standing on the yardarm of the USS *Constitution*, looking down at Boston Harbor two hundred feet below, I wished I had the natural defenses of a turkey buzzard. Then I could projectile vomit on Percy Jackson and make him go away.

The last time he'd made me try this jump, only an hour before, I'd broken every bone in my body. My friend Alex Fierro had rushed me back to the Hotel Valhalla just in time for me to die in my own bed.

Unfortunately, I was an *einherji*, one of Odin's immortal warriors. I couldn't die permanently as long as I expired within the boundaries of Valhalla. Thirty minutes later, I woke up as good as new. Now here I was again, ready for more pain. Hooray!

"Is this strictly necessary?" I asked.

Percy leaned against the rigging, the wind rippling little waves through his black hair.

He looked like a normal guy—orange T-shirt, jeans, battered white leather Reeboks. If you saw him walking down the street, you wouldn't think, *Hey, look, a demigod son of Poseidon! Praise the Olympians!* He didn't have gills or webbed fingers, though his eyes were sea green—about the same shade I imagined my face was just then. The only strange thing about Jackson was the tattoo on the inside of his forearm—a trident as dark as seared wood, with a single line underneath and the letters SPQR.

He'd told me the letters stood for *Sono Pazzi Quelli Romani*— *those Romans are crazy.* I wasn't sure if he was kidding.

"Look, Magnus," he told me. "You'll be sailing across hostile territory. A bunch of sea monsters and sea gods and who-knows-what-else will be trying to kill you, right?"

"Yeah, I suppose."

By which I meant: *Please don't remind me. Please leave me alone.*

"At some point," said Percy, "you're going to get thrown off the boat, maybe from as high up as this. You'll need to know how to survive the impact, avoid drowning, and get back to the surface ready to fight. That's going to be tough, especially in cold water."

I knew he was right. From what my cousin Annabeth had told me, Percy had been through even more dangerous adventures than I had. (And I lived in Valhalla. I died at least once a day.) As much as I appreciated him coming up from New York to offer me heroic aquatic-survival tips, though, I was getting tired of failing.

Yesterday, I'd gotten chomped by a great white shark, strangled by a giant squid, and stung by a thousand irate moon jellies. I'd swallowed several gallons of seawater trying to hold my breath, and learned that I was no better at hand-to-hand combat thirty feet down than I was on dry land.

This morning, Percy had walked me around Old Ironsides,

trying to teach me the basics of sailing and navigation, but I still couldn't tell the mizzenmast from the poop deck.

Now here I was: a failure at falling off a pole.

I glanced down, where Annabeth and Alex Fierro were watching us from the deck.

"You got this, Magnus!" Annabeth cheered.

Alex Fierro gave me two thumbs up. At least I think that was the gesture. It was hard to be sure from this distance.

Percy took a deep breath. He'd been patient with me so far, but I could tell the stress of the weekend was starting to get to him, too. Whenever he looked at me, his left eye twitched.

"It's cool, man," he promised. "I'll demonstrate again, okay? Start in skydiver position, spread-eagle to slow your descent. Then, right before you hit the water, straighten like an arrow—head up, heels down, back straight, butt clenched. That last part is really important."

"Skydiver," I said. "Eagle. Arrow. Butt."

"Right," Percy said. "Watch me."

He jumped from the yardarm, falling toward the harbor in perfect spread-eagle form. At the last moment, he straightened, heels downward, and hit the water, disappearing with hardly a ripple. A moment later, he surfaced, his palms raised like *See? Nothing to it!*

Annabeth and Alex applauded.

"Okay, Magnus!" Alex called up to me. "Your turn! Be a man!"

I suppose that was meant to be funny. Most of the time, Alex identified as female, but today he was definitely male. Sometimes I slipped up and used the wrong pronouns for him/her, so Alex liked to return the favor by teasing me mercilessly. Because friendship.

Annabeth hollered, "You got this, cuz!"

Below me, the dark surface of the water glinted like a freshly scrubbed waffle iron, ready to squash me flat.

Right, I muttered to myself.

I jumped.

For half a second, I felt pretty confident. The wind whistled past my ears. I spread my arms and managed not to scream.

Okay, I thought. *I can do this.*

Which was when my sword, Jack, decided to fly up out of nowhere and start a conversation.

"Hey, *señor!*" His runes glowed along his double-edged blade. "Whatcha doing?"

I flailed, trying to turn vertical for impact. "Jack, not now!"

"Oh, I get it! You're falling! You know, one time Frey and I were falling—"

Before he could continue his fascinating story, I slammed into the water.

Just as Percy had warned, the cold stunned my system. I sank, momentarily paralyzed, the air knocked out of my lungs. My ankles throbbed like I'd bounced off a brick trampoline. But at least I wasn't dead.

I scanned for major injuries. When you're an einherji, you get pretty good at listening to your own pain. You can stagger around the battlefield in Valhalla, mortally wounded, gasping your last breath, and calmly think, *Oh, so that's what a crushed rib cage feels like. Interesting!*

This time I'd broken my left ankle for sure. The right one was only sprained.

Easy fix. I summoned the power of Frey.

Warmth like summer sunlight spread from my chest into my limbs. The pain subsided. I wasn't as good at healing myself as I was at healing others, but I felt my ankles beginning to mend—as if a swarm of friendly wasps were crawling around inside my flesh, mud-daubing the fractures, reknitting the ligaments.

Ah, better, I thought, as I floated through the cold darkness. *Now, there's something else I should be doing. . . . Oh, right. Breathing.*

Jack's hilt nudged against my hand like a dog looking for attention. I wrapped my fingers around his leather grip and he hauled me upward, launching me out of the harbor like a rocket-powered Lady of the Lake. I landed, gasping and shivering, on the deck of Old Ironsides next to my friends.

"Whoa." Percy stepped back. "That was different. You okay, Magnus?"

"Fine," I coughed out, sounding like a duck with a chest cold.

Percy eyed the glowing runes on my weapon. "Where'd the sword come from?"

"Hi, I'm Jack!" said Jack.

Annabeth stifled a yelp. "It talks?"

"It?" Jack demanded. "Hey, lady, some respect. I'm *Sumarbrander!* The Sword of Summer! The weapon of Frey! I've been around for thousands of years! Also, I'm a dude!"

Annabeth frowned. "Magnus, when you told me about your magic sword, did you perhaps fail to mention that it—that *he* can speak?"

"Did I?" Honestly I couldn't remember.

The past few weeks, Jack had been off on his own, doing whatever sentient magic swords did in their free time. Percy and I had been using standard-issue Hotel Valhalla practice blades for sparring. It hadn't occurred to me that Jack might fly in out of nowhere and introduce himself. Besides, the fact that Jack talked was the *least* weird thing about him. The fact that he could sing the entire cast recording of *Jersey Boys* from memory . . . *that* was weird.

Alex Fierro looked like he was trying not to laugh. He was wearing pink and green today, as usual, though I'd never seen this particular outfit before: lace-up leather boots, ultra-skinny rose jeans, an untucked lime dress shirt, and a checkered skinny tie as loose as a necklace. With his thick black Ray-Bans and his choppy green hair, he looked like he'd stepped off a New Wave album cover circa 1979.

"Be polite, Magnus," he said. "Introduce your friends to your sword."

"Uh, right," I said. "Jack, this is Percy and Annabeth. They're demigods—the Greek kind."

"Hmm." Jack didn't sound impressed. "I met Hercules once."

"Who hasn't?" Annabeth muttered.

"Fair point," Jack said. "But I suppose if you're friends of Magnus's . . ." He went completely still. His runes faded. Then he leaped out of my hand and flew toward Annabeth, his blade twitching as if he was sniffing the air. "Where is she? Where are you hiding the babe?"

Annabeth backed toward the rail. "Whoa, there, sword. Personal space!"

"Jack, behave," Alex said. "What are you doing?"

"She's around here somewhere," Jack insisted. He flew to Percy. "Aha! What's in your pocket, sea boy?"

"Excuse me?" Percy looked a bit nervous about the magical sword hovering at his waistline.

Alex lowered his Ray-Bans. "Okay, now I'm curious. What *do* you have in your pocket, Percy? Inquiring swords want to know."

Percy pulled a plain-looking ballpoint pen from his jeans. "You mean this?"

"BAM!" Jack said. "Who is this vision of loveliness?"

"Jack," I said. "It's a pen."

"No, it's not! Show me! Show me!"

"Uh . . . sure." Percy uncapped the pen.

Immediately it transformed into a three-foot-long sword with a leaf-shaped blade of glowing bronze. Compared to Jack, the weapon looked delicate, almost petite, but from the way Percy wielded it, I had no doubt he'd be able to hold his own on the battlefields of Valhalla with that thing.

Jack turned his point toward me, his runes flashing burgundy. "See, Magnus? I *told* you it wasn't stupid to carry a sword disguised as a pen!"

"Jack, I never said that!" I protested. "*You* did."

Percy raised an eyebrow. "What are you two talking about?"

"Nothing," I said hastily. "So I guess this is the famous Riptide? Annabeth told me about it."

"*Her,*" Jack corrected.

Annabeth frowned. "Percy's sword is a she?"

Jack laughed. "Well, *duh.*"

Percy studied Riptide, though I could've told him from experience it was almost impossible to tell a sword's gender by looking at it.

"I don't know," he said. "Are you sure—?"

"Percy," said Alex. "Respect the gender."

"Okay, fine," he said. "It's just kinda strange that I never knew."

"On the other hand," Annabeth said, "you didn't know the pen could *write* until last year."

"That's low, Wise Girl."

"Anyway!" Jack interrupted. "The important thing is Riptide's here now, she's beautiful, and she's met me! Maybe the two of us can . . . you know . . . have some private time to talk about, er, sword stuff?"

Alex smirked. "That sounds like a wonderful idea. How about we let the swords get to know each other while the rest of us have lunch? Magnus, do you think you can handle eating falafel without choking?"

TWO

Falafel Sandwiches with a Side Order of Ragnarok

WE ATE ON the aft spar deck. (Look at me with the nautical terms.)

After a hard morning of failing, I felt like I'd really earned my deep-fried chickpea patties and pita bread, my yogurt and chilled cucumber slices, and my side order of extra-spicy lamb kebabs. Annabeth had arranged our picnic lunch. She knew me too well.

My clothes dried quickly in the sunlight. The warm breeze felt good on my face. Sailboats traced their way across the harbor while airplanes cut across the blue sky, heading out from Logan Airport to New York or California or Europe. The whole city of Boston seemed charged with impatient energy, like a classroom at 2:59 P.M., waiting for the dismissal bell, everybody ready to get out of town for the summer and enjoy the good weather.

Me, all I wanted to do was stay put.

Riptide and Jack stood propped nearby in a coil of rope, their hilts leaning against the gunnery rail. Riptide acted like your typical inanimate object, but Jack kept inching closer, chatting her up, his blade glowing the same dark bronze as hers. Fortunately, Jack was used to holding one-sided conversations. He joked. He flattered. He name-dropped like a maniac. "You know, *Thor* and *Odin* and I were at this tavern one time . . ."

If Riptide was impressed, she didn't show it.

Percy wadded up his falafel wrapper. Along with being a water-breather, the dude also had the ability to inhale food.

"So," he said, "when do you guys sail out?"

Alex raised an eyebrow at me like *Yeah, Magnus. When do we sail out?*

I'd been trying to avoid this topic with Fierro for the past two weeks, without much luck.

"Soon," I said. "We don't exactly know where we're headed, or how long it'll take to get there—"

"Story of my life," said Percy.

"—but we have to find Loki's big nasty ship of death before it sails at Midsummer. It's docked somewhere along the border between Niflheim and Jotunheim. We're estimating it'll take a couple of weeks to sail that distance."

"Which means," Alex said, "we really should've left already. We definitely have to sail by the end of the week, ready or not."

In his dark lenses, I saw the reflection of my own worried face. We both knew we were as far from *ready* as we were from Niflheim.

Annabeth tucked her feet underneath her. Her long blond hair was tied back in a ponytail. Her dark blue T-shirt was emblazoned with the yellow words COLLEGE OF ENVIRONMENTAL DESIGN, UC BERKELEY.

"Heroes never get to be ready, do we?" she said. "We just do the best we can."

Percy nodded. "Yep. Usually it works out. We haven't died yet."

"Though you keep *trying*." Annabeth elbowed him. Percy put his arm around her. She nestled comfortably against his side. He kissed the blond curls on the top of her head. This show of affection made my heart do a painful little twist.

I was glad to see my cousin so happy, but it reminded me how much was at stake if I failed to stop Loki.

Alex and I had already died. We would never age. We'd live in Valhalla until Doomsday came around (unless we got killed outside the hotel before that). The best life we could hope for was training for Ragnarok, postponing that inevitable battle as many centuries as possible, and then, one day, marching out of Valhalla with Odin's army and dying a glorious death while the Nine Worlds burned around us. Fun.

But Annabeth and Percy had a chance for a normal life. They'd already made it through high school, which Annabeth told me was the most dangerous time for Greek demigods. In the fall, they'd go off to college on the West Coast. If they made it through *that*, they had a decent chance of surviving adulthood. They could live in the mortal world without monsters attacking them every five minutes.

Unless my friends and I failed to stop Loki, in which case the world—*all* the worlds—would end in a few weeks. But, you know . . . no pressure.

I set down my pita sandwich. Even falafel could only do so much to lift my spirits.

"What about you guys?" I asked. "Straight back to New York today?"

"Yeah," Percy said. "I gotta babysit tonight. I'm psyched!"

"That's right," I remembered. "Your new baby sister."

Yet another important life hanging in the balance, I thought. But I managed a smile. "Congratulations, man. What's her name?"

"Estelle. It was my grandmother's name. Um, on my mom's side, obviously. Not Poseidon's."

"I approve," Alex said. "Old-fashioned and elegant. Estelle Jackson."

"Well, Estelle *Blofis,*" Percy corrected. "My stepdad is Paul Blofis. Not much I can do about that surname, but my little sis is awesome. Five fingers. Five toes. Two eyes. She drools a lot."

"Just like her brother," Annabeth said.

Alex laughed.

I could totally imagine Percy bouncing baby Estelle in his arms, singing "Under the Sea" from *The Little Mermaid.* That made me feel even more miserable.

Somehow I had to buy little Estelle enough decades to have a proper life. I had to find Loki's demonic ship full of zombie warriors, stop it from sailing off into battle and triggering Ragnarok, then recapture Loki and put him back in chains so he couldn't cause any more world-burning mischief. (Or at least not as *much* world-burning mischief.)

"Hey." Alex threw a piece of pita at me. "Stop looking so glum."

"Sorry." I tried to appear more cheerful. It wasn't as easy as mending my ankle by sheer force of will. "I'm looking forward to meeting Estelle someday, when we get back from our quest. And I appreciate you guys coming up to Boston. Really."

Percy glanced over at Jack, who was still chatting up Riptide. "Sorry I couldn't be more help. The sea is"—he shrugged—"kinda unpredictable."

Alex stretched his legs. "At least Magnus fell a lot better the second time. If worse comes to worst, I can always turn into a dolphin and save his sorry butt."

The corner of Percy's mouth twitched. "You can turn into a dolphin?"

"I'm a child of Loki. Want to see?"

"No, I believe you." Percy gazed into the distance. "I've got a friend named Frank who's a shape-shifter. He does dolphins. Also giant goldfish."

I shuddered, imagining Alex Fierro as a giant pink-and-green koi. "We'll make do. We've got a good team."

"That's important," Percy agreed. "Probably more important than having sea skills . . ." He straightened and furrowed his eyebrows.

Annabeth unfolded herself from his side. "Uh-oh. I know that look. You've got an idea."

"Something my dad told me . . ." Percy rose. He walked over to his sword, interrupting Jack in the middle of a fascinating tale about the time he'd embroidered a giant's bowling bag. Percy picked up Riptide and studied her blade.

"Hey, man," Jack complained. "We were just starting to hit it off."

"Sorry, Jack." From his pocket, Percy pulled out his pen cap and touched it to the tip of his sword. With a faint *shink*, Riptide shrank back into a ballpoint. "Poseidon and I had this conversation about weapons one time. He told me that all sea gods have one thing in common: they're really vain and possessive when it comes to their magic items."

Annabeth rolled her eyes. "That sounds like *every* god we've met."

"True," Percy said. "But sea gods even more so. Triton *sleeps* with his conch-shell trumpet. Galatea spends most of her time polishing her magic sea-horse saddle. And my dad is super-paranoid about losing his trident."

I thought about my one and only encounter with a Norse sea goddess. It hadn't gone well. Ran had promised to destroy me if I ever sailed into her waters again. But she *had* been obsessed with her magical nets and the junk collection that swirled inside them. Because of that, I'd been able to trick her into giving me my sword.

"You're saying I'll have to use their own stuff against them," I guessed.

"Right," Percy confirmed. "Also, what you said about having a good team—sometimes being the son of a sea god hasn't been enough to save me, even underwater. One time, my friend Jason and I got pulled to the bottom of the Mediterranean by this storm goddess, Kymopoleia? I was useless. Jason saved my butt by offering to make trading cards and action figures of her."

Alex almost choked on his falafel. *"What?"*

"The point is," Percy continued, "Jason knew nothing about the ocean. He saved me anyway. It was kind of embarrassing."

Annabeth smirked. "I guess so. I never heard the details about that."

Percy's ears turned as pink as Alex's jeans. "Anyway, maybe we've been looking at this all wrong. I've been trying to teach you sea skills. But the most important thing is to use whatever you've got on hand—your team, your wits, the enemy's own magical stuff."

"And there's no way to plan for that," I said.

"Exactly!" Percy said. "My work here is done!"

Annabeth frowned. "Percy, you're saying the best plan is no plan. As a child of Athena, I can't really endorse that."

"Yeah," Alex said. "And, personally, I still like *my* plan of turning into a sea mammal."

Percy raised his hands. "All I'm saying is the most powerful demigod of our generation is sitting right here, and it isn't me." He nodded to Annabeth. "Wise Girl can't shape-shift or breathe underwater or talk to pegasi. She can't fly, and she isn't superstrong. But she's *crazy* smart and good at improvising. That's what makes her deadly. Doesn't matter whether she's on land, in water, in the air, or in Tartarus. Magnus, you were training with me all weekend. I think you should've been training with Annabeth instead."

Annabeth's stormy gray eyes were hard to read. At last she said, "Okay, that was sweet." She kissed Percy on the cheek.

Alex nodded. "Not bad, Seaweed Brain."

"Don't you start with that nickname, too," Percy muttered.

From the wharf came the deep rumbling sound of warehouse doors rolling open. Voices echoed off the sides of the buildings.

"That's our cue to leave," I said. "This ship just got back from dry dock. They're reopening it to the public tonight in a big ceremony."

"Yeah," Alex said. "The glamour won't obscure our presence once the whole crew is aboard."

Percy arched an eyebrow. "Glamour? You mean like your outfit?"

Alex snorted. "No. Glamour as in illusion magic. It's the force that clouds the vision of regular mortals."

"Huh," Percy said. "We call that the Mist."

Annabeth rapped her knuckles on Percy's head. "Whatever we call it, we'd better hurry. Help me clean up."

We reached the bottom of the gangplank just as the first sailors were arriving. Jack floated along ahead of us, glowing different colors and singing "Walk Like a Man" in a terrible falsetto. Alex changed form from a cheetah to a wolf to a flamingo. (He does a great flamingo.)

The sailors gave us blank looks and a wide berth, but nobody challenged us.

Once we were clear of the docks, Jack turned into a runestone pendant. He dropped into my hand and I reattached him to the chain around my neck. It wasn't like him to shut up so suddenly. I figured he was miffed about his date with Riptide being cut short.

As we strolled down Constitution Road, Percy turned to me. "What was that back there—the shape-shifting, the singing sword? Were you *trying* to get caught?"

"Nah," I said. "If you flaunt the weird magical stuff, it confuses mortals even more." It felt good to be able to teach *him* something. "It kind of short-circuits mortal brains, makes them avoid you."

"Huh." Annabeth shook her head. "All these years sneaking around, and we could've just been ourselves?"

"You should *always* do that." Alex strolled alongside, back in human form, though he still had a few flamingo feathers stuck in his hair. "And you have to flaunt the weird, my friends."

"I'm going to quote you on that," Percy said.

"You'd better."

We stopped at the corner, where Percy's Toyota Prius was parked at a meter. I shook his hand and got a big hug from Annabeth.

My cousin gripped my shoulders. She studied my face, her gray eyes tight with concern. "Take care of yourself, Magnus. You *will* come back safely. That's an order."

"Yes, ma'am," I promised. "We Chases have to stick together."

"Speaking of that . . ." She lowered her voice. "Have you been over there yet?"

I felt like I was in free fall again, swan-diving toward a painful death.

"Not yet," I admitted. "Today. I promise."

The last I saw of Percy and Annabeth, their Prius was turning the corner on First Avenue, Percy singing along with Led Zeppelin on the radio, Annabeth laughing at his bad voice.

Alex crossed his arms. "If those two were any cuter together, they'd cause a nuclear explosion of cuteness and destroy the Eastern Seaboard."

"Is that your idea of a compliment?" I asked.

"Probably as close as *you'll* ever hear." He glanced over. "Where did you promise Annabeth you would go?"

My mouth tasted like I'd been chewing foil. "My uncle's house. There's something I need to do."

"Ohhh." Alex nodded. "I hate that place."

I'd been avoiding this task for weeks. I didn't want to do it alone. I also didn't want to ask any of my other friends— Samirah, Hearthstone, Blitzen, or the rest of the gang from floor nineteen of the Hotel Valhalla. It felt too personal, too painful. But Alex had been to the Chase mansion with me before. The idea of his company didn't bother me. In fact, I realized with surprise, I *wanted* him along pretty badly.

"Uh . . ." I cleared the last falafel and seawater out of my throat. "You want to come with me to a creepy mansion and look through a dead guy's stuff?"

Alex beamed. "I thought you'd never ask."

THREE

I Inherit a Dead Wolf
and Some Underwear

"THAT'S NEW," said Alex.

The brownstone's front door had been forced open, the dead bolt busted out of the frame. In the foyer, sprawled across the Oriental rug, lay the carcass of a wolf.

I shuddered.

You couldn't swing a battle-ax in the Nine Worlds without hitting some kind of wolf: Fenris Wolf, Odin's wolves, Loki's wolves, werewolves, big bad wolfs, and independently contracted small business wolves that would kill anybody for the right price.

The dead wolf in Uncle Randolph's foyer looked very much like the beasts that had attacked my mom two years ago, the night she died.

Wisps of blue luminescence clung to its shaggy black coat. Its mouth was contorted in a permanent snarl. On the top of its head, seared into the skin, was a Viking rune, though the fur around it was so badly burned I couldn't tell which symbol it was. My friend Hearthstone might have been able to say.

Alex circled its pony-size carcass. He kicked it in the ribs. The creature remained obligingly dead.

"Its body hasn't started to dissolve," he noted. "Usually monsters disintegrate pretty soon after you kill them. You can still smell the burning fur on this one. Must've happened recently."

"You think the rune was some kind of trap?"

Alex smirked. "I think your uncle knew a thing or two about magic. The wolf hit the carpet, triggering that rune, and BAM!"

I remembered all the times when, as a homeless kid, I'd broken into Uncle Randolph's house when he wasn't there to steal food, rifle through his office, or just be annoying. I'd never been *bammed*. I'd always considered Randolph a failure at home security. Now I felt a little nauseous, wondering if I could've ended up dead on the welcome mat with a rune burned into my forehead.

Was this trap the reason Randolph's will had been so specific about Annabeth and me visiting the property before we took possession? Had Randolph been trying to get some post-mortem revenge?

"You think the rest of the house is safe to explore?" I asked.

"Nope," Alex said cheerfully. "So let's do it."

On the first floor, we found no more dead wolves. No runes exploded in our faces. The most gruesome thing we discovered was in Uncle Randolph's refrigerator, where expired yogurt, sour milk, and moldy carrots were evolving into a pre-industrial society. Randolph hadn't even left me any chocolate in the pantry, the old villain.

On the second floor, nothing had changed. In Randolph's study, the sun streamed through the stained-glass window, slanting red and orange light across the bookshelves and the displays of Viking artifacts. In one corner sat a big runestone carved with the sneering red face of (naturally) a wolf. Tattered maps and faded yellow parchments covered Randolph's desk. I scanned the documents, looking for something new, something important, but I saw nothing I hadn't seen the last time I'd been here.

I remembered the wording of Randolph's will, which Annabeth had sent me.

It is critical, Randolph had stated, *that my beloved nephew Magnus examine my worldly belongings as soon as possible. He should pay special attention to my papers.*

I didn't know why Randolph had put those lines in his will. In his desk drawers, I found no letter addressed to me, no heartfelt apology like *Dear Magnus, I'm sorry I got you killed, then betrayed you by siding with Loki, then stabbed your friend Blitzen, then almost got you killed again.*

He hadn't even left me the mansion's Wi-Fi password.

I gazed out the office window. Across the street in the Commonwealth Mall, folks were walking their dogs, playing Frisbee, enjoying the nice weather. The statue of Leif Erikson stood on his pedestal, proudly flaunting his metal bra, surveying the traffic on Charlesgate, and probably wondering why he wasn't in Scandinavia.

"So." Alex came up next to me. "You inherit all of this, huh?"

During our walk over, I'd told him the basics about Uncle Randolph's will, but Alex still looked incredulous, almost offended.

"Randolph left the house to Annabeth and me," I said. "Technically, I'm dead. That means it's all Annabeth's.

Randolph's lawyers contacted Annabeth's dad, who told her, who told me. Annabeth asked me to check it out and"—I shrugged—"decide what to do with this place."

From the nearest bookshelf, Alex picked up a framed photo of Uncle Randolph with his wife and daughters. I'd never met Caroline, Emma, or Aubrey. They'd died in a storm at sea many years ago. But I'd seen them in my nightmares. I knew they were the leverage Loki had used to warp my uncle, promising Randolph that he could see his family again if he helped Loki escape his bonds. . . . And in a way, Loki had told the truth. The last time I'd seen Uncle Randolph, he was tumbling into a chasm straight to Helheim, the land of the dishonorable dead.

Alex turned over the photo, maybe hoping to find a secret note on the back. The last time we'd been in this office, we'd found a wedding invitation that way, and it had led us into all sorts of trouble. This time, there was no hidden message—just blank brown paper, which was a lot less painful to look at than the smiling faces of my dead relatives.

Alex put the picture back on the shelf. "Annabeth doesn't care what you do with the house?"

"Not really. She's got enough going on with college and, you know, demigod stuff. She just wants me to let her know if I find anything interesting—old photo albums, family history, that kind of thing."

Alex wrinkled his nose. "Family history." His face had the same slightly disgusted, slightly intrigued expression as when he'd kicked the dead wolf. "So what's upstairs?"

"I'm not sure. When I was a kid, we weren't allowed

above the first two floors. And the few times I broke in more recently . . ." I turned up my palms. "I guess I never made it that far."

Alex peered at me over the top of his glasses, his dark brown eye and his amber eye like mismatched moons cresting on the horizon. "Sounds intriguing. Let's go."

The third floor consisted of two large bedrooms. The front one was spotlessly clean, cold, and impersonal. Two twin beds. A dresser. Bare walls. Maybe a guest room, though I doubted Randolph entertained many people. Or maybe this had been Emma and Aubrey's room. If so, Randolph had removed all traces of their personalities, leaving a white void in the middle of the house. We didn't linger.

The second bedroom must have been Randolph's. It smelled like his old-fashioned clove cologne. Towers of musty books leaned against the walls. Chocolate-bar wrappers filled the wastebasket. Randolph had probably eaten his entire stash right before leaving home to help Loki destroy the world.

I supposed I couldn't blame him. I always say, *Eat chocolate first, destroy the world later.*

Alex hopped onto the four-poster bed. He bounced up and down, grinning as the springs squeaked.

"What are you doing?" I asked.

"Making noise." He leaned over and rifled through Randolph's nightstand drawer. "Let's see. Cough drops. Paper clips. Some wadded-up Kleenex that I am not going to touch. And . . ." He whistled. "Medication for bowel discomfort! Magnus, all this bounty belongs to you!"

"You're a strange person."

"I prefer the term *fabulously weird*."

We searched the rest of the bedroom, though I wasn't sure what I was looking for. *Pay special attention to my papers*, Randolph's will had urged. I doubted he meant the wadded-up tissues.

Annabeth hadn't been able to get much information out of Randolph's lawyers. Our uncle had apparently revised his will the day before he died. That might mean Randolph had known he didn't have long to live, felt some guilt about betraying me, and wanted to leave me some sort of last message. Or it might mean he'd revised the will because Loki had ordered him to. But if this was a trap to lure me here, then why was there a dead wolf in the foyer?

I found no secret papers in Randolph's closet. His bathroom was unremarkable except for an impressive collection of half-empty Listerine bottles. His underwear drawer was packed with enough navy-blue Jockeys to outfit a squadron of Randolphs—all briefs, perfectly starched, ironed, and folded. Some things defy explanation.

On the next floor, two more empty bedrooms. Nothing dangerous like wolves, exploding runes, or old-dude underwear.

The top floor was a sprawling library even larger than the one in Randolph's office. A haphazard collection of novels lined the shelves. A small kitchenette took up one corner of the room, complete with a mini fridge and an electric teapot and—CURSE YOU, RANDOLPH!—still no chocolate. The windows looked out over the green-shingled rooftops of Back Bay. At the far end of the room, a staircase led up to what I assumed would be a roof deck.

A comfy-looking leather chair faced the fireplace. Carved in the center of the marble surround was (of course) a snarling wolf's head. On the mantel, in a silver tripod stand, sat a Norse drinking horn with a leather strap and a silver rim etched with runic designs. I'd seen thousands of horns like that in Valhalla, but it surprised me to find one here. Randolph had never struck me as the mead-swilling type. Maybe he sipped his Earl Grey tea out of it.

"*Madre de Dios,*" Alex said.

I stared at him. It was the first time I'd ever heard him speak Spanish.

He tapped one of the framed photos on the wall and gave me a wicked grin. "*Please* tell me this is you."

The picture was a shot of my mother with her usual pixie haircut and brilliant smile, jeans, and flannel camping shirt. She stood in the hollowed-out trunk of a sycamore tree, holding a baby Magnus up to the camera—my hair a tuft of white gold, my mouth glistening with drool, my gray eyes wide like *What the heck am I doing here?*

"That's me," I admitted.

"You were *so* cute." Alex glanced over. "What happened?"

"Ha, ha."

I scanned the wall of photos. I was amazed Uncle Randolph had kept one of me and my mom right where he'd see it whenever he sat in his comfy chair, almost as if he actually cared about us.

Another photo showed the three Chase siblings as children—Natalie, Frederick, and Randolph—all dressed in World War II military uniforms, brandishing fake rifles.

Halloween, I guessed. Next to that was a picture of my grand-parents: a frowning, white-haired couple dressed in clashing 1970s-style plaid clothes, like they were either on their way to church or the senior citizens' disco.

Confession: I had trouble telling my grandfather and grandmother apart. They'd died before I could meet them, but from their pictures, you could tell they were one of those couples that had grown to resemble each other over the years until they were virtually indistinguishable. Same white helmet-hair. Same glasses. Same wispy mustaches. In the photo, a few Viking artifacts, including the mead horn that now sat on Randolph's mantel, hung on the wall behind them. I'd had no idea my grandparents were into Norse stuff, too. I wondered if they'd ever traveled the Nine Worlds. That might explain their confused, slightly cross-eyed expressions.

Alex perused the titles on the bookshelves.

"Anything good?" I asked.

He shrugged. "*The Lord of the Rings*. Not bad. Sylvia Plath. Nice. Oh, *The Left Hand of Darkness*. I love that book. The rest . . . meh. His collection is a little heavy on dead white males for my taste."

"I'm a dead white male," I noted.

Alex raised one eyebrow. "Yes, you are."

I hadn't realized Alex was a reader. I was tempted to ask if he liked some of my favorites: Scott Pilgrim or maybe *Sandman*. Those were fabulously weird. But I decided this might not be the right time to start a book club.

I searched the shelves for diaries or hidden compartments.

Alex meandered over to the last flight of stairs. He peered

upward and his complexion turned as green as his hair. "Uh, Magnus? You should probably see this."

I joined him.

At the top of the staircase, a domed Plexiglas hatch led to the roof. And on the other side, pacing and snarling, was another wolf.

FOUR

But Wait. Act Now, and You Get a *Second* Wolf Free!

"HOW DO you want to handle this?" I asked.

From his belt loops, Alex pulled the golden wire that served triple duty as fashion accessory, ceramic-cutting tool, and melee weapon. "I was thinking we should kill it."

The wolf growled and clawed at the hatch. Magical runes glowed on the Plexiglas. The beast's facial fur was already smoking and charred from previous attempts to bust in.

I wondered how long the wolf had been on the roof, and why it hadn't tried to gain access another way. Maybe it didn't want to end up dead like its friend downstairs. Or maybe it was single-mindedly focused on this particular room.

"It wants something," I guessed.

"To kill us," Alex said. "Which is why we should kill it first. You want to open the hatch or—?"

"Wait." Normally I would've been all in favor of killing a glowing blue wolf, but something about this animal bothered me . . . the way its cold dark eyes seemed to be looking past us, as if searching for different prey. "What if we let it in?"

Alex stared at me like I was crazy. He did that a lot. "You want to offer it a cup of tea? Maybe lend it a book?"

"It has to be here on a mission," I persisted. "Somebody

sent those wolves to retrieve something—maybe the same something I'm looking for."

Alex considered. "You think Loki sent the wolves."

I shrugged. "Loki's gonna Loki."

"And if we let the wolf in, you think it might make a bee-line for whatever it's hunting."

"I'm pretty sure it isn't here for the irritable bowel medicine."

Alex loosened his checkered tie even more. "Okay. We open the hatch, watch where the wolf goes, and *then* we kill it."

"Right." I pulled the runestone pendant off my neck chain. Jack grew into sword form, though he felt heavier than usual, like a kid having a meltdown on the floor of a department store.

"What is it now?" He sighed. "Can't you see I'm dying of a broken heart?"

I could have pointed out that he was incapable of dying, and he had no actual heart, but I thought that would be mean. "Sorry, Jack. We have a wolf to deal with."

I explained to him what was going on.

Jack's blade glowed violet. "But Riptide's razor-sharp edges," he said dreamily. "Did you see her edges?"

"Yeah. Great edges. Now how about we prevent Loki from launching his mighty death ship and starting Ragnarok? Then maybe we can arrange a second date for you and Riptide."

Another heavy sigh. "Wolf. Roof. Hatch. Got it."

I glanced at Alex and stifled a shriek. While I wasn't look-ing, he'd transformed into a large timber wolf.

"Do you *have* to turn into animals behind my back?" I asked.

Alex bared his fangs in a canine grin. He snout-pointed toward the top of the stairs like *What are you waiting for? I'm a wolf. I can't open that hatch.*

I climbed to the top of the stairs. The temperature was like the inside of a greenhouse. On the other side of the hatch, the wolf snuffled and chewed at the Plexiglas, leaving drool smears and fang marks. Those protective-barrier runes must have tasted great. Being this close to an enemy wolf made the hairs on the back of my neck do corkscrews.

What would happen if I opened the hatch? Would the runes kill me? Would they kill the wolf? Or would they deactivate if I let the wolf in of my own free will, since that was literally the stupidest thing I could do?

The wolf slavered at the Plexiglas.

"Hey, buddy," I said.

Jack buzzed in my hand. "What?"

"Not you, Jack. I'm talking to the wolf." I smiled at the beast, then remembered that showing teeth meant aggression to canines. I pouted instead. "I'm going to let you in. Won't that be nice? Then you can get whatever you came for, since I know you're not here to kill me, right?"

The wolf's snarl was not reassuring.

"Okay, then," I said. "One, two, three!"

I pushed against the hatch with all my einherji strength, shoving the wolf back as I surged onto the roof deck. I had time to register a barbecue grill, some planters overflowing with hibiscus, and two lounge chairs overlooking an amazing view of the Charles River. I wanted to slap Uncle Randolph for never telling me he had such a cool party spot.

The wolf stepped from behind the hatch and growled,

its hackles raised like a shaggy dorsal fin. One of its eyes was swollen shut, the eyelid burned from contact with my uncle's rune trap.

"Now?" Jack asked with no particular enthusiasm.

"Not yet." I flexed my knees, ready to spring into action if necessary. I would show this wolf how well I could fight . . . or, you know, how fast I could run away, depending on what the situation called for.

The wolf regarded me with its one good eye. It snorted dismissively and bolted down the stairwell into the town house.

I wasn't sure whether to be relieved or insulted.

I ran after it. By the time I reached the bottom of the stairs, Alex and the other wolf were having a snarl-off in the middle of the library. They bared their teeth and circled one another, looking for any signs of fear or weakness. The blue wolf was much larger. The neon wisps glowing in its fur gave it a certain cool factor. But it was also half-blind and wincing in pain. Alex, being Alex, showed no sign of being intimidated. He stood his ground as the other wolf edged around him.

Once our glowing blue visitor was confident Alex wasn't going to attack, it raised its snout and sniffed the air. I expected it to run toward the bookshelves and chomp some secret book of nautical maps, or maybe a copy of *How to Stop Loki's Ship of Death in Three Easy Steps!* Instead, the wolf lunged toward the fireplace, jumped at the mantel, and grabbed the mead horn in its mouth.

Some sluggish part of my brain thought, *Hey, I should probably stop it.*

Alex was way ahead of me. In one fluid movement, he morphed back into human form, stepped forward, and lashed out with his garrote like he was throwing a bowling ball. (Actually, it was a lot more graceful than that. I'd seen Alex bowl, and it wasn't pretty.) The golden cord wrapped around the wolf's neck. With one yank backward, Alex cured the wolf of any future headache problems.

The decapitated carcass flopped against the carpet. It began to sizzle, disintegrating until only the drinking horn and a few tufts of fur remained.

Jack's blade turned heavier in my grip. "Well, fine," he said. "I guess you didn't need me after all. I'll just go write some love poetry and cry a lot." He shrank back into a runestone pendant.

Alex crouched next to the mead horn. "Any idea why a wolf would want a decorative drinking vessel?"

I knelt next to him, picked up the horn, and looked inside. Rolled up and crammed into the horn was a small leather book like a diary. I pulled it out and fanned the pages: drawings of Viking runes, interspersed with paragraphs written in Uncle Randolph's cramped cursive.

"I think," I said, "we've found the right dead white male author."

We reclined in the lounge chairs on the roof deck.

While I flipped through my uncle's notebook, trying to make sense of his frenzied rune drawings and cursive crazy talk, Alex relaxed and sipped guava juice from the mead horn.

Why Uncle Randolph kept guava juice in his library's mini fridge, I couldn't tell you.

Every so often, just to annoy me, Alex slurped with exaggerated gusto and smacked his lips. "*Ahhhh.*"

"Are you sure it's safe to drink from that horn?" I asked. "It could be cursed or something."

Alex grabbed his throat and pretended to choke. "Oh, no! I'm turning into a frog!"

"Please don't."

He pointed at the diary. "Any luck with that?"

I stared at the pages. Runes swam in front of my eyes. The notations were in a mix of languages: Old Norse, Swedish, and some I couldn't begin to guess. Even the passages in English made little sense. I felt like I was trying to read an advanced quantum physics textbook backward in a mirror.

"Most of it's over my head," I admitted. "The earlier pages look like they're about Randolph's search for the Sword of Summer. I recognize some of the references. But here at the end . . ."

The last few pages were more hastily written. Randolph's writing turned shaky and frantic. Splotches of dried blood freckled the paper. I remembered that, in the tomb of the Viking zombies in Provincetown, Randolph had gotten several of his fingers lopped off. These pages might have been written after that, with his nondominant hand. The watery cursive reminded me of the way I used to write back in elementary school, when my teacher forced me to use my right hand.

On the last page, Randolph had scratched my name: *Magnus.*

Under that, he'd sketched two serpents interlocking in a figure eight. The quality of the drawing was terrible, but I recognized the symbol. Alex had the same thing tattooed on the nape of his neck: the sign of Loki.

Below that was a term in what I assumed was Old Norse:

mjöð. Then some notes in English: *Might stop L. Whetstone of Bolverk > guards. Where?*

That last word trailed downward, the question mark a desperate scrawl.

"What do you make of this?" I passed the book to Alex.

He frowned. "That's my mom's symbol, obviously."

(You heard right. Loki was normally a male god, but he happened to be Alex's mother. Long story.)

"And the rest of it?" I asked.

"This word looks like *moo* with a *j*. Perhaps Scandinavian cows have an accent?"

"I take it you don't read Old Norse, then, or whatever that language is?"

"Magnus, it may shock you to learn that I do not have every talent in the world. Just most of the important ones."

He squinted at the page. When he concentrated, the left corner of his mouth twitched like he was enjoying a secret joke. I found that tic distracting. I wanted to know what he found so funny.

"'Might stop L,'" Alex read. "Let's assume that's Loki. 'Whetstone of Bolverk.' You think that's the same thing as the Skofnung Stone?"

I shuddered. We'd lost the Skofnung Stone and Skofnung Sword during a wedding party in Loki's cavern, when he'd escaped the bindings that had held him for a thousand years. (Oops. Our bad.) I never wanted to see that particular whetstone again.

"I hope not," I said. "Ever heard the name Bolverk?"

"Nope." Alex finished his guava juice. "I'm kind of digging this mead horn, though. You mind if I keep it?"

"All yours." I found the idea of Alex taking a souvenir from my family mansion strangely pleasing. "So if Randolph wanted me to find that book, and Loki sent the wolves to get it before I could—"

Alex tossed the journal back to me. "Assuming what you just said is true, and assuming it's not a trap, and assuming those notes aren't the ramblings of a madman?"

"Uh . . . yeah."

"Then best-case scenario: Your uncle came up with an idea to stop Loki. It wasn't something he could do himself, but he hoped you could. It involves a whetstone, a Bolverk, and possibly a Scandinavian cow."

"When you put it like that, it doesn't sound so promising."

Alex poked the tip of the mead horn. "Sorry to burst your bubble, but most plans to stop Loki fail. We know this."

The bitter edge in his voice surprised me.

"You're thinking about your training sessions with Sam," I guessed. "How are they going?"

Alex's face told me the answer.

Among Loki's many disturbing qualities, he could command his children to do whatever he wanted whenever they were in his presence, which made family reunions a real drag.

Alex was the exception. He'd somehow learned to resist Loki's power, and for the past six weeks, he'd been trying to teach his half sister Samirah al-Abbas to do the same. The fact that neither of them talked much about their training suggested that it hadn't been a rousing success.

"She's trying," Alex said. "It doesn't make it easier that she's . . ." He stopped himself.

"What?"

"Never mind. I promised not to talk about it."

"Now I'm really curious. Is everything okay with her and Amir?"

Alex snorted. "Oh, yeah. They're still head over heels, dreaming of the day when they can get married. I swear, if those two didn't have me to chaperone them, they'd do something crazy like hold hands."

"Then what's the problem?"

Alex waved off my question. "All I'm saying is that you shouldn't trust anything you get from your Uncle Randolph. Not the advice in that book. Not this house. Anything you inherit from family . . . it *always* comes with strings attached."

That seemed a strange thing for him to say, considering he'd been enjoying the view from Randolph's magnificent roof deck while sipping chilled guava juice from his Viking mead horn, but I got the feeling Alex wasn't really thinking about my dysfunctional uncle.

"You never talk much about your family," I noted. "I mean your mortal family."

He stared at me darkly. "And I'm not going to start now. If you knew *half* the—"

BRAWK! In a flutter of black feathers, a raven landed on the tip of Alex's boot.

You don't see a lot of wild ravens in Boston. Canadian geese, seagulls, ducks, pigeons, even hawks, sure. But when a huge black raptor lands on your foot, that can only mean one thing: a message from Valhalla.

Alex held out his hand. (Not normally recommended with ravens. They have a vicious bite.) The bird hopped on his wrist, barfed up a hard pellet the size of a pecan right into Alex's palm, and then flew away, its mission accomplished.

Yes, our ravens deliver messages via barf-mail. Ravens have a natural ability to regurgitate inedible substances like bones and fur, so they have no qualms about swallowing a message capsule, flying it across the Nine Worlds, and vomiting it to the correct recipient. It wouldn't have been *my* chosen career, but hey, no judgment.

Alex cracked open the pellet. He unfolded the letter and began to read, the corner of his mouth starting to twitch again. "It's from T.J.," he said. "Looks like we're leaving today. Right now, in fact."

"What?" I sat up in my recliner. "Why?"

Of course, I'd known we were running out of time. We had to leave soon in order to reach Loki's ship before Midsummer. But there was a big difference between *soon* and *right now*. I wasn't a big fan of *right now*.

Alex kept reading. "Something about the tide? I dunno. I'd better go bust Samirah out of school. She'll be in Calculus. She's not going to be happy about leaving."

He rose and offered me a hand.

I didn't want to get up. I wanted to stay there on that deck with Alex and watch the afternoon sunlight change the color of the river from blue to amber. Maybe we could read some of Randolph's old paperbacks. We could drink all his guava juice. But the raven had barfed up our orders. You couldn't argue with raven barf.

I took Alex's hand and got to my feet. "You want me to come with you?"

Alex frowned. "No, dummy. You've got to get back to Valhalla. You're the one with the boat. Speaking of which, have you warned the others about—?"

"No," I said, my face burning. "Not yet."

Alex laughed. "That should be interesting. Don't wait for Sam and me. We'll catch up with you somewhere along the way!"

Before I could ask what he meant by that, Alex turned into a flamingo and launched himself into the sky, making it a banner day for Boston bird-watchers.

FIVE

I Bid Farewell to Erik, Erik, Erik, and Also Erik

LEGENDS TELL US that Valhalla has 540 doors, conveniently distributed across the Nine Worlds for easy access.

The legends don't mention that one of those entrances is in the Forever 21 store on Newbury Street, just behind the women's activewear rack.

It normally wasn't the entrance I liked to use, but it *was* the closest to Uncle Randolph's mansion. Nobody in Valhalla could explain to me why we had a gateway in Forever 21. Some speculated it was left over from a time when the building was not a retail store. Personally, I thought the location might be one of Odin's little jokes, since a lot of his einherjar were literally forever twenty-one, or sixteen, or sixty.

My dwarf friend Blitzen especially hated that entrance. Every time I mentioned Forever 21, he would launch into a rant about how *his* fashions were much better. Something about hemlines. I don't know.

I strolled through the lingerie section, getting a strange look from a saleslady, then dove into the activewear rack and popped out the other side in one of the Hotel Valhalla's game rooms. There was a pool tournament in progress, which Vikings play with spears instead of pool cues. (Hint: Never stand behind a Viking when he shoots.) Erik the Green from

floor 135 greeted me cheerfully. (From what I can tell, approximately 72 percent of the population of Valhalla is named
Erik.)

"Hail, Magnus Chase!" He pointed at my shoulder. "You've
got some spandex just there."

"Oh, thanks." I untangled the yoga pants that had gotten
stuck on my shirt and tossed them into the bin marked FOR
RESTOCKING.

Then I strode off to find my friends.

Walking through the Hotel Valhalla never got old. At
least it hadn't for me so far, and einherjar who'd been here
hundreds of years had told me the same thing. Thanks to the
power of Odin, or the magic of the Norns, or maybe just the
fact that we had an on-site IKEA, the decor was constantly
changing, though it always incorporated a lot of spears and
shields, and perhaps more wolf motifs than I would've liked.

Even just finding the elevators required me to navigate
hallways that had changed size and direction since the morning, past rooms I'd never seen before. In one enormous
oak-paneled lounge, warriors played shuffleboard with oars
for pushers and combat shields for pucks. Many of the players
sported leg splints, arm slings, and head bandages, because—
of course—einherjar played shuffleboard to the death.

The main lobby had been re-carpeted in deep crimson,
a great color to hide bloodstains. The walls were now hung
with tapestries depicting Valkyries flying into battle against
fire giants. It was beautiful work, though the proximity of so
many wall torches made me nervous. Valhalla was pretty lax
about safety codes. I didn't like burning to death. (It was one

of my least favorite ways to die, right up there with choking on the after-dinner mints in the feast hall.)

I took the elevator up to floor nineteen. Unfortunately, the elevator music hadn't changed. It was getting to the point that I could sing along with Frank Sinatra in Norwegian. I was just glad I lived on a low floor. If I lived somewhere up in the hundreds, I would have gone . . . well, berserk.

On floor nineteen, everything was strangely quiet. No sounds of video-game violence emanated from Thomas Jefferson Jr.'s room. (Dead Civil War soldiers *love* their video games almost as much as they love charging up hills.) I saw no signs that Mallory Keen had been practicing her knife-throwing in the hallway. Halfborn Gunderson's room was open and being serviced by a flock of ravens, who swirled through his library and his weapons collection, dusting books and battle-axes. The big man himself was nowhere to be seen.

My own room had recently been cleaned. The bed was made. In the central atrium, the trees had been pruned and the grass mowed. (I could never figure out how the ravens operated a lawn mower.) On the coffee table, a note in T.J.'s elegant script read:

We're at dock 23, sublevel 6. See you there!

The TV had been turned to the Hotel Valhalla Channel, which displayed a list of the afternoon's events: racquetball, machine-gun tag (like laser tag, except with machine guns), watercolor painting, Italian cooking, advanced sword-sharpening, and something called flyting—all done to the death.

I stared wistfully at the screen. I'd never wanted to practice watercolor painting to the death before, but now I was tempted. It sounded much easier than the trip I was about to take from dock twenty-three, sublevel six.

First things first: I showered off the smell of Boston Harbor. I changed into new clothes. I grabbed my *go* bag: camping supplies, some basic provisions, and, of course, some chocolate bars.

As nice as my hotel suite was, I didn't have much in the way of personal stuff—just a few of my favorite books, and some photos from my past that magically appeared over time, gradually filling up the fireplace mantel.

The hotel wasn't meant to be a forever home. We einherjar might stay here for centuries, but it was only a stopover on our way to Ragnarok. The whole hotel radiated a sense of impermanence and anticipation. *Don't get too comfortable,* it seemed to say. *You might be leaving any minute to go die your final death at Doomsday. Hooray!*

I checked my reflection in the full-length mirror. I wasn't sure why it mattered. I'd never cared much about appearances during the two years I'd lived on the streets, but lately Alex Fierro had been teasing me mercilessly, which made me more conscious of how I looked.

Besides, if you don't check yourself from time to time in Valhalla, you could be walking around for hours with raven poop on your shoulder, or an arrow in your butt, or a pair of yoga pants wrapped around your neck.

Hiking boots: check. New pair of jeans: check. Green Hotel Valhalla T-shirt: check. Down jacket, appropriate for cold-water expeditions and falling off masts: check. Runestone pendant that could turn into a heartbroken magical sword: check.

After living on the streets, I wasn't used to my face looking so clean. I definitely wasn't used to my new haircut, which Blitz had first given me during our expedition into Jotunheim. Since then, every time it started to grow out, Alex hacked it off again, leaving my bangs just long enough to fall in my eyes, the back chopped to collar level. I was used to my hair being much wilder and more wiry, but Alex took such glee in murdering my blond locks it was impossible to tell him no.

It's perfect! Alex said. *Now you at least look like you're groomed, but your face is still obscured!*

I slipped Randolph's notebook into my pack, along with one last item I'd been trying hard not to think about—a certain silk handkerchief I'd gotten from my father.

I sighed at the Magnus in the mirror. "Well, sir, you'd better get going. Your friends are eagerly waiting to laugh at you."

"There he is!" yelled Halfborn Gunderson, berserker extraordinaire, speaker of the obvious.

He barreled toward me like a friendly Mack truck. His hair was even wilder than mine used to be. (I was pretty sure he cut it himself, using a battle-ax, in the dark.) He wore a T-shirt today, which was unusual, but his arms were still a wild landscape of muscle and tattoo. Strapped across his back was his battle-ax named Battle-Ax, and holstered up and down his leather breeches were half a dozen knives.

He wrapped me in a bear hug and lifted me off my feet, perhaps testing to make sure my rib cage would not crack under pressure. He put me down and patted my arms, apparently satisfied.

"You ready for a quest?" he bellowed. "I'm ready for a quest!"

From the edge of the canal, where she was coiling ropes, Mallory Keen called, "Oh, shut up, you oaf! I still think we should use you as the rudder."

Halfborn's face mottled red, but he kept his eyes on me. "I'm trying not to kill her, Magnus. I really am. But it's *so* hard. I'd better keep busy or I'm going to do something I'll regret. You have the handkerchief?"

"Uh, yes, but—"

"Good man. Time's a-wasting!"

He tromped back to the dockside and began sorting his supplies—huge canvas duffels no doubt full of food, weapons, and lots of spare leather breeches.

I scanned the length of the cavern. Along the left-hand wall, a river rushed through the canal, emerging from a train-size tunnel on one end and disappearing into an identical tunnel on the other. The barreled ceiling was polished wood, amplifying the water's roar and making me feel like we were standing inside an old-fashioned root-beer keg. Supplies and baggage lined the dock, just waiting for a ship to be put on.

At the far end of the room, Thomas Jefferson Jr. stood deep in conversation with the hotel manager, Helgi, and his assistant, Hunding, all three of them looking over some paperwork on a clipboard. Since I had an aversion to paperwork and also to Helgi, I walked over to Mallory, who was now stuffing iron grappling hooks into a burlap sack.

She was dressed in black furs and black denim, her red

hair pulled back in a severe bun. In the torchlight, her freckles glowed orange. As usual, she wore her trusty pair of knives at her sides.

"Everything good?" I asked, because clearly it wasn't.

She scowled. "Don't you start, too, Mister—" She called me a Gaelic term I didn't recognize, but I was fairly sure it didn't mean *dearest friend.* "We've been waiting on you and the boat."

"Where are Blitzen and Hearthstone?"

It had been several weeks since I'd seen my dwarf and elf buddies, and I'd been looking forward to them sailing with us. (One of the few things I was looking forward to.)

Mallory grunted impatiently. "We're picking them up on the way."

That could have meant we were stopping by a different part of Boston, or stopping by a different world, but Mallory didn't look like she was in the mood to elaborate. She scanned the space behind me and scowled. "What about Alex and Samirah?"

"Alex said they'd meet us later."

"Well, then." Mallory made a shooing gesture. "Go sign us out."

"Sign us out?"

"Yeah . . ." She drawled the word to indicate just how slow she thought I was. "With Helgi. The manager. Off you go!"

Since she was still holding a fistful of grappling hooks, I did what she told me.

T.J. had his foot planted on a supply box, his rifle across his back. The brass buttons gleamed on his Union Army coat. He tipped his infantry cap at me in greeting. "Just in time, my friend!"

Helgi and Hunding exchanged nervous looks, the way they did whenever Odin announced one of his motivational staff retreats.

"Magnus Chase," Helgi said, tugging at his roadkill beard. He was dressed in his usual dark green pinstripe suit, which he probably thought made him look like a service-industry professional, but only made him look like a Viking in a pinstripe suit. "We were beginning to worry. The high tide will be here any minute."

I looked at the water raging down the canal. I knew that several subterranean rivers wove their way through Valhalla, but I didn't understand how they could be subject to tides. I also didn't see how the water level here could *get* any higher without flooding the entire room. Then again, I was having a conversation with two dead Vikings and a Civil War soldier, so I decided to give logic a rest.

"Sorry," I said. "I was . . ."

I waved vaguely, trying to indicate reading mysterious journals, killing wolves, breaking my leg in Boston Harbor.

T.J. practically vibrated with excitement. "You got the boat? I can't *wait* to see it!"

"Uh, yeah." I started rummaging in my knapsack, but the handkerchief seemed to have fallen to the bottom.

Hunding wrung his hands. His bellhop uniform was buttoned wrong, like he'd rushed to get dressed this morning. "You didn't lose it, did you? Oh, I warned you about leaving unattended magic items in your room! I told the cleaning ravens not to touch it. 'It's a warship!' I said. 'Not a napkin!' But they kept wanting to launder it with the linens. If it's missing—"

"Then *you'll* be held responsible," Helgi snarled at the bell-hop. "Floor nineteen is *your* service area."

Hunding winced. He and Helgi had a feud that went back several centuries. The manager welcomed any excuse to make Hunding work extra shifts shoveling garbage into the incinerators or hosing out the lindworm warrens.

"Relax." I pulled out the piece of cloth. "See? Here it is. And, Hunding, this is for you." I handed him one of my chocolate bars. "Thanks for keeping an eye on my room while I'm gone."

The bellhop's eyes turned misty. "Kid, you're the best. You can leave unattended magic items in your room anytime!"

"Hmph." Helgi scowled. "Well, then, Magnus Chase, I'll need you to sign out." He thrust the clipboard at me. "Read carefully and initial at the bottom of each page."

I flipped through a dozen pages of dense contract language. I skimmed over phrases like *In the event of death by squirrel attack* and *The proprietor shall not be held liable for off-site dismemberment.* No wonder my friends preferred to leave the hotel without permission. The release forms were brutal.

T.J. cleared his throat. "So, Magnus, maybe while you're doing that, I could set up the boat? Can I? I'm ready to get this regiment underway!"

I could tell. He was loaded down with enough ammunition pouches, haversacks, and canteens for a thirty-day march. His eyes gleamed as brightly as his bayonet. Since T.J. was usually the voice of reason on floor nineteen, I was glad to have him along, even if he did get a little too excited about full frontal charges on enemy positions.

"Yeah," I said. "Sure, man."

"YAY!" He plucked the handkerchief out of my hand and hustled toward the dock.

I signed the release forms, trying not to get hung up on the clauses about arbitration in case we got incinerated in the fires of Muspellheim or got pulverized by frost giants. I handed the clipboard back to Helgi.

The manager frowned. "You sure you read everything?"

"Uh . . . yeah. I'm a fast reader."

Helgi gripped my shoulder. "Then good luck, Magnus Chase, son of Frey. And remember, you *must* stop Loki's ship *Naglfar* from sailing at Midsummer—"

"I know."

"—or Ragnarok begins."

"Right."

"Which means our renovations to the banquet hall won't ever be complete, and we'll *never* get high-speed Internet restored on floor two hundred forty-two."

I nodded grimly. I did not need the extra pressure of being responsible for an entire floor's Internet connection. "We'll succeed. Don't worry."

Helgi tugged at his beard. "But if you *do* start Ragnarok, could you please get back here as soon as possible, or send us a text?"

"Okay. Um, a text?"

As far as I knew, the hotel staff just used ravens. They didn't know how to use mobile devices. None of them even had numbers. But that didn't stop them from talking a good game.

"We'll need to get everyone started on their checkout surveys before we march off to Doomsday," Helgi explained. "To expedite their deaths. If you can't make it back, you can also fill out your survey online. And if you wouldn't mind marking *excellent* wherever it mentions the manager, I'd appreciate it. Odin does read those."

"But if we're all going to die anyway—"

"Good man." He patted my shoulder. "Well, have a safe—er, successful journey!"

He tucked the clipboard under his arm and strolled off, probably going to inspect those renovations to the banquet hall.

Hunding sighed. "That man has no sense. Thanks for the chocolate, though, my boy. I just wish there was something more I could do for you."

My scalp tingled with inspiration. During my time at the hotel, Hunding had become my best source of information. He knew where all the bodies were buried (literally). He knew all the secret room service menu items, and how you could get from the lobby to the observation deck above the Grove of Glasir without having to pass through the gauntlet of gift shops. He was a walking Vikingpedia.

I pulled out Randolph's journal and showed him the last page. "Any idea what this word means?" I pointed to *mjöð*.

Hunding laughed. "It says *mead*, of course!"

"Huh. So it has nothing to do with cows."

"Pardon?"

"Never mind. What about this name here—Bolverk?"

Hunding flinched so violently he dropped his chocolate bar. "Bolverk? NO. No, no, no. What is this book, anyway? Why would you possibly—?"

"Argh!" Halfborn yelled from dockside. "Magnus, we need you over here, now!"

The river was starting to surge, frothing and lapping over the edge of the canal. T.J. shook the handkerchief desperately, yelling, "How does it work? How does it work?"

It hadn't occurred to me that the foldable ship, being a gift from my dad, might only work for me. I ran over to help.

Mallory and Halfborn were scrambling to gather their supplies.

"We've got a minute at most before the high tide comes flooding through here!" yelled Halfborn. "Ship, Magnus! Now!"

I took the handkerchief and tried to steady my shaking hands. I'd practiced this ship-unfolding trick a couple of times on calmer water, once by myself and once with Alex, but I could still hardly believe it would work. I definitely wasn't looking forward to the results.

I flicked the handkerchief toward the water. As soon as the cloth hit the surface, the corners unfolded and unfolded and kept unfolding. It was like watching the building of a Lego model in a sped-up stop-motion video. In the space of two breaths, a Viking longship lay at anchor in the canal, the turbulent water coursing around its stern.

But, of course, nobody complimented me on its beautifully trimmed hull, or the elaborate Viking shields lining the rails, or the five rows of oars ready for service. No one noted how the mainmast was hinged and folded over so it could pass through this low tunnel without breaking apart. No one gasped at the beauty of the carved dragon figurehead, or praised the fact that the ship was much larger and more spacious than your typical longship, even boasting a covered area belowdecks so we wouldn't have to sleep in the rain and snow.

Mallory Keen's first comment was, "Can we talk about the color?"

T.J. frowned. "Why is it—?"

"I don't know!" I wailed. "I don't *know* why it's yellow!"

My father, Frey, had sent me the boat weeks ago, promising that it was the perfect vessel to use on our voyage. It would get us where we needed to go. It would protect us on the most treacherous seas.

My friends had been excited. They had trusted me, even when I'd refused to give them a preview of our magical ship.

But why, oh, why had my father made the boat the color of I Can't Believe It's Not Butter!®?

Everything about it was neon, eye-melting yellow: the ropes, the shields, the hull, the sail, the rudder, even the dragon figurehead. For all I knew, the bottom of the keel was yellow, too, and we'd blind every fish we sailed past.

"Well, it doesn't matter now," Halfborn said, scowling at me like it mattered very much. "Load up! Hurry!"

A roar echoed from the upstream tunnel like an approaching freight train. The ship banged against the dock. Halfborn tossed our supplies on deck as T.J. hauled up the anchor, while Mallory and I held the mooring lines fast with all our einherji strength.

Just as Halfborn threw the last sacks, a wall of water burst out of the tunnel behind us.

"Let's go!" yelled T.J.

We jumped aboard as the wave slammed into our stern,

propelling us forward like the kick of a seventy-million-gallon mule.

I glanced back at the dock one last time. Hunding the bellhop stood knee-deep in water, clutching his chocolate bar, staring at me as we rocketed into the darkness, his face bleached with shock as if, after all these centuries of dealing with the dead in Valhalla, he'd finally seen an actual ghost.

SIX

I Have a Nightmare
About Toenails

I LIKE my rivers the way I like my enemies—slow, wide, and lazy.

I rarely get what I like.

Our boat shot down the rapids in near-total darkness. My friends scrambled around the deck, grabbing ropes and tripping over oars. The ship rocked side to side, making me feel like I was surfing on a pendulum. Mallory hugged the rudder with her full weight, trying to keep us in the middle of the current.

"Don't just stand there!" she yelled at me. "Help!"

The old saying is true: no nautical training survives first contact with the water.

I'm pretty sure that's an old saying.

Everything I'd learned from Percy Jackson evaporated out of my brain. I forgot starboard and port, stern and aft. I forgot how to discourage shark attacks and how to fall off a mast properly. I hopped across the deck yelling, "I'm helping! I'm helping!" without knowing what to do at all.

We swerved and sloshed through the tunnel at impossible speeds, our retracted mast barely clearing the roof. The tips of our oars scraped against the stone walls, leaving trails of bright yellow sparks that made it look like faeries were ice-skating alongside us.

T.J. rushed past me, heading for the prow, and nearly impaled me with his bayonet. "Magnus, hold that line!" he yelled, waving at pretty much every rope on the ship.

I grabbed the nearest bit of rigging and pulled as hard as I could, hoping I had the right line, or hoping I at least looked helpful while doing the wrong thing.

We bumped down a series of cataracts. My teeth clattered out telegraph messages. Frigid waves crashed over the shields on the railing. Then the tunnel widened and we sideswiped a rock that came out of nowhere. The boat spun a 360. We dropped down a waterfall toward certain death, and as the air turned to cold misty soup around us . . . everything went dark.

What a fantastic time to have a vision!

I found myself standing on the deck of a different ship.

In the distance, glacial cliffs rimmed a vast bay marbled with ice. The air was so cold, a layer of frost crackled over my coat sleeves. Beneath my feet, instead of wooden planking, spread a bumpy surface of glistening gray and black like the shell of an armadillo.

The entire ship, a Viking vessel the size of an aircraft carrier, was made of the same stuff. And unfortunately I knew what it was—the clipped toenails and fingernails of the dishonored dead, billions upon billions of nasty zombie cuttings, all cobbled together by evil pedicurist magic to create *Naglfar*, the Ship of Nails, also known as the Ship of the Dead.

Above me, gray sails rippled in the freezing wind.

Shuffling across the deck were thousands of desiccated human husks dressed in rusted armor: *draugr*, Viking zombies.

Giants strode among them, shouting orders and kicking them to form ranks. Out of the corners of my eyes, I caught glimpses of darker things, too: incorporeal shades that might have been wolves, or serpents, or skeletal horses made of smoke.

"Look who's here!" said a cheerful voice.

Standing before me, in the white uniform of a navy admiral, was Loki himself. His autumn-leaf-colored hair swept around the edges of his flag officer's hat. His intense irises glinted like rings of hardening amber, suffocating the life out of his poor trapped pupils. Despite the pitted wreckage of his face, damaged from centuries of snake venom dripping between his eyes, despite the scarred and twisted lips that had once been sewn together by an angry dwarf, Loki grinned in such a warm, friendly way it was almost impossible not to smile back.

"Coming to visit me?" he asked. "Awesome!"

I tried to yell at him. I wanted to berate him for getting my uncle killed, for torturing my friends, for ruining my life and causing me six solid months of indigestion, but my throat was filled with wet cement.

"Nothing to say?" Loki chuckled. "That's all right, because I've got *plenty* to tell you. First a friendly warning: I'd *really* think twice about following old Randolph's plan." His expression tightened with false sympathy. "I'm afraid the poor man got a little senile there toward the end. You'd have to be crazy to listen to him!"

I wanted to strangle Loki, but my hands felt strangely heavy. I looked down and saw that my fingernails were growing at unnatural speed, stretching toward the deck like taproots seeking soil. My feet felt too tight in my shoes. Somehow I knew that my toenails were also lengthening, pushing through my socks, trying to escape the confines of my hiking boots.

"What else?" Loki tapped his chin. "Oh, yes! Look!"

He gestured past the hordes of shuffling zombies, sweeping his arm across the bay as if revealing a fabulous prize I'd just won. On the misty horizon, one of the glacial cliffs had begun to calve, sheeting massive curtains of ice into the water. The sound hit me half a second later: a muffled rumble like thunder through thick clouds.

"Cool, huh?" Loki grinned. "The ice is melting much faster than I thought. I *love* global warming! We'll be able to sail before the week is out, so really, you're already too late. I'd turn around and go back to Valhalla if I were you. You've only got a few days to enjoy yourself before Ragnarok hits. Might as well take some of those fabulous yoga classes!"

My rebellious fingernails reached the deck. They wove their way into the glistening gray surface, pulling me down, forcing me to double over. My toenails burst through the tips of my boots. They rooted me in place while dead men's nails began to grow upward like saplings, curling eagerly around my shoelaces, vining their way up my ankles.

Loki looked down at me with a gentle smile, as if watching a toddler take his first steps. "Yes, it's a wonderful week for Doomsday. But if you do insist on challenging me . . ." He sighed and shook his head like *You crazy kids and your quests.* "Then *please* leave my children out of it, will you? Poor Sam and Alex. They've suffered enough. If you care for them at all . . . Well, this quest will destroy them. I promise you that. They have *no idea* what they'll be facing!"

I fell to my knees. I could no longer tell where my own

fingernails and toenails stopped and the ship began. Jagged branches of gray and black keratin tightened around my calves and wrists, chaining me to the deck, encircling my limbs, pulling me down into the fabric of the ship itself.

"Take care, Magnus!" Loki called. "One way or another, we'll talk again soon!"

A rough hand clamped my shoulder, shaking me awake.

"Magnus!" yelled Halfborn Gunderson. "Snap out of it, man! Grab an oar!"

I found myself back on the deck of our bright yellow ship. We were drifting sideways through a cold, dense fog, the current pulling us to port, where the river fell away into roaring darkness.

I swallowed the wet cement clogging my throat. "Is that another waterfall?"

Mallory dropped on the bench next to me. "One that'll send us straight into Ginnungagap and kill us, yeah. You feel like rowing now?"

T.J. and Halfborn took the bench in front of us. Together, we four rowed with all our strength, turning starboard and dragging our ship away from the precipice. My shoulders burned. My back muscles screamed in protest. Finally the roaring sound faded behind us. The fog burned away, and I saw that we were in Boston Harbor, not far from Old Ironsides. Rising on my left were the brick row houses and church steeples of Charlestown.

T.J. turned and grinned. "See? That wasn't so bad!"

"Sure," Mallory said. "Except for almost falling off the edge of the world and being vaporized."

Halfborn stretched his arms. "I feel like I've just carried

an elephant up Bunker Hill, but good job, all. . . ." He faltered when he saw my face. "Magnus? What is it?"

I stared at my trembling hands. I felt as if my fingernails were still growing, trying to find their way back to the Ship of the Dead.

"I had a little vision," I muttered. "Give me a sec."

My friends exchanged wary looks. They all knew there was no such thing as a *little* vision.

Mallory Keen scooted closer to me. "Gunderson, why don't you take the rudder?"

Halfborn frowned. "I don't take orders from—"

Mallory glared at him. Halfborn muttered under his breath and went to take the rudder.

Mallory fixed me with her eyes, the green irises flecked with brown and orange like the shells of cardinals' eggs. "Was it Loki you saw?"

Normally, I didn't get this close to Mallory unless she was pulling an ax out of my chest on the battlefield. She valued her personal space. There was something troubling about her gaze—a sort of free-floating anger, like a fire that jumped from rooftop to rooftop. You never knew what it would burn and what it would leave alone.

"Yeah." I explained what I'd seen.

Mallory's lip curled with disgust. "That trickster . . . We've all been seeing him in our nightmares lately. When I get my hands on him—"

"Hey, Mallory," T.J. chided. "I know you want revenge even more than most of us, but—"

Keen stopped him with a harsh look.

I wondered what T.J. was talking about. I'd heard that

Mallory had died trying to disarm a car bomb in Ireland, but beyond that, I knew very little of her past. Had Loki been responsible for her death?

She gripped my wrist, her calloused fingers reminding me uncomfortably of the keratin vines of *Naglfar*. "Magnus, Loki's calling you out. If you have that dream again, don't talk to him. Don't be baited."

"Baited into what?" I asked.

Behind us, Halfborn yelled, "Valkyrie at ten o'clock!" He pointed to the Charlestown waterfront. About a quarter mile ahead, I could just make out two figures standing on the dock—one with a green hijab, the other with green hair.

Mallory scowled back at Gunderson. "Do you have to be so loud, you oaf?"

"This is my regular voice, woman!"

"Yes, I know: loud and annoying."

"If you don't like it—"

"Magnus," she said, "we'll talk later." She stomped over to the deck hatch, where Halfborn had dropped his battle-ax during all the confusion. She scooped up the weapon and brandished it at Halfborn. "You can have this back when you start to behave."

She slid down the ladder and disappeared belowdecks.

"Oh, no, she didn't!" Halfborn abandoned his post and marched after her.

The ship began to list to starboard. T.J. scrambled back and took the rudder.

He sighed. "Those two picked a terrible time to break up."

"Wait, *what*?" I asked.

T.J. raised his eyebrows. "You didn't hear?"

Halfborn and Mallory argued so much, it was hard to tell when they were angry and when they were just showing affection. Now that I thought about it, though, they *had* been a little more aggressive with each other the last few days.

"Why the breakup?"

T.J. shrugged. "The afterlife is a marathon, not a sprint. Long-term relationships are tricky when you live forever. It's not uncommon for einherji couples to break up sixty, seventy times over the course of a few centuries."

I tried to imagine that. Of course, I'd never been in a relationship, long-term or otherwise, so . . . I couldn't.

"And we're stuck on a ship with them," I noted, "while they're working out their differences, surrounded by a wide assortment of weapons."

"They're both professionals," said T.J. "I'm sure it'll be fine."

THUNK. Below my feet, the deck shuddered with the sound of an ax impaling wood.

"Right," I said. "And the stuff Mallory was saying about Loki?"

T.J.'s smile melted. "We all have our problems with that trickster."

I wondered what T.J.'s were. I'd lived with my friends on floor nineteen for months now, but I was starting to realize how little I knew about their pasts. Thomas Jefferson Jr.— former infantryman in the Fifty-Fourth Massachusetts, son of the war god Tyr and a freed slave. T.J. never seemed to get flustered, even when he got killed on the battlefield, or when he had to intercept Halfborn Gunderson sleepwalking naked through the halls and get him back to his room. T.J. had the sunniest disposition of any dead person I knew, but he must have seen his share of horrors.

I wondered what sort of ammunition Loki used to taunt him in his dreams.

"Mallory said Loki was calling me out," I remembered. "And that I shouldn't take the bait?"

T.J. flexed his fingers, as if he were having sympathetic pains from his father, Tyr, who'd gotten his hand bitten off by Fenris Wolf. "Mallory's right. Some challenges you should never take, especially from Loki."

I frowned. Loki had used the term *challenge*, too. Not *fight*. Not *stop*. He'd said *if you do insist on challenging me*. . . .

"T.J., isn't your dad the *god* of personal challenges and duels and whatnot?"

"Exactly." T.J.'s voice was as stiff and flat as the hardtack bread he loved to eat. He pointed to the docks. "Look, Sam and Alex have company."

I hadn't noticed earlier, but lurking a few feet behind the children of Loki, leaning against the hood of his car in his jeans and teal work shirt, was my favorite supplier of fresh falafel sandwiches. Amir Fadlan, Samirah's fiancé, had come to see us off.

SEVEN

We All Drown

"WOW," SAID SAMIRAH as we approached the dock. "You're right, Alex. That ship is *really* yellow."

I sighed. "Not you, too."

Alex grinned. "I vote we name it the *Big Banana*. All in favor?"

"Don't you dare," I said.

"I love it," Mallory said, throwing Alex a mooring line.

Keen and Gunderson had emerged from belowdecks in an apparent truce, though both sported fresh black eyes.

"It's decided, then!" bellowed Halfborn. "The good ship *Mikillgulr*!"

T.J. scratched his head. "There's an Old Norse term for *big banana*?"

"Well, not exactly," Halfborn admitted. "The Vikings never sailed far enough south to discover bananas. But *Mikillgulr* means *big yellow*. That's close enough!"

I looked skyward with a silent prayer: *Frey, god of summer, Dad, thanks for the boat. But could I suggest that forest green is also a great summery color, and please stop embarrassing me in front of my friends? Amen.*

I climbed ashore and helped tie up the Big Yellow Humiliation, my legs still wobbly from the rough river ride and my vision of Loki. If I felt this grateful to be back on dry land after only a few minutes of travel, our journey across the sea promised to be tons of fun.

Amir shook my hand. "How are you, J— Magnus?"

Even after all these months, he sometimes slipped and called me *Jimmy*. That was my bad. During the two years I'd been homeless, Amir and his dad had been one of my few dependable sources of hot meals. They'd given me leftovers from their restaurant in the Transportation Building food court. In exchange for their kindness, I hadn't trusted them with my real name. I still felt guilty about that.

"Yeah, I'm good. . . ." I realized I was deceiving him yet again. "I mean, as good as can be expected given that we're heading off on another dangerous quest."

Samirah nudged my ribs with the butt of her ax. "Hey, don't get him agitated. I've spent the past few days trying to convince Amir not to worry."

Alex smirked. "And I've spent the past few days chaperoning them as she tried to convince him not to worry. It's been *very* cute."

Samirah blushed. She was dressed in her typical travel clothes: leather boots, sturdy cargo pants fitted with two axes, a long-sleeved turtleneck, and a dark green jacket that complemented her magical hijab. The fabric of the headscarf rippled in the breeze, catching the colors from her surroundings and ready to go into full camouflage mode at a moment's notice.

Sam's face, though, seemed a little *off*. Her lips were dry and peeling, her eyes sunken and dull like she was suffering from a vitamin deficiency.

"You okay?" I asked her.

"Of course. I'm fine!"

But I could smell the ketones on her breath—a stale sour scent like lemons left out in the sun. It was the smell of someone who hadn't eaten in a while. I'd gotten used to that on the streets. "Nah," I decided. "You're not okay."

She started to deny it, but Amir interceded.

"Ramadan started two weeks ago," he said. "We're both fasting."

"Amir!" Sam protested.

"Well? Magnus is a friend. He deserves to know."

Alex was working his jaw, trying to bite back his frustration. Of course Alex had known. That's what he'd been talking about at Uncle Randolph's—the reason Sam was having so much trouble focusing on her training. I didn't know much about Ramadan, but I knew a lot about going hungry. It can seriously mess up your concentration.

"So, uh, what are the rules about that?" I asked.

"It will not affect me on this quest," Sam promised. "I didn't want to say anything, because I didn't want anyone worrying. It's just no drinking or eating during daylight hours."

"Or bathing," Amir said. "Or cursing. Or smoking. Or violence."

"Which is fine," Alex said, "because our quests *never* involve violence."

Sam rolled her eyes. "I can still defend myself if attacked. It's only one month—"

"One *month*?" I asked.

"I've done this every year since I was ten," Sam said. "Believe me, it's no big deal."

It sounded like a pretty big deal to me, especially in the

summer when the days were so long, and we'd be facing all sorts of life-and-death situations that would not wait until after regular business hours. "Couldn't you, like, take a rain check until after our quest?"

"She *could*," Amir said. "That's allowable if you're traveling, or if fasting would be too dangerous, both of which are true in this case."

"But she won't," Alex chimed in. "Because she is as stubborn as a very devout mule."

Sam poked Alex in the ribs. "Watch it, brother."

"Ow," Alex complained. "What happened to no violence?"

"I was defending myself," Sam said.

"Hey, you all," Halfborn called from the ship. "We're loaded up and ready to sail. What are you gabbing about? Come on!"

I looked at Amir, as well-groomed as always, his clothes spotless and perfectly ironed, his dark hair cut to razor-straight perfection. You'd never guess he was a guy who was probably weak from hunger and thirst. But his facial muscles were more taut than usual. His gentle brown eyes kept blinking like he was expecting a drop of cold water to splash on his forehead. Amir was suffering, but it was from something that had nothing to do with Ramadan.

"Just be careful," he pleaded. "All of you. Magnus, I'd ask you to watch out for Samirah, but if I did that, she would hit me with her ax."

"I would never hit you with my ax," Sam said. "Anyway, I'll be watching out for Magnus, not the other way around."

"*I'll* watch out for Sam," Alex volunteered. "That's what family is for, right?"

Amir blinked even more. I got the sense that he still wasn't sure what to make of Alex Fierro, Sam's green-haired gender-fluid half-sibling chaperone of doom.

"Okay." Amir nodded. "Thanks."

I couldn't help feeling guilty about Amir's anguish. Months ago, when he'd started seeing into Samirah's weird double life as a Valkyrie of Odin, I'd healed his mind to keep him from going insane. Now his mortal eyes were permanently opened. Rather than living in blissful ignorance, he could see the earth giants that occasionally strolled down Commonwealth Avenue, the sea serpents that frolicked in the Charles River, and the Valkyries that flew overhead, bringing souls of fallen heroes to check in at the Hotel Valhalla. He could even see our huge Viking warship that looked like a heavily armed banana.

"We'll be careful," I told him. "Besides, nobody would dare attack this ship. It's *way* too yellow."

He mustered a faint smile. "That much is true." He reached behind him. From the hood of his car, he hefted a large green insulated pack—the kind Fadlan's Falafel used for deliveries. "This is for you, Magnus. I hope you enjoy."

The scent of fresh falafel wafted out. True, I'd eaten falafel just a few hours ago, but my stomach growled because . . . well, more falafel. "Man, you're the best. I can't believe— Wait. You're in the middle of a fast, and you brought me food? That seems wrong."

"Just because I'm fasting doesn't mean you can't enjoy." He clapped me on my shoulder. "You'll be in my prayers. All of you."

I knew he was sincere. Me, I was an atheist. I only prayed sarcastically to my own father for a better color of boat.

Learning about the existence of Norse deities and the Nine Worlds had just made me *more* convinced that there was no grand divine plan. What kind of God would allow Zeus and Odin to run around in the same cosmos, both claiming to be the king of creation, smiting mortals with lightning bolts and giving motivational seminars?

But Amir was a man of faith. He and Samirah believed in something bigger, a cosmic force that actually *cared* about humans. I suppose it was kind of comforting to know Amir had my back in the prayer department, even if I doubted there was anybody at the other end of that line.

"Thanks, man." I shook his hand one last time.

Amir turned to Sam. They stood a few feet apart, not touching. In all the years they'd known each other, they had never touched. I wondered if that was killing Amir even worse than the fasting.

I wasn't much of a toucher myself, but every once in a while, a hug from somebody I cared about could go a long way. Caring about each other as much as Sam and Amir did, and not even being able to hold hands . . . I couldn't imagine that.

"I love you," Amir told her.

Samirah stumbled backward like she'd been hit in the face with a giant eagle egg. Alex propped her up.

"I . . . yes," Sam squeaked. "Also. Too."

Amir nodded. He turned and got into his car. A moment later, his taillights disappeared down Flagship Way.

Samirah smacked her own forehead. "*Also? Too?* I am such an idiot."

Alex patted her arm. "I thought you were quite eloquent. Come on, sister. Your neon-yellow warship awaits."

We undid the mooring lines, extended the mast, hoisted the sail, and did a bunch of other nautical stuff. Soon we were leaving Boston behind, sailing through the mouth of the channel between Logan Airport and the Seaport District.

I liked the *Big Banana* a lot more when it wasn't bouncing through subterranean rapids or drifting toward inter-dimensional waterfalls. A strong wind filled the sail. The sunset turned the downtown skyline to red gold. The sea stretched ahead of us in silky sheets of blue, and for now, all I had to do was stand at the prow and enjoy the view.

After a long hard day, I might even have been able to relax, except I kept thinking about my Uncle Randolph. He had once sailed out of this same harbor, searching for the Sword of Summer. His family had never come back.

This is different, I told myself. *We've got a well-trained crew of einherjar and the stubbornest, most devout Valkyrie in Valhalla.*

Loki's voice echoed through my head. *Poor Sam and Alex. This quest will destroy them. They have no idea what they'll be facing!*

"Shut up," I murmured.

"Sorry?"

I hadn't realized Samirah was standing right next to me.

"Uh. Nothing. Well . . . not really nothing. I had a little visit from your dad." I told her the details.

Samirah grimaced. "So the usual, then. Alex has been having visions and nightmares, too, pretty much daily."

I scanned the deck, but Alex must have been below. "Really? He didn't say anything about that to me."

Samirah shrugged like *That's Alex.*

"What about you?" I asked. "Any visions?"

She tilted her head. "No, which is interesting. Ramadan

tends to focus the mind and strengthen the will. That could be why Loki hasn't been inside my head. I'm hoping . . ."

She let the thought trail off, but I caught her meaning. She hoped her fasting might make it harder for Loki to control her. It seemed like a long shot to me. Then again, if my dad could make me do anything he wanted simply by commanding me, I would've been willing to try anything, even forgoing falafel sandwiches, to thwart him. Every time Sam said her father's name, I heard the rage simmering inside her. She *hated* being under his power.

A passenger jet took off from Logan and roared overhead. From T.J.'s lookout at the top of the mast, he raised his arms and yelled, "WOOHOO!" as the wind ruffled through his dark curly hair.

Being from the 1860s, T.J. loved airplanes. I think they seemed more magical to him than dwarves, elves, or dragons.

I felt clanging and bumping below us—Alex and Mallory, probably, getting all our supplies stowed away. Halfborn Gunderson stood aft, leaning on the rudder and whistling "Fly Me to the Moon." (Stupid Valhalla elevator-music earworms.)

"Sam, you'll be ready," I said at last. "You'll beat Loki this time."

She turned to gaze at the sunset. I wondered if she was waiting for dusk, when she could eat and drink and, most important, curse again.

"The thing about that," she said, "is I won't know until I actually face Loki. Alex's training is all about loosening me up, getting me more comfortable with shape-shifting, but . . ." She swallowed. "I don't know that I *want* to be more comfortable with it. I'm not like Alex."

That was undeniable.

When Sam had first told me about her shape-changing abilities, she'd explained that she hated to use them. She saw it as giving in to Loki, becoming more like her father.

Alex believed in claiming Loki's power as his own. Sam saw her jotun heritage as poison that had to be expelled. She relied on discipline and structure: Pray more. Give up food and drink. Whatever it took. But shape-shifting, being fluid the way Alex and Loki were . . . that was alien to her, even though it was part of her blood.

"You'll find a way," I said. "A way that works for you."

She studied my face, perhaps trying to gauge whether I believed what I was saying. "I appreciate that. But in the meantime, we have other things to worry about. Alex told me what happened at your uncle's place."

Despite the warm evening, I shivered. Thinking about wolves does that to me. "You have any thoughts about what my uncle's notes meant? Mead? Bolverk?"

Sam shook her head. "We can ask Hearthstone and Blitzen when we pick them up. They've been traveling, doing a lot of— what did they call it?—long-range reconnaissance."

That sounded impressive. Maybe they'd been networking with their contacts in Mimir's strange interdimensional mafia, trying to find us the safest course through the seas of the Nine Worlds. But the image that kept coming to my mind was Blitzen shopping for new outfits while Hearthstone stood idly nearby, arranging runes into various spells to make time go faster.

I'd missed those guys.

"Where exactly are we meeting them?" I asked.

Sam pointed ahead. "Deer Island Lighthouse. They promised they'd be there at sunset today. Which is now."

Dozens of islands dotted the coastline off Boston. I could never keep them all straight, but the lighthouse Sam was talking about was easy enough to distinguish—a squat building with a mast thing on top, jutting out of the waves like the conning tower of a concrete submarine.

As we got closer, I waited to spot the glinting chain mail waistcoat of a fashionable dwarf, or an elf in black waving a candy-striped scarf.

"I don't see them," I muttered. I glanced up at T.J. "Hey, you see anything?"

Our lookout seemed paralyzed. His mouth hung open, his eyes wide in an expression I'd never associated with Thomas Jefferson Jr.—pure terror.

Next to me, Sam made a strangled sound. She backed away from the prow and pointed to the water between us and the lighthouse.

In front of us, the sea had started to churn, swirling into a downward funnel like someone had pulled the bathtub plug out of Massachusetts Bay. Rising from the maelstrom were the giant watery forms of women—nine in all, each as large as our ship, with dresses of foam and ice, and blue-green faces contorted with rage.

I just had time to think: *Percy didn't cover this in basic seamanship.*

Then the giant women fell on us like a vengeful tsunami, plunging our glorious yellow warship into the abyss.

EIGHT

In the Hall of the Huffy Hipster

HURTLING TO the bottom of the sea was bad enough.

I didn't need the singing, too.

As our ship tumbled, free-falling through the eye of a saltwater cyclone, the nine giant maidens spiraled around us, weaving in and out of the tempest so they appeared to drown over and over again. Their faces contorted in anger and glee. Their long hair lashed us with icy spray. Each time they emerged, they wailed and shrieked, but it wasn't just random noise. Their screams had a tonal quality, like a chorus of whale songs played through heavy feedback. I even caught snippets of lyrics: *boiling mead . . . wave daughters . . . death for you!* It reminded me of the first time Halfborn Gunderson played Norwegian black metal for me. After a few bars, it dawned on me . . . *Oh, wait. That's supposed to be music!*

Sam and I locked arms on the rigging. T.J. straddled the top of the mast, screaming like he was riding the world's most terrifying carousel pony. Halfborn wrestled the rudder, though I didn't see what good that would do in a downward plunge. Belowdecks, I heard Mallory and Alex getting thrown around, *KA-FLUMP, KA-FLUMP, KA-FLUMP,* like a pair of human dice.

The ship spun. With a cry of despair, T.J. lost his grip and hurtled into the maelstrom. Sam zoomed after him. Thank goodness for Valkyrie powers of flight. She tackled T.J. around the waist and zigzagged back to the ship with him, dodging the grasping hands of the sea giantesses and various pieces of luggage we were shedding like ballast.

As soon as she reached the deck—*BLOOOSH!* Our ship splash-landed and then sank.

The biggest shock was the heat. I'd been expecting a freezing death. Instead, I felt like I'd been dunked in a scalding bathtub. My back arched. My muscles contracted. I managed not to inhale any liquid, but when I blinked, trying to see which way was up, the water was a strange cloudy golden color.

That can't be good, I thought.

The deck surged beneath me. The *Big Banana* broke the surface of . . . wherever we were. The storm had vanished. The nine giantesses were nowhere to be seen. Our ship bobbed and creaked on the placid golden water that bubbled around the hull, exuding a smell like exotic spices, flowers, and baked goods. In every direction rose sheer brown cliffs—a perfect ring about a mile in diameter. My first thought was that we'd been dropped in the middle of a volcanic lake.

Our ship seemed to be in one piece, at least. The wet yellow sail flapped against the mast. The rigging glistened and steamed.

Samirah and T.J. got to their feet first. They slipped and staggered aft, where Halfborn Gunderson was slumped over the rudder, blood dripping from an ugly gash on his forehead.

For a moment, I thought, *Eh, Halfborn gets killed that way all the time.* Then I remembered we were not in Valhalla any-more. Wherever this was, if we died here, we would not get a do-over.

"He's alive!" Sam announced. "Knocked out cold, though!"

My ears still rang from the weird music. My thoughts moved sluggishly. I wondered why T.J. and Sam were looking at me.

Then I realized, *Oh, right. I'm the healer.*

I ran over to help. I channeled Frey-power to heal Gunderson's head wound as Mallory and Alex, both battered and bleeding, staggered out from belowdecks.

"What are you fools *doing* up here?" Mallory demanded.

As if in answer, a storm cloud rolled overhead, obscuring half the sky. A voice boomed from above:

"WHAT ARE YOU DOING IN MY CAULDRON?"

The storm cloud descended, and I realized it was a face—a face that did not look happy to see us.

From my previous dealings with giants, I'd learned that the only way to process their immense size was to focus on one thing at a time: a nose the size of an oil tanker, a beard as thick and vast as a redwood forest, round gold-rimmed glasses that looked like crop circles. And on the giant's head, what I'd taken for a storm front was the rim of the universe's largest panama hat.

The way his voice echoed in the basin, pinging off the cliffs with tinny reverberations, made me realize we were not, in fact, in a volcanic crater. Those cliffs were the metal rim of a huge pot. The steaming lake was some kind of brew. And we'd just become the secret ingredient.

My friends stood with their mouths open, trying to make

sense of what they were seeing—all except for Halfborn Gunderson, who wisely remained unconscious.

I was the first to regain my wits. I hate it when that happens.

"Hello," I said to the giant.

I'm diplomatic that way, always knowing the right greeting.

Frowny McHugeface furrowed his brow, giving me flashbacks to my sixth-grade science lesson on plate tectonics. He glanced to either side and called out, "Daughters! Get over here!"

More gigantic faces popped up around the rim of the pot: the nine women from the maelstrom, but much larger now, their frothy hair floating about their faces, their smiles a little too manic, their eyes bright with excitement or hunger. (I hoped it wasn't hunger. . . . It was probably hunger.)

"We got them, Dad!" one of the women squeaked—or it would have been a squeak if she hadn't been the size of South Boston.

"Yes, but *why*?" their father asked.

"They're yellow!" another giantess chimed in. "We noticed them right away! With a ship that color, we figured they deserved to drown!"

I mentally began composing a list of words that began with *F*: Frey. Father. False. Friend. Frick. Frack. And some others.

"Also," said a third daughter, "one of them mentioned *mead*! We knew you'd want to talk to them, Dad! That's your favorite word!"

"Whoa, whoa, whoa!" Alex Fierro waved his hands like there was a flag on the play. "Nobody here was talking about mead. There's been some kind of mistake—" He hesitated, then frowned at me. "Right?"

"Uh . . ." I pointed to Samirah, who backed away, out of range of Alex's cutting wire. "I was just explaining—"

"DOESN'T MATTER!" boomed Frowny. "You're here now, but I can't have you in my cauldron. I'm just cooking down the mead. A Viking ship could totally ruin the flavor of the honey!"

I glanced at the bubbling liquid around us. I was suddenly glad I hadn't inhaled any of it.

"Honey?" I asked.

"Don't you *dare* call me that," Alex growled. Possibly he was kidding. I didn't want to ask.

A massive hand loomed over us, and Frowny plucked up our ship by the mast.

"They're too small to see properly," he complained. "Let's scale things down."

I hated it when gigantic people changed the proportions of reality. Instantly the world telescoped around me. My stomach imploded. My ears popped. My eyes expanded painfully in their sockets.

BOOM! SCRAPE! THUMP!

I stumbled over my own feet, and found myself standing with my friends in the middle of a vast Viking hall.

In one corner, our ship lay on its side, hot mead still dripping from the hull. The room's walls were columned with dozens of ship keels, soaring hundreds of feet up and curving inward to form the rafters of a peaked ceiling. Instead of planks or plaster filling in the space between the columns, there was nothing except rippling green water, held in place by no physics that made sense to me. Here and there, doors lined the watery walls, leading to other undersea chambers, I guessed. The floor was carpeted in squishy kelp that made me glad I had shoes on.

The hall's layout wasn't much different than your typical Viking party pad. A rectangular feasting table dominated the space, with chairs of carved red coral along either side, and an elaborate throne at the far end, decorated with pearls and shark jaws. Freestanding braziers burned with ghostly green flames, filling the hall with a smell like toasted seaweed. Hanging over the main hearth fire was the cauldron we'd been floating in, though it now appeared much less massive—maybe just big enough to cook a team of oxen in. The pot's polished bronze sides were engraved with designs of waves and snarling faces.

Our host/captor, the frowny-daddy giant guy, stood before us, his arms crossed, his brow knit. He was now only twice as tall as a human. The cuffs of his army-green skinny jeans were turned up over pointy black boots. His suit vest was buttoned over a white dress shirt, the sleeves pushed back to show lots of swirling runic tattoos on his forearms. With his panama hat and his gold-rimmed glasses, he looked like an agitated Whole Foods shopper, stuck in the express line behind a bunch of people with too many items, when all he wanted to do was purchase his macrobiotic matcha smoothie and leave.

Behind him, in a loose semicircle, stood the nine wave girls—who were not (shockingly) doing the wave. Each giantess was terrifying in her own special way, but they all leered and giggled and pushed each other around with the same level of excitement, like fans waiting for a star to come through the stage door so they could tear him to pieces to show their love.

I recalled my encounter with the sea goddess Ran, who

had described her husband as a hipster who liked micro-brewing. At the time, the description had been too weird to comprehend. Afterward, it had seemed funny. Now it seemed a little too real, because I was pretty sure the hipster god in question was standing right in front of me.

"You are Aegir," I guessed. "God of the sea."

Aegir grunted in a way that implied *Yeah, so? You still tainted my mead.*

"And these . . ." I gulped. "These lovely ladies are your daughters?"

"Of course," he said. "The Nine Giantesses of the Waves! This is Himminglaeva, Hefring, Hrönn—"

"I'm Hefring, Dad," said the tallest girl. "She's Hrönn."

"Right," said Aegir. "And Unn. And Bylgya—"

"Bigly?" asked Mallory, who was doing her best to hold up a half-conscious Halfborn.

"Nice to meet you all!" Samirah yelped, before Aegir could introduce Comet, Cupid, and Rudolph. "We claim guest rights!"

Samirah was smart. In certain polite jotun households, claiming guest rights could get you a free pass from being slaughtered, at least temporarily.

Aegir harrumphed. "What do you take me for, a savage? Of *course* you have guest rights. Despite the fact that you ruined my mead and you have an insultingly yellow ship, you're in my house now. We at least have to have a meal together before I decide what to do with you. Unless one of you is Magnus Chase, of course, in which case I'd have to kill you right away. One of you isn't he, I hope?"

No one responded, though my friends all glared at me like *Dang it, Magnus.*

"Just hypothetically . . ." I said. "If we had a Magnus Chase, why would you kill him?"

"Because I promised my wife, Ran!" Aegir cried. "For some reason, she *hates* that guy!"

The nine daughters nodded vigorously, muttering, "Hates him. A lot. Yes, tons."

"Ah." I was glad I was drenched in mead. Maybe it would hide the sweat popping up on my forehead. "And where is your lovely wife?"

"Not here tonight," Aegir said. "She's out collecting trash in her nets."

"Thank gods!" I said. "I mean . . . thank gods we at least get to spend some quality time with the rest of you!"

Aegir tilted his head. "Yes. . . . Well, daughters, I suppose you should set extra places at the table for our guests. I'll talk to our chef about cooking up those juicy prisoners!"

He waved toward one of the side doors, which swung open by itself. Inside was a vast kitchen. When I saw what was suspended above the oven, it took all my willpower not to scream like a wave giantess. Hanging in two matching extra-large canary cages were our long-range reconnaissance experts, Blitzen and Hearthstone.

NINE

I Become a Temporary Vegetarian

THAT AWKWARD moment when you lock eyes with two friends hanging in cages in a giant's kitchen. And one of them recognizes you and begins to shout your name, but you do not want your name shouted.

Blitzen staggered to his feet, gripped the bars of his cage, and yelled, "MAG—"

"—NIFICENT!" I bellowed over him. "What beautiful specimens!"

I jogged toward the cages, Sam and Alex on my heels.

Aegir frowned. "Daughters, see to our other guests!" He made a sweeping take-out-the-trash gesture toward Mallory and T.J., who were still trying to keep our semiconscious berserker from face-planting in the kelp. Then the sea god followed us into the kitchen.

The appliances were all twice human size. The oven knobs alone would have made decent dinner plates. Hearthstone and Blitzen, looking unharmed but humiliated, dangled over the four-burner cooktop, their cages knocking against a tile backsplash that was painted with *buon appetito!* in garish red cursive.

Hearthstone wore his usual black biker outfit, his

candy-striped scarf the only flourish of color. His pale face and white-blond hair made it difficult to tell if he was anemic or terrified or just mortified by the *buon appetito!* sign.

Blitzen straightened his navy-blue blazer, then made sure his mauve silk dress shirt was properly tucked into his jeans. His matching handkerchief and ascot were a little askew, but the dude looked pretty good for a prisoner who was on today's dinner menu. His curly black hair and beard were well trimmed. His dark complexion coordinated beautifully with the iron bars of his cage.

If nothing else, Aegir should have let him go for being a fellow snazzy dresser.

I used a quick flurry of sign language to warn them: *Don't say my name. A-E-G-I-R will kill me.*

I spelled out the god's name since I didn't know what name sign we might use for him. *Frowny*, *Beer Man*, or *H* for *hipster* were all logical choices.

The god appeared at my side. "They *are* magnificent specimens," he agreed. "We always try to have a fresh catch of the day in case guests stop by."

"Right! Very smart," I said. "But do you normally eat dwarves and elves? I didn't think gods—"

"*Gods?*" Aegir barked a laugh. "Well, there's your mistake, little mortal. I'm not one of those namby-pamby Aesir or Vanir gods! I'm a jotun deity, one hundred percent giant!"

I hadn't heard the term *namby-pamby* since third-grade PE class with Coach Wicket, but I seemed to recall it not being a compliment. "So . . . you *do* eat dwarves and elves?"

"Sometimes." Aegir sounded a bit defensive. "And the

occasional troll or human, though I draw the line at hobgob-
lins. Too gamey. Why do you ask?" He narrowed his eyes. "Do
you have special dietary restrictions?"

Sam, again, was quickest on the draw. "Yes, actually! I'm
Muslim."

Aegir winced. "I see. Sorry. Yes, I don't think dwarves are
halal. I'm not sure about elves."

"They're not, either," Sam said. "In fact, it's Ramadan,
which means I need to break my fast in the *company* of dwarves
and elves, rather than eating them or being around anyone
who does eat them. It's strictly forbidden."

I was pretty sure she was making that up, but what did I
know? I suppose she was counting on Aegir knowing even less
about Quranic restrictions than I did.

"What a pity." Our host sighed. "And the rest of you?"

"I'm a vegetarian," I said, which wasn't true, but hey, falafel
was a vegetable. I glanced at Blitz and Hearth. They gave me
four enthusiastic thumbs up.

"And I have green hair." Alex spread his hands like *What
are you gonna do?* "I'm afraid eating dwarves or elves goes
against my beliefs. But I very much appreciate the offer."

Aegir glowered, as if we were testing the limits of his culi-
nary hospitality. He stared at Blitzen and Hearthstone, now
leaning casually against the bars of their cages and trying to
look as non-halal as possible.

"So much for the catch of the day," Aegir grumbled. "But
we always do our best to accommodate our guests. *Eldir!*"

He yelled the last word so loudly I jumped and hit my head
on the oven door handle.

A side door swung open, and an old man shuffled out of

the pantry in a cloud of smoke. He was dressed in a white chef's outfit, complete with poufy hat, but his clothes seemed to be in the process of combusting. Flames danced across his sleeves and apron. Smoke streamed from his collar like his chest was coming to a boil. Sparks wormed through his gray eyebrows and beard. He looked about six hundred years old, his expression so sour he might have spent that entire time smelling terrible things.

"What is it?" he snapped. "I was preparing my elfish salt rub!"

"We'll need something different for dinner," Aegir ordered. "No elf. No dwarf."

"*What?*" Eldir grumbled.

"Our guests have food restrictions: halal, vegetarian, green-hair friendly."

"And it's Ramadan," Sam added. "So you'll need to free those prisoners so they can break my fast with me."

"Humph," said Eldir. "Expect me to *(mutter, mutter)* short notice *(mutter, mutter)* green-hair-friendly menu. I may have some kelp patties in the freezer." He tromped back into the pantry, still complaining and smoldering.

"I don't mean to be rude," I said to Aegir, "but is your chef on fire?"

"Oh, Eldir has been like that for centuries. Ever since my other servant, Fimafeng, got killed by Loki, which left Eldir with twice as much work and made him *burning* mad!"

A little bubble of hope formed in my chest. "Killed by Loki, you say?"

"Yes!" Aegir frowned. "Surely you heard how that scoundrel disgraced my hall?"

I glanced at Sam and Alex like *Hey, guys, Aegir is another enemy of Loki!*

Then I remembered that Sam and Alex were both children of Loki. Aegir might not like my friends any more than he liked people named Magnus Chase.

"Lord Aegir," Sam said. "That time Loki disgraced your hall . . . was that the feast of the gods?"

"Yes, yes," Aegir said. "A complete disaster! The gossip bloggers had a field day with it!"

I could almost see Sam's mind working. If she'd been Eldir, steam would've been pouring from the edges of her hijab.

"I remember the story," Sam said. She grabbed Alex's arm. "I have to pray. Alex needs to help me."

Alex blinked. "I do?"

"Lord Aegir," Sam continued, "may I use a corner of your hall for a quick prayer?"

The sea god tugged on his vest. "Well, I suppose."

"Thanks!"

Sam and Alex scurried out of the kitchen. I hoped they were going to formulate a cunning plan to get us all out of Aegir's hall alive. If Sam was really just going to pray . . . well, I wondered if she'd ever tried to say a Muslim prayer in the home of a Norse god (sorry, *jotun deity*) before. I was afraid the entire place might collapse from religious paradox.

Aegir stared at me. That awkward dinner-party silence when you've tried to serve dwarf and elf to a vegetarian.

"I'm going to retrieve some mead from the cellar," he said at last. "Please tell me you and your friends don't have dietary restrictions against mead?"

"I think we're good!" I said, because I did not want to see a grown jotun cry.

"Thank the waves." Aegir dug a set of keys from his vest pocket and tossed them to me. "Unlock the dinner—I mean the prisoners, would you? Then make yourself . . ."

He waved vaguely toward the feast hall then stomped off, leaving me to imagine how he might've finished that sentence: *comfortable, scarce, a sandwich.*

I climbed the oven and freed Blitz and Hearth from their canary cages. We had a tearful reunion on the front left burner.

"Kid!" Blitzen gave me a hug. "I knew you'd come rescue us!"

"Uh, actually, I didn't know you guys were here." I used sign language as I talked, for Hearthstone's benefit, though it had been several weeks and my hands were slow. You get out of practice fast. "But I'm really glad I found you."

Hearthstone snapped his fingers for attention. *I'm glad too,* he signed. He patted the bag of runes at his belt. *Stupid cages were magic-proof. Blitzen was crying a lot.*

"I was not," Blitzen protested, signing along. "You were."

I was not, Hearthstone said. *You were.*

At that point, the ASL conversation deteriorated into the two of them poking each other in the chest.

"Guys," I interrupted. "What happened? How did you end up here?"

"Long story," Blitz said. "We were waiting for you guys at the lighthouse, minding our own business."

Fighting a sea serpent, Hearth signed.

"Doing nothing wrong," Blitz said.

Hitting serpent on the head with rocks.

"Well, it was threatening us!" Blitz said. "Then this wave came up and swallowed us!"

Wave contained nine angry women. Serpent was their pet.

"How was I supposed to know that?" Blitz grumbled. "The serpent didn't *look* like it was trying to play fetch. But that's not important, kid. We found out some information on our reconnaissance, and it isn't good—"

"Guests!" Aegir called from main hall. "Come! Join us for mead and food!"

Put a pin in that, Hearthstone signed, poking Blitz in the chest one last time.

Back in the days when we were three homeless guys on the streets of Boston, if somebody had called us for dinner, we would've come running. Now we trudged over reluctantly. This was one free meal I wasn't so pumped about.

The nine daughters of Aegir hustled about, setting the table with plates and forks and goblets. Aegir hummed as he fiddled with a rack of mead kegs, each labeled with runes. T.J., Mallory, and Halfborn were already seated, looking very uncomfortable in their red coral seats, with empty chairs spaced between them. Halfborn Gunderson, more or less conscious now, kept blinking and staring at his surroundings like he hoped he was dreaming.

Over by the *Big Banana*, Samirah finished her prayers. She rolled up her portable rug, had a brief, urgent conversation with Alex, then they both came over to join us. If Sam did have a brilliant plan, I was glad it didn't involve her and Alex turning into dolphins, yelling, *See you, suckers!*, and escaping on their own.

The dining table looked like it had been made from the world's largest mast, cut in half lengthwise and folded out to make two leaves. Overhead, suspended from the rafters by an anchor chain, was a sea-glass chandelier. Instead of candles or electric lights, glowing souls of the dead swirled in oversize sconces. Just to set the mood, I guessed.

I was about to sit down between Blitz and Hearth when I realized there were name tags at the place settings: DWARF. HRÖNN. ELF. HEFRING. GREEN HEADSCARF. I found mine on the other side of the table: BLOND GUY.

Great. We had assigned seating.

A daughter of Aegir sat down on either side of me. According to the name tags, the lady on my left was Kolga. The one on my right . . . oh, boy. Apparently her name was Blodughadda. I wondered if that was the sound her mom had made on anesthesia after giving birth to daughter number nine. Maybe I could just call her Blod.

"Hi," I said.

Blod smiled. Her teeth were stained red. Her wavy hair was flecked with blood. "Hello. It was a pleasure dragging you under the sea."

"Yeah. Thanks."

Her sister Kolga leaned in. Frost started to form on my forearm. Kolga's dress appeared to be woven from ice shards and slush. "I hope we get to keep them, sister," she said. "They'd make fine tortured spirits."

Blod cackled. Her breath smelled like fresh ground beef

just out of the fridge. "Yes, indeed! Perfect for our chandelier."

"Appreciate the offer," I said. "But we actually have a pretty full calendar."

"Where are my manners?" Blod said. "In your language, I am called Blood-Red Hair. My sister here is Freezing Wave. And your name is . . ." She frowned at my card. "Blond Guy?"

I didn't see how that was any worse than Blood-Red Hair or Bigly.

"You can call me Jimmy," I offered. "In your language that's . . . Jimmy."

Blod didn't look satisfied with that. "There's something about you." She sniffed my face. "Have you sailed over my bloodred waters in a naval battle before?"

"Pretty sure not."

"Perhaps my mother, Ran, described you to me. But why would she—?"

"Guests!" Aegir boomed, and I had never been happier for an interruption. "Here is my first microbrew of the evening. This is a peach lambic mead that makes a lovely aperitif. I welcome your comments after you try it."

His nine daughters oohed and aahed as Aegir hefted the mead cask and carried it around the table, pouring everyone a serving.

"I think you'll find this has a fruity edge," Aegir said. "With just a hint of—"

"Magnus Chase!" Blod yelled, surging to her feet and pointing at me. "This is MAGNUS CHASE!"

TEN

Can We Talk About Mead?

TYPICAL. SOMEBODY says *fruity edge* and immediately my name comes to mind.

Come on, people. A little respect.

The daughters of Aegir shot to their feet. Some picked up steak knives, forks, or napkins to stab, poke, or strangle us with.

Aegir screamed, "Magnus Chase? What is this deception?"

My friends and I didn't move a muscle. We all knew how guest rights worked. We still might be able to talk our way out of a fight, but once we drew our weapons, we stopped being considered guests and started being the catch of the day. Against an entire family of jotun deities on their home turf, I didn't like our odds.

"Wait!" I said, as calmly as I could with a woman named Blood-Red Hair holding a knife over me. "We're still guests at your table. We haven't broken any rules."

Steam rolled beneath the brim of Aegir's panama hat. His gold-rimmed glasses fogged up. Under his arm, the mead cask began to creak like a pecan in a nutcracker.

"You lied to me," Aegir snarled. "You said you weren't Magnus Chase!"

"You're going to break your cask," I warned.

That got his attention. Aegir shifted the mead cask forward and held it in both arms like a baby. "Guest rights do not apply! I granted you a place at my table under false pretenses!"

"I never actually *said* I wasn't Magnus Chase," I reminded him. "Besides, your daughters also brought us here because we mentioned mead."

Kolga snarled. "And because you have an ugly yellow ship."

I wondered if everyone could see my heart beating through my shirt. It definitely felt that strong. "Right, but also mead. We're here to talk about mead!"

"We are?" Halfborn asked.

Mallory looked like she would have hit him, except there was a sea giantess in the way. "Of course we are, you oaf!"

"So, you see," I continued, "that wasn't a false pretense. That pretense was completely true!"

The daughters of Aegir muttered to themselves, unable to counter my flawless logic.

Aegir cradled his cask. "What exactly do you have to say about mead?"

"I'm glad you asked!" Then I realized I had no answer.

Once again, Samirah to the rescue. "We will explain!" she promised. "But stories are better told over dinner, with good mead, are they not?"

Aegir stroked his cask affectionately. "An aperitif, with a fruity edge."

"Exactly," Sam agreed. "So, let's break our fast together. If you are not completely satisfied with our explanations at the end of the dinner, then you can kill us."

"He can?" T.J. asked. "I mean . . . sure. He can."

On my right, Blod's clawlike fingernails dripped with red

salt water. On my left, a miniature hailstorm swirled around Kolga. Interspersed between my friends, the other seven daughters snarled like Tasmanian devil waterspouts.

Blitzen put his hands on his chain mail vest. After getting stabbed by the Skofnung Sword a few months ago, he was a little sensitive about knife attacks. Hearthstone's eyes flicked from face to face, trying to keep track of the conversation. Lip-reading a single person was hard enough. Trying to read an entire room was nearly impossible.

Mallory Keen gripped her mead goblet, ready to imprint its decorative design on the nearest giantess's face. Halfborn frowned sleepily, no doubt *convinced* now that this was all a dream. T.J. tried to look inconspicuous as he dug into his pack of firing caps, and Alex Fierro just sat back calmly, sipping his peach lambic mead. Alex needed no preparation for battle. I'd seen how fast he could draw his garrote.

The sea god Aegir was the tipping point. All he had to say was *kill them*, and we were cooked like honey mead. We'd fight ferociously, no doubt. But we would die.

"I don't know . . ." Aegir mused. "My wife said to kill you if I ever saw you. I was to drown you slowly, revive you, then drown you again."

That sounded like Ran talking.

"Great Lord," Blitzen chimed in. "Did you swear a formal *oath* to kill Magnus Chase?"

"Well, no," Aegir admitted. "But when my wife asks—"

"You have to consider her wishes, of course!" Blitz agreed. "But you also have to weigh that against guest rights, eh? And how can you be sure what to do, until you've given us time to tell our whole story?"

"Let me kill them, Father!" growled the daughter with exceptionally big hands. "I will grasp them until they scream!"

"Silence, Grasping Wave," Aegir commanded.

"Let me do the honors!" said another daughter, throwing her plate to the floor. "I will pitch them into Jormungand's mouth!"

"Hold, Pitching Wave." Aegir frowned. "The dwarf has a point. This is a quandary. . . ."

He stroked his keg. I waited for him to say: *My mead cask is angry. And when my mead cask is angry, people DIE!*

Instead, finally, he heaved a sigh. "It would be a shame to waste all this good mead. We will eat and drink together. You will tell me your story, paying special attention to how it relates to mead."

He gestured to his daughters to be seated again. "But I warn you, Magnus Chase, if I decide to kill you, my vengeance shall be terrible. I am a jotun deity, a primordial force! Like my brothers Fire and Air, I, the Sea, am a raging power that will not be contained!"

The kitchen door burst open. In a cloud of smoke, Eldir appeared, his beard still smoldering and his chef's hat now on fire. In his arms was a leaning tower of covered platters.

"Who had the gluten-free meal?" he growled.

"Gluten-free?" Aegir asked. "I don't think we had gluten-free."

"That's mine," said Blod. She noticed my expression and scowled defensively. "What? I'm on an all-blood diet."

"That's fine," I squeaked.

"Okay, then," Aegir said, taking charge of the orders.

"Halal meal—that is Samirah's. The vegetarian is Magnus Kill-Him-Later Chase. The green-hair entrée—"

"Right here," said Alex, which was probably unnecessary. Even in a room filled with sea giantesses, he was still the only one present with green hair.

Platters were distributed. Mead was poured.

"Right," Aegir said, lowering himself into his throne. "Everybody good?"

"Got one left!" Eldir yelled. "The Buddhist meal?"

"That's me," said Aegir.

Don't stare, I told myself, as the primordial deity uncovered his platter of tofu and bean sprouts. *This is all completely normal.*

"Now, where was I?" Aegir said. "Oh, yes. A raging power that cannot be contained! I will rip you all limb from limb!"

The threat would have been more frightening if he hadn't been waving a steamed snow pea at us.

Alex sipped from his goblet. "Can I just say that this mead is *excellent*? If I'm not mistaken, it has a fruity edge. How do you brew it?"

Aegir's eyes lit up. "You have a discerning palate! You see, the secret is in the temperature of the honey."

Aegir began to hold forth. Alex nodded politely and asked more questions.

I realized he was buying us time, hoping to draw out the meal while we thought of amazing things to say about mead. But I was fresh out of mead-related ideas.

I glanced at Blod's plate. Big mistake. She was slurping away at a large red gelatin mold.

I turned the other direction. Kolga's meal was a plate of different colored snow cones, arranged in a fan like peacock feathers.

Kolga noticed me looking and snarled, her teeth like chiseled ice cubes. The temperature dropped so fast, frost crystals crackled in my ear canals.

"What are you staring at, Magnus Chase? You can't have my snow cones!"

"No, no! I was just wondering, uh . . . what side are you guys fighting on in Ragnarok?"

She hissed. "The sea swallows everything."

I waited for more. That seemed to be her entire battle plan.

"Okay," I said. "So, you're kind of neutral? That's cool."

"Cool is good. Cold is better."

"Right. But your dad isn't friends with Loki."

"Of course not! After that horrible flyting? Loki disgraced this hall, the gods, my father, even my father's mead!"

"Right. The flyting."

The word seemed familiar. I was pretty sure I'd seen it on the TV screen in Valhalla, but I had no idea what it meant.

"I don't suppose you've heard the name Bolverk?" I asked, pressing my luck. "Or what it might have to do with mead?"

Kolga sneered at me as if I were a fool. "Bolverk was the alias of the mead thief, of course."

"The mead thief." That sounded like the title of a really bad novel to me.

"The one who stole Kvasir's Mead!" Kolga said. "The only mead my father cannot brew! Bah, you're clueless. I'll look forward to stuffing your soul in our chandelier." She went back to enjoying her snow cones.

Kvasir. Great. I asked about one name I didn't know, and I got another name I didn't know. But I felt like I was getting close to something important—some combination of puzzle pieces that would explain Uncle Randolph's journal, give me his plan for beating Loki, and maybe even provide a mead-based solution for getting us out of this hall alive.

Aegir continued holding forth about mead-brewing, explaining to Alex the virtues of staggered yeast nutrients and hydrometers. Alex heroically managed to look interested.

I caught Hearthstone's eye across the table. I signed, *What is a f-l-y-t-i-n-g?*

He frowned. *Contest.* He raised his index finger and twirled it around like he was sticking it up . . . Ah, yes. The ASL symbol for *insults.*

And K-V-A-S-I-R? I asked.

Hearthstone pulled back his hands like he'd touched a hot stove. *Then you know?*

Sam rapped her knuckles on the table to get my attention. Her hands flew in small furious ASL gestures: *Been trying to tell you! Loki was here. Long ago. Insult contest. Have to promise Aegir revenge. Alex and I think there is mead we can use—*

I got this, I signaled back.

Amazingly, I felt like I had a plan. Not all the details. Not even most of the details. More like I'd been spun around blindfolded, then somebody had put a stick in my hand and faced me in the general direction of the piñata and said *Start swinging.*

But it was better than nothing.

"Great Aegir!" I jumped up in my seat and climbed onto the table before I could think about what I was doing. "I will now explain to you why you should not kill us, and what it has to do with mead!"

Silence fell around the table. Nine storm giantesses glared at me as if considering all the different ways they could pitch, grasp, hurl, or freeze me to death.

At the edge of my vision, Alex flashed me a message in ASL: *Your fly is open.*

With superhuman willpower, I managed not to look down. I stayed focused on frowning Aegir and the single bean sprout dangling from his beard.

The sea god grumbled, "I was just explaining how to sanitize a fermenter. This interruption had better be good."

"It is!" I promised, slyly checking my zipper, which was not in fact open. "Our crew is sailing forth to bring Loki to justice! He has escaped his bonds, but we mean to find his ship, *Naglfar*, before it can sail at Midsummer, recapture Loki, and put him back in chains. Help us, and you will have vengeance for that terrible flyting."

A puff of steam lifted Aegir's panama hat like the lid of a popcorn popper. "You dare speak of that disgrace?" he demanded. "Here, at the very table where it happened?"

"I know, he flyted you!" I yelled. "He flyted you bad! You and all your godly guests got a *mean* flyting. He even flyted your mead! But we can defeat Loki and pay him back. I—I will challenge Loki myself!"

Sam put her head in her hands. Alex stared at the ceiling and mouthed, *Wow. No.*

My other friends stared at me aghast, as if I'd just pulled the pin out of a grenade. (I did that once on the battlefield in Valhalla before I fully understood how grenades worked. It had not ended well for the grenade or for me.)

Aegir became deadly calm. He leaned forward, the lenses flashing in his golden glasses. "You, Magnus Chase, would challenge Loki to a flyting?"

"Yes." Despite my friends' reactions, I still felt certain this was the correct answer, even though I didn't quite understand what it meant. "I will flyte the heck out of him."

Aegir stroked his beard, found the bean sprout, flicked it away. "How would you achieve this? Not even the gods could match Loki in a flyting! You would need some incredible secret weapon to give you an edge!"

Perhaps even a fruity edge, I thought, because this was the other thing I was sure of, even if I didn't totally understand it. I stood up straight and announced in my deepest quest-accepting voice: "I will use the mead of Kevin!"

Alex joined Samirah in the bury-your-face-in-your-hands club.

Aegir narrowed his eyes. "You mean the Mead of Kvasir?"

"Yes!" I said. "That!"

"Impossible!" Kolga protested, her mouth dyed six different colors from her snow cones. "Father, don't believe them!"

"And, great Aegir," I persisted, "if you let us go, we'll even . . . uh, bring you a sample of Kvasir's Mead, since it is the only mead you can't brew yourself."

My friends and the nine giantesses all turned to Aegir, waiting for his verdict.

A thin smile played across the sea god's mouth. He looked

like he'd managed to jump into a newly opened express lane at Whole Foods and finally scored his matcha smoothie.

"Well, this changes everything," he said.

"It does?" I asked.

He rose from his throne. "I would love to see Loki brought to justice, and in a flyting, no less. I would also love to get a sample of Kvasir's Mead. And I would prefer not to kill you all, since I did grant you guest rights."

"Great!" I said. "So, you'll let us go?"

"Unfortunately," Aegir said, "you're still Magnus Chase, and my wife wants you dead. If I let you go, she'll be mad at me. But if you were to escape, say, while I wasn't looking, and my daughters didn't manage to kill you in the attempt . . . well, I think we'd just have to consider that the will of the Norns!"

He straightened his vest. "I am going to the kitchen to get some more mead now! I sure hope nothing unpleasant happens while I'm gone. Come along, Eldir!"

The cook gave me one last smoldering leer. "Flyte Loki once for Fimafeng, will you?" Then he followed his master into the kitchen.

As soon as the door closed, all nine daughters of Aegir rose from their seats and attacked.

ELEVEN

My Sword Takes You to (Dramatic Pause) Funkytown

BACK WHEN I was a regular mortal kid, I didn't know much about combat.

I had some murky ideas that armies would line up, blow trumpets, and then march forward to kill one another in an orderly fashion. If I thought about *Viking* combat at all, I would envision some dude yelling *SHIELD WALL!* and a bunch of hairy blond guys calmly forming ranks and merging their shields into some cool geometric pattern like a polyhedron or a Power Ranger Megazord.

Actual battle was nothing like that. At least, not any version *I'd* ever been in. It was more like a cross between interpretive dance, *lucha libre* wrestling, and a daytime talk show fight.

The nine sea giantesses fell upon us with a collective howl of glee. My friends were ready. Mallory Keen flipped onto Grasping Wave's back and plunged her knives into the giantess's shoulders. Halfborn Gunderson dual-wielded mead goblets, slamming Hefring in the face and Unn in the gut.

T.J. lost valuable time trying to load his rifle. Before he could fire, the lovely Himminglaeva turned into a tidal wave and washed him across the hall.

Hearthstone threw a runestone I hadn't seen before:

ᚱ

It hit Bigly—I mean Bylgya—with a bright flash, liquefying her into a large angry puddle.

Sam's spear of light shimmered in her hand. She flew upward, just beyond reach, and began blasting giantesses with arcs of pure Valkyrie radiance. Meanwhile Blitzen hopped around the chaos, distracting the nine sisters with blistering fashion critiques like "Your hem is too high! You've got a run in your stocking! That scarf does *not* go with your dress!"

Kolga and Blod lunged at me from either side. I valiantly slipped under the table and tried to crawl away, but Blod grabbed me by the leg and pulled me out.

"Oh, no," she snarled, her teeth dripping red. "I'm going to rip your soul from your body, Magnus Chase!"

Then a silverback mountain gorilla crashed into her, knocked her to the floor, and ripped her face off. (That sounds gross. Actually, when the gorilla swiped Blod's face, the giantess's whole head simply dissolved into salt water, soaking the kelp carpet.)

The gorilla turned toward me, his eyes mismatched brown and gold. He grunted at me impatiently, like *Get up, you idiot. Fight!*

The gorilla turned to face Kolga.

I staggered backward. Magic explosions, beams of light, axes, swords, and bad-fashion insults flew everywhere, answered by blasts of salt water, shards of ice, and globs of blood-tinted gelatin.

My gut told me that the giantesses would be much more powerful if they combined forces, like they had when they sank our ship. We were only alive so far because each of the sisters was intent on killing her own target. We had succeeded at being just that individually annoying. If the nine giantesses started singing their weird music again, working together as a team, we would be done for.

Even fighting them separately, we were in trouble. Every time a giantess got vaporized or reduced to a puddle, she quickly re-formed. We were outnumbered nine to eight. No matter how well my friends fought, the giantesses had the home-court advantage—and also immortality, which was a pretty big fruity edge.

We had to find a way to get on our boat and get out of here, back to the surface and far away. For that, we would need a distraction, so I called on the most distracting being I knew.

I pulled the runestone from my neck chain.

Jack sprang into sword form. "Hey, señor! You know, I was thinking about that Riptide girl. Who needs her, right? There are plenty of other swords in the armory and—WHOA! Aegir's palace? Awesome! What mead is he serving today?"

"Help!" I yelled as Blod rose in front of me, her face reattached, her talons dripping blood.

"Sure!" Jack said amiably. "But, man, Aegir's Oktoberfest Pumpkin Spice Mead is to die for!"

He zipped over to Blood-Red Hair, placing himself between my assailant and me.

"Hey, lady!" Jack said. "Wanna dance?"

"No!" Blod snarled.

She tried to get around him, but Jack was nimble. (Yes, and quick, though I'd never seen him jump over candlesticks.)

He swerved side to side, presenting his edge to the giantess and singing "Funkytown."

Blod seemed unwilling or unable to get past Jack's magical blade, which bought me a few seconds of safety as Jack disco-danced.

"Magnus!" Samirah zoomed by, ten feet above me. "Prepare the ship!"

My heart sank. I realized my friends were playing interference for me, hoping that I could somehow make our ship ready to sail again. Sad, deluded friends.

I ran back to the *Big Banana*.

The ship lay on its side, its mast piercing the wall of water. The current outside must have been strong, because it pushed the ship along the carpet ever so slightly, the keel leaving gouge marks in the kelp.

I touched the hull. Thankfully, the boat responded, collapsing into a handkerchief, which I clutched in my hand. If I could get all my friends together, maybe we could jump through the wall of water simultaneously and summon the ship as the current carried us away from here. Maybe the ship, being magic, would bring us back to the surface. Maybe we wouldn't drown or get crushed by the water pressure.

That was a lot of maybes. Even if we managed it, the nine daughters of Aegir had sucked us under the ocean once before. I didn't see why they couldn't do it again. Somehow, I needed to stop them from following us.

I scanned the battle. Hearthstone raced past me, throwing runes at the giantesses trying to chase him. The ᚠ rune seemed to do the best job. Every time it blasted a giantess, she turned into a puddle for several seconds. Not much, but it was something.

I glanced at the walls of the feast hall, and had an idea.

"Hearth!" I yelled.

I cursed my own stupidity. One of these days, I would get over my habit of yelling for my deaf friend's attention. I ran after him, ducking past Grasping Wave, who Mallory Keen was driving around the room with her dagger handles like a combat robot.

I grabbed Hearth's sleeve for his attention. *That rune,* I signed. *What?*

L-A-G-A-Z, he finger-spelled. *Water. Or . . .* He made a gesture I'd never seen: one hand horizontal, the fingers of the other hand trickling from it. I got the idea: *drip, leak.* Or maybe *liquefy.*

Can you do that to the wall? I asked. *Or the ceiling?*

Hearth's mouth quirked, which for him was a diabolical grin. He nodded.

Wait for my signal, I signed.

Pitching Wave surged between us, yelling, "RAAARR!" and Hearthstone plunged back into the melee.

I had to figure out how to separate my friends from the giantesses. Then we might be able to collapse part of the feast hall on top of the nine sisters while we made our getaway. I doubted that would hurt our enemies, but it might at least surprise them and slow them down. The problem was, I didn't know how to break up the fight. I doubted I could blow a whistle and call for a jump ball.

Jack flew back and forth, harassing giantesses with his

deadly blade and his even deadlier rendition of a 70s disco classic. Kolga blasted sheets of ice across the carpet, causing Halfborn Gunderson to wipe out. Bylgya fought with T.J., red coral sword against bayonet. Grasping Wave finally managed to pull Mallory off her back. The giantess would have ripped her apart, but Blitzen tossed a dinner plate that smashed the giantess in the face.

(One of Blitz's unsung skills: he was *killer* at dwarven Ultimate Frisbee.)

Himminglaeva lunged for Samirah. She caught Sam's legs, but Alex lashed out with his garrote. The giantess suddenly lost several inches around her waistline—actually her *entire* waistline. She crumpled to the floor, neatly bisected, and dissolved into sea foam.

Hearthstone caught my eye. *When the rune?*

I wished I had an answer. My friends couldn't keep up the fight forever. I considered summoning the Peace of Frey—my super *time out* power that blasts everybody's weapons out of their hands—but the giantesses weren't really using weapons, and I didn't think my friends would appreciate being disarmed.

I needed help. Desperately. So, I did something that didn't come easy for me. I looked toward the watery ceiling and prayed earnestly, not snarkily: "Okay, Frey, Dad, please. I know I sounded ungrateful earlier about the bright yellow ship. But we're about to die down here, so if you've got any help you could send me, I'd really appreciate it. Amen. Love, Magnus. Magnus *Chase*, in case you were wondering."

I winced. I really sucked at praying. I also wasn't sure what help a god of summer could send me at the bottom of Massachusetts Bay.

"Hello," said a voice right next to me.

I leaped about a foot into the air, which I thought was pretty restrained under the circumstances.

Standing at my side was a man in his late fifties, stout, and sun-weathered as if he'd spent decades as a lifeguard. He wore a pale blue polo shirt and cargo shorts, and his feet were bare. His feathery hair and close-cropped beard were the color of honey, flecked with gray. He smiled like we were old friends, though I was sure I'd never seen him before.

"Uh, hi?" I said.

Living in Valhalla, you get used to strange entities popping up out of nowhere. Still, this seemed like an odd time for a casual encounter.

"I'm your grandfather," he offered.

"Right," I said. Because what was I supposed to say? The guy looked nothing like Grandpa (or Grandma) Chase, but I figured he was talking about the other side of my family tree. The Vanir side. Now if I could just remember the name of Frey's dad, I would've been all set. "Hi . . . Grandpa."

"Your father can't do much in the ocean," said Grandpa Frey-Dad. "But I can. Want some help?"

"Yes," I said, which perhaps was foolish. I couldn't be sure this guy was who he said he was, and accepting help from a powerful being always puts you in their debt.

"Great!" He patted me on the arm. "I'll meet you on the surface when this is all done, okay?"

I nodded. "Mm-hmm."

My newfound grandfather strode into the midst of the battle. "Hello, girls! How's it going?"

The fighting fizzled to a stop. The giantesses retreated

warily toward the dinner table. My friends staggered and stumbled in my direction.

Blod bared her red-stained teeth. "Njord, you are not welcome here!"

Njord! That's his name! I made a mental note to send him a card on Grandparents' Day. Was Grandparents' Day a thing with Vikings?

"Oh, come now, Blodughadda," the god said cheerfully. "Can't an old friend get a cup of mead? Let's talk like civilized sea deities."

"These mortals are ours!" growled Grasping Wave. "You have no right!"

"Ah, but you see, they are under my protection now. Which means we're back to our old conflict of interests, eh?"

The giantesses hissed and snarled. Clearly, they wanted to tear Njord to pieces but were afraid to try.

"Besides," Njord said, "one of my friends here has a trick to show you. Don't you, Hearthstone?"

Hearthstone locked eyes with me. I nodded.

Hearth tossed the lagaz rune straight up, past the lost-soul chandelier. I didn't see how it could reach the ceiling a hundred feet above, but the stone seemed to get lighter and faster as it ascended. It hit the peak of the rafters, exploding into a blazing golden ↑, and the watery roof crashed inward, burying the giantesses and Njord in a million-gallon shower.

"Now!" I yelled to my friends.

We plowed together in a desperate group hug as the wave hit us. My handkerchief expanded around us. The collapsing hall squirted us into the deep like toothpaste from a tube, and we shot toward the surface on our bright yellow Viking warship.

TWELVE

The Guy with the Feet

THERE'S NOTHING like erupting from the depths of the ocean on a magical Viking ship!

It sucks. A lot.

My eyes felt like grapes that had been lagaz-ed. My ears popped with such force I thought I'd been shot in the back of the head. I gripped the rail, shivering and disoriented, as the *Big Banana* landed on the waves—*WHOMMMM!*—and knocked my jaw out of alignment.

The sail unfurled on its own. The oars unlocked, pushed into the water, and began to row by themselves. We sailed under starry skies, the waves calm and glittering, no land to be seen in any direction.

"The ship . . . is self-driving," I noted.

Next to me, Njord popped into existence, looking no worse for being caught in the collapse of Aegir's hall.

Njord chuckled. "Well, yes, Magnus, of course the ship is self-driving. Were you trying to row it the old-fashioned way?"

I ignored my friends glaring at me. "Um, maybe."

"All you have to do is will the ship to take you where you want to go," Njord told me. "Nothing else is required."

I thought about all that time I'd spent with Percy Jackson learning bowlines and mizzenmasts, only to find out the

Viking gods had invented Google-boats. I bet the ship would even magically assist me if I needed to fall off the mast.

"Magnus?" Alex spat a clump of sea giantess hair out of his mouth. Wait. *Her* mouth. I wasn't sure when it had happened, but I was pretty certain Alex had shifted gender. "Aren't you going to introduce us to your friend?"

"Right," I said. "Everybody, this is Frey-Dad. I mean Njord."

Blitzen scowled. He muttered under his breath, "Might have known."

Halfborn Gunderson's eyes widened. "Njord? God of ships? *The* Njord?" Then the berserker turned and vomited over the railing.

T.J. stepped forward, hands raised like *We come in peace.* "Halfborn wasn't making an editorial comment, great Njord. We appreciate your help! He just has a head injury."

Njord smiled. "That's perfectly fine. You all should get some rest. I did what I could to ease your decompression sickness, but you're going to feel bad for a day or two. Also, you have blood trickling from your nose. Oh, and coming out your ears."

I realized he was talking about everyone. We were leaking red like Blodughadda, but at least all my friends seemed to be in one piece.

"So, Njord," said Mallory, wiping her nose. "Before we rest, are you sure those nine giantesses aren't going to pop up again any minute and, you know, destroy us?"

"No, no," he promised. "You're under my protection and safe for the present! Now perhaps you would give me some time to talk with my grandson?"

Alex picked a last strand of giantess hair off her tongue.

"No problem, Frey-Dad. Oh, and by the way, guys, my pronouns are *she* and *her* now. It's a new day!"

(Hooray for me being right.)

Samirah stepped forward, her fists clenched. Her wet hijab clung to her head like an affectionate octopus. "Magnus, down in the feast hall . . . do you realize what you agreed to? Do you have any idea—?"

Njord raised his hand. "My dear, perhaps you'd let me discuss that with him? Dawn is coming. Shouldn't you eat your *suhur* meal?"

Sam gazed east, where the stars were beginning to fade. She worked her jaw muscles. "I suppose you're right, though I don't feel much like it. Anybody want to join me?"

T.J. shouldered his rifle. "Sam, when it comes to eating, I always have your back. Let's go below and see if the galley is still in one piece. Anybody else?"

"Yep." Mallory eyed the sea god. For some reason, she seemed fascinated by his bare feet. "We'll give Magnus some family time."

Alex followed, doing her best to steady Halfborn Gunderson. Maybe it was just my imagination, but before Alex went down the ladder, she gave me a look like *You okay?* Or maybe she was just wondering why I was so weird, as per usual.

That left only Blitz and Hearth, who were fussing with each other's outfits. Hearth's scarf had somehow gotten tied around his arm like a sling. Blitzen's ascot had wrapped around his head like a fancy do-rag. They were trying to help while swatting each other away, thus not accomplishing much.

"Dwarf and elf." Njord's tone was relaxed, but my friends

immediately stopped their fussing and faced the god. "Stay with us," Njord said. "We should confer."

Hearthstone looked agreeable enough, but Blitz scowled even deeper.

We settled on the foredeck, which was the only place where we wouldn't get tripped by the self-rowing oars, bonked by the boom, or strangled by the magical rigging.

Njord sat with his back to the railing, his legs far apart. He wriggled his toes as if to get them a good tan. This didn't give the rest of us a lot of room to sit, but since Njord was the god and he'd just saved us, I figured he'd earned the privilege of manspreading.

Blitz and Hearth sat side by side across from the god. I squatted against the prow, though I'd never done well sitting backward in a moving vehicle. I hoped I wasn't going to become the second crewmember to vomit in the god's presence.

"Well," Njord said, "this is nice."

I felt like my head had been run through a Play-Doh press. I'd been drenched in mead and salt water. I'd barely touched my vegetarian-option meal, and my stomach was devouring itself. Drops of blood from my nose splattered in my lap. Otherwise, yeah. It was real nice.

Sometime during our ascent, Jack had returned to pendant form. He hung from my neck chain, buzzing against my sternum as if humming a message: *Compliment his feet.*

I must have either imagined it or misunderstood him. Maybe Jack meant *Compliment his feat.*

"Uh, thanks again for the help, Granddad," I said.

Njord smiled. "Just call me Njord. *Granddad* makes me feel old!"

I figured he'd been alive for two or three thousand years, but I didn't want to insult him. "Right. Sorry. So, did Frey send you, or did you just happen to be in the neighborhood?"

"Oh, I hear all desperate prayers spoken at sea."

Njord wriggled his toes. Was it my imagination or was he intentionally showing off his feet? I mean, they *were* well manicured. No calluses. Not a fleck of dirt or tar. Toenails trimmed, buffed to perfection. Zero toe gunk or weird hobbit foot fur. But still . . .

"I was happy to assist," Njord continued. "Aegir and I go back a long way. He and Ran and their daughters represent the raging forces of nature, the sea's raw power, blah, blah, blah. Whereas I—"

"You're the god of fishing," Blitzen said.

Njord frowned. "Other things as well, Mr. Dwarf."

"Please, call me Blitz," said Blitz. "Mr. Dwarf was my father."

Hearthstone grunted impatiently, the way he often does when Blitzen is about to get himself killed by a deity.

Njord is god of many things, he signed. *Sailing. Shipbuilding.*

"Exactly!" Njord said, apparently having no difficulty with Hearth's ASL. "Trading, fishing, navigation—any occupation that involves the ocean. Even farming, since the tides and storms affects crop-growing! Aegir is the nasty, brutal side of the ocean. I'm the guy you pray to when you want the sea to work for you!"

"Hmph," Blitz said.

I didn't know why he was being antagonistic. Then I remembered that his father, Bilì, had died checking the chains that bound Fenris Wolf on his island. Bilì's slashed and torn clothing had eventually washed up on the shores of Nidavellir.

No safe homeward voyage for him. Why would Blitzen consider the sea anything but cruel?

I wanted to let Blitz know that I understood, that I was sorry, but he kept his gaze firmly on the deck.

"Anyway," Njord said, "Aegir and his family have been my, ah, *competitors* for centuries. They try to drown mortals: I try to save them. They destroy ships; I build better ships. We're not enemies, exactly, but we do keep each other on our toes!"

He emphasized the word *toes*, stretching out his feet a little more. This was now officially getting weird.

Jack's voice buzzed in my head more forcefully. *Compliment. His. Feet.*

"You have beautiful feet, Grand—er, Njord."

The god beamed. "Oh, these old things? Well, you're kind. Did you know I once won a beauty contest with my feet? The prize was my wife!"

I glanced at Blitz and Hearth, to see if I was imagining this entire conversation.

Please, Hearth signed with zero enthusiasm. *Tell us the story.*

"Well, if you insist." Njord gazed at the stars, perhaps recalling his glory days in the foot-beauty-pageant circuit. "Most of the story isn't important. The gods killed this giant, Thjassi. His daughter Skadi demanded vengeance. Blood. Killing. Blah, blah, blah. To prevent further war and stop the blood feud, Odin agreed to let Skadi marry a god of her choosing."

Blitzen scowled. "And she chose . . . you?"

"No!" Njord clapped his hands in delight. "Oh, it was *so* funny. You see, Odin only let Skadi choose her husband by looking at the gods' feet!"

"Why?" I asked. "Why not . . . noses? Or elbows?"

Njord paused. "I never considered that. Not sure! Anyway, Skadi figured the most handsome husband would have the most handsome feet, right? So, we all stood behind a curtain and she went down the line, looking for Balder, because he was always the one everyone thought was the most handsome." He rolled his eyes and mouthed, *Overrated*. "But I had the most beautiful feet of all the gods, as Odin must have known. Skadi picked me! You should've seen the look on her face when she pulled back the curtain and saw who she had to marry!"

Blitzen crossed his arms. "So, Odin used you to trick the poor lady. You were a booby prize."

"Of course not!" Njord looked more startled than angry. "It was a great match!"

"I'm sure it was," I said, anxious to prevent Blitzen from getting turned into a dinghy or whatever other punishment the ship god could deal out. "You two lived happily ever after?"

Njord shifted his back against the rail. "Well, no. We separated shortly thereafter. She wanted to live in the mountains. I liked the beach. Then Skadi had an affair with Odin. Then we got a divorce. But that's not the point! My feet on the day of the contest—they were *amazing*. They won the hand of Skadi, the beautiful ice giantess!"

I was tempted to ask if he only won her hand or the rest of her, too, but I decided against it.

Blitzen stared at me. He twitched his hands like he wanted to sign something ugly about Njord but then remembered that Njord could read ASL. He sighed and stared at his lap.

Njord frowned. "What's wrong, Mr. Dwarf? You don't look impressed!"

"Oh, he is," I promised. "Just speechless. We can all tell that . . . uh, your feet are very important to you."

What is your beauty secret? Hearthstone asked politely.

"Several centuries of standing in the surf," Njord confided. "It smoothed my feet into the perfectly sculpted masterpieces you see today. That, and regular pedicures with a paraffin-wax treatment." He wiggled his shiny toenails. "I was debating about buffing or no buffing, but I think the buffing really makes those piggies shine."

I nodded and agreed that he had very shiny piggies. I also wished I didn't have such an odd family.

"In fact, Magnus," said Njord, "that is one of the reasons I wanted to meet you."

"To show me your feet?"

He laughed. "No, silly." By which, I was pretty sure, he meant yes. "To give you some advice."

"On how to buff his toenails?" Blitz asked.

"No!" Njord hesitated. "Although I *could* do that. I have two important bits of wisdom that may help you on your quest to stop Loki."

We enjoy bits of wisdom, Hearth signed.

"The first is this," Njord said. "To reach the Ship of the Dead, you must pass through the borderlands between Niflheim and Jotunheim. This is harsh territory. Mortals can perish from the cold in seconds. If that does not kill you, the giants and draugrs will."

Blitz grumbled, "I'm not enjoying this particular bit of wisdom."

"Ah, but there is one safe harbor," Njord said. "Or at least one *potentially* safe harbor. Or at least one harbor where you might not be instantly killed. You should seek out Thunder Home, the fortress of my beloved Skadi. Tell her I sent you."

"Your beloved?" I asked. "Aren't you divorced?"

"Yes."

"But you're still friends."

"I haven't seen her in centuries." Njord got a distant look in his eyes. "And we didn't exactly part on good terms. But I have to believe she still holds some affection for me. Seek her out. If she grants you safe harbor for my sake, that will tell me she's forgiven me."

And if she doesn't welcome us? Hearth asked.

"That would be disappointing."

I took this to mean: *You will all end up in Skadi's meat locker.*

I didn't like the idea of being my grandfather's test balloon for a reconciliation with his ex-wife. Then again, a potentially safe harbor sounded better than freezing to death in twenty seconds.

Unfortunately, I got the feeling we hadn't heard Njord's worst "helpful" advice yet. I waited for the other shoe to drop, even though Njord did not appear to own any shoes.

"What's the second bit of wisdom?" I asked.

"Hmm?" Njord's focus snapped back to me. "Oh, yes. The point of my story about my beautiful feet."

"There was a point?" Blitz sounded genuinely surprised.

"Of course!" Njord said. "The most unexpected thing can be the key to victory. Balder was the most handsome of the gods, but because of my feet, *I* won the girl."

"Whom you later separated from and divorced," Blitz said.

"Would you stop dwelling on that?" Njord rolled his eyes at me like *Dwarves these days.* "My point, dear grandson, is that you will need to use unexpected means to defeat Loki. You began to realize that in Aegir's hall, didn't you?"

I didn't remember biting off any clumps of sea giantess hair, but a ball of the stuff seemed to be forming in my throat.

"A flyting," I said. "I'll have to beat Loki in a contest . . . of insults?"

New gray whiskers spread like frost through Njord's beard. "A flyting is much more than a series of simple put-downs," he warned. "It's a duel of prestige, power, confidence. I was present at Aegir's hall when Loki flyted with the gods. He shamed us so badly. . . ." Njord seemed to deflate, as if just thinking about it made him older and weaker. "Words can be more lethal than blades, Magnus. And Loki is a master of words. To beat him, you must find your inner poet. Only one thing can give you a chance to beat Loki at his own game."

"Mead," I guessed. "Kvasir's Mead."

The answer didn't sit right with me. I'd been on the streets long enough to see how well "mead" improved people's skills. Pick your poison: beer, wine, vodka, whiskey. Folks claimed they needed it to get through the day. They called it liquid courage. It made them funnier, smarter, more creative. Except it didn't. It just made them less able to tell how unfunny and stupid they were acting.

"It's not merely mead," my grandfather said, reading my expression. "Kvasir's Mead is the most valuable elixir ever created. Finding it will not be easy." He turned to Hearthstone and Blitzen. "You know this, don't you? You know that the quest may claim both your lives."

THIRTEEN

Stupid Exploding Grandfathers

"YOU SHOULD have led with that," I said, my pulse jack-hammering in my neck. "Hearth and Blitz do *not* die. That's a deal-breaker."

Njord's toothy smile was as white as Scandinavian snow. I wished I knew his secret for staying so calm. Zen meditation? Fishing? Hotel Valhalla yoga classes?

"Ah, Magnus, you are so much like your father."

I blinked. "We're both blond and like the outdoors?"

"You both have kind hearts," said Njord. "Frey would do anything for a friend. He always loved easily and deeply, sometimes unwisely. You have the proof of that around your neck."

I curled my fingers around Jack's runestone. I knew the story: Frey had given up the Sword of Summer so he could win the love of a beautiful giantess. Because he had forsaken his weapon, he would be slain at Ragnarok. The moral of the story, as Jack liked to put it: *Blades before babes.*

The thing was, pretty much everybody would be slain at Ragnarok anyway. I didn't blame my dad for his choices. If he didn't fall in love easily, I would never have been born.

"Fine, I'm like my dad," I said. "I still choose my friends over a cup of mead. I don't care if it's pumpkin spice or peach lambic."

"It's blood, actually," Njord said. "And god spit."

I started to feel seasick, and I didn't think it was because of the direction I was facing. "Come again?"

Njord opened his hand. Above his palm floated the miniature glowing figure of a bearded man in woolen robes. His face was open and cheerful, his expression caught in mid-laugh. Seeing him, it was hard not to lean forward, smile, and want to hear what he was laughing about.

"This was Kvasir." Njord's tone took on an edge of sadness. "The most perfect being ever created. Millennia ago, when the Vanir and Aesir gods ended their war, all of us spit into a golden cup. From that mixture sprang Kvasir, our living peace treaty!"

Suddenly I didn't want to lean so close to the little glowing man. "The dude was made of spit."

"Makes sense," Blitzen grunted. "God saliva is an excellent crafting ingredient."

Hearthstone tilted his head. He seemed fascinated by the holographic figure. He signed, *Why would anyone murder him?*

"Murder?" I asked.

Njord nodded, lightning flickering in his eyes. For the first time, I got the impression that my grandfather wasn't just some laid-back guy with nice feet. He was a powerful deity who could probably crumple our warship with a single thought. "Kvasir wandered the Nine Worlds, bringing wisdom, advice, and justice wherever he went. Everyone loved him. And then he was slaughtered. Horrible. Inexcusable."

"Loki?" I guessed, because that seemed like the logical next word in that list.

Njord barked a short, sour laugh. "Not this time, no. It was dwarves." He glanced at Blitzen. "No offense."

Blitzen shrugged. "Dwarves aren't all the same. Like gods."

If Njord sensed an insult, he didn't let on. He closed his hand and the tiny spit man disappeared. "The details of the murder aren't important. Afterward, Kvasir's blood was drained and mixed with honey to create a magical mead. It became the most prized, most coveted drink in the Nine Worlds."

"Ugh." I put my hand to my mouth. My idea of which details should be left out of a story was very different from Njord's. "You want me to drink mead that is made from blood that is made from god spit."

Njord stroked his beard. "When you put it that way, it sounds bad. But yes, Magnus. Whoever drinks Kvasir's Mead finds their inner poet. The perfect words come to you. The poetry flows. The oration dazzles. The stories enthrall all who listen. With such power, you could stand toe-to-toe, insult-to-insult in a flyting with Loki."

My mind pitched and swayed along with my stomach. Why did *I* have to be the one to challenge Loki?

My inner voice responded, or maybe it was Jack: *Because you volunteered at the feast, dummy. Everybody heard you.*

I rubbed my temples, wondering if it was possible for a brain to literally explode from too much information. That's one death I'd never experienced in Valhalla.

Hearthstone stared at me with concern. *You want a rune?* he signed. *Or some aspirin?*

I shook my head.

So Uncle Randolph's notebook hadn't been a trick. He'd left an actual, viable plan for me to follow. In the end, despite all he'd done, it seemed like the old fool had experienced some remorse. He had tried to help me. I wasn't sure if that made me feel better or worse.

"What about the name Bolverk?" I asked. "Who is that?"

Njord smiled. "That was Odin's alias. For a long time, the giants possessed all of Kvasir's Mead. Odin went in disguise to steal some back for the gods. He succeeded. He even scattered drops of mead around Midgard to inspire mortal bards. But the gods' supply of the elixir was exhausted centuries ago. The only mead that remains is a tiny portion, jealously guarded by the giants. To get it, you will have to follow in Bolverk's footsteps and steal what only Odin was ever able to steal."

"Perfect," Blitz muttered. "So how do we do *that*?"

"More important," I said, "why is it so dangerous for Hearth and Blitz? And how can we make it not be?"

I had an overwhelming desire to write a letter for Hearth and Blitz: *Dear Cosmic Forces, Please excuse my friends from their deadly fate. They are not feeling well today.* At the very least, I wanted to outfit them with safety helmets, life jackets, and reflective decals before sending them off.

Njord faced Hearthstone and Blitzen. He signed, *You already know your task.*

He made a stick figure man standing in his palm: *ground*; then two fists, one tapping the top of the other: *work*.

Lay the groundwork. At least, I thought that's what he meant. Either that or: *You farm the fields.* Since Njord was a god of crops, I couldn't be sure.

Hearthstone touched his scarf. He signed, reluctantly, *The stone?*

Njord nodded. *You know where you must look for it.*

Blitzen broke into the conversation, signing so fast his words got a little muddled. *Leave my elf alone! We can't do that again! Too dangerous!*

Or he could have meant, *Leave my elf in the bathroom! We can't do that wristwatch! Too much garbage!*

"What are you guys talking about?" I asked.

My spoken words sounded jarring and unwelcome in the silent dialogue.

Blitzen brushed his chain mail vest. "Our long-range reconnaissance work, kid. Mimir told us to look for the Mead of Kvasir. Then we heard rumors about a certain item we'd need—"

"Bolverk's whetstone," I guessed.

He nodded unhappily. "It's the only way to defeat"—he spread his hands—"whatever's guarding the mead. We're not clear on the who, how, or why."

Those all seemed like pretty important points to me.

"The thing is," Blitz continued, "if this stone is where we *think* it is . . ."

It's all right, Hearthstone signed. *We must. So we will.*

"Buddy, no," Blitz said. "You can't—"

"The elf is right," Njord said. "You two must find the stone while Magnus and the rest of the crew sail on to discover the location of the mead. Are you ready?"

"Whoa, whoa, whoa," I said. "You're sending them away *right now*? They just got here!"

"Grandson, you have very little time before Loki's ship is ready to sail. Only by dividing can you conquer."

I was pretty sure the old *divide and conquer* saying meant that the divided army *got* conquered, but Njord didn't sound like he was in the mood for a debate.

"Let me go instead." I staggered to my feet. I'd just had the longest day in the history of days. I was ready to fall over. But there was no way I was going to stand by while my two oldest friends got sent into mortal danger. "Or at least let me go with them."

"Kid," Blitz said, his voice cracking. "It's okay."

My burden, Hearth signed, both hands pushing down on one of his shoulders.

Njord gave me another calm smile. I was about ready to punch in my grandfather's perfect teeth.

"The crew of this ship will need you with them, Magnus," he said. "But I promise you this: once Hearthstone and Blitzen have found the location of the whetstone, once they have laid the groundwork for the assault, I will send them back to get you. Then the three of you can face the true danger together. If you fail, you'll die as a team. How is that?"

That didn't make me yell *hooray*, but I figured it was the best offer I was going to get.

"All right." I helped Blitz to his feet and gave him a hug. He smelled like toasted kelp and Dwarf Noir eau de toilette. "Don't you dare die without me."

"Do my best, kid."

I faced Hearthstone. I put my hand gently on his chest, an elfish gesture of deep affection. *You,* I signed. *Safe. Or me. Angry.*

The corners of his mouth pulled upward, though he still looked distracted and worried. His heartbeat fluttered under my fingertips like a scared dove.

You, too, he signed.

Njord snapped his fingers, and my friends broke into sea spray, like waves crashing against the bow.

I swallowed down my anger.

I told myself Njord had only sent Hearth and Blitz away. He hadn't actually vaporized them. He'd promised I would see them again. I had to believe that.

"Now what?" I asked him. "What do I do while they're gone?"

"Ah." Njord crossed his legs in lotus position, probably just to show off the soles of his wave-sculpted feet. "Your task is equally difficult, Magnus. You must discover the location of Kvasir's Mead. This is a closely guarded secret, known only to a few giants. But there is one who might be convinced to tell you: Hrungnir, who prowls the human land of Jorvik."

The ship hit a swell, jarring my stomach loose from its undercarriage. "I've had some bad encounters with giants."

"Haven't we all?" Njord said. "Once you reach Jorvik, you must find Hrungnir and challenge him. If you beat him, demand that he give you the information you need."

I shuddered, thinking about the last time I was in Jotunheim. "Please tell me this challenge won't be a bowling tournament."

"Oh, no, rest easy!" Njord said. "It will most likely be personal combat to the death. You should bring a couple of friends along. I would recommend the attractive one, Alex Fierro."

I wondered if Alex would be flattered by that or grossed

out, or if she'd just laugh. I wondered if Alex's feet were as well-groomed as Njord's. What a stupid thing to wonder about.

"Okay," I said. "Jorvik. Wherever that is."

"Your ship knows the way," Njord promised. "I can grant you safe passage that far, but if you survive and sail onward, your ship will once again be vulnerable to attack by Aegir, Ran, their daughters, or . . . worse things."

"I will try to contain my happiness."

"That's wise," Njord said. "Your elf and dwarf will find the whetstone you require. You will discover the secret location of the mead. Then you will retrieve the Mead of Kvasir, defeat Loki, and return him to his chains!"

"I appreciate the vote of confidence."

"Well, it's more that if you don't, Loki will flyte you into a pathetic, powerless shadow of yourself. Then you will have to watch all your friends die, one by one, until you alone are left to suffer in Helheim for eternity while the Nine Worlds burn. That is Loki's plan."

"Oh."

"Anyway!" Njord said brightly. "Good luck!"

My grandfather exploded in a fine sea mist, splattering my face with salt.

FOURTEEN

Nothing Happens. It's a Miracle

SMOOTH SAILING.

I never appreciated that term until I'd actually had some. The next two days were shockingly, perversely uneventful. The sky remained cloudless, the winds gentle and cool. The sea stretched in all directions like green silk, reminding me of pictures my mom used to show me from her favorite artist, this dude named Christo, who worked outside and wrapped entire forests, buildings, and islands in shimmering cloth. It looked like Christo had turned the North Atlantic into one huge art installation.

The *Big Banana* sailed merrily onward. Our yellow oars churned by themselves. The sail tacked and jibed as needed.

When I told the crew we were going to Jorvik, Halfborn grunted unhappily, but whatever he knew about the place, he wouldn't share. At least the ship seemed to understand where we were heading.

The second afternoon, I found myself standing amidships with Mallory Keen, who'd been acting even more disgruntled than usual.

"I still don't understand why Blitz and Hearth had to leave," she grumbled.

I had a sneaking suspicion Miss Keen had a crush on

Blitzen, but I was not brave enough to ask. Every time Blitz visited Valhalla, I would catch Mallory checking out his immaculate beard and perfect outfit, then glancing at Halfborn Gunderson as if wondering why her boyfriend/ex-boyfriend/re-boyfriend/ex-boyfriend couldn't dress so nattily.

"Njord swore it was necessary," I said, though I'd been doing little else but worrying about Blitz and Hearth. "Something about maximizing our time."

"Hmph." Mallory waved at the horizon. "Yet here we are, sailing and sailing. Your grandpa couldn't have just zapped us to Jorvik? That would've been more useful."

Halfborn Gunderson walked by with a mop and bucket. "Useful," he muttered. "Unlike *some* people."

"Shut up and swab!" Mallory snapped. "As for you, Magnus, I warned you about taking Loki's bait. And what did you do? Stepped up and volunteered for a flyting. You're as stupid as this berserker!"

With that, she climbed to the top of the mast, the most solitary place on the ship, and proceeded to glare daggers at the ocean.

Halfborn mumbled as he swabbed the deck, "Redheaded Irish vixen. Pay her no mind, Magnus."

I wished we didn't have to make our voyage while the two of them were feuding. Or while Sam was fasting for Ramadan. Or while Alex was trying to teach Sam how to foil Loki's control. Come to think of it, I wished we didn't have to make this voyage at all.

"What's Mallory's history with Loki?" I asked. "She seems . . ."

I wasn't sure which word to use: *Worried? Resentful? Homicidal?*

Halfborn knotted his shoulders, making the serpent tattoos undulate across his back. He glanced at the top of the mast, as if considering more curse words at Mallory's expense. "Not my place to say. But being baited into doing something you later regret . . . Mallory knows about that. It's how she died."

I thought back to my first days in Valhalla, when Halfborn had teased Mallory for trying to disarm a car bomb with her face. Her death must have had more to it. She'd been brave enough to attract the attention of a Valkyrie.

"Magnus, you've got to understand," Halfborn said, "we're both heading toward the places where we died. It may be different for you. You died in Boston, stayed in Boston. You haven't been dead long enough to see the world change around you. But for us? Mallory's got no wish to see Ireland again, even if we just sail past its shores. And me . . . I never wanted to return to Jorvik."

I felt a pang of guilt. "Man, I'm sorry. Is that where you died?"

"Eh. Not the exact spot, but close. I helped conquer the city with Ivar the Boneless. It served as our base camp. Not much of a town, back in the day. I just hope they don't still have *vatnavaettir* in the river." He shuddered. "Bad."

I had no idea what vatnavaettir were, but if Halfborn Gunderson considered them bad, I did not want to meet them.

Later that evening I checked in on T.J., who was standing at the prow, staring over the waves, drinking coffee, and nibbling a piece of hardtack. Why he liked hardtack, I couldn't tell you. It was like a big saltine cracker made with cement instead of flour, and no salt.

"Hey," I said.

He had trouble focusing on me. "Oh, hey, Magnus." He offered me a cement cracker. "Want one?"

"I'm good, thanks. I might need my teeth later on."

He nodded as if he hadn't gotten the joke.

Ever since I'd told the crew about my conversation with Njord, T.J. had been quiet and withdrawn, about as close as he ever got to brooding.

He dipped his hardtack in the coffee. "I've always wanted to go to England. I just never thought it would be after I was dead, on a quest, on a bright yellow warship."

"England?"

"That's where we're heading. Didn't you know?"

When I thought about England, which wasn't very often, I thought of the Beatles, Mary Poppins, and guys wearing bowler hats, carrying umbrellas, and saying *pip, pip cheerio*. I didn't think about hordes of Vikings or places called *Jorvik*. Then I remembered that when I first met Halfborn Gunderson, he'd told me he died invading East Anglia. That had been a kingdom in England, like, twelve hundred years ago. Those Vikings really got around.

T.J. leaned on the rail. In the moonlight, a thin streak of amber glowed across his neck—the path of a minié ball that had grazed him during his first battle as a Union Army soldier. It seemed strange to me that you could die, reach Valhalla, get resurrected daily for a hundred and fifty years, and still carry a tiny scar you got in your mortal life.

"Back in the war," he said, "we all worried that Great Britain would declare for the Rebels. The British had abolished slavery *way* before we did—the Union, I mean—but they needed Southern cotton for their textile mills. The fact that the UK stayed neutral and *didn't* side with the South—that was a huge factor in the North winning the war. It always gave me a warm feeling toward the Brits. I dreamed about going there someday and saying thank you in person."

I tried to detect sarcasm or irony in his tone. T.J. was the son of a freed slave. He'd fought and died for a country that kept his family in chains for generations. He even carried the name of a famous slaveholder. But T.J. said *we* when he talked about the Union. He wore his uniform proudly after more than a century. He dreamed about crossing the ocean to thank the British just because they'd done him the favor of staying neutral.

"How do you always find the bright side?" I marveled. "You're so . . . positive."

T.J. laughed, nearly choking on his hardtack. "Magnus, buddy, if you'd seen me right after I got to Valhalla? Nah. Those first few years were rough. Union soldiers weren't the only ones who made it to Valhalla. Plenty of Rebels died with swords in their hands. Valkyries don't care which side of the war you fight on, or how just your cause is. They look for personal bravery and honor." There. Just a hint of disapproval in his voice. "First couple of years I was an einherji, I saw some familiar faces come through the feast hall—"

"How did you die?" I asked. "The real story."

He traced the rim of his cup. "Told you. Charging the battlements at Fort Wagner, South Carolina."

"There's more to it. A few days ago, you warned me about accepting challenges. You talked like you had personal experience."

I studied the line of T.J.'s jaw, the tension bottled up there. Maybe that was why he liked hardtack. It gave him something difficult to grind his teeth against.

"A Confederate lieutenant singled me out," he said at last. "I have no idea why. Our regiment was hunkered down, waiting for the order to charge the battlements. The enemy fire was withering. None of us could move."

He glanced over. "And then this Reb officer stood up on the enemy lines. He pointed across no-man's-land with his sword, *right* at me, like somehow he knew me. He shouted, '*You, n–*' Well, you can guess what he called me. '*Come out and fight me man-to-man!*' "

"Which would have been suicide."

"I prefer to think of it as a hopeless display of bravery."

"You mean you *did* it?"

His coffee cup trembled between his hands. The piece of hardtack in it started to dissolve, expanding like a sponge, brown liquid soaking into the white starch.

"When you're a child of Tyr," he said, "you can't turn down a personal duel. Somebody says *fight me*, and you do it. Every muscle in my body responded to that challenge. Believe me, I didn't want to go one-on-one with that . . . guy."

He'd obviously been thinking of a word other than *guy*. "But I couldn't refuse. I went over the top, charged the Reb fortifications all by myself. I heard later, after I was dead, that my action triggered the offensive that led to the fall of Fort Wagner. The rest of the fellows followed my example. Guess they figured I was so crazy, they'd better back me up. Me, I just wanted to kill that lieutenant. I did, too. Jeffrey Toussaint. Shot him once in the chest, then got close enough to jab my bayonet right into his gut. Of course, by then the Rebs had shot me about thirty times. I fell in their ranks and died smiling up at a bunch of angry Confederate faces. Next thing I knew, I was in Valhalla."

"Odin's undies," I muttered, which was a curse I saved for special occasions. "Wait . . . the lieutenant you killed. How did you learn his name?"

T.J. gave me a rueful smile.

Finally, I understood. "He ended up in Valhalla, too."

T.J. nodded. "Floor seventy-six. Me and old Jeffrey . . . we spent about fifty years killing each other over and over again, every day. I was so filled with hate. That man was everything I despised and vice versa. I was afraid we'd end up like Hunding and Helgi—immortal enemies, still sniping at each other thousands of years later."

"But you didn't?"

"Funny thing. Eventually . . . I just got tired of it. I stopped looking for Jeffrey Toussaint on the battlefield. I figured something out. You can't hold on to hate forever. It won't do a thing to the person you hate, but it'll poison you, sure enough."

He traced the minié ball scar with his finger. "As for Jeffrey, he stopped showing up in the feast hall. Never saw him again. That happened to a lot of the Confederate einherjar. They didn't last. They locked themselves in their rooms, never came out. They faded away."

T.J. shrugged and continued. "I guess it was harder for them to adjust. You think the world is one way, then you find out it's much bigger and stranger than you ever imagined. If you can't expand your thinking, you're not going to do well in the afterlife."

I recalled standing with Amir Fadlan on the rooftop of the Citgo building, cradling his head and willing his mortal mind not to fracture under the weight of seeing the Bifrost Bridge and the Nine Worlds.

"Yeah," I agreed. "Expanding your brain hurts."

T.J. smiled, but I no longer thought of it as an easy smile. It was hard-won, as courageous as a solitary soldier charging enemy lines. "You've accepted your own personal challenge now, Magnus. You're going to have to face Loki one-on-one. There's no going back. But if it helps, you won't be charging those fortifications by yourself. We'll be right there with you."

He patted my shoulder. "Now, if you'll excuse me . . ." He handed me his coffee-and-hardtack soup like this was a fantastic gift. "I'm off to get some shut-eye!"

Most of the crew slept belowdecks. The *Big Banana*, we had discovered, would unfold as many rooms as we needed to be comfortable, regardless of the exterior size of the hull. I wasn't sure how that worked. Even though I was a *Doctor Who* fan, I didn't feel like testing the limits of our bright yellow TARDIS. I preferred sleeping on the deck, under the stars, which is where I was on our third morning at sea, when Alex shook me awake.

"Let's go, Chase," she announced. "We're running Samirah through her paces. I'm going to teach her how to defy Loki even if it kills us. And by us, I mean you."

FIFTEEN

Monkey!

I SAW my problem immediately.

I should never have introduced Alex to Percy Jackson. She had learned *way* too much from his relentless training methods. Maybe Alex couldn't summon sea animals, but she could turn into them. That was just as bad.

We started with Samirah and Alex fighting each other—on the deck, in the water, in the air. My job was to call out random animals from a stack of flash cards Alex had made. I'd shout, "MONKEY!" and Sam was supposed to turn into a monkey mid-combat, while Alex shape-shifted continually from human to animal to human, doing her best to beat up Sam.

Whenever Alex was in human form, she tossed out taunts like "Come on, al-Abbas! You call that a cotton-topped tamarin? Do better!"

After an hour of combat charades, Samirah's face gleamed with sweat. She'd taken off her hijab and tied back her long brown hair so she could fight better. (She considered us all family, so she had no problem going hijab-less when required.) She leaned against the rail, taking a breather. I almost offered her some water, then I remembered she was fasting.

"Maybe we should take a break until tonight," I suggested. "After dark, you can eat and drink. This must be killing you."

"I'm fine." Sam wasn't a very good liar, but she forced a smile. "Thanks, though."

Alex paced the deck, consulting her clipboard. *A clipboard*, y'all, like she was gunning to be assistant manager at the Hotel Valhalla. She wore green skinny jeans with a pink tank top, the front stitched with an inappropriate hand gesture in glittery sequins. Her hair had started to grow out, the black roots making her look even more imposing, like a lion with a healthy mane.

"Okay, Magnus, your turn," she told me. "Get Jack and prepare to fight."

Jack was pleased to help. "Combat time? Cool!" He floated in a circle around me. "Who are we fighting?"

"Sam," I said.

Jack froze. "But I like Sam."

"We're just practicing," I said. "Try to kill her without really killing her."

"Oh, phew! Okay. I can do that."

Alex had a clicker. Her cruelty knew no bounds. Jack and I double-teamed Sam—Jack attacking with his blade, obviously; me with a mop handle, which I doubt struck terror into Sam's heart. Sam dodged and weaved and tried to land hits on us with her ax, the blade wrapped in sail canvas. Sam was supposed to shape-shift whenever Alex clicked her clicker, which she did at random intervals with no regard for Sam's situation.

The idea, I guessed, was to condition Samirah to change shape whenever, wherever she had to without second-guessing herself.

Jack held back, I could tell. He only whacked Sam a couple of times. Me, I was less than successful with my mop. Combat maneuvering on the deck of a Viking ship turned out to be one of the many important skills I did not have. I tripped over the oars. I got snagged in the rigging. Twice, I bonked my head on the mast and fell into the ocean. About average for me, in other words.

Sam had no such trouble. She left me bruised and battered. The only time I landed a hit was when Alex clicked at a particularly bad time. Mid-lunge, Sam turned into a parrot and flew beak-first into my mop handle. She squawked, turned back into a human, and sat down hard on the deck, a cloud of blue and red feathers fluttering around her.

"Sorry, Sam." I felt mortified. "I've never hit a parrot before."

Despite her bloody nose, she laughed. "It's fine. Let's try that again."

We fought until we were both spent. Alex called our practice done, and the three of us slumped against the rail shields.

"Whew!" Jack propped himself next to me. "I'm exhausted!"

Since all the energy he expended would come out of *me* as soon as I took hold of him, I decided to let Jack stay in blade form a while longer. I wasn't ready to go comatose until after I had lunch.

But at least I could *have* lunch.

I glanced at Samirah. "This Ramadan thing. I seriously don't know how you do it."

She raised an eyebrow. "You mean *why* I do it?"

"That, too. You really have to endure the fast for a whole month?"

"Yes, Magnus," she said. "It may surprise you to learn that the month of Ramadan lasts one month."

"Glad you haven't completely lost your snark."

She dabbed her face with a towel, which was apparently not forbidden. "I'm more than halfway through the month. It's not so bad." She frowned. "Of course, if we all die before the end of Ramadan, that would be irritating."

"Yeah," Alex agreed. "Loki burns down the Nine Worlds while you're fasting, and you can't even have a drink of water? Ouch."

Sam swatted her arm. "You have to admit, Fierro, I was more focused today. Ramadan helps."

"Eh, maybe," Alex said. "I still think you're crazy to fast, but I'm not as worried as I was."

"I feel clearer," Sam said. "Emptier, in a *good* way. I'm not freezing up as much. I'll be ready when I face Loki, inshallah."

Sam didn't use that term much, but I knew it meant *God willing*. Though it obviously helped her, it never inspired much confidence in me. *I'm going to do great, inshallah* was sort of like saying *I'm going to do great, assuming I don't get run over by a truck first.*

"Well," Alex said, "we won't know what'll happen until you're facing dear old Mom-slash-Dad. But I'm cautiously optimistic. And you didn't kill Magnus, which I suppose is good."

"Thanks," I muttered.

Even that little bit of consideration from Alex—the idea that my death might be slightly disagreeable to her—gave me a warm and fuzzy feeling. Yeesh. I was pathetic.

The rest of the afternoon, I helped out around the *Big Banana*. Despite the automatic sailing, there was still plenty to do: swabbing decks, untangling lines, preventing Mallory and Halfborn from killing each other. The chores kept me from thinking too much about my impending confrontation with Loki, or what Blitz and Hearth might be up to. They'd already been gone three days, and we now had just under two weeks until Midsummer, maybe even less time until the ice melted enough to let Loki's ship sail. How long could it take Blitz and Hearth to find a rock?

Naturally, the idea of searching for a whetstone brought back bad memories of my last quest with Blitz and Hearth, when we'd been trying to find the Skofnung Stone. I told myself there was no connection. This time there would be no brutal Alfheim sunlight, no evil violin-playing *nøkks*, no scowling, sadistic elf father.

Soon, Hearth and Blitz would come back and report on a completely different set of dangerous obstacles for us to overcome! Every time a wave broke over the bow, I watched the sea spray, hoping it would solidify into my friends. But they did not reappear.

A couple of times during the afternoon, small sea serpents swam by—like, twenty-footers. They eyed the ship but didn't attack. I guessed they either didn't like banana-flavored prey or were scared off by Jack's singing.

Jack followed me around the deck, alternating between Abba hits (Vikings are huge Abba fans) and telling me stories about the old days when he and Frey would roam the Nine Worlds, spreading sunshine and happiness and occasionally killing people.

As they day wore on, this became a personal test of endurance: Did I want to return Jack to runestone form and pass out from the toll of our combined exertions, or did I want to listen to him sing some more?

Finally, around sunset, I couldn't stand it any longer. I stumbled aft to where I'd set up my sleeping bag. I lay down, enjoying the sound of Samirah doing her evening prayer on the foredeck, the singsong poetry soft and relaxing.

It seemed strange, the Muslim Maghrib prayer aboard a Viking ship full of atheists and pagans. Then again, Samirah's ancestors had been dealing with Vikings since the Middle Ages. I doubted this was the first time prayers to Allah had been said aboard a longship. The world, the *worlds*, were a lot more interesting because of constant intermixing.

I returned Jack to runestone form and barely had time to reattach him to my neck chain before I passed out.

In my dreams, I got to witness a murder.

SIXTEEN

Spit Man Versus Chain Saw. Guess Who Wins

I STOOD with four gods at the crest of a hill, next to the ruins of a thatched hut.

Odin leaned on a thick oaken staff, chain mail glinting under his blue travel cloak. A spear was strapped across his back. A sword hung at his side. His one good eye gleamed under the shade of his blue wide-brimmed hat. With his grizzled beard, eye patch, and assorted weapons, he looked like a guy who couldn't decide whether to go to a Halloween party as a wizard or a pirate.

Next to him stood Heimdall, the guardian of the Bifrost Bridge. Smartphones must not have been invented yet, because he wasn't doing his usual thing of taking pictures every five seconds. He was dressed in armor of thick white wool, with two swords sheathed in an X across his back. Gjallar, the Horn of Doomsday, dangled from his belt, which didn't strike me as very safe. Anybody could've run up behind him, blown that horn, and started Ragnarok as a practical joke.

The third god, my father, Frey, knelt next to the ashes of a campfire. He wore faded jeans and a flannel shirt, though I didn't see how those clothes could have been invented yet. Maybe Frey was a medieval beta-tester for REI. His blond hair swept across his shoulders. His bristly beard glowed in the sunlight. If there had been any justice in the world, the thunder god Thor would've looked like this—blond and handsome and regal, not like a muscle-bound redheaded fart machine.

The fourth god I had never met, but I recognized him from Njord's holographic show-and-tell: Kvasir, the living peace treaty between the Aesir and Vanir. He was a handsome guy considering that he originated as a cup of divine spit. His dark curly hair and beard rippled in the breeze. Homespun robes enfolded him, giving him that Jedi-master vibe. He knelt next to my father, his fingers hovering over the charred remnants of the campfire.

Odin leaned toward him. "What do you think, Kvasir?"

That question alone told me how much the gods respected Kvasir. Normally Odin did not ask for the opinions of others. He simply gave answers, usually in the form of riddles or PowerPoint presentations.

Kvasir touched the ashes. "This is Loki's fire, all right. He was here recently. He is still close by."

Heimdall scanned the horizon. "I don't see him anywhere in a five-hundred-mile radius, unless . . . No, that's an Irishman with a nice haircut."

"We must catch Loki," Odin grumbled. "That flyting was the last straw. He must be imprisoned and punished!"

"A net," Kvasir announced.

Frey scowled. "What do you mean?"

"See? Loki was burning the evidence." Kvasir traced a barely discernible pattern of crossed lines in the ashes. "He was trying to anticipate our moves, considering all the ways we might capture him. He wove a net, then quickly burned it."

Kvasir rose. "Gentlemen, Loki has disguised himself as a fish. We need a net!"

The others looked amazed, like *Holmes, how did you do that?* I waited for Kvasir to cry, *The game's afoot!* Instead he shouted "To the nearest river!" and strode off, the other gods hurrying after him.

My dream changed. I saw flashes of Kvasir's life as he traveled the Nine Worlds, advising the locals on everything from farming to childbirth to tax deductions. All mortal beings loved him. In every town, castle, and village, he was greeted like a hero.

Then one day, after filling out some particularly difficult tax forms for a family of giants, he was on the road to Midgard when he was stopped by a pair of dwarves—stunted, warty, hairy little guys with malicious smiles.

Unfortunately, I recognized them—the brothers Fjalar and Gjalar. They'd once sold me a one-way boat ride. According to Blitzen, they were also notorious thieves and murderers.

"Hello!" Fjalar called to Kvasir from the top of a boulder. "You must be the famous Kvasir!"

Next to him, Gjalar waved enthusiastically. "Well met! We've heard wonderful things about you!"

Kvasir, being the wisest being ever created, should have known enough to say *Sorry, I gave at the office* and keep walking.

Unfortunately, Kvasir was also kind. He raised his hand in greeting. "Hello, good dwarves! I am indeed Kvasir. How may I help you?"

Fjalar and Gjalar exchanged glances, like they couldn't believe their good luck. "Uh, well, you can be our guest for dinner!" Gjalar gestured to a nearby hillside, where the entrance to a cave was covered with curtains of ragged leather.

"We are not interested in murdering you," Fjalar promised. "Or stealing your stuff. Or draining your blood, which probably has incredible magical properties. We simply want to show you our hospitality!"

"Much appreciated," Kvasir said. "But I am expected in Midgard tonight. Many humans need my help."

"Oh, I see," Fjalar said. "You like . . . helping people." He said it the way one might say *You like raw beef.* "Well, as it happens, we're having a terrible time with our, uh, quarterly estimated taxes."

Kvasir frowned in sympathy. "I see. Those can be difficult to calculate."

"Yes!" Gjalar clasped his hands. "Could you help us, O Wise One?"

This was like the part in every horror movie when the audience yells DON'T DO IT! But Kvasir's compassion overcame his wisdom.

"Very well," he said. "Show me your paperwork!"

He followed the dwarves into their cave.

I wanted to run after him, to warn him what was going to happen, but my feet remained rooted to the ground. Inside the cave, Kvasir began to scream. A few moments later, I heard a sound like a chain saw, then liquid gurgling into a large cauldron. If I'd been able to throw up in my sleep, I would have.

The scene shifted one last time.

I found myself in the front yard of a three-story mansion, one in a line of Colonials facing a public green. It might have been Salem or Lexington—one of those sleepy pre-Revolutionary towns outside Boston. White-painted columns flanked the house's entrance. Honeysuckle bushes filled the air with sugary perfume. An American flag fluttered on the porch. The scene was so bucolic it could have been Alfheim if the sunlight had been a little harsher.

The front door swung open, and a skinny figure tumbled down the brick steps as if she'd been thrown.

Alex Fierro looked about fourteen, maybe two or three years younger than when I'd met her. A trickle of blood ran from her left temple. She crawled down the front walk on her hands and knees, her palms shredded from breaking her fall and leaving dabs of blood across the cement like a sponge painting.

She didn't look scared so much as bitter and angry, with tears of frustration in her eyes.

In the doorway of the house, a middle-aged man appeared—short dark hair streaked with gray, pressed black slacks, shiny black shoes, a white dress shirt so crisp and bright it hurt my eyes. I could imagine Blitzen saying *You really need a splash of color, sir!*

The man had Alex's petite build. His face was handsome in the same harsh angular way—like a diamond you could admire but not touch without getting cut.

He shouldn't have been scary. He wasn't big or strong or tough-looking. He dressed like a banker. But there was something terrifying about the set of his jaw, the intensity of his stare, the way his lips twitched and tightened across his teeth as if he hadn't quite mastered human expressions. I wanted to put myself between him and Alex, but I couldn't move.

In one hand, the man hefted a ceramic object the size of a

football—a brown-and-white ovoid. I saw that it was a bust with two different faces side by side.

"NORMAL!" The man threw the ceramic sculpture at Alex. It shattered on the walkway. "That's all I want from you! To be a *normal* kid! Is that so damn hard?"

Alex struggled to her feet. She turned to face her father. A mauve skirt hung to her knees over black leggings. Her green sleeveless top had given her arms no protection from the pavement. Her elbows looked like they'd been struck by a meat tenderizer. Her hair was longer than I'd ever seen it, a green ponytail sprouting from her black roots like a flame from Aegir's hearth fire.

"I *am* normal, *Father*." She hissed the word as if it was the most twisted insult she could think of.

"No more help." His tone was hard and cold. "No more money."

"I don't *want* your money."

"Well, that's good! Because it's going to my *real* children." He spat on the steps. "You had so much potential. You understood the craft almost as well as your grandfather. And look at you."

"The art," Alex corrected.

"What?"

"It's art. Not craft."

Her father waved in disgust at the broken ceramic pieces. "That is not art. It's trash."

The sentiment was clear, even if he didn't say it: *You have chosen to be trash, too.*

Alex glared at her father. The air between them turned dry and bitter. Both seemed to be waiting for the other to make a definitive gesture—to apologize and give in, or to cut the thread between them forever.

Alex got no such resolution.

Her father shook his head in dismay, as if he couldn't believe his life had come to this. Then he turned and went inside, slamming the door behind him.

I woke with a start. "WHAT?"

"Relax, Sleepy." Alex Fierro stood over me—*today's* Alex, wearing a raincoat of such bright yellow I wondered if our ship had begun to assimilate her. The banging sound I'd heard in my dream had been her dropping a full canteen next to my head. She lobbed an apple at my chest.

"Breakfast," she said. "And also lunch."

I rubbed my eyes. I could still hear the voice of her father and smell the honeysuckle in their front yard. "How long was I out?"

"About sixteen hours," she said. "You didn't miss much, so we let you sleep. But now it's time."

"For what?"

I sat up in my sleeping bag. My friends moved around the deck, tying off lines and securing the oars. Cold drizzle hung in the air. Our longship was moored at a stone embankment, on a river lined with brick town houses not too different than those back home in Boston.

"Welcome to Jorvik." Halfborn glowered. "Or as you modern folk call it, York, England."

SEVENTEEN

We Are Ambushed
by a Pile of Rocks

IN CASE you're wondering, Old York looks absolutely nothing like New York.

It looks older.

Magnus Chase, master of description. You're welcome.

Halfborn wasn't thrilled to be back at his old base camp. "No self-respecting Viking city should be so far from the sea," he grumbled. "I don't know why Ivar the Boneless even bothered with this place. We wasted all morning sailing here—about twenty-five miles up the River Ouse!"

"The River Ooze?" I asked.

"Ouse," T.J. corrected, breaking into a grin. "It rhymes with *moose*. I read about it in a travel guide!"

I shuddered. Nothing good rhymes with *moose*. *Excuse. Noose. Caboose.* I also found it disturbing that T.J. had done so much research on England. Then again, a hundred and fifty years is a long time to hang around Valhalla, and the hotel library *is* impressive.

I glanced over the port side. Murky green water curled and swelled around our hull, the rain stippling the surface of the river with overlapping bull's eyes. The current seemed too alive, too *awake*. No matter how much Percy Jackson had trained me, I did not want to fall in there.

"You sense them, don't you?" Halfborn gripped his ax as if ready to cut loose on the Ouse. "The vatnavaettir."

Halfborn said the word as if he found it truly awful—like *cowardice* or *beard trimmer*. "What are they?" I asked.

"And do they have a more pronounceable name?" Alex added.

"They're nature spirits," Mallory said. "We have similar legends in Ireland. We call them *each-uisce*—water horses."

Halfborn snorted. "You Irish have similar legends because you got them from the Norse."

"Lies," Mallory growled. "The Celts were in Ireland *long* before you louts invaded."

"*Louts?* The Viking kingdom of Dublin was the only power worth mentioning on your miserable island!"

"Anyway . . ." Samirah stepped between the two lovebirds. "Why are these water horses dangerous?"

Halfborn frowned. "Well, they can form a herd and, if they get riled up, stampede and destroy our ship. I imagine they've only held off this long because they're not sure what to make of us being bright yellow. Also, if anyone is foolish enough to touch them—"

"They'll adhere to your skin," Mallory said, "drag you under, and drown you."

Her words made my stomach clench. I'd once gotten myself adhered to a magical eagle that proceeded to take me on a demolition-derby tour over the rooftops of Boston. The idea of being dragged into the Ouse sounded even less fun.

Alex threw her arms around Mallory and Halfborn. "Well, then. It sounds like you two are the water-horse experts. You should stay on board and defend the *Big Banana* while the rest of us go giant hunting!"

"Uh," I said. "I can just turn the ship into a handkerchief—"

"Oh, no!" Halfborn said. "I have *no* desire to set foot in Jorvik again. I wouldn't be of any use to you, anyway. Place has changed a bit in twelve hundred years. I'll stay on the ship, but I don't need *Mallory's* help defending it."

"You think not?" Mallory glared up at him, her hands on the hilts of her knives. "Do *you* know any Gaelic songs for calming water horses? I'm not leaving this ship in *your* care."

"Well, I'm not leaving it in *your* care!"

"Guys!" Samirah raised her hands like a boxing referee. She'd never been much of a curser, but I got the sense she was struggling with the Ramadan *no cursing* rule again. Funny how that works: as soon as you're told you can't do something, you have the overwhelming desire to do it.

"If you both insist on staying aboard," she said, "I'll stay, too. I'm good with horses. I can fly if I get in trouble. And in a pinch"—she flicked her wrist, telescoping her spear of light into existence—"I can blast anything that attacks us. Or I can blast the two of you, if you don't behave."

Halfborn and Mallory looked equally unhappy about that arrangement, which meant it was a good compromise.

"You heard the lady," Alex said. "The landing party will consist of me, T.J., and Blond Guy."

"Excellent!" T.J. rubbed his hands. "I can't wait to thank the British!"

T.J. wasn't kidding.

As we walked the narrow streets of York in a cold gray

drizzle, he greeted everyone he saw and tried to shake hands. "Hello!" he said. "I'm from Boston. Thank you for not supporting the Confederacy!"

The reactions of the locals ranged from "Eh?" to "Leave off!" to some phrases so colorful I wondered if the speakers had descended from Halfborn Gunderson.

T.J. wasn't deterred. He strolled along, waving and pointing. "Anything you guys need!" he offered. "I owe you." He grinned at me. "I love this place. The people are *so* friendly."

"Uh-huh." I scanned the low rooftops, figuring that if there was a giant in this city, I should be able to spot him. "So, if you were a jotun in York, where would you be hiding?"

Alex stopped in front of a collection of street signs. With her green hair sticking out the hood of her yellow raincoat, she looked like a punk spokesperson for frozen fish sticks. "Maybe we could start there." She pointed at the top sign. "The Jorvik Viking Centre."

It sounded like as good a plan as any, especially since we had no other plans.

We followed the signs, winding our way through narrow crooked streets lined with brick town houses, pubs, and storefronts. It could have been the North End of Boston, except York was even more of a historical patchwork. Victorian brick butted up against medieval stone, which butted up against black-and-white Elizabethan magpie, which butted up against a tanning salon offering twenty minutes for five pounds.

We passed only a few people. Traffic was light. I wondered if it was a holiday, or if the locals had heard about the bright yellow Viking ship invading the Ouse and had run for the hills.

I decided it was just as well. If there'd been more English

folk to meet and greet, T.J. would have really slowed us down.

We made our way down a street called the Shambles, which struck me as an honest description but poor branding. The road itself was just wide enough for a bicycle, assuming the rider was skinny. The houses overhung the sidewalk at fun-house-mirror angles, each story a little wider than the one below it, giving the impression that the entire neighborhood would collapse in on itself if we took one wrong step. I barely breathed until we emerged onto a wider avenue.

Finally, the signs led us to a pedestrian shopping area, where a squat brick building was festooned with green banners: VIKINGS! LIVING HISTORY! THRILLS! FULL INTERACTIVE EXPERIENCE!

All of which sounded pretty good, except for the sign across the front entrance: CLOSED.

"Huh." T.J. rattled the door handle. "Should we break in?"

I didn't see what good that would do. The place was obviously a museum for tourists. No matter how good this interactive experience was, it would be a letdown after actually living in Valhalla. I didn't need any Viking paraphernalia from the gift shop, either. My runestone pendant/talking sword was as much as I could handle.

"Guys," Alex said, her voice tight. "Did that wall just move?"

I followed her gaze. Across the pedestrian plaza, jutting from the side of a Tesco Express grocery store, was a crumbling section of rough-hewn limestone blocks that might have been part of a castle or the old city walls.

At least that's what I thought, until the pile of limestone shifted.

A few times, I had watched Samirah emerge from beneath

her camouflage hijab—it would look like she had stepped out of a tree trunk or a plain white wall or the display case at a Dunkin' Donuts. This sight gave me a similar kind of vertigo.

My mind had to reprocess what I was looking at: not a section of ruined wall, but a giant, twenty feet tall, whose appearance perfectly mimicked limestone. His rough brown-and-beige skin was beaded like a Gila monster's. A flocking of rubble crusted his long shaggy hair and beard. He wore a tunic and leggings of quilted heavy canvas, giving him that fortress-wall look. Why he'd been leaning against the grocery store, I had no idea. Dozing? Panhandling? Did giants panhandle?

He fixed us with his amber eyes—the only part of him that seemed truly alive.

"Well, well," rumbled the giant. "I've been waiting ages for Vikings to appear at the Viking Centre. Can't wait to kill you!"

"Good idea, Alex," I squeaked. "Let's follow the signs to the Viking Centre. Yay."

For once, she had no scathing comeback. She stared at the giant, her mouth hanging open, her raincoat hood slipping back from her head.

T.J.'s rifle quivered in his hands like a dowsing rod.

I didn't feel much braver. Sure, I'd seen taller giants. I'd seen eagle giants, fire giants, drunk giants, and giants in gaudy bowling shirts. But I'd never had a stone giant appear right in front of me and cheerfully offer to kill me.

Standing upright, his shoulders were level with the two-story rooftops around us. The few pedestrians on the streets simply walked around him as if he were an inconvenient construction project.

He grabbed the nearest telephone pole and yanked it out

of the ground along with a large circular chunk of pavement. Only when he rested the pole across his shoulder did I realize it was his weapon—a maul with a head the size of a hot tub.

"Vikings used to be more social," he rumbled. "I thought surely they'd come to their community center for trials by combat. Or at least for bingo! But you're the first ones I've seen in . . ." He tilted his shaggy head, a gesture that looked like an avalanche of sheepdogs. "How long *was* I sitting there? I must have dozed off! Ah, well. Tell me your names, warriors. I would like to know who I am killing."

At that point, I would have screamed *I claim guest rights!* But, sadly, we were not inside the giant's home. I doubted guest rights would apply on a public street in a human city.

"Are you the giant Hrungnir?" I asked, hoping I sounded more confident than panic-stricken. "I'm Magnus Chase. This is Thomas Jefferson Jr. and Alex Fierro. We're here to bargain with you!"

The shaggy stone colossus looked from side to side. "Of course I am Hrungnir! Do you see any other giants around? I'm afraid killing you is nonnegotiable, little einherji, but we can haggle about the details, if you like."

I gulped. "How did you know we're einherjar?"

Hrungnir grinned, his teeth like the crenellations of a castle turret. "You *smell* like einherjar! Now, come. What were you hoping to bargain for—a quick death? A death by squeezing? Perhaps a lovely death by stomping followed by being scraped off the bottom of my shoe!"

I glanced at T.J., who shook his head vigorously like *Not the shoe!*

Alex still hadn't moved. I only knew she was still alive because she blinked the rain out of her eyes.

"O Large and Beige Hrungnir," I said, "we seek the location of Kvasir's Mead!"

Hrungnir scowled, his rocky eyebrows furrowing, his brick-like lips forming a segmental arch. "Well, well. Playing Odin's thievery game, are you? The old Bolverk trick?"

"Uh . . . maybe."

Hrungnir chuckled. "I could give you that information. I was with Baugi and Suttung when they sequestered the mead in its new hiding place."

"Right." I silently added *Baugi* and *Suttung* to my mental list of Things I Am Clueless About. "That's what we have come to bargain for. The location of the mead!"

I realized I had already said that. "What is your price, O Beige One?"

Hrungnir stroked his beard, causing rubble and dust to sift down the front of his tunic. "For me to consider such a trade, your deaths would have to be very entertaining." He studied T.J., then me. His eyes came to rest on Alex Fierro. "Ah. This one smells of clay! You have the necessary skills, do you not?"

I glanced at Alex. "Necessary skills?"

"Eep," Alex said.

"Excellent!" Hrungnir boomed. "It's been centuries since the stone giants found a worthy opponent for a traditional two-on-two duel! A fight to the death! Shall we say tomorrow at dawn?"

"Whoa," I said. "Couldn't we do a healing contest?"

"Or bingo," T.J. offered. "Bingo is good."

"No!" Hrungnir cried. "My very name means *brawler*, little einherji. You won't cheat me out of a good fight! We will follow the ancient rules of combat. Me versus . . . Hmm."

I didn't want to volunteer, but I'd seen Jack take down bigger giants than this guy before. I raised my hand. "Very well, I—"

"No, you're too scrawny." Hrungnir pointed to T.J. "I challenge him!"

"I ACCEPT!" T.J. yelled.

Then he blinked, as if thinking *Thanks a lot, Dad.*

"Good, good," the giant said. "And my second will fight your second, who will be made by her!"

Alex staggered back as if she'd been pushed. "I—I can't. I've never—"

"Or I can just kill all three of you now," Hrungnir said. "Then you'll have *no* chance of finding Kvasir's Mead."

My mouth felt as dusty as the giant's beard. "Alex, what's he talking about? What are you supposed to make?"

By the trapped look in her eyes, I could tell she understood Hrungnir's demand. I'd only seen her this panicked once before—on her first day in Valhalla, when she thought she might be stuck in one gender for the rest of eternity.

"I—" She licked her lips. "All right. I'll do it."

"That's the spirit!" Hrungnir said. "As for the little blond guy here, I guess he can be your water boy or something. Well, I'm off to make my second. You should do the same. I will meet you tomorrow, at dawn, at Konungsgurtha!"

The giant turned and strode through the streets of York, pedestrians moving out of his way as if he were a veering bus.

I turned to Alex. "Explain. What did you just agree to?"

The contrast between her heterochromatic eyes seemed even greater than usual, as if the gold and the brown were separating, pooling to the left and right.

"We need to find a pottery studio," she said. *"Fast."*

EIGHTEEN

I Roll Play-Doh to the Death

YOU DON'T hear heroes say that a lot.

Quick, Boy Wonder! To the pottery studio!

But Alex's tone left no doubt it was a matter of life and death. The nearest ceramics workshop—a place called the Earthery—turned out to be on my favorite street, the Shambles. I didn't see that as a good omen. While T.J. and I waited outside, Alex spent a few minutes talking with the proprietor, who at last emerged, grinning and holding a large wad of multicolored money. "Have fun, lads!" he said as he hurried down the street. "Brilliant! Ta!"

"Thank you!" T.J. waved. "And thanks for not getting involved in our Civil War!"

We headed inside, where Alex was taking inventory—worktables, potter's wheels, metal shelves lined with half-finished pots, tubs filled with tools, a cabinet stacked with slabs of wet clay in plastic bags. In the back of the studio, one door led to a small bathroom, another to what looked like a storage room.

"This might work," Alex muttered. "Maybe."

"Did you buy this place?" I asked.

"Don't be silly. I just paid the owner for twenty-four hours' exclusive use. But I paid well."

"In British pounds," I noted. "Where'd you get so much local cash?"

She shrugged, her attention on counting bags of clay. "It's called preparation, Chase. I figured we'd be traveling through the UK and Scandinavia. I brought euros, kronor, kroner, and pounds. Compliments of my family. And by *compliments*, I mean I stole it."

I remembered my dream of Alex in front of her house, the way she'd snarled *I don't want your money*. Maybe she'd meant she only wanted it on her terms. I could respect that. But how she'd gotten so many different currencies, I couldn't guess.

"Stop gawping and help me," she ordered.

"I'm not— I wasn't gawping."

"We need to push these tables together," she said. "T.J., go see if there's more clay in the back. We need a *lot* more."

"On it!" T.J. dashed to the supply room.

Alex and I moved four tables together, making a work surface big enough to play Ping-Pong on. T.J. hauled out extra bags of clay until I estimated we had an adequate amount to make a ceramic Volkswagen.

Alex looked back and forth between the clay and the potter's wheels. She tapped her thumbnail nervously against her teeth. "Not enough time," she muttered. "Drying, glazing, firing—"

"Alex," I said. "If you want us to help you, you're going to have to explain what we're doing."

T.J. edged away from me, in case Alex brought out the garrote.

She just glared at me. "You would *know* what I'm doing if you'd taken Pottery 101 in Valhalla with me like I asked you."

"I—I had a scheduling conflict." In fact, I hadn't liked the idea of pottery to the death, especially if it involved getting thrown in a fiery kiln.

"Stone giants have a tradition called *tveirvigi*," said Alex. "Double combat."

"It's like Viking single combat, *einvigi*," T.J. added. "Except with *tveir* instead of *ein*."

"Fascinating," I said.

"I know! I read about it in—"

"Please don't say a travel guide."

T.J. looked at the floor.

Alex picked up a box of assorted wooden tools. "Honestly, Chase, we don't have time to bring you up to speed. T.J. fights Hrungnir. I make a ceramic warrior who fights the giant's ceramic warrior. You play water boy, or heal, or whatever. It's pretty straightforward."

I stared at the bags of clay. "A ceramic warrior. As in *magic* pottery?"

"Pottery 101," Alex repeated, like that was obvious. "T.J., would you start cutting those slabs? I need slices one inch thick, about sixty or seventy of them."

"Sure! Do I get to use your garrote?"

Alex laughed long and hard. "Absolutely not. There should be a cutter in that gray tub."

T.J. sulked off to find a regular clay cutter.

"And you," Alex told me, "you're going to be making coils."

"Coils."

"I know you can roll clay into coils. It's just like making snakes out of Play-Doh."

I wondered how she knew my dark secret—that I had

enjoyed Play-Doh as a kid. (And when I say *kid*, I mean up to, like, age eleven.) I grudgingly admitted that this was within my scope of talents. "And you?"

"The hardest part is using the wheel," she said. "The most important components have to be thrown."

By *thrown*, I knew she meant *shaped on the wheel*, not *thrown across the room*, though with Alex the two activities often went together.

"All right, boys," she said. "Let's get to work."

After a few hours spent rolling coils, my shoulders ached. My shirt stuck to my sweaty skin. When I closed my eyes, clay snakes flopped around on the backs of my eyelids.

My only relief was getting up to change the station on the proprietor's little radio whenever Alex or T.J. didn't like a song. T.J. preferred martial music, but English radio had a shocking lack of marching-band tunes. Alex favored songs from Japanese anime—also in short supply on the AM/FM dial. Finally, they both settled on Duran Duran, for reasons I can't explain.

From time to time, I brought Alex soft drinks from the proprietor's mini fridge. Her favorite was Tizer, a sort of cherry soda with extra twang. I didn't like it, but Alex quickly got addicted. Her lips turned bright red like a vampire's, which I found both disturbing and strangely fascinating.

Meanwhile T.J. ran back and forth between his slab-cutting and the kiln, which he was heating up for an epic day of firing. He seemed to take special pleasure in poking pencil-stub-size dents in the slabs so they wouldn't crack when baked. He did this while humming "Hungry Like the Wolf"—not my favorite song, given my personal history. T.J. seemed cheerful for a guy who had a duel scheduled with a twenty-foot-tall stone giant in the morning. I decided not to remind him that if he died here in England, he would stay dead, no matter how friendly the locals were.

I had placed my worktable as close as I could to Alex's wheel so I could talk to her. Usually I waited to ask her a question until she was centering a new lump of clay. With both her hands engaged, she was less likely to hit me.

"Have you done this before?" I asked. "Made a pottery guy?"

She glanced over, her face flecked with white porcelain. "Tried a few times. Nothing this big. But my family . . ." She bore down on the clay, molding it into a beehive-like cone. "Like Hrungnir said, we have the necessary skills."

"Your family." I tried to imagine Loki sitting at a table, rolling clay snakes.

"The Fierros." Alex shot me a wary look. "You really don't know? Never heard of Fierro Ceramics?"

"Uh . . . should I have?"

She smiled, as if she found my ignorance refreshing. "If you knew anything about cooking or home décor, maybe. It was a hot brand about ten years ago. But that's fine. I'm not talking about the machine-made crap my dad sells, anyway. I'm talking about my grandfather's art. He started the business when he emigrated from Tlatilco."

"Tlatilco." I tried to place the name. "I'm guessing that's outside I-95?"

Alex laughed. "No reason you'd have heard of it. Tiny place in Mexico. These days it's really just a subsection of Mexico City. According to my grandfather, our family has been making pottery there since before the Aztecs. Tlatilco used to be this super-ancient culture." She pressed her thumbs into the center of her beehive, opening up the sides of the new pot.

It still seemed like magic to me the way she did it, shaping such a delicate and perfectly symmetrical vase with nothing but strength and spin. The few times I'd tried to use a wheel, I'd nearly broken my fingers and managed to turn a lump of clay into a slightly uglier lump of clay.

"Who knows what's true?" Alex continued. "These are just family stories. Legends. But my abuelo took them seriously. When he moved to Boston, he kept doing things the old way. Even if he was just making a plate or a cup, he'd create every piece by hand, with lots of pride and attention to detail."

"Blitzen would like that."

Alex sat back, regarding her pot. "Yeah, my granddad would have made a good dwarf. Then my dad took over the business and decided to go commercial. He sold out. He mass-produced lines of ceramic dishware, entered into deals with home-furnishing-supply chains. He made millions before people started realizing the quality was going downhill."

I recalled her father's bitter words in my dream: *You had so much potential. You understood the craft almost as well as your grandfather.*

"He wanted you to carry on the family business."

She studied me, no doubt wondering how I'd guessed. I almost told her about the dream, but Alex *really* did not like having people inside her head, even unintentionally. And I didn't like being yelled at.

"My father is an idiot," she said. "He didn't understand

how I could like pottery but not want to make money off it. He definitely didn't appreciate me listening to my granddad's crazy ideas."

"Such as?"

Over at his worktable, T.J. kept poking holes in the clay slices with a dowel, creating different patterns, like stars and spirals. "This is kind of fun," he admitted. "Therapeutic!"

Alex's Tizer-red lips curled up at the edges. "My abuelo made pottery for a living, but his real interest was in our ancestors' sculptures. He wanted to understand the spirituality of them. That wasn't easy. I mean . . . after so many centuries, trying to figure out your heritage when it's been buried under so much else—Olmec, Aztec, Spanish, Mexican. How do you even know what's true? How do you reclaim it?"

I got the feeling her questions were rhetorical and didn't require answers from me, which was just as well. I couldn't think clearly with T.J. humming "Rio" and doweling smiley faces in his clay.

"But your granddad managed," I guessed.

"He thought so." Alex spun up the wheel again, sponging the sides of her pot. "So did I. My dad . . ." Her expression soured. "Well, he liked to blame . . . you know, the way I am . . . on Loki. He didn't like it *at all* when I found validation on the Fierro side of the family."

My brain felt like my hands—as if a layer of clay was tightening over it, sucking out all the moisture. "Sorry, I don't understand. What does this have to do with magic ceramic warriors?"

"You'll see. Fish the phone out of my pocket and call

Sam, will you? Give her an update. Then shut up so I can concentrate."

Even under orders, pulling something out of Alex's pants pocket while she was wearing said pants seemed like a good way to get myself killed.

I managed, with only a couple of small panic attacks, and found that Alex's phone had data service in the UK. She must have arranged that when she arranged her multicurrency theft.

I texted Samirah and gave her the lowdown.

A few minutes later, the phone buzzed with her reply. *K. GL. Fighting. GTG.*

I wondered if *GTG* in this context meant *got to go, Gunderson throttling girlfriend,* or *giants torturing Gunderson.* I decided to think optimistically and went with the first option.

As the afternoon wore on, the back tables filled up with fired porcelain squares that looked like armored plates. Alex taught me how, by combining my coils, to form cylinders that would serve as arms and legs. Her efforts at the pottery wheel produced feet, hands, and a head, all shaped like vases and meticulously decorated with Viking runes.

She spent hours on the faces—two of them, side by side, like the piece of art that Alex's father had shattered in my dream. The left face had heavy-lidded, suspicious eyes, a cartoon villain's curly mustache, and a huge grimacing mouth. The right face was a grinning skull with hollow eyeholes and a lolling tongue. Looking at the two visages pressed together, I couldn't help thinking about Alex's own different-colored eyes.

By evening, we'd laid out all the pieces of the ceramic

warrior on our quadruple table, creating an eight-foot-long Frankenstein's monster, some assembly required.

"Well." T.J. wiped his forehead. "That thing would scare me if *I* had to face it in battle."

"Agreed," I said. "And speaking of faces—?"

"It's a duality mask," Alex explained. "My ancestors from Tlatilco—they made a lot of the figurines with two faces, or one face with two halves. Nobody's sure why. My grandfather thought they represented two spirits in a single body."

"Like my old Lenape friend Mother William!" T.J. said. "So, I guess the native cultures down in Mexico had *argr*, too!" He corrected himself quickly. "I mean trans folks, gender-fluid folks."

Argr, the Viking word for someone of shifting gender, literally meant *unmanly*, which was not an Alex-approved term.

I studied the mask. "No wonder the duality art spoke to you. Your granddad . . . he *got* who you were."

"He got it," Alex agreed, "and he honored it. When he died, my dad did his best to discredit my abuelo's ideas, destroy his art, and turn me into a good little businessperson. I wouldn't let him."

She rubbed the nape of her neck, maybe subconsciously touching the tattooed symbol of the figure-eight serpents. She had embraced shape-shifting, refusing to let Loki ruin it for her. She had done the same with pottery, even though her father had turned the family business into something she despised.

"Alex," I said, "the more I find out about you, the more I admire you."

Her expression was a mix of amusement and exasperation, like I was a cute puppy that had just peed on the carpet. "Hold the admiration until I can bring this thing to life, Smooth Talker. *That's* the real trick. In the meantime, we all need some fresh air." She threw me another wad of money. "Let's go get some dinner. You're buying."

NINETEEN

I Attend a Zombie Pep Rally

DINNER WAS fish and chips at a place called Mr. Chippy. T.J. found the name hilarious. While we ate, he kept saying "MR. CHIPPY!" in a loud, bubbly voice, which did not amuse the guy at the register.

Afterward, we returned to the pottery studio to lay low for the night. T.J. suggested going back to the ship to be with the rest of the crew, but Alex insisted she needed to keep an eye on her ceramic warrior.

She texted Sam an update.

Sam's response: *NP. OK here. Fighting water horses.*

Fighting water horses was written in emojis: fist, wave, horse. I guessed Sam had fought so many of them today she'd decided to make a text shortcut.

"You got her international coverage, too," I noted.

"Well, yeah," Alex said. "Gotta keep in touch with my sister."

I wanted to ask why she hadn't done the same for me. Then I remembered I didn't have a phone. Most einherjar didn't bother with them. For one thing, getting a number and paying the bill is hard when you're officially dead. Also, no data plan covers the rest of the Nine Worlds. And the reception in Valhalla is horrible. I blame the roof of golden shields. Despite all that, Alex insisted on keeping a phone. How she managed,

I didn't know. Maybe Samirah had registered her in some kind of *friends & family & also dead family* program.

As soon as we reached the studio, Alex checked on her ceramic project. I wasn't sure whether to be relieved or disappointed that it hadn't assembled itself and come to life yet.

"I'll check it again in a few hours," she said. "Gonna . . ."

She staggered to the only comfy chair in the room—the proprietor's clay-spattered Barcalounger—then passed out and began to snore. Yikes, she could *snore*. T.J. and I decided to bunk in the storage room, where we'd be better insulated from Alex's impression of a dying lawn mower.

We made some impromptu mattresses out of canvas tarps.

T.J. cleaned his rifle and sharpened his bayonet—a nighttime ritual for him.

I lay down and watched the rain patter against the skylights. The glass leaked, dripping on the metal shelves and filling the room with the smell of damp rust, but I didn't mind. I was grateful for the steady drumming.

"So, what happens tomorrow?" I asked T.J. "I mean exactly?"

T.J. laughed. "Exactly? I fight a twenty-foot-tall giant until one of us dies or can't fight anymore. Meanwhile, the giant's clay warrior fights Alex's clay warrior until one of them is rubble. Alex, I dunno, cheers on her creation, I guess. You heal me if you can."

"That's allowed?"

T.J. shrugged. "Far as I know, anything's allowed for you and Alex as long as you don't actually fight."

"Doesn't it bother you that your opponent is fifteen feet taller than you?"

T.J. straightened his back. "Do you think I look that short? I'm almost six feet!"

"How can you be so calm?"

He inspected the edge of his bayonet, holding it up to his face so it seemed to cut him in half like a duality mask. "I've already beat the odds so many times, Magnus. On James Island, South Carolina? I was standing right next to a friend of mine, Joe Wilson, when a Reb sniper—" He made a finger gun and pulled the trigger. "Could have been me. Could have been any of us. I hit the dirt, rolled over and stared up at the sky, and this sense of calm washed over me. I wasn't afraid anymore."

"Yeah, that's called shock."

He shook his head. "Nah, I saw *Valkyries*, Magnus—ladies on horses, swirling in the skies above our regiment. I finally believed what my ma had always told me about my dad being Tyr. Those crazy stories about Norse gods in Boston. Right then I decided . . . okay. What happens happens. If my dad is the god of bravery, I'd better make him proud."

I wasn't sure that would've been my reaction. I was glad I had a father who was proud of me for healing people, enjoying the outdoors, and tolerating his talking sword.

"You've met your dad?" I asked. "He gave you that bayonet, right?"

T.J. folded the blade in its chamois cloth like he was tucking it into bed. "The bayonet was waiting for me when I checked into Valhalla. I never met Tyr face-to-face." T.J. shrugged. "Still, every time I accept a challenge, I feel closer to him. The more dangerous, the better."

"You must feel *super* close to him right now," I guessed.

T.J. grinned. "Yep. Good times."

I wondered how a god could go a hundred and fifty years without acknowledging a son as brave as T.J., but my friend wasn't alone. I knew a lot of einherjar who had never met their parents. Face time with the kids wasn't a priority for Norse deities—maybe because they had hundreds or thousands of children. Or maybe because the gods were jerks.

T.J. lay back on his tarp mattress. "Now I just gotta figure out how to kill that giant. I'm worried a direct frontal charge might not work."

For a Civil War soldier, this was creative thinking.

"So what's your plan?" I asked.

"No idea!" He tipped his Union cap over his eyes. "Maybe something will come to me in my dreams. 'Night, Magnus."

He began to snore almost as loudly as Alex.

I couldn't win.

I lay awake, wondering how Sam, Halfborn, and Mallory were doing on board the ship. I wondered why Blitzen and Hearthstone weren't back yet, and why it would take them five days just to scout the location of a whetstone. Njord had promised I'd see them again before the really dangerous stuff went down. I should've gotten him to swear an oath on his immaculately groomed feet.

Mainly though, I worried about my own impending duel with Loki: a contest of insults with the most eloquent Norse deity. What had I been thinking? No matter how magical Kvasir's Mead was, how could it possibly help me beat Loki at his own game?

No pressure, of course. If I lost I'd just be reduced to a shadow of myself and imprisoned in Helheim while all my friends died and Ragnarok destroyed the Nine Worlds. Maybe

I could buy a book of Viking insults at the Viking Centre gift shop.

T.J. snored on. I admired his courage and positivity. I wondered if I'd have a tenth of his presence of mind when I had to face Loki.

My conscience answered *NO!* then broke down in hysterical sobbing.

Thanks to the rain, I finally managed to sleep, but my dreams were not relaxing, nor were they reassuring.

I found myself back on *Naglfar*, the Ship of the Dead. Masses of draugr swarmed the deck, rags and mildewed armor hanging from their bodies, their spears and swords corroded like burnt matchsticks. The warriors' spirits fluttered inside their rib cages like blue flames clinging to the last remnants of kindling.

Thousands upon thousands shambled toward the foredeck, where hand-painted banners hung along the rails and waved from the yardarms in the frigid wind: MAKE SOME NOISE!, GO, DRAUGR, GO!, RAGNAROK AND ROLL!, and other slogans so terrible they could only have been written by the dishonored dead.

I did not see Loki. But standing at the helm, on a dais cobbled together from dead men's nails, was a giant so old I almost thought he might be one of the undead. I'd never seen him before, but I'd heard stories about him: Hrym, the captain of the ship. His very name meant *decrepit*. His bare arms were painfully emaciated. Wisps of white hair clung to his leathery head like icicles, making me think of pictures I'd seen of prehistoric men found in melting glaciers. Moldy white furs covered his wasted frame.

His pale blue eyes, though, were very much alive. He couldn't have been as frail as he looked. In one hand, he brandished a battle-ax bigger than I was. In the other hand was a shield made from the sternum of some huge animal, the space between the ribs fitted with sheets of studded iron.

"Soldiers of Helheim!" the giant bellowed. "Behold!"

He gestured across the gray water. At the other end of the bay, the glacial cliffs crumbled more rapidly, ice cracking and sloughing into the sea with a sound like distant artillery.

"The way will soon be clear!" the giant shouted. "Then we sail to battle! Death to the gods!"

The cry went up all around me—hollow, hateful voices of the long dead taking up the chant.

Mercifully, my dream shifted. I stood in a recently plowed wheat field on a warm sunny day. In the distance, wildflowers blanketed rolling hills. Beyond that, milk-white waterfalls tumbled down the sides of picturesque mountains.

Some part of my brain thought: *At last, a pleasant dream! I'm in a commercial for organic whole wheat bread!*

Then an old man in blue robes hobbled toward me. His clothes were tattered and mud-stained from long travel. His wide-brimmed hat shaded his face, though I could make out his graying beard and secretive smile.

When he reached me, he looked up, revealing one eye that gleamed with malicious humor. The other eye socket was dark and empty.

"I am Bolverk," he said, though of course I knew it was Odin. Aside from his less-than-creative disguise, once you've heard Odin give a keynote address on best berserker practices, you never forget his voice. "I'm here to make you the deal of a lifetime."

From beneath his cloak, he produced an object the size of

a cheese round, covered in cloth. I was afraid it might be one of Odin's inspirational CD collections. Then he unwrapped it, revealing a circular whetstone of gray quartz. It reminded me of the bashing end of Hrungnir's maul, only smaller and less maul-worthy.

Odin/Bolverk offered it to me. "Will you pay the price?"

Suddenly Odin was gone. Before me loomed a face so large I couldn't take it all in: glowing green eyes with vertical slits for pupils, leathery nostrils dripping with mucus. The stench of acid and rotten meat burned my lungs. The creature's maw opened to reveal rows of jagged triangular teeth ready to shred me—and I sat bolt upright, screaming in my bed of tarps.

Above me, dim gray light filtered through the skylights. The rain had stopped. T.J. sat across from me, munching a bagel, a strange pair of glasses on his face. Each lens had a clear center, bordered by a ring of amber glass, making T.J. look like he'd acquired a second set of irises.

"Finally up!" he noted. "Bad dreams, huh?"

My whole body felt jittery, like coins rattling inside a change-separator machine.

"Wh-what's going on?" I asked. "What's with the glasses?"

Alex Fierro appeared in the doorway. "A scream that high could only be Magnus. Ah, good. You're awake." She tossed me a brown paper bag that smelled of garlic. "Come on. Time's wasting."

She led us to the main room, where her ceramic duality dude still lay in pieces. She circled the table, checking her work and nodding with satisfaction, though I couldn't see that anything had changed. "Okay! Yep. We're good."

I opened the paper bag and frowned. "You left me a garlic bagel?"

"Last awake, last choice," Alex said.

"My breath is going to be terrible."

"*More* terrible," Alex corrected. "Well, that's fine. *I'm* not kissing you. Are *you* kissing him, T.J.?"

"Wasn't planning on it." T.J. popped the last of his bagel in his mouth and grinned.

"I—I didn't say anything about—" I stammered. "I didn't mean . . ." My face felt like it was crawling with fire ants. "Whatever. T.J., why are you wearing those glasses, anyway?"

I'm good at subtly changing the conversation like that when I'm embarrassed. It's a gift.

T.J. wiggled his new specs. "You helped jog my memory, Magnus, talking about that sniper last night! Then I dreamed about Hrungnir and those weird amber eyes of his, and I saw myself laughing and shooting him dead. Then, when I woke up, I remembered I had these in my haversack. Completely forgot about them!"

It sounded like T.J. had way better dreams than I did, which was no surprise.

"They're sniper glasses," he explained. "They're what we used before scopes were invented. I bought this pair in Valhalla, oh, a hundred years ago, I guess, so I'm pretty sure they're magic. Can't wait to try them out!"

I doubted Hrungnir was going to stand still while T.J. sniped at him from a safe distance. I also doubted any of us would be doing much laughing today. But I didn't want to spoil T.J.'s pre-combat buzz.

I turned to the ceramic warrior. "So, what's going on with Pottery Barn guy? Why is he still in pieces?"

Alex beamed. "Pottery Barn? Good name! But let's not assume Pottery Barn's gender."

"Uh. Okay."

"Wish me luck." She took a deep breath, then traced her fingers across the ceramic warrior's two faces.

The ceramic pieces clattered and flew together as if they'd been magnetized. Pottery Barn sat up and focused on Alex. The faces were still hardened clay, but the frozen twin sneers suddenly seemed angrier, hungrier. The right side's eye sockets glowed with golden light.

"Yes!" Alex exhaled with relief. "Okay. Pottery Barn is non-binary, as I suspected. Preferred pronouns are *they* and *them*. And they are ready to fight."

Pottery Barn jumped off the table. Their limbs grinded and scraped like stones against cement. They stood about eight feet tall, which was plenty scary to me, but I wondered if they stood a chance against whatever clay warrior Hrungnir had created.

Pottery Barn must have sensed my doubt. They turned their faces toward me and raised their right fist—a heavy clay vase glazed bloodred.

"Stop!" Alex ordered. "He's not the enemy!"

Pottery Barn turned to Alex as if asking *You sure about that?*

"Maybe they don't like garlic," Alex speculated. "Magnus, finish that bagel quickly and let's get on the road. We can't keep our enemies waiting!"

TWENTY

Tveirvigi = Worst Vigi

AS WE WALKED through the early-morning streets of York, I ate my garlic bagel and told my friends about my dreams. Our new buddy Pottery Barn clanked along beside us, drawing disapproving looks from the sleepy locals, like *Bah, tourists.*

At least my story kept T.J.'s attention, so he didn't pester too many Yorkshire folk with thank-yous and handshakes.

"Hmm," he said. "I wish I knew why we needed the whetstone. I think maybe Odin discussed the Bolverk incident in one of his books—*The Aesir Path to Winning?* Or was it *The Art of the Steal?* I can't remember the details. A big beast with green eyes, you say?"

"And lots of teeth." I tried to shake off the memory. "Maybe Odin killed the beast to get the stone? Or maybe he hit the beast in the face *with* the stone, and that's how he got the mead?"

T.J. frowned. He'd propped his new glasses on the rim of his cap. "Neither sounds right. I don't remember any monster. I'm pretty sure Odin stole the mead from giants."

I recalled my earlier dream of about Fjalar and Gjalar's chain-saw massacre. "But didn't dwarves kill Kvasir? How did giants get the mead?"

T.J. shrugged. "All the old stories are basically about one

group murdering another group to steal their stuff. That's probably how."

This made me proud to be a Viking. "Okay, but we don't have much time to figure it out. Those glaciers I saw are melting fast. Midsummer is in, like, twelve days now, but I think Loki's ship will be able to sail *long* before that."

"Guys," Alex said. "How about this? First, we beat the giant, *then* we talk about our next impossible task?"

That sounded sensible, though I suspected Alex just wanted me to shut up so I wouldn't breathe more garlic in her direction.

"Anyone know where we're going?" I asked. "What's a Konungsgurtha?"

"It means *king's court*," T.J. said.

"Was that in your travel book?"

"No." T.J. laughed. "Old Norse 101. Didn't you take that class yet?"

"I had a scheduling conflict," I muttered.

"Well, this is England. There's got to be a king with a court around here somewhere."

Alex stopped at the next crossroads. She pointed to one of the signs. "What about King's Square? Will that do?"

Pottery Barn seemed to think so. They turned their double faces in that direction and strode off. We followed, since it would've been irresponsible to let an eight-foot-tall pile of ceramics walk through town unaccompanied.

We found the place. Hooray.

King's Square wasn't a square, and it wasn't very kingly. The streets made a Y around a triangular park paved in gray slate, with some scrubby trees and a couple of park benches.

The surrounding buildings were dark, the storefronts shuttered. The only soul in sight was the giant Hrungnir, his boots planted on either side of a pharmacy named, appropriately enough, Boots. The giant was dressed in his same quilted armor, his shaggy limestone beard freshly avalanched, his amber eyes bright with that can't-wait-to-kill-you gleam. His maul stood upright beside him like the world's largest Festivus pole.

When Hrungnir saw us, his mouth split in a grin that would've made masons' and bricklayers' hearts flutter. "Well, well, you showed up! I was beginning to think you'd run away." He knit his gravelly eyebrows. "Most people run away. It's very annoying."

"Can't imagine why," I said.

"Mmm." Hrungnir nodded at Pottery Barn. "That's your ceramic second, eh? Doesn't look like much."

"You just wait," Alex promised.

"I look forward to it!" the giant boomed. "I love killing people here. You know, long ago"—he gestured toward a nearby pub—"the Norse king of Jorvik's court stood right there. And where you are standing, the Christians had a church. See? You're walking on somebody's grave."

Sure enough, the slab of slate under my feet was etched with a name and dates too faded to read. The whole square was paved with tombstones, maybe from the floor of the old church. The idea of walking over so many dead people made me queasy, even though I was technically a dead person myself.

The giant chuckled. "Seems fitting, doesn't it? Already so many dead humans here, what's a few more?" He faced T.J. "Are you ready?"

"Born ready," T.J. said. "Died ready. Resurrected ready. But I'm giving you one last chance, Hrungnir. It's not too late to opt for bingo."

"Ha! No, little einherji! I worked all night on my fighting partner. I don't intend to waste him on bingo. Mokkerkalfe, get over here!"

The ground shook with a squishy *THUMP, THUMP*. From around the corner appeared a man of clay. He was nine feet tall, crudely shaped, still glistening wet. He looked like something *I* might make in Pottery 101—an ugly, lumpy creature with arms too thin and legs too thick, his head no more than a blob with two eyeholes and a frowny face carved into it.

Next to me, Pottery Barn started to clatter, and I didn't think it was from excitement.

"Bigger doesn't mean stronger," I told them under my breath.

Pottery Barn turned their faces toward me. Of course, their expressions didn't change, but I sensed that both mouths were telling me the same thing: *Shut up, Magnus.*

Alex crossed her arms. She'd tied her yellow raincoat around her waist, revealing the plaid pink-and-green sweater-vest I thought of as her combat uniform. "You do sloppy work, Hrungnir. You call that a clay man? And what kind of name is Mokkerkalfe?"

The giant raised his eyebrows. "We'll see whose work is sloppy when the fighting begins. Mokkerkalfe means *Mist Calf*! A poetic, honorable name for a warrior!"

"Uh-huh," Alex said. "Well, this is Pottery Barn."

Hrungnir scratched his beard. "I must admit, that is also a poetic name for a warrior. But can it fight?"

"*They* can fight just fine," Alex promised. "And they'll take down that slag heap of yours, no problem."

Pottery Barn looked at their creator like *I will?*

"Enough talk!" Hrungnir hefted his maul and scowled at T.J. "Shall we begin, little man?"

Thomas Jefferson Jr. put on his amber-rimmed glasses. He unslung his rifle and pulled a small cylindrical paper packet—a gunpowder cartridge—from his kit.

"This rifle has a poetic name, too," he said. "It's a Springfield 1861. Made in Massachusetts, just like me." He tore open the cartridge with his teeth, then poured the contents into the rifle's muzzle. He pulled the ramrod and jammed down the powder and ball. "I used to be able to shoot three rounds a minute with this beauty, but I've been practicing for several hundred years. Let's see if I can do five rounds a minute today."

He fished out a little metal cap from his side pouch and set it under the hammer. I'd seen him do all this before, but the way he could load, talk, and walk at the same time was as magical as Alex's skill at the pottery wheel. For me, it would've been like trying to tie my shoes and whistle "The Star-Spangled Banner" while jogging.

"Very well!" yelled Hrungnir. "LET THE TVEIRVIGI BEGIN!"

My first task was my favorite one—getting out of the way.

I scrambled right as the giant's mallet slammed into a tree, smashing it to kindling. With a dry *CRACK*, T.J.'s rifle discharged. The giant roared in pain. He staggered backward, smoke streaming from his left eye, which was now black instead of amber.

"That was rude!" Hrungnir raised his mallet again, but T.J. circled to his blind side, calmly reloading. His second shot sparked off the giant's nose.

Meanwhile, Mokkerkalfe lumbered forward, swinging his tiny arms, but Pottery Barn was quicker. (I wanted to credit the great work I'd done on their coil joints.) P.B. ducked to one side and came up behind Mokkerkalfe, slamming both vase-fists into his back.

Unfortunately, their fists sank into Mokkerkalfe's soft gooey flesh. As Mokkerkalfe turned, trying to face his opponent, P.B. got yanked off their feet and dragged around like a ceramic tail.

"Let go!" Alex yelled. "Pottery Barn! Oh, *meinfretr.*"

She loosened her garrote, though how she could help without actually fighting, I wasn't sure.

CRACK! T.J.'s musket ball ricocheted off the giant's neck, shattering a second-story window. I was amazed the locals hadn't already come out to investigate the commotion. Maybe there was a strong glamour at work. Or maybe the good people of York were used to early-morning Viking/giant smack-downs.

T.J. reloaded as the giant pressed him back.

"Stand still, little mortal!" roared Hrungnir. "I want to smash you!"

King's Square was close quarters for a jotun. T.J. tried to stay on Hrungnir's blind side, but the giant only needed one well-timed step or one lucky swipe to flatten T.J. into an infantry pancake.

Hrungnir swung his maul again. T.J. leaped aside just in time as the maul splintered a dozen tombstones, leaving a ten-feet-deep hole in the courtyard.

Meanwhile, Alex lashed out with her wire. She lassoed Pottery Barn's legs and yanked them free. Unfortunately, she put a little too much muscle into it just as Mokkerkalfe swung in the same direction. With the excessive momentum, Pottery Barn went flying across the square and smashed through the window of a store offering payday loans.

Mokkerkalfe turned toward Alex. The clay man made a wet gurgling sound in his chest, like the growl of a carnivorous toad.

"Whoa there, boy," Alex said. "I wasn't actually fighting. I'm not your—"

GURGLE! Mokkerkalfe launched himself like a wrestler, more quickly than I would've thought possible, and Alex disappeared under three hundred pounds of wet clay.

"NO!" I screamed.

Before I could move or even process how to help Alex, T.J. screamed at the other end of the courtyard.

"HA!" Hrungnir raised his fist. Wrapped in his fingers, struggling helplessly, was Thomas Jefferson Jr.

"One squeeze," the giant boasted, "and this contest is over!"

I stood paralyzed. I wanted to break into two parts, to become a duality like our ceramic warrior. But even if I could, I didn't see how I could help either of my friends.

Then the giant tightened his fist, and T.J. howled in agony.

TWENTY-ONE

Fun with Open-Heart Surgery

POTTERY BARN saved the day.

(And, no. That's not a line I ever thought I would use.)

Our ceramic friend exploded from a third-story window above the payday loan office. They hurled themselves onto Hrungnir's face, clamping their legs around the giant's upper lip and whaling his nose with both their vase-fists.

"PFBAH! GET OFF!" Hrungnir staggered, releasing T.J., who landed in an unmoving heap.

Meanwhile, Mokkerkalfe struggled to get up, which must have been difficult with Alex Fierro imprinted on his chest. From beneath his weight, Alex groaned. Relief washed over me. At least she was alive and might stay that way for a few more seconds. Triage decision: I ran toward T.J., whose condition I wasn't so optimistic about.

I knelt at his side, put my hand against his chest. I almost snatched my hand away again because the damage I sensed was so bad. A trickle of red etched the corner of his mouth like he'd been drinking Tizer—but I knew it wasn't Tizer.

"Hang on, buddy," I muttered. "I got you."

I glanced over at Hrungnir, who was still stumbling around trying to grab Pottery Barn off his face. So far so good. At the other side of the square, Mokkerkalfe had peeled himself away from Alex and now stood over her, gurgling angrily and pounding his blobby fists together. Not so good.

I yanked the runestone from my neck chain and summoned Sumarbrander.

"Jack!" I yelled.

"What?" he yelled back.

"Defend Alex!"

"What?"

"But do it without actually fighting!"

"What?"

"Just keep that clay giant off her!"

"What?"

"Distract him. GO!"

I was glad he didn't say *what* again, or I would've worried that my sword was going deaf.

Jack flew over to Mokkerkalfe, positioning himself between the clay man and Alex. "Hey, buddy!" Jack's runes pulsed up and down his blade like equalizer lights. "You want to hear a story? A song? Wanna dance?"

While Mokkerkalfe struggled to comprehend the strange hallucination he was having, I returned my attention to T.J.

I put both hands against his sternum and summoned the power of Frey.

Sunlight spread across the blue wool fibers of his jacket. Warmth sank into his chest, knitting his broken ribs, mending his punctured lungs, un-flattening several internal organs that did not function well when they were flattened.

As my healing power flowed into Thomas Jefferson Jr., his memories backwashed into my mind. I saw his mother in a faded gingham dress, her hair prematurely gray, her face stretched thin from years of hard work and worry. She knelt in front of ten-year-old T.J., her hands tightly clasping his shoulders as if she were afraid he might blow away in a storm.

"Don't you *ever* point that at a white man," she scolded.

"Ma, it's just a stick," T.J. said. "I'm playing."

"You don't *get* to play," she snapped. "You play-shoot at a white man with a stick, he's going to real-shoot you back with a gun. I'm not losing another child, Thomas. You hear me?"

She shook him, trying to rattle the message into him.

A different image: T.J. as a teenager, reading a flyer posted on a brick wall by the wharf:

TO COLORED MEN!

FREEDOM! PROTECTION, PAY, AND A CALL TO MILITARY SERVICE!

I could sense T.J.'s pulse racing. He had never been so excited. His hands itched to hold a rifle. He felt a calling—an undeniable impulse, like all those times he'd been challenged to fistfights in the alley behind his ma's tavern. This was a personal challenge, and he could not refuse it.

I saw him in the hold of a Union ship, the seas pitching as his comrades threw up in buckets on either side of him. A friend of his, William H. Butler, groaned in misery. "They bring our people over on slave ships. They free us. They promise to pay us to fight. Then they put us right back into the belly of a ship." But T.J. held his rifle eagerly, his heart pumping with excitement. He was proud of his uniform. Proud of those stars and stripes flapping on the mast somewhere over their heads. The Union had given him a *real* gun. They were *paying* him to shoot rebels—white men who would most definitely kill him given a chance. He grinned in the dark.

Then I saw him running across no-man's-land at the battle of Fort Wagner, gun smoke rising like volcanic gas all around him. The air was thick with sulfur and the screams of the wounded, but T.J. stayed focused on his nemesis, Jeffrey Toussaint, who had dared to call him out. T.J. leveled his bayonet and charged, exhilarated by the sudden fear in Toussaint's eyes.

Back in the present, T.J. gasped. Behind his amber-rimmed glasses, his vision cleared.

He croaked, "My left, your right."

I dove to one side. I'll admit I didn't have time to distinguish left from right. I rolled onto my back as T.J. raised his rifle and fired.

Hrungnir, now free of Pottery Barn's affections, loomed over us, his maul raised for one final strike. T.J.'s musket ball caught him in the right eye, snuffing out his sight.

"RARG!" Hrungnir dropped his weapon and sat down hard in the middle of King's Square, crushing two park benches under his ample butt. In a nearby tree, Pottery Barn hung broken and battered, their left leg dangling from a branch ten feet above their head, but when they saw Hrungnir's predicament, they grinded their head against their neck with a sound like laughter.

"Go!" T.J. snapped me out of my shock. "Help Alex!"

I scrambled to my feet and ran.

Jack was still trying to entertain Mokkerkalfe, but his song-and-dance routine was wearing thin. (That happens quickly with Jack.) Mokkerkalfe tried to swat him aside. The blade got stuck on the back of the clay man's sticky hand.

"Yuck!" Jack complained. "Let me go!"

Jack was a little obsessive about cleanliness. After lying at the bottom of the Charles River for a thousand years, he wasn't a fan of mud.

As Mokkerkalfe stomped around, trying to dislodge the talking sword from his hand, I ran to Alex's side. She was spread-eagled, shellacked in clay from head to foot, groaning and twitching her fingers.

I knew Alex didn't like my healing powers. She hated the idea of me peeking into her emotions and memories, which just happened automatically as part of the process. But I decided her survival outweighed her right to privacy.

I clamped my hand on her shoulder. Golden light seeped through my fingers. Warmth poured into Alex's body, working its way from her shoulder into her core.

I steeled myself for more painful images. I was ready to face her awful father again, or see how badly Alex had been bullied at school, or how she'd been beaten up in the homeless shelters.

Instead, a single clear memory hit me: nothing special, just breakfast at Café 19 in Valhalla, a quick snapshot of me, stupid Magnus Chase, the way Alex saw me. I was sitting across the table from her, grinning at something she'd just said. A little glob of bread was stuck between my front teeth. My hair was messy. I looked relaxed and happy and utterly dorky. I held Alex's gaze for a second too long and things got awkward. I blushed and looked away.

That was her entire memory.

I recalled that morning. I remembered thinking at the time: *Well, I've made a complete idiot of myself, as usual.* But it had hardly been an earthshaking event.

So why was it at the top of Alex's memories? And why did

I feel such a rush of satisfaction seeing my dorky self from Alex's perspective?

Alex opened her eyes abruptly. She swatted my hand off her shoulder. "Stop that."

"Sorry, I—"

"My right, your left!"

I dove one way. Alex rolled the other. Mokkerkalfe's fist, now free of Jack's blade, slammed into the slate pavement between us. I caught a glimpse of Jack, leaning in the doorway of the Boots pharmacy, covered with mud and groaning like a dying soldier, "He got me! He got me!"

The clay man rose, ready to kill us. Jack would be no help. Alex and I were not up to this fight. Then a pile of pottery hurtled out of nowhere and landed on Mokkerkalfe's back. Somehow, Pottery Barn had extricated themselves from the tree. Despite their missing left leg, despite their right vase hand being cracked to shards, Pottery Barn went into ceramic-berserker overdrive. They ripped into Mokkerkalfe's back, gouging out chunks of wet clay as if excavating a collapsed well.

Mokkerkalfe stumbled. He tried to grab Pottery Barn, but his arms were too short. Then, with a sucking *POP*, Pottery Barn pulled something from Mokkerkalfe's chest cavity and both warriors collapsed.

Mokkerkalfe steamed and began to melt. Pottery Barn rolled off their enemy's carcass, their double faces turning toward Alex. Weakly, they lifted the thing they were holding. When I realized what it was, my garlic-bagel breakfast threatened to come back up again.

Pottery Barn was offering Alex the heart of their enemy— an actual heart muscle, much too big for a human. Maybe it had belonged to a horse or a cow? I decided I'd rather remain ignorant.

Alex knelt by Pottery Barn's side. She placed her hand across the warrior's double foreheads. "You did well," she said, her voice quavering. "My Tlatilcan ancestors would be proud of you. My grandfather would be proud. Most of all, *I'm* proud."

The gold light flickered in the skull face's eye sockets, then went out. Pottery Barn's arms collapsed. Their pieces lost magical cohesion and fell apart.

Alex allowed herself the space of three heartbeats to grieve. I could count them, because that gross muscle between Pottery Barn's hands was still beating. Then she rose, clenched her fists, and turned toward Hrungnir.

The giant was not doing so well. He lay curled on his side, blind and gurgling in pain. T.J. walked around him, using his bone-steel bayonet to cut the giant's sinews. Hrungnir's Achilles tendons were already severed, making his legs useless. T.J. worked with cold, vicious efficiency to give the jotun's arms the same treatment.

"Tyr's tush," Alex swore, the anger draining from her face. "Remind me never to duel Jefferson."

We walked over to join him.

T.J. pressed the tip of his bayonet against the giant's chest. "We won, Hrungnir. Give us the location of Kvasir's Mead and I don't have to kill you."

Hrungnir cackled weakly. His teeth were spattered with gray liquid, like the buckets of slip back at the pottery studio.

"Oh, but you *do* have to kill me, little einherji," he croaked. "It's part of the duel! Better than leaving me here hobbled and in agony!"

"I could heal you," I offered.

Hrungnir curled his lip. "How typical of a weak, pathetic Frey-son. I welcome death! I will re-form from the icy abyss of Ginnungagap! And on the day of Ragnarok, I will find you on the field of Vigridr and crack your skull between my teeth!"

"Okay, then," T.J. said. "Death it is! But first, the location of Kvasir's Mead."

"Heh." Hrungnir gurgled more gray slip. "Very well. It won't matter. You'll never get past the guards. Go to Fläm, in the old Norse land you call Norway. Take the train. You'll see what you're after quick enough."

"Fläm?" I got a mental image of a tasty caramel dessert. Then I remembered that was *flan*.

"That's right," Hrungnir said. "Now kill me, son of Tyr! Go on. Right in the heart, unless you are as weak-willed as your friend!"

Alex started to say, "T.J. . . ."

"Wait," I muttered.

Something was wrong. Hrungnir's tone was too mocking, too eager. But I was slow to compute the problem. Before I could suggest we should kill the giant some other way, T.J. accepted Hrungnir's final challenge.

He jabbed his bayonet into the giant's chest. The point hit something inside with a hard *clink!*

"Ahh." Hrungnir's death gasp sounded almost smug.

"Hey, guys?" Jack's weak voice called from over at the pharmacy. "Don't pierce his heart, okay? Stone giants' hearts explode."

Alex's eyes widened. "Hit the deck!"

KA-BLAM!

Shards of Hrungnir sprayed the square, breaking windows, destroying signs, and peppering brick walls.

My ears rang. The air smelled of flint sparks. Where the giant Hrungnir had lain, nothing remained but a smoking line of gravel.

I seemed unhurt. Alex looked okay. But T.J. knelt, groaning, with his hand cupped over his bleeding forehead.

"Let me see!" I rushed to his side, but the damage wasn't as bad as I'd feared. A piece of shrapnel had embedded itself above his right eye—a triangular gray splinter like a flint exclamation point.

"Get it out!" he yelled.

I tried, but as soon as I pulled, T.J. howled in pain. I frowned. That made no medical sense. The shard couldn't be that deep. There wasn't even that much blood.

"Guys?" Alex said. "We have visitors."

The locals were finally starting to come outside to check on the commotion, probably because Hrungnir's exploding heart had shattered every window on the block.

"Can you walk?" I asked T.J.

"Yeah. Yeah, I think so."

"Then let's get you back to the ship. We'll heal you there."

I helped him to his feet, then went to retrieve Jack, who was still moaning about being covered in mud. I put him back into runestone form, which did not help my level of exhaustion. Alex knelt next to the remnants of Pottery Barn. She picked up their detached head, cradling it like an abandoned infant.

Then the three of us staggered back through York to find the *Big Banana*. I just hoped the water horses hadn't sunk it along with our friends.

TWENTY-TWO

I Have Bad News and— No, Actually I Just Have Bad News

THE SHIP was still intact. Halfborn, Mallory, and Samirah looked like they'd paid a heavy price to keep it that way.

Halfborn's left arm was in a sling. Mallory's wild red hair had been shorn off at chin-level. Sam stood at the rail dripping wet, wringing out her magic hijab.

"Water horses?" I asked.

Halfborn shrugged. "Nothing we couldn't handle. Half a dozen attacks since yesterday afternoon. About what I figured."

"One pulled me into the river by my hair," Mallory complained.

Halfborn grinned. "I think I gave you a pretty good haircut, considering I only had my battle-ax to work with. Let me tell you, Magnus, with the blade so close to her neck, I was tempted—"

"Shut up, oaf," Mallory growled.

"Exactly my point," said Halfborn. "But Samirah, now— you should've seen her. *She* was impressive."

"It was nothing," Sam muttered.

Mallory snorted. "Nothing? You got dragged under the river and came up *riding* a water horse. You mastered that beast. I've never heard of anyone who could do that."

Samirah winced slightly. She gave her hijab another twist,

as if she wanted to squeeze out the last drops of the experience. "Valkyries get on well with horses. That's probably all it was."

"Hmm." Halfborn pointed at me. "What about you all? You're alive, I see."

We told him the story of our night in the pottery studio and our morning destroying King's Square.

Mallory frowned at Alex, who was still covered in clay. "That would explain Fierro's new coat of paint."

"And the rock in T.J.'s head." Halfborn leaned closer to inspect the shrapnel. T.J.'s forehead had stopped bleeding. The swelling was down. But for reasons unknown, the sliver of flint still refused to come out. Whenever I tried to pull it, T.J. yelped in pain. Fixed above his eyebrow, the little shard gave him a look of permanent surprise.

"Does it hurt?" Halfborn asked.

"Not anymore," T.J. said sheepishly. "Not unless you try to remove it."

"Hold on, then." With his good hand, Halfborn rummaged through his belt pouch. He pulled out a box of matches, fumbled one free, then struck it against T.J.'s flint. The match burst into flames immediately.

"Hey!" T.J. complained.

"You have a new superpower, my friend!" Halfborn grinned. "That could be useful!"

"Right, enough of that," Mallory said. "Glad you all survived, but did you get information from the giant?"

"Yeah," Alex said, cradling the head of Pottery Barn. "Kvasir's Mead is in Norway. Some place called Fläm."

The lit match slipped from Halfborn's fingers and landed on the deck.

T.J. stomped out the flame. "You all right, big guy? You look like you've seen a draugr."

An earthquake seemed to be happening under Halfborn's whiskers. "Jorvik was bad enough," he said. "Now Fläm? What are the odds?"

"You know the place," I guessed.

"I'm going below," he muttered.

"Want me to heal that arm first?"

He shook his head miserably, as if he was quite used to living with pain. Then he made his way down the ladder.

T.J. turned to Mallory. "What was that about?"

"Don't look at me," she snapped. "I'm not his keeper."

But there was a twinge of concern in her voice.

"Let's get under way," Samirah suggested. "I don't want to be on this river any longer than we have to."

On that, we all agreed. York was pretty. It had good fish and chips and at least one decent pottery studio, but I was ready to get out of there.

Alex and T.J. went below to change clothes and rest up from their morning of combat. That left Mallory, Sam, and me to man the ship. It took us the rest of the day to navigate our way down the River Ouse and back out to sea, but the voyage was mercifully uneventful. No water horses stampeded us. No giants challenged us to combat or bingo. The worst thing we encountered was a low bridge, forcing us to fold down the mainmast, which may or may not have collapsed on top of me.

At sunset, as we left the coast of England behind, Sam did her ritual washing. She prayed facing southwest, then sat down next to me with a satisfied sigh and unwrapped a package of dates.

She passed me one, then took a bite of hers. She closed her eyes as she chewed, her face transformed by pure bliss like the fruit was a religious experience. Which I guess it was.

"Every sunset," she said, "the taste of that date is like experiencing the joy of food for the first time. The flavor just explodes in your mouth."

I chewed my date. It was okay. It did not explode or fill me with bliss. Then again, I hadn't worked for it by fasting all day.

"Why dates?" I asked. "Why not, like, Twizzlers?"

"Just tradition." She took another bite and made a contented *mmm*. "The Prophet Muhammad always broke fast by eating a few dates."

"But you can have other stuff afterward, right?"

"Oh, yes," she said gravely. "I intend to eat *all* the food. I understand Alex brought back some cherry soda? I want to try that as well."

I shuddered. I could escape giants, countries, and even whole worlds, but it seemed I was never going to get away from Tizer. I had nightmares about all my friends grinning at me with red lips and cherry-tinted teeth.

While Sam went below to eat all the food, Mallory lounged at the rudder, keeping an eye on the horizon, though the ship seemed to know where we were going. From time to time, she touched her shoulders where her hair used to fall, then sighed unhappily.

I sympathized. Not long ago, Blitz had hacked off my hair to make magic embroidering thread for a bowling bag. I still had traumatic flashbacks.

"Sailing to Norway will take us a few days," Mallory said.

"The North Sea can get pretty rough. Unless anybody has a friendly sea god they can call on."

I focused on my date. I wasn't about to call for Njord's help again. I'd seen enough of my granddad's beautiful feet for one eternal lifetime. But I remembered what he had told me: After Jorvik, we were on our own. No divine protection. If Aegir or Ran or their daughters found us . . .

"Maybe we'll get lucky," I said weakly.

Mallory snorted. "Yep. That happens a lot. Even if we get to Fläm safely, what's this business about the mead having unbeatable guardians?"

I wished I knew. *Guardians of the Mead* sounded like another book I never wanted to read.

I recalled my dream of Odin offering me the whetstone, then his face morphing into something else: a leathery visage with green eyes and rows of teeth. I'd never faced a creature like that in real life, but the cold rage in its gaze had seemed uncomfortably, terrifyingly familiar. I thought about Hearthstone and Blitzen, and where Njord might have sent them to search for a rare stone. An idea began to coalesce, swirling into symmetry like a lump of clay on Alex's wheel, but I didn't like the shape it was taking on.

"We'll need the whetstone to defeat the guardians," I said. "I have no idea why. We just have to trust—"

Mallory laughed. "Trust? Right. I've got as much of that as I have luck."

She drew one of her knives. Casually, holding the blade by the tip, she threw the knife at my feet. It impaled the yellow planking and quivered there like a Geiger-counter needle.

"Take a look," she offered. "See why I don't trust 'secret weapons.'"

I pulled the knife from the deck. I'd never held one of Mallory's weapons before. The blade was surprisingly light—so light it might get you into trouble. If you handled it like a standard dagger, wielding it with more force than necessary, this was the kind of knife that could leap out of your hand and cut your own face off.

The blade was a long, dark isosceles triangle etched with runes and Celtic knot designs, the handle wrapped in soft worn leather.

I wasn't sure what Mallory wanted me to notice about it, so I just said the obvious, "Nice blade."

"Eh." From her belt, Mallory unsheathed its twin. "They aren't as sharp as Jack. They don't do anything magical, as far as I can tell. They were supposed to save my life, but as you can see"—she spread her arms—"I'm dead."

"So . . . you had the knives when you were alive."

"For the last five, six minutes of my life, yeah." She twirled the blade between her fingers. "First my mates . . . they goaded me into setting the bomb."

"Hold on. *You* set the—"

She cut me off with a harsh look, like *Never interrupt a lady with a knife.*

"That was Loki, egging me on," she said. "His voice among my crew—the trickster disguised as one of us. Didn't realize that at the time, of course. Then, after I did the deed, my conscience got the better of me. That's when the old hag appeared."

I waited. I'll admit I wasn't following Mallory's story very well. I knew she had died disarming a car bomb, but a car bomb she had set *herself*? Seeing her as somebody who would do that was even harder than seeing her with short hair. I had no idea who I was looking at.

She brushed away a tear as if it were an annoying insect. "The hag says, 'Oh, girl. Follow your heart.' Blah, blah. Nonsense like that. She gives me these knives. Tells me they are indestructible. Can't be dulled. Can't be broken. And she's right about that, far as I can tell. But she also says, 'You'll need them. Use them well.' And I go back to—to undo what I did. I waste time, trying to figure out how these bloody daggers are supposed to solve my problem. But they don't. And . . ." She opens her fingertips in a silent explosion.

My head buzzed. I had a lot of questions I was afraid to ask. Why had she set that bomb? Who was she trying to blow up? Was she completely insane?

She sheathed her knife, then gestured for me to throw her the other. I was afraid I might accidentally toss it overboard or kill her, but she caught it easily.

"The hag was also Loki," she said. "Had to be. Wasn't enough for him to fool me once. He had to fool me twice and get me killed."

"Why did you keep the daggers then, if they're from Loki?"

Her eyes glistened. "Because, my friend, when I see him again, I'm going to sheathe these blades right in his throat."

She put the second dagger away, and I exhaled for the first time in several minutes.

"Point is, Magnus," she said, "I wouldn't put my faith in any magic weapon, knife or otherwise, to solve all our problems—whether it's Kvasir's Mead, or this whetstone that's supposed to get us the mead. In the end, all that counts is us. Whatever Blitzen and Hearthstone are off searching for—"

As if their names were an incantation, a wave surged out of nowhere, crashing across the ship's bow. Out of the sea spray stumbled two weary figures. Our elf and dwarf had returned.

"Well, well." Mallory got to her feet, wiping away another tear. She forced some cheerfulness into her tone. "Nice of you boys to drop by."

Blitzen was covered head to toe in anti-sun protection gear. Salt water glittered on his dark trench coat and gloves. Black netting circled the rim of his pith helmet, obscuring his expression until he lifted the veil. His facial muscles twitched. He blinked repeatedly, like someone who had just walked away from a car accident.

Hearthstone sat down right where he was. He draped his hands over his knees and shook his head, *No, no, no.* Somehow, he'd lost his scarf, leaving his outfit as black as hearse upholstery.

"You're alive," I said, dizzy with relief. My stomach had been knotted up for days worrying about them. Yet now, looking at their shocked expressions, I couldn't savor having them back.

"You found what you were looking for," I guessed.

Blitzen swallowed. "I—I'm afraid so, kid. Njord was right. We're going to need your help for the hard stuff."

"Alfheim." I wanted to say it before he could, just to take the sting out of the word. I hoped I was wrong. I would have preferred a trip to the wildest corner of Jotunheim, the fires of Muspellheim, or even a public bathroom in Boston's South Station.

"Yeah," Blitzen agreed. He glanced at Mallory Keen. "Dear heart, would you let your friends know? We need to borrow Magnus. Hearthstone has to face his father one last time."

TWENTY-THREE

Follow the Smell of Dead Frogs (to the Tune of "Follow the Yellow Brick Road")

WHAT WAS it about dads?

Almost everyone I knew had a garbage father, like they were all competing for the Worst Dad of the Universe award.

I was lucky. I'd never met my dad until last winter. Even then I'd only talked to him for a few minutes. But at least Frey seemed cool. We hugged. He let me keep his talking disco sword and sent me a bright yellow boat in my time of need.

Sam had Loki, who put the *con* in *conniving*. Alex's dad was an abusive raging butt-hat with dreams of global dishware domination. And Hearthstone . . . he had it worse than any of us. Mr. Alderman had made Hearthstone's childhood a living Helheim. I never wanted to spend another night under that man's roof, and I'd only been there once. I couldn't imagine how Hearthstone would bear it.

We fell out of the golden sky, the way one does when tumbling into the airy world of the elves. We landed gently on the street in front of the Alderman mansion. As before, the wide suburban lane stretched out in either direction, hedged with stone walls and carefully tended trees, obscuring the elf millionaires' multi-acre estates from one another. The weak gravity made the ground seem squishy under my feet, as if

I could trampoline right back into the stratosphere. (I was tempted to try.)

The sunlight was as harsh as I remembered, making me grateful for the dark glasses Alex had lent me, even if they did have thick pink Buddy Holly frames. (There had been much snickering about this aboard the *Big Banana*.)

Why we had left Midgard at sunset and arrived in Alfheim during what looked like early afternoon, I wasn't sure. Maybe the elves observed Alf-light Saving Time.

Alderman's elaborate gates still gleamed with their fili-greed *A* monogram. On either side, the high walls still bristled with spikes and barbed wire to discourage riffraff. But now the security cameras were dark and motionless. The gates were laced shut with a chain and padlock. On either side of the gates, nailed to the brick columns, were matching yellow signs with glaring red letters:

PROPERTY OFF-LIMITS

BY ORDER OF ALFHEIM POLICE DEPARTMENT

TRESPASSERS WILL DIE

Not prosecuted. Not arrested or shot. That simple warning—step inside these boundaries and you'll die—was much more sinister.

My gaze wandered over the grounds, which were roughly the size of the Boston Public Garden. Since our last visit, the grass had grown high and wild in the rich Alfheim light. Spiky balls of moss festooned the trees. The pungent smell of scum from the swan lake came wafting through the gates.

The half-mile driveway was littered with white feathers,

possibly from the aforementioned swans; bones and tufts of
fur that might have once been squirrels or raccoons; and a
single black dress shoe that looked as if it had been chewed
and spit out.

At the top of the hill, the once imposing Alderman Manor
lay in ruins. The left side of the complex had collapsed in a
heap of rubble, girders, and charred beams. Kudzu vines had
completely overtaken the right side, growing so heavy that the
roof had caved in. Only two picture windows remained intact,
their glass panes smoked brown around the edges from the
fire. Glinting in the sun, they reminded me uncomfortably of
T.J.'s sniper glasses.

I turned to my friends. "Did *we* do this?"

I felt more amazement than guilt. The last time we fled
Alfheim, we'd been pursued by evil water spirits and elfish
police with guns, not to mention Hearth's maniacal father. We
may have busted a few windows in the process of escaping. I
supposed it was possible we'd caused a fire to break out, too. If
so, it couldn't have happened to a viler mansion.

But still . . . I didn't understand how the place could have
been so thoroughly destroyed, or how quickly such a suburban
paradise had turned into this creepy wilderness.

"We only started it." Blitzen's face was again covered by
netting, making it impossible to read his expression. "This
destruction is the ring's fault."

In the harsh warm light, it shouldn't have been possible to
get a chill. Nevertheless, ice trickled down my back. On our
last visit, Hearth and I had stolen a hoard of gold from a slimy
old dwarf, Andvari, including the little dude's cursed ring.

He'd tried to warn us that the ring would only bring misery, but had we listened? Nooooo. At the time, we'd been more focused on stuff like, oh, saving Blitzen's life. The only thing that could do that was the Skofnung Stone in Mr. Alderman's possession. His price for it? A gazillion dollars in gold, because evil fathers don't take American Express.

Long story short: Alderman took the cursed ring. He put it on and turned even crazier and eviler, which I hadn't thought possible.

Personally, I liked my cursed rings to at least do something cool, like turn you invisible and let you see the Eye of Sauron. Andvari's ring had no upside. It brought out the worst in you—greed, hate, jealousy. According to Hearth, it would eventually change you into a bona fide monster so your outside could be as repulsive as your inside.

If the ring was still working its magic on Mr. Alderman, and if it had overtaken him as quickly as the wilderness had overtaken his estate . . . Yeah, that wasn't good.

I turned to Hearth. "Is your dad . . . is he still *in* there?"

Hearthstone's expression was grim and stoic, like a man who had finally accepted a terminal diagnosis. *Nearby,* he signed. *But not himself.*

"You don't mean . . ."

I stared at the chewed-up shoe in the drive. I wondered what had happened to its owner. I remembered my dream of large green eyes and rows of teeth. No, that couldn't be what Hearth meant. No cursed ring could work so fast, could it?

"You—you scouted around inside?" I asked.

"Afraid so." Blitz signed as he talked, since Hearth could

not see his lips moving. "Alderman's whole collection of rare stones and artifacts—gone. Along with all the gold. So, if the whetstone we're looking for was somewhere in that house—"

It has been moved, Hearthstone signed. *Part of his hoard.*

The sign Hearth used for *hoard* was a grasping fist in front of his chin, like he was clutching something valuable: *Treasure. Mine. Don't touch, or you'll die.*

I swallowed a mouthful of sand. "And . . . did you find this hoard?" I knew my friends were brave, but the idea of them poking around inside the walls of that estate terrified me. Definitely it hadn't been good for the local squirrel population.

"We think we found his lair," Blitz said.

"Oh, good." My voice sounded higher and softer than usual. "Alderman has a lair now. And, uh, did you see him?"

Hearthstone shook his head. *Only smelled him.*

"Okay," I said. "That's not creepy."

"You'll see," Blitz said. "It's easiest just to show you."

That was one offer I definitely wanted to refuse, but there was no way I would let Hearth and Blitz go through those gates again without me.

"W-why haven't the local elves done something about the estate?" I asked. "Last time we were here, they wouldn't even tolerate us loitering. Haven't the neighbors complained?"

I waved at the ruins. An eyesore like this, especially if it killed swans, rodents, and the occasional door-to-door sales elf, had to be against the rules of the neighborhood association.

"We talked to the authorities," Blitz said. "Half the time we've been gone, we've been dealing with elfish bureaucracy." He shuddered in his heavy coat. "Would it surprise you that the police didn't want to listen to us? We can't prove Alderman is dead or missing. Hearthstone doesn't have any legal rights to the land. As for clearing the property, the best the police would do is put up those stupid warning signs. They aren't going to risk their necks, no matter how much the neighbors complain. Elves pretend to be sophisticated, but they're as superstitious as they are arrogant. Not all elves, of course. Sorry, Hearth."

Hearthstone shrugged. *Can't blame the police,* he signed. *Would you go in there if you didn't have to?*

He had a point. Just the thought of traipsing through the property, unable to see whatever lurked in the tall grass, made jumping beans hop around in my stomach. The Alfheim police were great at bullying transients out of the neighborhood. Facing an actual threat in the ruins of a madman's mansion . . . maybe not so much.

Blitzen sighed. "Well, no sense waiting. Let's go find dear old Dad."

I would have preferred another dinner with Aegir's murderous daughters, or a battle to the death with a pile of pottery. Heck, I would have even shared guava juice with a pack of wolves on Uncle Randolph's roof deck.

We climbed the gates and picked our way through the tall grass. Mosquitoes and gnats swarmed our faces. The sunlight made my skin prickle and my pores pop with sweat. I decided Alfheim was a pretty world as long as it was manicured and trimmed and kept up by the servants. Allowed to go wild, it went wild in a *big* way. I wondered if elves were similar. Calm,

delicate, and formal on the outside, but if they let loose . . .
I really did *not* want to meet the new-and-unimproved Mr.
Alderman.

We skirted the ruins of the house, which was fine by me.
I remembered too well the blue fur rug in Hearthstone's old
room, which we'd been forced to cover with gold to pay the
wergild for his brother's death. I remembered the menu board
of infractions on Hearthstone's wall, keeping tally of his never-
ending debt to his dad. I didn't want to get near that place
again, even if it was in ruins.

As we picked our way through the backyard, something
crunched under my foot. I looked down. My shoe had gone
straight through the rib cage of a small deer skeleton.

"Ugh," I said.

Hearthstone frowned at the desiccated remains. Nothing
but a few strips of meat and fur clung to the bones.

Eaten, he signed, putting his closed fingertips under his
mouth. The sign was very similar to *hoard/treasure.* Sometimes
sign language was a little too accurate for my liking.

With a silent apology to the poor deer, I freed my foot. I
couldn't tell what might have devoured the animal, but I hoped
the prey hadn't suffered much. I was surprised wildlife that
large was even allowed to exist in the tonier neighborhoods of
Alfheim. I wondered if the cops harassed the deer for loitering, maybe cuffing their little hooves and shoving them into
the backs of squad cars.

We made our way toward the woods at the back of the
property. The grounds had become so overgrown I couldn't
tell where the lawn stopped and the underbrush began.

Gradually, the canopy of trees grew thicker, until the sunlight was reduced to yellow buckshot across the forest floor.

I estimated we weren't far from the old well where Hearthstone's brother had died—another place high on my Never Visit Again list. So, naturally, we stumbled right into it.

A cairn of stones covered the spot where the well had been filled in. Not a weed or blade of grass grew in the barren dirt, as if even they didn't want to invade such a poisoned clearing. Still, I had no trouble imagining Hearthstone and Andiron playing here as children—Hearth's back turned as he happily stacked rocks, not hearing his brother scream when the *brunnmigi*, the beast who lived in the well, rose from the darkness.

I started to say, "We don't have to be here—"

Hearth walked to the cairn as if in a trance. Sitting at the top of the pile, where Hearthstone had left it during our last visit, was a runestone:

$$\diamondsuit$$

Othala, the rune of family inheritance. Hearthstone had insisted he would never use that rune again. Its meaning had died for him in this place. Even his new set of rowan runes, the ones he'd received as a gift from the goddess Sif, did not contain othala. Sif had warned him this would cause him trouble. Eventually, she'd said, he would have to return here to reclaim his missing piece.

I hated it when goddesses were right.

Should you take it? I signed. In a place like this, silent conversation seemed better than using my voice.

Hearthstone frowned, his gaze defiant. He made a quick chopping gesture—sideways then down, like he was tracing a backward question mark. *Never.*

Blitzen sniffed the air. *We're close now. Smell it?*

I smelled nothing except the faint scent of rotting plant matter. *What?*

"Yeesh," he said aloud. *Human noses are pathetic.*

Useless, Hearthstone agreed. He led the way deeper into the forest.

We didn't make for the river, as we had last time to find Andvari's gold. This time we moved roughly parallel to the water, picking our way through briars and the gnarled roots of giant oak trees.

After another quarter mile, I started to smell what Hearth and Blitz had talked about. I had a flashback to my eighth-grade biology class, when Joey Kelso hid our teacher's frog habitat in the ceiling tiles. It wasn't discovered until a month later, when the glass terrarium crashed back into the classroom and broke all over the teacher's desk, spraying the front row with glass, mold, slime, and rancid amphibian bodies.

What I smelled in the forest reminded me of that, except *much* worse.

Hearthstone stopped at the edge of another clearing. He crouched behind a fallen tree and gestured for us to join him.

In there, he signed. *Only place he could have gone.*

I peered through the gloom. The trees around the clearing had been reduced to charcoal stick figures. The ground was thick with rotting mulch and animal bones. About fifty feet from our hiding place rose an outcropping of boulders, two of the largest rocks leaning together to form what looked like the entrance of a cave.

"Now we wait," Blitz whispered as he signed, "for what passes for nighttime in this dwarf-forsaken place."

Hearth nodded. *He will emerge at night. Then we see.*

I was having a hard time breathing, much less thinking in the miasma of dead-frog stench. Staying here sounded like a terrible idea.

Who's going to emerge? I signed. *Your dad? From there? Why?*

Hearthstone looked away. I got the feeling he was trying to be merciful by not answering my questions.

"We'll find out," Blitz murmured. "If it's what we fear . . . Well, let's enjoy our ignorance while we still can."

TWENTY-FOUR

I Liked Hearthstone's Dad Better as a Cow-Abducting Alien

WHILE WE waited, Hearthstone provided us with dinner.

From his rune bag, he drew this symbol:

It looked like a regular *X* to me, but Hearthstone explained it was *gebo*, the rune of gifts. In a flash of gold light, a picnic basket appeared, overflowing with fresh bread, grapes, a wheel of cheese, and several bottles of sparkling water.

"I like gifts," I said, keeping my voice low. "But won't the smell draw . . . uh, unwanted attention?" I pointed to the cave entrance.

"Doubtful," said Blitzen. "The smell coming out of that cave is more powerful than anything in this basket. But just to be safe, let's eat everything quickly."

"I like the way you think," I said.

Blitzen and I dug in, but Hearth merely settled himself behind the fallen tree trunk and watched us.

"Not eating?" I asked him.

He shook his head. *Not hungry,* he signed. *Also, g-e-b-o makes gifts. Not for the giver. For giver, it must be sacrifice.*

"Oh." I looked down at the wedge of cheese I'd been about to shove in my mouth. "That doesn't seem fair."

Hearthstone shrugged, then motioned for us to continue. I didn't like the idea of him sacrificing so we could eat dinner. Just him being back home, waiting for his father to emerge from a cave, seemed like sacrifice enough. He didn't need his very own Ramadan rune.

On the other hand, it would've been rude to refuse his gift. So, I ate.

As the sun sank, the shadows lengthened. I knew from experience that Alfheim never got fully dark. Like Alaska in summer, the sun would just dip to the horizon and pop back up again. Elves were creatures of light, which was proof that *light* did not equal *good*. I'd met plenty of elves (Hearth excepted) who proved that.

The gloom intensified, but not enough for Blitz to take off his anti-sun gear. It must have been a thousand degrees inside that heavy jacket, but he didn't complain. Once in a while he pulled a handkerchief from his pocket and dabbed under his netting, wiping the sweat from his neck.

Hearthstone fidgeted with something on his wrist—a bracelet of woven blond hair that I'd never seen before. The color of the locks seemed vaguely familiar. . . .

I tapped his hand for attention. *Is that from Inge?*

Hearth winced, like this was an awkward subject. On our last visit, Mr. Alderman's long-suffering house servant Inge had helped us a lot. A *hulder*, a sort of elf with the tail of a cow, she'd known Hearth since they were both kids. As it turned out, she also had a massive crush on him, even kissing him on

the cheek and declaring her love before she fled the chaos of
Mr. Alderman's last party.

We visited her a few days ago, Hearth signed. *While scouting.
She is living with her family now.*

Blitz sighed in exasperation, which, of course, Hearth
couldn't hear.

Inge is a good lady, the dwarf signed. *But . . .* He made Vs
with both hands and circled them in front of his forehead, like
he was pulling things out of his mind. In this context, I imagined the sign meant something like *delusional.*

Hearthstone frowned. *Not fair. She tried to help. Hulder
bracelet is good luck.*

If you say so, Blitz signed.

Glad she is safe, I signed. *Is the bracelet magic?*

Hearth started to respond. Then his hands froze. He
sniffed the air and gestured *DOWN!*

The birds had stopped chattering in the trees. The whole
forest seemed to be holding its breath.

We crouched lower, our eyes barely peeking over the top
of the fallen tree. On my next inhalation, I got such a snootful
of dead-frog stench I had to repress a gag.

Just inside the cave entrance, twigs and dry leaves crackled
under the weight of something huge.

The hairs on my neck quivered. I wished I had summoned
Jack so I would be ready to fight if needed, but Jack wasn't good
in stakeout situations, what with his tendency to glow and sing.

Then, from the doorway of the cave came . . . *Oh, gods of
Asgard.*

I'd been holding out hope that Alderman had turned
into something not so bad. Maybe his cursed form was a

Weimaraner puppy, or a chuckwalla iguana. Of course, deep down I'd known the truth all along. I just hadn't wanted to admit it.

Hearth had told me horror stories about what happened to previous thieves who dared to take Andvari's ring. Now I saw that he hadn't been bluffing.

Emerging from the cave was a beast so hideous I couldn't comprehend it all at once.

First I focused on the ring glinting on its middle right fore-toe—a tiny band of gold biting into the scaly flesh. It must have hurt badly, throbbing like a tourniquet. The end of the toe had blackened and shriveled.

The monster's four feet were each the diameter of a trashcan lid. Its short thick legs dragged along a lizard-like body, maybe fifty feet from nose to tail, its spine ridged with spikes bigger than my sword.

The face I had seen in my dreams: glowing green eyes, a snub-nosed snout with slimy nostrils, a horrible maw with rows of triangular teeth. Its head was maned with green quills. The monster's mouth reminded me of Fenris Wolf's—too large and expressive for a beast, its lips too human. Worst of all: tufts of white clung to its forehead—the last remnants of Mr. Alderman's once-impressive hair.

The new, dragonish Alderman pulled himself from his lair, muttering, grinning, snarling, then cackling hysterically— all for no apparent reason.

"No, Mr. Alderman," he hissed. "You mustn't leave, sir!"

With a roar of frustration, he belched a column of fire across the forest floor, roasting the trunks of the nearest trees. The heat made my eyebrows crinkle like rice paper.

I didn't dare move. I couldn't even look at my friends to see how they were taking this.

Now you may be thinking *Magnus, you've seen dragons before. What was the big deal?*

Okay, sure. I'd seen the occasional dragon. I even fought an elder lindworm once.

But I'd never faced a dragon that used to be someone I *knew*. I'd never seen a person transformed into something so awful, so smelly, so malevolent, and yet . . . so obviously *correct*. This was Mr. Alderman's true self, his worst qualities given flesh.

That terrified me. Not just the knowledge that this creature could broil us alive, but the idea that *anyone* could have this much monster inside them. I couldn't help but wonder . . . if I'd put on that ring, if the worst thoughts and failings of Magnus Chase had been given a form, what would've happened to me?

The dragon took another step, until only the tip of his tail remained in the cave. I held my breath. If the dragon went out to hunt, maybe we could dash into the cave while he was gone, find the whetstone we needed, and get out of Alfheim without a fight. I could've really gone for an easy win like that.

The dragon moaned. "So thirsty! The river isn't far, Mr. Alderman. Just a quick drink, perhaps?"

He chuckled to himself. "Oh, no, Mr. Alderman. Your neighbors are tricky. Posers! Wannabes! They'd *love* for you to leave your treasure unguarded. Everything you have worked so hard for—your wealth! Yours alone! No, sir. Back you go! Back!"

Hissing and spitting, the dragon retreated into his cave,

leaving behind only dead-frog stench and a few smoldering trees.

I still couldn't move. I counted to fifty, waiting to see if the dragon would reemerge, but tonight's show seemed to be over.

Finally my muscles began to thaw. I sank back behind our log. My legs shook uncontrollably. I had an overwhelming urge to pee.

"Gods," I muttered. "Hearthstone, I . . ."

Words and sign language failed me. How could I commiserate, or even begin to understand what Hearthstone must be feeling?

He set his mouth in a hard line. His eyes glinted with steely determination, a look that reminded me too much of his father.

He made an open hand and tapped his thumb to his chest. *I'm fine.*

Sometimes you lie to deceive people. Sometimes you lie because you need the lie to become the truth. I guessed Hearth was doing the latter.

"Hey, buddy," Blitzen whispered as he signed. His voice sounded like it had been crushed under the weight of the dragon. "Magnus and I can figure this out. Let us take the hit."

The idea of Blitzen and me facing that monster alone didn't do much for my bladder problems, but I nodded. "Yeah. Yeah, sure. Maybe we can lure the dragon out and sneak in—"

You're both wrong, Hearthstone signed. *We must kill him. And I must help.*

We Devise a Fabulously
Horrible Plan

WORST PLACE for a council of war?

How about the collapsed well where Hearthstone's brother had died, in the middle of a creepy forest, in my least favorite of the Nine Worlds, where we could expect absolutely no backup?

Yep, that's where we went.

I brought out Jack and filled him in on the situation. For once, he did not squeal with excitement or burst into song.

"A ring dragon?" His runes dimmed to gray. "Oh, that's bad. Cursed rings always make the *worst* dragons."

I signed along for Hearth's benefit.

Hearthstone grunted. *The dragon has a weak spot. The belly.*

"What's he saying?" Jack asked.

Among Hearthstone's friends, Jack was a stubborn holdout when it came to learning to read ASL. He claimed the gestures didn't make sense to him because he didn't have hands. Personally, I thought it was just payback for Hearth not being able to read Jack's lips since, you know, Jack didn't have lips. Magic swords can be petty like that.

"He said the belly is the dragon's weak spot," I repeated.

"Oh, well, yeah." Jack sounded unenthused. "Their hide is almost impossible to cut, but they do have chinks in their belly armor. If you could somehow get the dragon to roll over—and good luck with that—you might be able to stab me through and reach its heart. But even if you could, have you ever pierced a ring dragon's belly? I have. It's gross. Their blood is acid!"

I translated all that for Hearth.

"Jack, did the blood damage you?" I asked.

"Of course not! I'm the Sword of Summer! I was forged with a magical finish that resists all wear and tear!"

Blitzen nodded. "It's true. Jack's got a nice finish."

"*Thank* you," Jack said. "Somebody here appreciates good workmanship! Piercing a dragon's belly won't damage *me*, but I'm thinking about *you*, señor. You get one drop of that blood on you while you're cutting the dragon, and you're done. That stuff will eat right through you. *Nothing* can stop it."

I had to admit that didn't sound fun. "Can't you fight on your own, Jack? You could just fly up to the dragon and—"

"Ask it nicely if it will roll over?" Jack snorted, which sounded like a hammer hitting a corrugated metal roof. "Ring dragons crawl on their bellies for a reason, guys. They know better than to present their weak spot. Besides, killing a ring dragon is a very personal thing. You would have to wield me yourself. An act like that affects your *wyrd*."

I frowned. "You mean it affects you weirdly?"

"No. Your *wyrd*."

"*You're* weird," I muttered.

"He means *fate*," Blitzen put in, signing as he spoke for Hearth's benefit.

The sign for *fate* was one hand pushing forward, like everything was going along just fine, la-di-da, then both hands suddenly dropping into Blitz's lap like they'd run into a wall and died. I may have mentioned that ASL can be a little too descriptive.

"When you kill a ring dragon," Blitz said, "especially one who used to be someone you knew, you're messing with serious magic. The dragon's own curse can reverberate through your future, change the course of your destiny. It can . . . stain you."

He said the word *stain* like it was worse than ketchup or grease—like dragon-killing wouldn't come out of your wyrd even with a good presoaking.

Hearthstone signed in clipped gestures, the way he did when he was irritated: *Must be done. I will do it.*

"Buddy . . ." Blitz shifted uncomfortably. "This is your dad."

Not anymore.

Hearth, I signed. *Some way to get whetstone without killing the dragon?*

He shook his head adamantly. *Not the point. Dragons can live for centuries. I can't leave him like that.*

His pale eyes moistened. With a shock, I realized he was crying. It may sound dumb, but elves were usually so in control and subdued about their emotions, it surprised me to know they were *capable* of tears.

Hearth wasn't just angry. He didn't want vengeance. Despite everything Alderman had done to him, Hearthstone didn't want his dad to suffer as a twisted monster. Sif had warned Hearth that he would have to come back here to reclaim his lost inheritance rune. That meant closing the sad story of his family, putting Mr. Alderman's tortured soul to rest.

"I get it," I said. "I do. But let me strike the killing blow. You shouldn't have that on your conscience, or your wyrd, or whatever."

"Kid's right," Blitz said. "It won't stain his destiny as badly. But you—killing your own dad, even if it's a mercy? Nobody should ever have to face a choice like that."

I thought Samirah and Alex might disagree. They might welcome the chance to put Loki out of our collective misery. But, generally speaking, I knew Blitz was right.

"Besides," Jack chimed in, "I'm the only blade that can do the job, and I wouldn't let the elf handle me!"

I decided not to translate that. "What do you say, Hearthstone? Will you let me do this?"

Hearthstone's hands hovered in front of him like he was about to play the air piano. At last, he signed, *Thank you, Magnus*—a gesture like blowing a kiss, then a fist with the thumb under three fingers, *M*, my name sign.

Normally he wouldn't have bothered with my name. When you talk to somebody in ASL, it's obvious who you are addressing. You just look at them or point. Hearth used my name sign to show respect and love.

"I got you, man," I promised. My insides fluttered at the thought of killing the dragon, but there was no way I'd let Hearthstone take the fall for that act. His wyrd had already suffered enough, thanks to Mr. Alderman. "So how do we do this, preferably without acid dissolving me into a pile of Magnus foam?"

Hearth gazed at the cairn. His shoulders sagged, as if somebody was piling invisible rocks on top of him. *There is a way. Andiron* . . . He hesitated at his brother's name sign. *You know we used to play around here. There are tunnels, made by wild*– Here he used a sign I'd never seen before.

"He means *nisser*," Blitzen explained. "They're like . . ."

He held his hand about two feet off the ground. "Little guys. They're also called hobs. Or *di sma*. Or brownies."

I guessed he didn't mean the Girl Scout Junior type of brownie, or the baked chocolate kind.

Hundreds used to live in the woods, Hearth signed, *before Dad called exterminator.*

A chunk of bread swelled in my throat. A minute before, I hadn't even known brownies existed. Now I felt sorry for them. I could imagine Mr. Alderman making the call. *Hello, Pest-Away? There's a civilization in my backyard I'd like exterminated.*

"So . . . the brownies' tunnels are still there?" I asked.

Hearth nodded. *They are narrow. But you could use one to crawl close to the cave. If we can taunt dragon to walk over the spot where you are hiding–*

"I could strike from beneath," I said. "Right into its heart."

Jack's runes glowed an angry chartreuse. "That's a terrible idea! You'll get showered with dragon's blood!"

I wasn't crazy about the idea either. Hiding in a tunnel made by exterminated brownies while a five-ton dragon dragged itself overhead presented all kinds of possibilities for a painful demise. On the other hand, I wasn't going to let Hearthstone down. Getting the whetstone now seemed almost beside the point. I had to help my friend get free of his horrible past once and for all, even if it meant risking an acid bath.

"Let's try a dry run," I said. "If we can find a good tunnel, maybe I'll be able to stab the dragon quickly and scramble to the exit before I get splashed."

"Hmph." Jack sounded awfully grumpy. Then again, I *was* asking him to slay a dragon. "I suppose that means you'd leave me stuck in the dragon's heart?"

"Once the dragon's dead, I'll come back and get you . . . uh, assuming I can figure out how to do that without getting destroyed by acid."

Jack sighed. "All right, I suppose the idea's worth exploring. Just, if you live through this, you'll have to promise to clean me really well afterward."

Blitzen nodded, as if Jack's priorities made perfect sense to him. "We'll still need a way to draw the dragon out of his cave," he said. "To make sure he crawls over the right spot."

Hearth rose. He walked to his dead brother's cairn. He stared at it for a long while, as if wishing it would go away. Then, with trembling fingers, he reclaimed the othala rune. He held it out for us to see. He didn't sign, but his meaning was clear:

Leave that to me.

TWENTY-SIX

Things Get Wyrd

IN VALHALLA, we spent a lot of time waiting.

We waited for our daily call to battle. We waited for our final glorious deaths at Ragnarok. We waited in line for tacos at the food court, because the Viking afterlife only had one taqueria, and Odin should really do something about that.

A lot of einherjar said waiting was the hardest part of our lives.

Normally, I disagreed. I was happy to wait for Ragnarok as long as possible, even if it meant long lines for my pollo asado fix.

But waiting to fight a dragon? Not my favorite thing.

We found a brownie tunnel easily enough. In fact, so many nisser holes peppered the forest floor I was surprised I hadn't broken my leg in one already. The tunnel we scouted had an exit in the woods outside the clearing, and another only thirty feet from the cave entrance. It was perfect, except for the fact that the passage was claustrophobic and muddy and smelled of—I am not making this up—baked brownies. I wondered if the exterminator had used a blowtorch to eliminate the poor little guys.

Carefully, quietly, we laid branches over the hole near-est the cave. That's where I would hide with my sword ready, waiting for the dragon to crawl over me. Then we did a few dry runs (which weren't very dry in that damp crawlspace) so I could practice jabbing upward with my blade and scrambling out of the tunnel.

On my third try, as I crawled out gasping and sweaty, Jack announced, "Twenty-one seconds. That's worse than last time! You'll be acid soup for sure!"

Blitzen suggested I try it again. He assured me we had time, since ring dragons were nocturnal, but we were operating so close to the dragon's lair I didn't want to push our luck. Also, I just didn't want to go back into that little hole.

We retreated to the cairn, where Hearthstone had been practicing his magic in private. He wouldn't tell us what he'd been doing or what he was planning. I figured the guy had been traumatized enough without me interrogating him. I just hoped his dragon lure worked, and he wasn't going to be the bait.

We waited for nightfall, taking turns napping. I couldn't sleep much, and when I did, my dreams were bad. I found myself back on the Ship of the Dead, though now the deck was strangely empty. In his admiral's uniform, Loki paced back and forth in front of me, tsking as if I'd failed a uniform inspection. "Sloppy, Magnus. Going after that silly whetstone with so little time remaining?" He got in my face, his eyes so close I could see flecks of fire in his irises. His breath smelled of venom poorly masked with peppermint. "Even if you find it, what then? Your uncle's idea is foolishness. You know you can never beat me." He tapped my nose. "Hope you've got a Plan B!"

His laughter crashed over me like an avalanche, knocking me to the deck, squeezing the air from my lungs. Suddenly I was back in the nisser tunnel, little brownie dudes frantically pushing at my head and feet, screaming as they tried to get past. The mud walls collapsed. Smoke stung my eyes. Flames roared at my feet, roasting my shoes. Above my head, drops of acid ate through the mud, sizzling all around my face.

I woke with a gasp. I couldn't stop shaking. I wanted to grab my friends and get out of Alfheim. Forget the stupid whetstone of Bolverk. Forget Kvasir's Mead. We could find a Plan B. *Any* Plan B.

But the rational part of me knew that wasn't the answer. We were following the most insane, horrifying Plan A imaginable, which meant it was probably the right one. Just once I wished I could go on a quest that involved walking across the hall, pushing a SAVE THE WORLD button, and going back to my room for a few more hours' sleep.

Around sunset, we approached the dragon's lair. We'd now spent over a day in the forest, and we didn't smell so good. This brought back memories of our homeless days, the three of us huddled together in filthy sleeping bags in the alleys of Downtown Crossing. Ah, yes, the good ol' bad times!

My skin crawled with grime and sweat. I could only imagine how Blitz felt in his heavy anti-sun outfit. Hearthstone looked as clean and spotless as ever, though the Alfheim evening light tinted his hair the color of Tizer. As usual, being an elf, the most pungent body odor he produced was no worse than diluted Pine-Sol.

Jack weighed heavily in my hand. "Remember, señor, the heart is located at the *third* chink in the armor. You have to count the lines as the dragon drags itself overhead."

"Assuming I can see?" I asked.

"I'll glow for you! Just remember: stab quick and get out of there. That blood will shoot out like water from a fire hose—"

"Got it," I said queasily. "Thanks."

Blitzen clapped my shoulder. "Good luck, kid. I'll be waiting at the exit to pull you out. Unless Hearth needs backup . . ."

He glanced at the elf as if hoping for more details besides *I have it covered.*

Hearthstone signed, *I have it covered.*

I took a shaky breath. "If you guys have to run, run. Don't wait for me. And if—if I don't make it, tell the others—"

"We'll tell them," Blitzen promised. He sounded like he knew what I wanted to say to everybody, which was good, because I didn't. "But you *will* make it back."

I hugged Hearth and Blitz, which they both tolerated despite my BO.

Then, like a great hero of old, I crawled into my hole.

I wriggled through the nisser tunnel, my nose full of the smell of loam and burnt chocolate. When I reached the opening near the dragon's lair, I balled myself up, grunting, shoving, and turning my legs until my head was facing the way I'd come. (As bad as crawling out of this tunnel would be, crawling out backward, feetfirst, would've been even worse.)

I lay faceup, staring at the sky through the lattice of branches. Carefully, so as not to kill myself, I summoned Jack. I positioned him along my left side, his hilt at my belt, his point resting against my collarbone. When I stabbed upward, the angle would be tricky. Using my right hand, I would have to lever the sword diagonally, guide the tip to the chink in the dragon's belly armor, then thrust it through, into the dragon's heart with all my einherji strength. After that, I'd have to scramble out of the tunnel before I was sautéed in acid.

The job seemed impossible. Probably because it was.

Time passed slowly in the muddy tunnel. My only companions were Jack and a few earthworms that were crawling across my calves, checking out my socks.

I started to think the dragon wouldn't go out for dinner. Maybe he'd call for pizza instead. Then I'd end up with an elfish Domino's delivery guy falling on my face. I was about to lose hope when Alderman's putrid smell hit me like a thousand burning frogs kamikaze-diving into my nostrils.

Above, the woven branches rattled as the dragon emerged from his cave.

"I'm thirsty, Mr. Alderman," he growled to himself. "And hungry, too. Inge hasn't served me a proper dinner in days, weeks, months? Where *is* that worthless girl?"

He dragged himself closer to my hiding place. Dirt rained on my chest. My lungs constricted as I waited for the whole tunnel to collapse on top of me.

The dragon's snout eclipsed my hole. All he had to do was look down and he'd see me. I'd be toasted like a nisser.

"I can't leave," Mr. Alderman muttered. "The treasure must be guarded! The neighbors, can't trust them!"

He snarled in frustration. "Back, then, Mr. Alderman. Back to your duties!"

Before he could retreat, from somewhere in the woods a bright flash of light painted the dragon's snout amber—the color of Hearthstone's rune magic.

The dragon hissed. Smoke curled between his teeth. "What was that? Who is there?"

"Father." The voice turned my marrow to ice. The sound

echoed, weak and plaintive, like a child calling from the bottom of a well.

"NO!" the dragon stomped the ground, shaking the earthworms off my socks. "Impossible! You are not here!"

"Come to me, Father," the voice pleaded again.

I'd never known Andiron, Hearth's dead brother, but I guessed I was hearing his voice. Had Hearthstone used the othala rune to summon an illusion, or had he managed something even more terrible? I wondered where elves went when they died, and if their spirits could be brought back to haunt the living. . . .

"I have missed you," said the child.

The dragon howled in agony. He blew fire across my hiding place, aiming for the sound of the voice. All the oxygen was sucked from my chest. I fought down the impulse to gasp. Jack buzzed gently against my side for moral support.

"I am here, Father," the voice persisted. *"I want to save you."*

"Save me?" The dragon edged forward.

Veins pulsed on the underside of his scaly green throat. I wondered if I could stab him in the gullet. It looked like a soft target. But it was too far above me, out of my blade's reach. Also, Jack and Hearthstone had been very specific: I had to aim for the heart.

"Save me from what, my precious boy?" The dragon's tone was tortured and ragged, almost human—or rather almost *elfish.* "How can you be here? He killed you!"

"No," said the child. *"He sent me to warn you."*

The dragon's snout quivered. He lowered his head like a threatened dog. "He—he sent you? He is your enemy. *My* enemy!"

"*No, Father,*" said Andiron. "*Please, listen. He has given me a chance to persuade you. We can be together in the next life. You can redeem yourself, save yourself, if you willingly give up the ring–*"

"THE RING! I knew it! Show yourself, deceiver!"

The dragon's neck was so close now. I could slide Jack's blade right up to its carotid artery and— Jack hummed a warning in my mind: *No. Not yet.*

I wished I could see what was happening at the edge of the clearing. I realized Hearth had not just created a magic distraction. He had summoned the spirit of Andiron, hoping against hope that his brother might be able to save their father from his wretched fate. Even now, after all Alderman had done to him, Hearthstone was willing to give his dad a chance at redemption, even if it meant standing in his brother's shadow one last time.

The clearing grew still and silent. In the distance, briars rustled.

Alderman hissed. "YOU."

I could only imagine one person Alderman would address with so much familiar contempt. Hearthstone must have revealed himself.

"*Father,*" pleaded Andiron's ghost. "*Do not do this–*"

"Worthless Hearthstone!" the dragon cried. "You dare use magic to sully your brother's memory?"

A pause. Hearthstone must have signed something, because Alderman bellowed in reply, "Use your board!"

I clenched my teeth. As if Hearth would carry around that awful little board Alderman used to make him write on—not because Alderman couldn't read ASL, but because he enjoyed making his son feel like a freak.

"I will kill you," the dragon said. "You *dare* try to trick me with this grotesque charade?"

He barreled forward—too fast for me to react. His belly covered the nisser hole and plunged me into darkness. Jack lit his runes, illuminating the tunnel, but I was already disoriented from fear and shock. An opening in the dragon's belly armor appeared just above me, but I had no idea how much of his body had charged past. If I struck now, would I hit his heart? His gallbladder? His lower intestine?

Jack hummed in my mind: *No good! That's the sixth chink! The dragon needs to back up!*

I wondered if Mr. Alderman would respond to a politely worded request. I doubted it.

The dragon had stopped moving. Why? The only reason I could think of: Alderman was in the process of chewing Hearthstone's face off. I panicked. I almost stabbed the beast in the sixth chink, desperate to get the dragon off my friend. Then, through the muffling bulk of the monster's body, I heard a mighty voice yell:

"BACK OFF!"

My first thought: Odin himself had appeared in front of the dragon. He had intervened to save Hearthstone's life so that his rune-magic training sessions would not go to waste. That commanding roar was so loud it *had* to be Odin. I'd heard jotun war horns less forceful.

The voice boomed again: "GET AWAY, YOU FOUL, SMELLY EXCUSE FOR A FATHER!"

Now I recognized the accent—a little Southie with a hint of Svartalf.

Oh, no. No, no, no. It wasn't Odin.

"YOU'RE NOT GETTING ANYWHERE CLOSE TO MY FRIEND, SO PUT YOUR SMELLY DEAD-FROG CARCASS IN REVERSE!"

With crystal clarity, I envisioned the scene: the dragon, stunned and perplexed, stopped cold in its tracks by a new opponent. How such small lungs could possibly produce so much volume, I had no idea. But I was certain that the only thing standing between Hearthstone and fiery death was a well-dressed dwarf in a pith helmet.

I should have been amazed, impressed, inspired. Instead, I wanted to cry. As soon as the dragon recovered his senses, I knew he would kill my friends. He would blowtorch Blitzen and Hearthstone and leave nothing for me to clean up but a pile of fashionable ashes.

"GO!" Blitz bellowed.

Amazingly, Alderman slid backward, revealing the fifth chink in his armor.

Maybe he wasn't used to being spoken to in such a manner. Perhaps he feared some sort of terrible demon was hiding under Blitz's black mosquito netting.

"BACK TO YOUR SMELLY CAVE!" Blitzen yelled. "HYAH!"

The dragon snarled, but it retreated one more chink. Jack hummed in my hands, ready to do our job. Just one more section of belly armor to go . . .

"He's only a stupid dwarf, Mr. Alderman," the dragon muttered to himself. "He wants your ring."

"I DON'T CARE ABOUT YOUR STUPID RING!" Blitz yelled. "SCAT!"

Maybe the dragon was stunned by Blitzen's earnestness.

Or maybe Alderman was confused by the sight of Blitzen standing in front of Hearthstone and the ghost of Andiron, like a father protecting his young. That instinct would have made as little sense to Alderman as a person who wasn't motivated by greed.

He scooted back another few inches. Almost there . . .

"The dwarf is no threat, sir," the dragon assured himself. "He'll make a tasty dinner."

"YOU THINK SO?" Blitz roared. "TRY ME!"

Hiss.

Alderman retreated another inch. The third chink came into view.

Fumbling and panicked, I positioned Jack's point against the weak spot in the hide.

Then, with all my strength, I drove the sword into the dragon's chest.

TWENTY-SEVEN

We Win a Small Rock

I'D LIKE TO tell you I had qualms about leaving Jack buried up to his hilt in dragon flesh.

I didn't. My hand left the grip and I was *out* of there—scrambling down the tunnel like a brownie on fire. The dragon roared and stomped above me, shaking the earth. The tunnel collapsed behind me, sucking at my feet, filling the air with acidic fumes.

Yikes! I thought. *Yikes, yikes, yikes!*

I am eloquent in times of danger.

The crawl seemed to take much longer than twenty-one seconds. I didn't dare breathe. I imagined that my legs were burning off. If I made it out, I would look down and realize I was a sawed-off Magnus.

Finally, black spots dancing in my eyes, I clawed my way out of the tunnel. I gasped and flailed, kicking off my shoes and jeans as if they were poison. Because they were. As I'd feared, dragon blood had splattered my pants and was sizzling through the denim. My shoes smoked. I dragged my bare legs across the forest floor, hoping to smear off any remaining drops of blood. When I checked my feet and the backs of my calves, I saw nothing wrong. No new craters in my flesh. No smoke. No smell of burning einherji.

I could only guess that the collapsing tunnel had saved me, the mud mixing with the acid to slow down the tide of corrosion. Or maybe I'd just used up my luck for the next century.

My heart hammered at a less frantic pace. I staggered into the clearing and found the green dragon Alderman lying on his side, tail flopping, legs twitching. He vomited up a feeble blast of napalm, torching a swath of dead leaves and squirrel skeletons.

Jack's hilt protruded from the dragon's chest. My former hiding place was now a steaming sinkhole, slowly eating its way to the core of Alfheim.

At the dragon's snout stood Hearthstone and Blitzen, both unharmed. Next to them, flickering like a weak candle flame, was the specter of Andiron. I'd only seen Hearth's brother once before, in the portrait above their father's fireplace. That painting had made him look like a young god, perfect and confident, tragically beautiful. What I saw in front of me, though, was just a boy—fair-haired, skinny, knobby-kneed. I wouldn't have picked him out of a lineup of elementary schoolers unless I was trying to identify kids likely to be bullied.

Blitz had raised the front of his anti-sun netting, despite the risk of petrification. The skin around his eyes was starting to turn gray. His expression was grim.

The dragon managed to draw a ragged breath. "Traitor. Murderer."

Blitzen balled his fists. "You've got some nerve—"

Hearthstone touched his sleeve. *Stop.* He knelt next to the dragon's face so Alderman could see him signing.

I did not want this, Hearthstone signed. *I am sorry.*

The dragon's lips curled over his fangs. "Use. Your. Board. Traitor."

Alderman's inner eyelid shut, filming over his greasy green iris. A final plume of smoke escaped his nostrils. Then Alderman's massive body went still.

I waited for him to return to elfish form. He didn't.

His corpse seemed perfectly content to stay a dragon.

Hearthstone rose. His expression was distant and confused—as if he'd just watched a movie made by an alien civilization and was trying to figure out what it meant.

Blitzen turned to me. "You did good, kid. It had to happen."

I stared at him in amazement. "You faced down a dragon. You made him back off."

Blitzen shrugged. "I don't like bullies." He pointed at my legs. "We might need to get you some new pants, kid. Dark khakis would go with that shirt. Or gray denim."

I understood why he wanted to change the subject. He didn't want to talk about how brave he'd been. He didn't see his actions as praiseworthy. It was simply a fact: you didn't mess with Blitzen's bestie.

Hearthstone faced the ghost of his brother.

Andiron signed, *We tried, Hearth. Don't blame yourself.* His features were hazy, but his expression was unmistakable. Unlike Mr. Alderman, Andiron felt nothing but love for his brother.

Hearth wiped his eyes. He stared into the woods as if trying to find his bearings, then signed to Andiron, *I don't want to lose you again.*

I know, the ghost gestured. *I don't want to go.*

Father—

Andiron chopped his palm, the symbol for *stop.*

Don't waste another minute on him, Andiron said. *He took enough of your life. Will you eat his heart?*

That made no sense, so I figured I must have interpreted the signs wrong.

Hearth's face darkened. He signed, *I don't know.*

Andiron gestured, *Come here.*

Hearthstone hesitated. He edged closer to the ghost.

I will tell you a secret, Andiron said. *When I whispered into that well, I made a wish. I wanted to be as kind and good as you, brother. You are perfect.*

The little boy stretched out his phantom arms. Hearthstone leaned down to embrace him, and the ghost burst into white vapor.

The othala runestone fell into Hearth's palm. Hearth studied it for a moment, as if it were something he'd never seen before—a dropped jewel that the owner would surely want back. He curled his fingers around the stone and pressed it to his forehead. For once, it was my turn to read *his* lips. I was pretty sure he whispered, *Thank you.*

Something rattled in the dragon's chest. I was afraid Alderman had started to breathe again, but then I realized it was Jack quivering angrily, trying to get free.

"STUCK!" he shouted in a muffled voice. *"GEMME-OUTTAEEER!"*

Careful of my bare feet, I stepped toward the acidic cesspool. Blood still oozed from the dragon's chest, forming a steamy, muddy lake. There was no way I could get close enough to grab the hilt. "Jack, I can't reach you! Can't you pull yourself out?"

"PULLMYWHATNO!" he yelled. "JUSTSAIDI'MSTUCK!"

I frowned at Blitz. "How can we get him out of there?"

Blitz cupped his hands and shouted to Jack as if he were on the other side of the Grand Canyon. "Jack, you'll just have to wait! The dragon's blood will lose its potency in about an hour. Then we can pull you free!"

"ANHOURAREYOUKIDDINGME?" His hilt vibrated, but he remained firmly embedded in Alderman's rib cage.

"He'll be fine," Blitz assured me.

Easy for him to say. He didn't have to live with the sword.

Blitz touched Hearth's shoulder for attention. *Need to check cave for the whetstone,* he signed. *You up for that?*

Hearth clutched the othala rune tightly. He studied the dragon's face as if trying to see anything familiar there. Then he slipped the rune into his bag, making his set complete.

You two go ahead, he signed. *I need a minute.*

Blitz grimaced. "Yeah, buddy, no problem. You've got a big decision to make."

"What decision?" I asked.

Blitz gave me a look like *Poor naïve kid.* "Come on, Magnus— let's check out this monster's treasure."

The treasure was easy to find. It took up most of the cave. In the middle of the hoard was a dragon-shaped impression where Alderman used to sleep. No wonder he'd been so cranky. That mound of coins, swords, and jewel-encrusted goblets couldn't have afforded much back support.

I walked around the edges of the hoard, pinching my nose

shut to block out the overwhelming stench. My mouth still tasted like a biology class terrarium.

"Where's the stone?" I asked. "I don't see any of Alderman's old artifacts."

Blitz scratched his beard. "Well, dragons are vain. He probably wouldn't put his dull geology specimens on top. He'd bury those and show off the shiny stuff. I wonder. . . ."

He crouched next to the treasure. "Ha! Just as I figured. Look."

Sticking out from the landslide of gold was the end of a braided cord.

It took me a second to recognize it. "Is that . . . the magic bag we got from Andvari?"

"Yep!" Blitz grinned. "The hoard is sitting right on top of it. Alderman might have been greedy, cruel, and horrible, but he wasn't stupid. He wanted his treasure to be easy to transport in case he had to find a new lair."

It seemed to me that this also made the treasure really easy to steal, but I wasn't going to argue with the logic of a dead dragon.

Blitz pulled the cord. A canvas tsunami engulfed the treasure, shuddering and shrinking until lying on the floor at our feet was a simple tote bag, suitable for grocery shopping or concealing several billion dollars' worth of priceless objects. Blitz lifted the bag with just two fingers.

Against the back wall of the cave, underneath where the treasure had been piled, lay dozens of Alderman's artifacts. Many had been crushed by the weight of the gold. Fortunately for us, rocks were pretty durable. I picked up the round gray whetstone I'd seen in my dream. Holding it did not fill me with ecstasy. Angels did not sing. I did not feel all-powerful, like I could defeat the mysterious invincible guardians of Kvasir's Mead.

"Why this?" I asked. "Why is it worth . . . ?" I couldn't put into words the sacrifices we'd made. Especially Hearthstone.

Blitzen took off his pith helmet. He ran his fingers through his sticky hair. Despite the cave's smell of death and decay, he looked relieved to be out of the sun.

"I don't know, kid," he said. "I can only assume we'll need the stone to sharpen some blades."

I looked around at Alderman's other artifacts. "Anything else we should take while we're here? Because I *really* don't want to come back."

"Hope not, because I'm in *complete* agreement." With obvious reluctance, he put his helmet back on. "Let's go. I don't want to leave Hearthstone alone too long."

As it turned out, Hearth was not alone.

Somehow, he had freed Jack from the dragon's chest. Now the sword, being a contrary weapon, was diving right back into the dragon's carcass, wrenching the chest apart through a chink like he was performing an autopsy. Hearth seemed to be directing him.

"Whoa, whoa, whoa!" I said. "What are you guys doing?"

"Oh, hey, señor!" Jack floated over. He sounded cheerful for a gore-covered blade. "The elf asked me to open the rib cage. At least I'm pretty sure that's what he was asking. I figured since he used his magic to pull me free, it was the least I could do! Oh, and I already chopped off the ring. It's right there, ready to go!"

I looked down. Sure enough, a few inches from my bare foot, Andvari's ring glittered on the swollen severed toe of the dragon. I swallowed down a surge of bile. "Ready to go? What are we doing with it?"

Hearth signed, *Put it with the treasure. Take it back to river and return it to Andvari.*

Blitz scooped up the dragon toe and dropped it in his magical tote. "We'd best do this quick, kid, before the ring starts tempting us to use it."

"Okay, but . . ." I pointed to the partially dissected dragon. I'd never been a hunter, but one time my mom dated a guy who hunted. He'd taken us into the woods and tried to impress my mom by teaching me how to gut a carcass. (That hadn't gone so well. Neither had their relationship.)

Anyway, looking at the dragon, I was sure Jack was trying to cut out Mr. Alderman's no-longer-vital organs.

"Why?" I managed.

Jack laughed. "Oh, come on, señor, I thought you knew! After killing a ring dragon, you have to cut out its heart, roast it, and eat it!"

That's when I lost my lunch.

TWENTY-EIGHT

Don't Ever Ask Me to Cook My Enemy's Heart

SO FAR on our quest, I'd done well not puking. I was on my way to being a not-puking professional.

But the idea of eating a dragon's heart—*Alderman's* disgusting evil excuse for a heart—nope. That was too much.

I staggered into the woods and retched for so long I almost passed out. At last, Blitz clamped his hand on my shoulder and steered me away from the clearing. "Okay, kid. I know. Come on."

By the time I was somewhat coherent again, I realized Blitzen was leading me toward the river where we'd met Andvari. I didn't trust myself to speak, except for the occasional "Ow!" when I stepped barefoot on a rock or a branch or a nest of Alfheim fire ants.

Finally, we reached the water. Standing at the edge of a little waterfall, I peered down into Andvari's pool. It hadn't changed much since last time. It was impossible to tell if the slimy old dwarf still lived down there, disguised as a slimy old fish. Maybe after we robbed him, he'd given up, moved to Key West, and retired. If so, I was tempted to join him.

"You ready?" Blitz's voice was strained. "I'm going to need your help."

I squinted at him through the yellow film in my eyes. Blitz held the tote bag over the edge, ready to drop it into the pool, but his arm trembled. He yanked the bag back, as if to save the treasure from its fate, then extended his arm again with difficulty, like he was bench-pressing the entire weight of the gold.

"Going—to—fight—me," Blitz grumbled. "Dwarves—throwing away—treasure. Not—*easy*."

Somehow I managed to get my head out of *eat-dragon-heart?-what-the-Helheim?* mode. I grabbed the bag's other strap. Immediately I felt what Blitz was talking about. My mind was flooded with glorious ideas about what I could do with all this treasure—buy a mansion! (But wait . . . I already had Uncle Randolph's mansion, and I didn't even want it.) Get a yacht! (I already had a big yellow boat. No thanks.) Save for retirement! (I was dead.) Send my kids to college! (Einherjar can't have kids. We're dead.)

The bag shuddered and kicked. It seemed to be rethinking its strategy. *Okay,* it whispered in my thoughts, *how about helping the homeless? Think of all the good you could do with the gold, and this bagful is just the down payment! Put on that lovely ring, and you'll get infinite wealth! You could build housing! Provide meals! Job-training!*

These possibilities were more tempting. . . . But I knew it was a trick. This treasure would never do anyone any good. I looked down at my bare legs, scraped and muddy. I remembered the suffocating smell of dragon belly. I recalled Hearthstone's miserable expression as he said good-bye to his father.

I muttered, "Stupid treasure."

"Yeah," said Blitz. "On three? One, two—"

We tossed the bag into the pool. I resisted the urge to jump in after it.

"There you go, Andvari," I said. "Enjoy."

Or maybe Andvari was gone. In which case, we'd just made a family of trout billionaires.

Blitz sighed with relief. "Okay, that's one burden gone. Now . . . the other thing."

My stomach rebelled all over again. "I'm not really supposed to—?"

"Eat the dragon's heart? You?" Blitz shook his head. "Well, you *are* the one who killed him. . . . But in this case, no. You don't eat the heart."

"Thank the gods."

"Hearth has to do that."

"*What?*"

Blitz's shoulders slumped. "The dragon was Hearth's kin, Magnus. When you kill a ring dragon, you can put its spirit to rest by destroying its heart. You can either burn it up—"

"Yeah, let's do that."

"—or you can consume it, in which case you inherit all the dragon's memories and wisdom."

I tried to imagine why Hearthstone would *want* any of his father's memories or so-called wisdom. For that matter, why would he even feel obliged to put Alderman's evil spirit to rest? Andiron had told him not to waste a minute longer worrying about dead old Dad, and that sounded like excellent brotherly advice.

"But if Hearth . . . I mean, isn't that cannibalism, or dragonbalism or something?"

"I can't answer that." Blitz sounded like he badly wanted to answer that with a loud *YES, I KNOW IT'S DISGUSTING.* "Let's go help him with . . . whatever he decides."

Jack and Hearthstone had built a campfire. Hearthstone turned a spit over the flames while Jack floated next to him singing "Roll Out the Barrel" at the top of his nonexistent lungs. Being deaf, Hearthstone was the ideal audience.

The scene would have been charming except for the six-ton dragon carcass rotting nearby, the sickly expression on Hearthstone's pale face, and the basketball-size black glistening thing sizzling on the spit, filling the air with the smell of barbecue. The fact that Alderman's heart actually smelled like food made me even sicker.

Hearthstone signaled with his free hand. *Done?*

Yeah, Blitzen signed back. *Treasure and ring gone. Very wealthy fish.*

Hearthstone nodded, apparently satisfied. His blond hair was speckled with mud and leaves, which reminded me, ridiculously, of parade confetti, like the forest was throwing him a grim celebration for his father's death.

"Hearth, man . . ." I pointed at the heart. "You don't have to do this. There's got to be another way."

"That's what I told him!" Jack said. "Of course, he can't hear me, but still!"

Hearth started to sign with one hand, which is like trying to talk without vowels. He gave up in frustration. He pointed to me, then to the spit: *Take this for me.*

I didn't want to get anywhere close to that dragon heart, but I was the only one who could talk and turn the spit at the same time. Hearth could at least read my lips. Blitzen could sign, but his face was covered with netting. And Jack . . . well, he just wasn't very helpful.

I took over organ-roasting duty. The heart seemed much too heavy and wobbly for the spit, which was placed across two makeshift tree-branch stakes. Keeping it balanced over the flames took a lot of concentration.

Hearthstone flexed his fingers, warming up for a long conversation. His Adam's apple bobbed up and down as if his throat was already protesting tonight's dinner special.

If I eat the heart, Hearthstone signed, *it means Father's knowledge not lost forever.*

"Yeah," I said, "but why would you *want* that?"

His fingers hesitated in the air. *Memories of Mother, Andiron. Older family knowledge. Knowing my . . .*

He made an *H* with two fingers extended, then whacked the back of his opposite hand. I guessed it was the sign for *history*, though it looked a lot like a teacher slapping a bad student with a ruler.

"But you'd know things only from your father's perspective," I said. "He was *poison*. Like Andiron told you, you don't owe your father anything. He's got no wisdom to give."

Jack laughed. "Right? Dude collected rocks, after all!"

I decided it was just as well Hearth and my sword couldn't communicate.

Hearth's mouth tightened. He understood *me* just fine, but I could tell I wasn't saying anything he didn't already know. He didn't want to eat that disgusting thing. But he felt . . . I didn't know the right word in English or sign language. *Obliged? Honor-bound?* Maybe Hearth hoped against hope that if he knew his father's inner thoughts, he would find some glimmer of love in there, something that could redeem his memory.

I knew better. I wasn't about digging up the painful past. Look behind somebody's horrible exterior, and you usually found a horrible interior, shaped by a horrible history. I didn't want Alderman's thoughts affecting Hearthstone, literally being ingested by him. There had to be a vegetarian option. Or a Buddhist one. I would even have settled for a green-hair-friendly meal.

Blitzen sat down, crossing his legs at the ankles. He patted his friend's knee. *Your choice. But the soul will still rest if you make the other choice.*

"Yes!" I asked. "Destroy the heart. Just let it go—"

That's when I messed up. I got too excited. I was focusing on Hearth and not paying attention to my job as chef. I turned the spit a little too forcefully. The heart wobbled. The braces collapsed inward, and the whole thing toppled into the fire.

Oh, but wait. It gets worse. With my lightning-fast and incredibly stupid einherji reflexes, I grabbed for the heart. I almost caught it in one hand, but it rolled off my fingertips and crashed into the flames, combusting like its ventricles were filled with gasoline. In a red flash, the heart was gone.

Oh, but wait. It gets worse still. The sizzling heart left boiling grease on my fingertips. And dumb Magnus, incredibly gross Magnus—I did what most people do when they touch something hot. I instinctively put my fingers to my mouth.

The taste was like ghost chili mixed with concentrated Hawaiian Punch syrup. I pulled my fingertips out and tried to spit away the blood. I retched and wiped my tongue. I crawled around sputtering, "No! *Pfffttss.* No! *Pfffttss.* No!"

But it was too late. Even that little taste of dragon heart's blood had infiltrated my system. I could feel it seeping into my tongue, humming through my capillaries.

"Señor!" Jack flew toward me, his runes glowing orange. "You shouldn't have done that!"

I bit back an insult about my sword's godlike powers of hindsight.

Blitzen's face was obscured by netting, but his posture was even stiffer than the time he'd been petrified. "Kid! Ah, gods, you feel okay? Dragon blood can . . . well, it can bring out some strange stuff in your DNA. Humans have DNA, don't they?"

I wished we didn't. I gripped my gut, worried that I might already be turning into a dragon. Or worse, an evil elf father.

I forced myself to meet Hearthstone's eyes. "Hearth, I—I'm so sorry. It was an accident, I swear. I didn't mean to . . ."

My voice faltered. I wasn't sure *I* believed me. I didn't know why Hearth would. I'd suggested destroying the heart. Then I'd done it. Worse, I'd tasted it.

Hearth's face was a mask of shock.

"Tell me what to do," I pleaded. "I'll find some way to make it right—"

Hearthstone held up his hand. I'd seen the wall of ice he put up on those rare occasions when he was truly furious, but I saw none of that now. Instead, his muscles seemed to be unknotting, his tension draining away. He looked . . . relieved.

It is wyrd, Hearth signed. *You killed the dragon. Fate decided that you would taste his blood.*

"But . . ." I stopped myself from making another apology. Hearth's expression made it clear he didn't want that.

You put my father's soul to rest, Hearth signed. *You saved me from that deed. It may cost you, though. It is I who am sorry.*

I was relieved he wasn't angry with me. Then again, I didn't like the new wariness in his gaze, as if he was waiting to see how the dragon blood would affect me.

Then, somewhere above, a chittering voice said, *What a knucklehead.*

I flinched.

"You okay, señor?" asked Jack.

I scanned the canopy of trees. I saw no one.

Another tiny voice said, *He doesn't even know what he's done, does he?*

Not a clue, the first voice agreed.

I spotted the source of the voices. On a branch about twenty feet up, two robins were eyeing me. They spoke in a series of chirps, as birds do, but somehow their meaning was clear to me.

Ah, eggshells, the first robin cursed. *He sees us. Fly! Fly!*

The two birds darted away.

"Kid?" Blitz asked.

My heart raced. What was happening to me? Was I hallucinating?

"I—I—yes." I gulped. "Yeah. I'm okay. I guess."

Hearthstone studied me, clearly unconvinced, but he decided not to argue. He rose to his feet, then glanced one last time at the corpse of his dragon father.

We've lingered too long, he signed. *Should take the whetstone back to the ship. It may already be too late to stop Loki.*

TWENTY-NINE

We Almost Become a Norwegian Tourist Attraction

JUMPING OFF a cliff was the *least* strange thing I did in Alfheim.

Blitz, Hearth, and I hiked to an outcropping of rock at the edge of the Alderman property—the sort of place where a megalomaniac businessman could stand, survey the neighbors' estates in the valley below, and think *Someday, all this will be mine! BWAHAHA!*

We were just high enough to break our legs if we fell, so Hearth declared the spot perfect. He cast *raidho*, ᚱ, the rune of traveling, as we jumped. The air rippled around us, and instead of smashing into the ground below, we landed in a heap on the deck of the *Big Banana*, right on top of Halfborn Gunderson.

"*Eldhusfifls!*" Halfborn roared.

(That was another of his favorite insults. As he explained it, an eldhusfifl was a fool who sat by the communal fire all day, so basically, a village idiot. Plus, it just *sounded* insulting: *el-doos-feef-full*.)

We climbed off him and apologized. Then I healed his broken arm, which was still in a sling and had been re-broken by the weight of a falling dwarven butt.

"Hmph," he said. "I suppose I forgive you, but I just washed my hair. You ruined my 'do!"

His hair looked no different than usual, so I couldn't tell if he was joking. He didn't kill us with his battle-ax, though, so I guess he wasn't too upset.

Night had fallen in Midgard. Our ship sailed the open sea under a net of stars. Blitz stripped off his overcoat, gloves, and pith helmet and took in a lungful of air. "Finally!"

The first person to emerge from belowdecks was Alex Fierro, dressed like a 1950s greaser—her green-black hair slicked back, her white T-shirt tucked into lime-colored jeans.

"Thank the gods!" She rushed toward me, which lifted my spirits for about a microsecond until she plucked the pink Buddy Holly glasses off my face. "My outfit wasn't complete without these. I hope you didn't scratch them."

While she polished her specs, Mallory, T.J., and Samirah clambered up to the deck.

"Whoa!" Sam averted her eyes. "Magnus, where are your pants?"

"Um, long story."

"Well, put on some clothes, Beantown!" Mallory ordered. "*Then* tell us the story."

I went below to get pants and shoes. When I came back, the crew was gathered around Hearth and Blitz, who were recounting our adventure in the magical land of elves, light, and reeking dragon carcasses.

Sam shook her head. "Oh, Hearthstone. I am so sorry about your dad."

The others murmured in agreement.

Hearth shrugged. *It had to be done. Magnus bore the worst of it. Tasting the heart.*

I winced. "Yeah, about that . . . I should probably tell you guys something."

I explained about the conversation I'd overheard between the two robins.

Alex Fierro snorted, then covered her mouth. "I'm sorry. It's not funny." She signed: *Hearth, your father, the heart. Awful. I can't imagine.* She continued aloud: "In fact, I have something for you."

From her pocket, she pulled a diaphanous silk scarf of pink and green. "I noticed you lost your other one."

Hearth took the scarf like it was a holy relic. He solemnly wrapped it around his collar. *Thank you,* he signed. *Love.*

"You bet." Alex faced me, her mouth curling in a mischievous smile. "But honestly, Magnus. You fumbled the heart. You tasted the blood. And now you're talking to the animals—"

"I didn't talk," I protested. "I only listened."

"—like Dr. Dolittle?"

T.J. frowned. "Who is Dr. Dolittle? Does he live in Valhalla?"

"He's a character from a book." Samirah bit a chunk off her cucumber sandwich. Since it was nighttime, she was doing her best to eat all the ship's food rations as fast as possible. "Magnus, any *other* effects you've noticed from the heart's blood? I'm worried about you."

"I—I don't think so."

"The effects might only be temporary," T.J. suggested. "Do you still feel weird?"

"Weirder than usual?" Alex clarified.

"No," I said. "But it's hard to be sure. There aren't any animals around to listen to."

"I could turn into a ferret," Alex offered, "and we could have a conversation."

"Thanks anyway."

Mallory Keen had been trying out our new whetstone on one of her knives. Now she flung the newly sharpened blade against the deck. The knife sank up to its hilt in the solid wood. "Well, well."

"Try not to destroy our boat, woman," Halfborn said. "We're still sailing in it."

She made a face at him. "This is quite a good sharpener the boys brought back."

T.J. coughed. "Yeah, could I see that for my bayonet?"

"No, indeed." Mallory slipped the stone in the pocket of her jacket. "I don't trust you lot with this little beauty. I think I'll hold on to it so you all don't hurt yourselves. As for the dragon blood, Magnus, I wouldn't worry. You *are* a son of Frey, one of the most powerful nature gods. Perhaps the dragon's blood simply enhanced your natural abilities. Makes sense for you to understand forest creatures."

"Huh." I nodded, slightly encouraged. "Maybe you're right. Still, I'd feel bad if I took away part of Hearthstone's heritage. I mean, what if Mr. Alderman could understand animals—?"

Hearth shook his head. *Father was not Doctor Dolittle. Do not feel guilty. I have the othala rune back. That is enough for me.*

He looked exhausted but relieved, like he'd just finished a six-hour test he'd been dreading all semester. He might not be sure he passed, but at least the ordeal was over.

"Well," said Samirah, "we have the whetstone. Now we

have to get to Fläm, find Kvasir's Mead, and figure out how to defeat its guardians."

"Then feed the mead to Magnus," Alex said, "hoping it gives him the gift of speaking in complete sentences."

Mallory frowned as if she found this unlikely. "Then we find the Ship of the Dead and pray Magnus can beat Loki in a flyting."

"Then somehow recapture that meinfretr," Halfborn said, "stop *Naglfar* from launching, and prevent Ragnarok. Assuming, of course, we're not too late already."

That seemed like a big assumption. We'd burned two more days in Alfheim. Midsummer was roughly ten days away now, and I was pretty sure Loki's ship would be able to sail well before that.

Also, my mind stuck on Mallory's words: *pray Magnus can beat Loki in a flyting*. I didn't have Sam's faith in prayer, especially when it was a prayer about me.

Blitz sighed. "I'm going to wash up. I smell like a troll. Then I'm going to sleep for a very long time."

"Good idea," Halfborn said. "Magnus and Hearth, you should, too."

I could get behind that plan. Jack had returned to runestone form on my neck chain, which meant my arms and shoulders now ached like I'd spent the day sawing through dragon hide. My skin itched all over, as if my anti-acid finish had been sorely tested.

T.J. rubbed his hands with excitement. "Tomorrow morning, we should enter the fjords of Norway. I can't wait to see what we get to kill there!"

• • •

I slept without dreams, which was a nice change, until eventually Samirah shook me awake. She was grinning way too much for someone on a fast. "You really should see this."

I struggled out of my sleeping bag. When I got to my feet and looked over the railing, I lost the ability to breathe.

On either side of the ship, so close I could almost touch them, sheer cliffs rose out of the water—thousand-foot-high walls of rock marbled with waterfalls. White rivulets of snowmelt coursed down the ridges, bursting into mist that fractured the sunlight into rainbows. The sky had been reduced to a jagged ravine of deep blue directly above. Around the hull, the water was so green it might have been algae puree.

In the shadow of those cliffs, I felt so small I could only think of one place we might be. "Jotunheim?"

T.J. laughed. "No, it's just Norway. Pretty, huh?"

Pretty didn't do it justice. I felt like we'd sailed into a world meant for much larger beings, a place where gods and monsters roamed freely. Of course, I knew gods and monsters roamed freely all over Midgard. Heimdall was fond of a certain bagel place near Fenway. Giants often strolled through the marshes in Longview. But Norway seemed like a proper stomping ground for them.

I got a little ache in my heart, thinking how much my mom would've loved this place. I wished I could share it with her. I could picture her hiking along those cliff-tops, relishing the sun and the crisp, clean air.

At the prow stood Alex and Mallory, both silent in amazement. Hearth and Blitz must have still been asleep below. Halfborn sat at the rudder, a sour look on his face.

"What's wrong?" I asked him.

The berserker eyed the cliffs as if they might collapse on us if he made a bad comment. "Nah. It's beautiful. Hasn't really changed since I was a boy."

"Fläm was your hometown?" I guessed.

He let out a bitter laugh. "Well, wasn't much of a town. And it wasn't called Fläm back then. Just a nameless fishing village at the end of the fjord. You'll see the spot in a minute."

His knuckles whitened on the rudder. "As a boy, I couldn't get out of here fast enough. Joined Ivar the Boneless when I was twelve and went a-Viking. I told my mom . . ." He grew silent. "I told her I wouldn't come back until the skalds were singing about my heroic deeds. I never saw her again."

The boat glided onward, the soft applause of the waterfalls echoing through the fjord. I remembered what Halfborn had told me about not liking to go backward, not revisiting his past. I wondered if he felt guilty about leaving his mom, or disappointed that the skalds hadn't made him a great hero. Or maybe they *had* sung about his deeds. From what I'd seen, fame rarely lasted longer than a few years, much less centuries. Some einherjar in Valhalla got bitter when they realized nobody born after the Middle Ages had a clue as to who they were.

"You're famous to us," I offered.

Halfborn grunted.

"I could ask Jack to write a song about you."

"Gods forbid!" His brow remained furrowed, but his mustache quirked like he was trying not to smile. "Enough of that. We'll be docking soon. Keen, Fierro, stop gawking at the scenery and help! Trim the sail! Ready the mooring lines!"

"We're not your pirate wenches, Gunderson," Mallory grumbled, but she and Alex did as he asked.

We rounded a curve, and again I caught my breath. At the end of the fjord, a narrow valley split the mountains—layer upon layer of green hills and forests zigzagging into the distance like an infinite reflection. At the rocky shore, shadowed by cliffs, a few dozen red, ochre, and blue houses clustered together as if for protection. Parked at the dock was a giant white cruise ship bigger than the entire town—a twenty-story floating hotel.

"Well, *that* wasn't here before," Halfborn grumbled.

"Tourists," Mallory said. "What do you think, T.J.? Are they exciting enough for you to fight?"

T.J. tilted his head as if considering the idea.

I decided it might be a good time to refocus the conversation.

"So, back in York," I said, "Hrungnir told us to take the train in Fläm, then we'd find what we were looking for. Anybody see a train?"

T.J. frowned. "How could anybody lay tracks across terrain like that?"

It did seem improbable. Then I glanced off our port side. A car zipped along the base of a cliff. It made a hairpin turn and disappeared into a tunnel, straight through the side of the mountain. If Norwegians were crazy enough to build and drive on highways like that, maybe they were crazy enough to lay train tracks the same way.

"Let's go ashore and find out," Alex suggested. "I recommend we dock as far as possible from that cruise ship."

"You don't like tourists?" Sam asked.

"That's not it," said Alex. "I'm afraid they'll notice this bright yellow Viking boat and think we're a local attraction. You want to give rides around the fjord all day?"

Sam shuddered. "Good point."

We slipped into the dock farthest from the cruise ship. Our only neighbors were a couple of fishing boats and a Jet Ski with the dubious name *Odin II* painted on the side. I considered one Odin quite enough. I wasn't anxious for a sequel.

As Mallory and Alex tied the mooring lines, I scanned the town of Fläm. It was small, yes, but more convoluted than it had appeared from a distance. Streets wound up and down hills, through pockets of houses and shops, stretching out about half a mile along the shore of the fjord. I would have thought a train station would be easy to spot, but I didn't see one from the dock.

"We could split up," Mallory suggested. "Cover more ground that way."

I frowned. "That never works in horror movies."

"Then you come with me, Magnus," Mallory said. "I'll keep you safe." She frowned at Halfborn Gunderson. "But I refuse to be stuck with *this* lout again. Samirah, you're useful in a pinch. How about it?"

The invitation seemed to surprise Sam, although Mallory had been treating her with a lot more deference since the incident with the water horses. "Uh, sure."

Halfborn scowled. "Fine by me! I'll take Alex and T.J."

Mallory arched her eyebrows. "You're going ashore? I thought you wouldn't set foot—"

"Well, you thought wrong!" He blinked twice, as if he'd surprised himself. "This isn't my home anymore, just a random tourist stop! What does it matter?"

He sounded less than certain. I wondered if it would be helpful to offer to switch up the teams. Mallory had a gift for distracting Halfborn. I would've been willing to trade her for . . . I don't know, Alex, maybe. But I didn't think the offer would be appreciated by anybody else.

"What about Hearthstone and Blitz?" I said. "Shouldn't I wake them up?"

"Good luck with that," Alex said. "They are *out.*"

"Could you fold up the ship with them inside?" T.J. asked.

"Doesn't sound safe," I said. "They could wake up and find themselves stuck in a handkerchief."

"Ah, leave 'em here," Halfborn said. "They'll be fine. This place was never dangerous, unless it bored you to death."

"I'll leave them a note," Sam volunteered. "How about we scout around for half an hour? We'll meet back here. Then, assuming somebody's found the train, we can all go there together."

We agreed that plan had a low possibility of violent death. A few minutes later, Halfborn, T.J., and Alex headed off in one direction, while Mallory, Sam, and I headed the other way—wandering the streets of Fläm to find a train and some interesting enemies to kill.

THIRTY

Fläm, Bomb, Thank You, Mom

AN OLD LADY was not what I had in mind.

We walked about three blocks through crowds of tourists, past shops selling chocolate and moose sausage and little wooden troll souvenirs. (You would think anybody descended from Vikings would know better than to create *more* trolls.) As we passed a small grocery store, Mallory grabbed my arm with enough force to leave a bruise.

"It's *her*." She spat the word like a mouthful of poison.

"Who?" Sam asked. "Where?"

Mallory pointed to a store called Knit Pickers, where tourists were oohing and aahing over a sidewalk display of locally produced wool yarn. (Norway offered something for everyone.)

"The lady in white," Mallory said.

I spotted the one she meant. In the midst of the crowd stood an old woman with rounded shoulders and a hunched back. Her head craned forward like it was trying to get away from her body. Her white knit sweater was so fuzzy it might have been cotton candy, and cocked on her head was a matching floppy hat that made it hard to see her face. Dangling from one arm was a bag stuffed with yarn and knitting needles.

I didn't understand what had attracted Mallory's attention. I could easily have picked out ten other folks from the cruise ship who looked stranger. Then the old lady glanced in our direction. Her cloudy white eyes seemed to pierce right through me as if she'd ninja-chucked her knitting needles into my chest.

The crowd of tourists shifted, engulfing her, and the feeling passed.

I gulped. "Who was—?"

"Come on!" Mallory said. "We can't lose her!"

She dashed toward the knitting store. Samirah and I exchanged a worried look, then followed.

A senior citizen dressed in cotton candy shouldn't have been able to hobble very fast, but the lady was already two blocks away when we got to Knit Pickers. We ran after her, dodging tour groups, bicyclists, and guys carrying kayaks. Mallory didn't wait for us. By the time Sam and I caught up, she was clinging to a chain-link fence outside a small train depot, cursing as she scanned for her lost prey.

"You found the train," I noted.

Parked at the platform were half a dozen brightly painted old-fashioned railcars. Tourists were piling on board. The tracks wound from the station and up the hills into the ravine beyond.

"Where is she?" Mallory muttered.

"*Who* is she?" asked Sam.

"There!" Mallory pointed to the last car, where the cotton candy grandma was just getting on board.

"We need tickets," Mallory barked. "Quickly."

"We should get the others," Sam said. "We told them we'd rendezvous—"

"NO TIME!"

Mallory nearly mugged Sam for her Norwegian kroner. (Currency provided, of course, by the ever-resourceful Alex.) With much cursing and hand-waving, Mallory managed to purchase three tickets from the station attendant, then we bolted through the turnstile and made it aboard the last car just as the doors were closing.

The cabin was hot, stuffy, and packed with tourists. As the train rattled up the hillside, I felt queasier than I had since . . . well, the day before, roasting that dragon heart in Alfheim. It didn't help that I would occasionally catch snippets of bird chatter from outside—conversations I could still understand, mostly about where one could find the juiciest worms and bugs.

"Okay, Mallory, explain," Sam demanded. "Why are we following this old lady?"

Mallory slowly made her way up the aisle, checking the faces of the passengers. "She's the woman who got me killed. She's Loki."

Sam almost fell into an old man's lap. *"What?"*

Mallory gave her the quick version of what she'd told me a few days ago: how she'd set a car bomb, then regretted it, then gotten a visit from an old woman who convinced her to go back and disarm the bomb using a couple of super-useful daggers that turned out to be super-useless. And then *ka-boom.*

"But *Loki*?" Sam asked. "Are you sure?"

I understood the anxiety in Sam's voice. She'd been training to fight her dad, but she hadn't expected it to happen here, today. Fighting Loki was *not* a class in which you wanted a pop quiz.

"Who else could it be?" Mallory scowled. "She's not here. Let's try the next car."

"And if we catch him?" I asked. "Or her?"

Mallory unsheathed one of her knives. "I told you. That lady got me killed. I intend to return her daggers, points-first."

In the next car, tourists pressed against the windows, taking pictures of ravines, waterfalls, and quaint villages. Squares of farmland quilted the valley floor. Mountains cast shadows as sharp as sundial needles. Every time the train rounded a bend, the view seemed more scenic than before.

Samirah and I kept stopping, dumbfounded by the scenery outside, but Mallory had no interest in pretty stuff. The old lady wasn't in the second car, so we moved on.

In the next car, halfway up the aisle, Mallory froze. The last two rows on the right were arranged in a sort of conversation nook, with three backward-facing seats and three that faced forward. The rest of the cabin was jammed with people, but that little nook was empty except for the old lady. She sat facing our direction, humming as she knit, paying no attention to the scenery or to us.

A low growl started in Mallory's throat.

"Hold on." Sam grabbed her wrist. "There are a lot of mortals on this train. Can we at least *confirm* that this lady is Loki before we start killing and destroying?"

If *I* had tried to make that argument, I imagined Mallory would've hilt-bashed me in the groin. Since it was Sam asking, Mallory sheathed her dagger.

"Fine," she snapped. "We'll try to talk to her first. *Then* I'll kill her. Happy?"

"Delirious," Sam said.

That didn't describe my mood. Jumpy and confuzzled came closer. But I followed the girls as they approached the old lady in white.

Without looking up from her knitting, she said, "Hello, my dears! Please, sit."

Her voice surprised me. It sounded young and beautiful, like a radio announcer on a wartime propaganda station trying to convince enemy soldiers she was on their side. Norway Nancy, maybe. Or Fläm Flo.

Her face was hard to see—and not just because of the floppy hat. Her features glowed with a white light as fuzzy as her sweater. She seemed to be every age at once: a little girl, a teenager, a young lady, an old grandmother, all the faces existing in the present like the layers of a transparent onion. Maybe she hadn't been able to decide which glamour to wear today, so she'd just worn them all.

I glanced at my friends. We took a silent vote.

Sit? I asked.

Kill? Mallory asked.

Sit, Sam ordered.

We edged into the three seats across from the old lady. I kept one eye on her knitting needles, waiting for her to bust out some dual-wielding moves, but she just kept working on her fuzzy white yarn, making what looked like a cotton candy scarf.

"Well?" Mallory snapped. "What do you want?"

The old lady clucked disapprovingly. "My dear, is that any way to treat me?"

"I should treat you worse, Loki," Mallory growled. "You got me killed!"

"Mallory," Sam said. "This isn't Loki."

The relief was obvious in her voice. I wasn't sure how Sam knew, but I hoped she was right. There wasn't room in this train car to wield a blazing spear of light or a singing broadsword.

Mallory's face mottled red. "What do you mean *not Loki?*"

"Mallory Audrey Keen," the old woman chided. "Did you really think, for all these years, I was *Loki?* For shame. Few beings in the Nine Worlds hate Loki as much as I do."

I considered that good news, but when I met Sam's eyes I could tell she had the same question I did: *Audrey?*

Mallory shifted, her hands on the hilts of her daggers like she was a downhill skier approaching a difficult jump. "You were there in Belfast," she insisted. "In 1972. You gave me these useless knives, said I should run back and disarm the bomb on that school bus."

Sam caught her breath. "School bus? You targeted a *school bus?*"

Mallory did her best to avoid our eyes. Her face was the color of cherry juice.

"Don't be too hard on her," said the old lady. "She was told the bus would be full of soldiers, not children. It was July twenty-first. The Irish Republican Army was planting bombs all across Belfast against the British—retaliation for retaliation, as it usually goes. Mallory's friends wanted in on the action."

"Two of my friends had been shot by the police the month before," Mallory murmured. "They were fifteen and sixteen. I wanted revenge." She glanced up. "But Loki was one of the lads in our gang that day. He *must* have been. I've heard his voice since then, taunting me in dreams. I know how his power can tug—"

"Oh, yes." The old lady continued to knit. "And do you hear his voice right now?"

Mallory blinked. "I . . . I suppose not."

The old lady smiled. "You're correct, my dear. Loki *was* there that Friday in July, disguised as one of you, egging you on to see how much mischief he could create. You were the angriest of the bunch, Mallory—the doer, not the talker. He knew just how to manipulate you."

Mallory stared at the floorboards. She swayed with the rattling of the train. Behind us, tourists gasped with delight every time a new vista came into view.

"Uh, ma'am?" I didn't usually insert myself into conversations with creepy godly ladies, but I felt bad for Mallory. No matter what she'd done in her past, she seemed to be shrinking under the woman's words. I remembered that feeling well from my most recent dream about Loki.

"If you're not Loki," I said, "which is great, by the way, then who are you? Mallory said you were there, too, the day she died. After she set the bomb, you appeared and told her—"

The intensity of the woman's gaze pinned me to my seat. Within her white irises, gold pupils glowed like tiny suns.

"I told Mallory what she already suspected," the woman said. "That the bus would be full of children, and that she had been used. I encouraged her to follow her conscience."

"You got me killed!" Mallory said.

"I urged you to become a hero," the woman said calmly. "And you did. Around twenty other bombs went off in Belfast on July 21, 1972. It became known as Bloody Friday. How much worse would it have been if you hadn't acted?"

Mallory scowled. "But the knives—"

"—were my gifts to you," said the woman, "so that you would die with blades in your hands and go to Valhalla. I suspected they would be useful to you someday, but—"

"*Someday?*" Mallory demanded. "You might have mentioned that part before I got myself blown up trying to cut bomb wires with them!"

The woman's frown seemed to ripple outward through her layers of ages—the little girl, the young woman, the crone. "My powers of prophecy are short-range, Mallory. I can only see what will happen within twenty-four hours, give or take. That's why I'm here. You will need those knives. *Today.*"

Sam sat forward. "You mean . . . to help us retrieve Kvasir's Mead?"

The woman nodded. "You have good instincts, Samirah al-Abbas. The knives—"

"Why should we listen to you?" Mallory blurted out. "Whatever you tell us to do, it'll probably get us killed!"

The woman laid her knitting needles across her lap. "My dear, I am the goddess of foresight and the immediate future. I would never tell you what to do. I am only here to give you the information you need to make a good choice. As to why you should listen to me, I hope you would do so because I love you."

"*LOVE ME?*" Mallory looked at us in disbelief, like *Are you hearing this?* "Old woman, I don't even know who you *are!*"

"Of course you do, dear."

The woman's form shimmered. Before us sat a middle-aged woman of regal beauty, her long hair the same color as Mallory's, plaited down both shoulders. Her hat became a war helm of white metal, glowing and flickering like trapped neon gas. Her white dress seemed made of the same stuff, only woven into gentle folds. In her knitting bag, her fuzzy yarn had become swirling puffs of mist. The goddess, I realized, had been knitting with clouds.

"I am Frigg," she said, "queen of the Aesir. And I am your mother, Mallory Keen."

THIRTY-ONE

Mallory Gets Nuts

YOU KNOW how it goes. You're minding your own business, taking a train up a ravine in the middle of Norway, when an old lady with a bag of knitting supplies introduces herself as your godly mother.

If I had a krone for every time that happened . . .

When Frigg broke the news, the train screeched to a stop as if the locomotive itself were asking *SAY WHAT?*

Over the intercom, an announcement crackled in English: something about a photo opportunity with a waterfall. I didn't know why that rated a stop, since we'd already passed about a hundred scenic waterfalls, but all the tourists got up and piled out of the car until we were alone: just Sam, Mallory, me, and the Queen of the Universe.

Mallory had been frozen for a good twenty seconds. When the aisle was clear, she shot to her feet, marched to the end of the car and back again, then shouted at Frigg, "You don't just ANNOUNCE something like that out of NOWHERE!"

Yelling at a goddess isn't generally a good idea. You run the risk of getting impaled, zapped, or eaten by giant house cats. (It's a Freya thing. Don't ask.) Frigg didn't seem bothered, though. Her calmness made me question how she could be related to Mallory.

Now that Frigg's appearance had resolved into one clear image, I saw faint scars under her white-and-gold eyes, scoring her cheeks like the tracks of tears. On an otherwise divinely perfect face, the streaks were jarring, especially since they reminded me of another goddess with similar scars: Sigyn, the strange silent wife of Loki.

"Mallory," Frigg said. "Daughter—"

"Don't call me that."

"You already know it is true. You've had suspicions for years."

Samirah gulped, as if she'd forgotten how to swallow for the past few minutes. "Wait. You are Frigg. Wife of Odin. Mrs. Odin. *The* Frigg."

The goddess chuckled. "As far as I know, dear, I'm the only Frigg. It's not a very popular name."

"But . . . *nobody* ever sees you." Sam patted her clothes like she was looking for an autograph pen. "I mean . . . *never*. I don't know a single Valkyrie or einherji who has ever met you. And Mallory is your *daughter?*"

Mallory threw her hands in the air. "Will you stop fangirling, Valkyrie?"

"But don't you see—?"

"—another deadbeat parent? Yeah, I do." Keen scowled at the goddess. "If you're my ma, you're no better than my da."

"Oh, child." Frigg's voice turned heavy. "Your father wasn't always as broken as when you knew him. I'm sorry you never got to see him the way I did, before the drinking and the rage."

"Wouldn't that have been peachy." Mallory blinked her red-tinged eyes. "But since you apologized, I suppose all's forgiven!"

"Mallory," Sam chided, "how can you be so callous? This is your *mom*. Frigg is your mom!"

"Right. I heard."

"But . . ." Sam shook her head. "But that's *good*!"

"I'll be the judge of that." Mallory plopped back into her seat. She crossed her arms and glared at the clouds in her mother's knitting bag.

I tried to see similarities between mother and daughter. Beyond the red hair, I couldn't. Frigg wrapped herself in gentle white clouds. She radiated calm, cool, and melancholy. Mallory was more like a dust devil, all agitation and fury. Despite the goddess's war helm, I couldn't imagine Frigg dual-wielding knives any more than I could imagine Mallory sitting quietly, knitting a cloud scarf.

I understood why Mallory was angry. But I also got the wistful yearning in Samirah's voice. Sam and I had both lost our moms. We would have given anything to have them back. *Gaining* a mom, even one who had waited fifty-odd years to reveal herself . . . That wasn't something to throw away lightly.

From the left side of the train, music drifted in through the open windows. Somewhere, a woman was singing.

Frigg turned her ear toward the sound. "Ah . . . that's just a mortal singer performing for the tourists. She's pretending to be a spirit of the waterfall. She's not a real nøkk."

I shuddered. "Good."

"Indeed," Frigg said. "You have quite enough on your plate today with the giant's thralls."

Sam leaned forward. "Giant's thralls? As in slaves?"

"I'm afraid so," Frigg said. "The thralls of the giant Baugi guard the mead. To defeat them, you will need the stone in my daughter's pocket."

Mallory's hand moved to the side of her jacket. I'd forgotten she was carrying the whetstone. Apparently, she had, too.

"I don't like the idea of fighting slaves," Mallory said. "I also don't like you calling me *daughter*. You haven't earned the right. Not yet. Maybe not ever."

On Frigg's cheeks, the tear scars glistened like veins of silver. "Mallory . . . *ever* is a very long time. I've learned not to try seeing that far into the future. Whenever I attempt it . . ." She sighed. "Always tragedy, like what happened to my poor son Balder."

Balder, I thought. *Which one was Balder?* Dealing with the Norse gods, I really needed a program with glossy color pictures of all the players, along with their season stats.

"He died?" I guessed.

Sam elbowed me, though I thought it was a perfectly legitimate question. "He was the most handsome of the gods," Sam explained. "Frigg had a dream that he would die."

"And so I tried to prevent it." Frigg picked up her needles. She knitted a stitch of cloud vapor. "I exacted promises from everything in the Nine Worlds not to harm my son. Each type of stone. Each type of metal. Salt water. Freshwater. Air. Even fire. Fire was hard to convince. But there are many, many things in the Nine Worlds. Toward the end . . . I'll admit, I got tired and absent-minded. I neglected one tiny plant, mistletoe. When I realized my oversight, I thought *Oh, well, it doesn't matter. Mistletoe is much too small and insignificant to hurt Balder.* Then, of course, Loki found out—"

"I remember this part," Mallory said, still glaring at the

bag of clouds. "Loki tricked a blind god into killing Balder with a mistletoe dart. Which means Loki murdered . . . my brother."

She tasted the word, trying it out. From her expression, I guessed she didn't like it. "So, *Ma*, do you fail all your children spectacularly? Is that a thing with you?"

Frigg frowned, and a hint of storm darkened her cloud-white irises. I wished the seats were wider so I could scoot away from Mallory.

"The death of Balder was a hard lesson," said the goddess. "I learned that even I, queen of the Aesir, have limits. If I concentrate, I can glean the destiny of any living thing. I can even manipulate their wyrd to some extent. But *only* in the short term—twenty-four hours, sometimes less. If I try to look beyond that, to shape someone's long-term fate . . ." She separated her needles. Her knitting unraveled into wisps of smoke.

"You may hate me, Mallory," Frigg said. "But it is too painful for me to visit my children, to see what will befall them and not be able to change it. That is why I only appear in times when I *know* I can make a difference. Today, for you, is one of those times."

Mallory seemed to be struggling internally—her anger battling her curiosity.

"All right, I'll bite," she relented. "What's my future?"

Frigg pointed out the window on our right. My vision telescoped, zooming across the valley. If I hadn't been sitting down, I would have fallen. I guessed Frigg was enhancing my sight, giving me Heimdall-level clarity for just a moment.

At the base of a mountain, a waterfall split against a granite promontory as if it were the prow of a ship. In the center of the rock, between twin white curtains of water, stood a massive set of iron doors. And spread out before those doors, on a strip of land between the two rivers, was a field of ripe wheat. Nine burly men, wearing only iron neck collars and loincloths, worked the field, swinging their scythes like a squadron of grim reapers.

My vision snapped back to normal. Looking across the valley, I could now just make out the spot where the waterfall split on the rock—maybe ten miles away.

"That is the place," Frigg said. "And there is the path you must use to reach it."

She pointed to the base of the railroad tracks. Just out the window, a streak of rubble zigzagged down the side of the cliff. Calling it a *path* was generous. I would've called it a *landslide*.

"Today, Mallory," the goddess announced, "you will need those daggers, and your wits. You are the key to retrieving Kvasir's Mead."

Mallory and Sam both looked queasy. I guessed they'd also gotten a free trial of Heimdall-Vision.

"I don't suppose you could be any vaguer?" Mallory asked.

Frigg gave her a sad smile. "You have your father's fierce spirit, my dear. I hope you can master it and use it, as he could not. You have everything you need to retrieve the mead, but there is one last gift I can give you—something that will help you when you finally face Loki. As I learned when I underestimated mistletoe . . . even the smallest thing can make a vast difference."

She reached into her knitting bag and pulled out a small wrinkled brown orb. . . . A chestnut? Walnut? One of those big nuts. She pulled apart the two halves, showing that the shell was empty, then fit them back together. "If Magnus defeats Loki in the flyting, you will have to imprison the trickster in this shell."

"Wait, *if*?" I asked. "Can't you see my future?"

The goddess fixed me with her strange white gaze. "The future is a brittle thing, Magnus Chase. Sometimes merely revealing someone's destiny can cause that destiny to shatter."

I gulped. I felt like a high-pitched tone was reverberating through my bones, ready to crack them like glass. "Okay. Let's not shatter anything, then."

"If you defeat Loki," Frigg continued, "bring him back to the Aesir, and we will deal with him."

From the tone of Frigg's voice, I doubted the Aesir planned on throwing Loki a welcome-back party.

She threw the nut.

Mallory caught it in her fingertips. "Bit small for a god, isn't it?"

"It won't be if Magnus succeeds," Frigg said. "The ship *Naglfar* has not yet sailed. You have at least twenty-four hours. Perhaps even forty-eight. After that . . ."

Blood roared in my ears. I didn't see how we could do everything we needed to do in a day—or even two. I *definitely* didn't see how I could insult Loki down to the size of a walnut.

The train's whistle blew—a plaintive sound like a bird calling for its dead mate. (And you can trust me on that, because I understood birdcalls.) Tourists began piling back onto the train.

"I must go," Frigg said. "And so must you."

"You just *got* here." Mallory's scowl deepened. Her expression hardened. "But fine. Whatever. Leave."

"Oh, my dear." Frigg's eyes misted over, the light dimming in her golden pupils. "I am never far, even if you do not see me. We will meet again. . . ." A new tear trickled down the scarred path of her left cheek. "Until then, trust your friends. You are right: they are more important than any magic items. And whatever happens, whether you choose to believe me or not, I love you."

The goddess dissolved, knitting bag and all, leaving a sheen of condensation on the seat.

The tourists piled back into the train car. Mallory stared at the moist impression left by her godly mother, as if hoping the water droplets might reconstitute into something that made sense: a target, an enemy, even a bomb. A mother who showed up out of nowhere and proclaimed *I love you*—that was something no knives, no wits, no walnut shell could help her conquer.

I wondered if I could say anything to make her feel better. I doubted it. Mallory was about action, not talk.

Apparently, Sam reached the same conclusion. "We should go," she said, "before—"

The train lurched into motion. Unfortunately, tourists were still shuffling to their seats, blocking the aisles. We'd never be able to muscle our way to the door before the train got back up to full speed and left the mountainside trail far behind.

Sam glanced at the open window on our right. "Another exit?"

"That's suicidal," I said.

"That's typical," Mallory corrected.

She led the way, leaping out the window of the moving train.

THIRTY-TWO

Mallory Also Gets Fruit

DON'T GET me wrong.

If you're going to fall down the side of a mountain, Norway is a beautiful place to do it. We skidded past lovely creeks, bounced off majestic trees, fell from imposing cliffs, and tumbled through fields of fragrant wildflowers. Somewhere off to my left, Mallory Keen cursed in Gaelic. Somewhere behind me, Samirah kept yelling, "Magnus, take my hand! Magnus!"

I couldn't see her, so I couldn't comply. Nor did I understand why she wanted to hold hands as we fell to our demise.

I shot from the side of a ridge, pinballed off a spruce, and finally rolled to a stop on a more level slope, my head coming to rest against something fuzzy and warm. Through a haze of pain, I found myself staring up at the brown-and-white face of a goat.

"Otis?" I mumbled.

Baaaaaa, said the goat.

I could understand his meaning, not because he was Thor's talking goat Otis, but because regular goat bleats now made as much sense to me as bird chirps. He'd said *No, stupid. I'm Theodore. And my belly is not a pillow.*

"Sorry," I mumbled.

The goat got to his feet and capered off, depriving me of my comfy headrest.

I sat up, groaning. I did a self-check and found nothing broken. Amazing. Frigg really knew how to suggest the safest trails to hurtle down at life-threatening speeds.

Samirah swooped down from the sky, her green hijab rippling around her face. "Magnus, didn't you hear me calling? You didn't have to *fall*! I was going to *fly* you both down here."

"Ah." That awkward moment when you jump out a window because your friend jumped out a window, then you remember that your other friend can fly. "When you say it like that, it does make more sense. Where's Mallory?"

"*Cailleach!*" she shouted from somewhere nearby.

I recognized the word: Gaelic for *witch* or *hag*, which I assumed Mallory was using as a term of endearment for her newly discovered maternal unit. In case you're curious, the word is pronounced: *Ki*— followed by clearing a large amount of mucus from your throat. Try it at home, kids! It's fun!

Finally, I spotted Mallory. She had fused herself with a blackberry bush, her head wedged firmly between its two largest boughs, its thorny branches woven into her clothes. She was hanging upside down with her left arm bent at a strange angle.

"Hold on!" I yelled, which in retrospect was dumb, since she obviously wasn't going anywhere.

Sam and I managed to extricate her from her new fruit-bearing friend. Then I summoned the power of Frey and healed a thousand small cuts and a fractured bone, though I couldn't do much about her wounded pride or her foul mood.

"Better?" I asked.

She spat a leaf from her mouth. "Compared to five minutes ago? Yeah. Compared to this morning, when I didn't know that cailleach was my ma? Not so much."

She pulled the walnut from her pocket. It had left quite a bruise against her hip during her tumble down the mountain, but the shell itself was undamaged. Mallory seemed to take this as a personal affront. She stuck the nut in her jacket along with the whetstone, muttering various insults about the walnut's parentage.

Sam reached out to pat Mallory's shoulder, then clearly thought better of it. "I—I know you're angry."

"Yeah?" Mallory snapped. "What gave it away?"

"But . . . *Frigg*," Sam said, as if the name alone was an entire persuasive essay with three examples per paragraph and a conclusion. "You see the similarities, don't you?"

Mallory flexed her healed arm. "What similarities would those be, Valkyrie? Choose your words carefully."

Sam ignored the threat. When she spoke, her voice was full of awe. "Frigg's the power behind the throne! Odin's the king, but he's always traveling. Frigg controls Asgard. She does it without anybody even noticing. You've heard the story about when Odin was exiled, right?"

Sam looked at me for support.

I had no clue what she was referring to, so I said, "Yep, absolutely."

Sam pointed at me like *See? Magnus knows what's up!*

"Odin's brothers Vili and Ve took over in his absence," she said. "But to do so, they had to marry Frigg. Different kings. Same queen. Asgard got along just fine, because Frigg was the one in charge."

Mallory frowned. "You're saying I'm like my ma because I'll hook up with anybody to get power?"

"No!" Sam blushed. "I'm saying Frigg is always below the radar, never seen, but she is the cement that holds the Aesir together."

Mallory tapped her foot. "Now you're comparing me to easily ignored cement."

"I'm saying you're like your mother because you're the Frigg of floor nineteen. T.J. and Halfborn never would have become friends if you hadn't goaded them into it. They used to hate each other."

I blinked. "They did?"

"True enough," Mallory muttered. "When I arrived—ugh. They were insufferable. I mean even *more* insufferable."

"Exactly," said Sam. "You made them a *team*. Then, when Odin disguised himself as an einherji, do you think it was an *accident* he chose to live on your floor? You're Frigg's chosen agent in Valhalla. The All-Father wanted to see what you were made of."

I hadn't thought about that for a while. When I first arrived in Valhalla, Odin had been slumming with us on floor nineteen disguised as X the half-troll. X had liked dogs, was good in battle, and never said much. I liked Odin a lot better in that form.

"Huh," Mallory grunted. "You really believe that?"

"I do," Sam said. "And when Magnus came along, where did he end up? On *your* team. Same with Alex. Same with me." Sam spread her hands. "So, excuse me if I fangirled a little when I met Frigg, but she has *always* been my favorite Aesir. She's kind of the *anti*-Loki. She keeps things together while

Loki is trying to pick them apart. And knowing you're her daughter . . . well, that makes perfect sense to me. I am even more honored to fight at your side."

More red splotches appeared on Mallory's face, but this time I didn't think they were from anger. "Well, Valkyrie, you've got your father's silver tongue. I don't see any reason to kill you for what you've said."

That was Mallory's way of saying *thank you.*

Sam inclined her head. "Then let's find Kvasir's Mead, shall we?"

"One more thing," I said, because I couldn't help myself. "Mallory, if your middle name is Audrey, and your initials are *M. A. K.—*"

She raised an index finger. "Don't say it, Beantown."

"We are totally calling you Mack now."

Mallory fumed. "My friends in Belfast used to call me that. *Constantly.*"

That wasn't a *no*, so I decided we had permission.

The next hour we spent trekking across the valley floor. Sam tried to text Alex to let her know we were okay, but she couldn't get a signal. No doubt the Norse god of cell-phone service had decreed *THOU SHALT HAVE NO BARS!* and was now laughing at our expense.

We walked over a creaky wooden bridge spanning white-water rapids. We navigated a pasture full of goats who were not Otis. We passed from frigid shadows into baking sunlight as we moved in and out of the woods. All the while, I did my best to tune out the voices of birds, squirrels, and goats, none of whom had anything good to say about us walking through their territory. Slowly, we made our way toward the split waterfall we'd seen from the train. Even in this colossal countryside, it was an easy landmark.

We stopped once for lunch—consisting only of some trail mix Mallory happened to have, along with a few wild blackberries we picked, and water from a stream so cold it made my teeth hurt. Sam didn't join us, of course. She just did her noon prayers on a carpet of fluffy green grass.

I'll say this about Ramadan: it cut down my impulse to whine. Whenever I started thinking I had it rough, I remembered that Samirah was doing everything I was doing but without food or water.

We trekked up the other side of the valley, using the twin rivers from the waterfall as our guidelines. At last, as the falls loomed close, we heard harsh rasping sounds coming from over the ridge in front of us—*whisk, whisk, whisk,* like metal files being scraped across bricks.

I recalled the vision Frigg had shown us of nine burly dudes with scythes. I thought, *Magnus, if those guys are over that hill, you might want a plan.*

"So, what exactly is a thrall?" I asked my friends.

Mallory wiped her brow. Our trip through the valley hadn't done her fair complexion any favors. She'd be suffering a bad case of sunburn if we lived through the day. "Like I said earlier, a thrall is a slave. The ones we're going to face—I'm pretty sure they're giants."

I tried to square that with what I knew about giants, which, granted, wasn't much. "So . . . jotuns enslave other jotuns?"

Sam wrinkled her nose in distaste. "All the time. Humans gave up the practice centuries ago—"

"Some might dispute that," Mallory grumbled.

"Fair point," Sam agreed. "What I mean is, giants do it the way Vikings used to. Clans go to war against one another. They take prisoners of war and declare them personal property. Sometimes, the thralls can earn their freedom, sometimes not. Depends on the master."

"Then maybe we can free these guys," I suggested. "Get them on our side."

Mallory snorted. "Unbeatable guardians of the mead—unless you offer them their freedom, in which case they're pushovers!"

"I'm just saying—"

"Won't be that easy, Beantown. Let's stop dreaming and start fighting."

She led the way over the hill, which struck me as only slightly less reckless than jumping out of a moving train.

THIRTY-THREE

We Devise a Horribly Fabulous Plan

SO MUCH for strategy.

We popped over the ridge and found ourselves at the edge of a wheat field several acres across. The wheat grew taller than us, which would have made it perfect for sneaking through, except that the guys working the field were taller still—nine giants, all swinging scythes. The setup reminded me of a video game level I'd played with T.J. once, but I had no wish to try it with my actual body.

Each thrall had an iron collar around his neck. Otherwise they wore nothing but loincloths and a whole lot of muscles. Their bronze skin, shaggy hair, and beards all dripped with perspiration. Despite their size and strength, they seemed to be having a hard time cutting the wheat. The stalks just bent against their scythe blades with a whisking sound like laughter, then sprang back up again. Because of this, the thralls looked almost as miserable as they smelled . . . and they smelled like Halfborn Gunderson's sandals.

Beyond the field loomed the wishbone-shaped waterfall. In the cliff face that jutted from the middle was a set of massive iron doors.

Before you could say *Darn it, Mallory*, the nearest thrall— who had a mop of red hair even more impressive than Miss

Keen's—sniffed the air, stood up straight, and turned to face us. "Ho, ho!"

The other eight stopped working and turned toward us as well, adding, "Ho, ho! Ho, ho! Ho, ho!" like a flock of strange birds.

"What have we here?" asked the redheaded thrall.

"What indeed?" asked another with an impressively tattooed face.

"What indeed?" asked a third, maybe just in case we hadn't heard the tattooed guy.

"Kill them?" Red polled his buddies.

"Yes, probably kill them," Tattoo agreed.

"Hold on!" I yelled before they could take a vote, which I had a feeling would be unanimous. "We're here for a very important reason—"

"—which does *not* entail our deaths," Sam added.

"Good point, Sam!" I nodded vigorously, and the thralls all nodded along, apparently impressed by my earnestness. "Tell them why we're here, Mack!"

Mallory gave me her standard I'll-kill-you-later-with-both-knives look. "Well, Beantown, we're here to—to help these fine gentlemen!"

The nearest thrall, Red, frowned at his scythe. Its curved iron blade was almost as corroded as Jack had been when I first pulled him out of the Charles River.

"Don't know how you could help," Red said. "Unless you could harvest the field for us? Master only gives us these dull blades."

The others muttered in agreement.

"And the wheat stalks are as hard as flint!" said Tattoo.

"Harder!" said another thrall. "And the wheat keeps growing back as soon as we cut it! We can only take a break when all the wheat is cut, but . . . we can't ever finish!"

Red nodded. "It's almost like . . ." His face darkened with effort. "Like Master doesn't *want* us to ever take a break."

The others nodded, pondering this theory.

"Ah, yes, your master!" Mallory said. "Who is your master again?"

"Baugi!" said Red. "Great thane of the stone giants! He's off in the north getting ready for Doomsday." He said this as if Baugi had just gone to the store to get some milk.

"He is a hard master," Mallory noted.

"Yes!" Tattoo agreed.

"No," Red said.

The others chimed in. "No. No, not at all! Kind and good!"

They glanced suspiciously from side to side, as if their master might be hiding in the wheat.

Sam cleared her throat. "Does Baugi give you any other duties?"

"Oh, yes!" said a thrall in the back. "We guard the doors! So no one can take Suttung's mead or free Suttung's prisoner!"

"The prisoner?" I asked. "Suttung?"

Nine thrall heads nodded solemnly. They would have made an excellent kindergarten class if the teacher could have found large enough coloring books and crayons.

"Suttung is the master's brother," said Red. "He owns the mead and the prisoner in the cave."

Another thrall shrieked. "You are not supposed to say what is in the cave!"

"Right!" Red turned even redder. "Suttung owns the mead and the prisoner who—who may or may not be in the cave."

The other thralls nodded, apparently satisfied Red had thrown us off the scent.

"If anyone tries to get past us," said Tattoo, "we get to take a break from cutting wheat, just long enough to kill the trespassers."

"So," Red said, "if you are not here to cut the wheat, then do we get to kill you? That would be helpful! We could use a good killing break!"

"Killing break?" asked a guy in the back.

"Killing break!" said another.

The rest took up the call.

Nine giants shouting *killing break* tended to make me a little jumpy. I thought about pulling out Jack and having him cut the wheat for the thralls, but that would still leave us facing nine big dudes who were under orders to kill trespassers. Jack might be able to slay nine giants before they slew us, but I still didn't like the idea of chopping down thralls when I could be chopping down their masters.

"What if we freed you?" I asked. "Just for the sake of argument. Would you turn on your master? Would you run away to your homeland?"

The thralls got dreamy looks in their eyes.

"We might do those things," Tattoo agreed.

"And would you help us?" Sam asked. "Or even just leave us alone?"

"Oh, no!" Red said. "No, first we would kill you. We love killing humans."

The other eight nodded enthusiastically.

Mallory glared at me like *I told you so.* "Also for the sake of argument, noble thralls, what if we fought you? Could we kill you?"

Red laughed. "That is very funny! No, we are under strong magic spells. Baugi is a great sorcerer! We cannot be killed by anyone except each other."

"And we like each other!" said another thrall.

"Yes!" said a third.

The giants started to bring it in for a group hug, then seemed to remember they were holding scythes.

"Well, then!" Mallory's eyes gleamed like she had a wonderful idea I was going to hate. "I know exactly how we can help you!"

She fished around in her jacket pocket and brought out the whetstone. "Ta-da!"

The thralls looked less than impressed.

"It is a rock," Red said.

"Oh, no, my friend," Mallory said. "This whetstone can magically sharpen *any* blade and make your work much easier. May I show you?"

She held out her empty hand. After a few minutes of deep thought, Red flinched. "Oh, you want my scythe?"

"To sharpen it," Sam explained.

"So . . . I can work faster?"

"Exactly."

"Huh." Red handed over his weapon.

The scythe was huge, so it took all three of us to do the job. I held the handle. Sam kept the top of the blade flat against the ground while Mallory scraped the whetstone along the edges. Sparks flew. Rust vanished. In a couple of passes, both sides of the scythe blade glinted like new in the sunlight.

"Next scythe, please!" Mallory said.

Soon, all nine thralls had shiny sharpened weapons.

"Now," Mallory said, "try them out on your field!"

The thralls went to work, cutting through the wheat like it was wrapping paper. In a matter of minutes, they had reaped the entire field.

"Amazing!" said Red.

"Hooray!" said Tattoo.

The other thralls cheered and hooted.

"We can finally have water!" said one.

"I can eat lunch!" said another.

"I have needed to pee for five hundred years!" said a third.

"We can kill these trespassers now!" said a fourth.

I hated that guy.

"Ah, yes." Red frowned at us. "Sorry, my new friends, but by helping us, you have clearly trespassed on our master's field, and so you are not our friends and we must kill you."

I wasn't a fan of this giantish logic. Then again, we'd just given nine huge enemies sharper weapons to kill us with, so I wasn't in a position to criticize.

"Hold on, boys!" Mallory shouted. She waggled the whetstone between her fingertips. "Before you kill us, you should decide who gets the stone!"

Red frowned. "Who gets . . . the stone?"

"Well, yes," Mallory said. "Look, the field is already growing back!"

Sure enough, the wheat stubble was already up to the giants' ankles.

"You'll need the whetstone to keep your blades sharp," Mallory continued. "Otherwise they'll just get dull again. The wheat will eventually grow back as high as it was before, and you won't have any more breaks."

"And that would be bad," Red concluded.

"Right," Mallory agreed. "You can't share custody of the stone, either. It can only be owned by one of you."

"Really?" said Tattoo. "But why?"

Mallory shrugged. "Those are the rules."

Red nodded sagely. "I think we can trust her. She has red hair."

"Well, then!" Mallory said. "Who gets it?"

All nine thralls shouted, "ME!"

"Tell you what," Mallory said, "how about a toss-up? Whoever catches it wins."

"That sounds fair," Red agreed.

I saw where this was going a little too late. Sam said uneasily, "Mallory . . ."

Mallory tossed the stone above the thralls' heads. All nine rushed in to catch it, piling into each other while holding sharp, long, awkward blades. In such a situation, what you end up with is a large pile of dead thralls.

Sam stared wide-eyed at the scene. "Wow. Mallory, that was—"

"Did you have a better idea?" Mallory snapped.

"I'm not criticizing. I just—"

"I killed nine giants with one stone." Mallory's voice sounded hoarse. She blinked as if sparks from the whetstone were still flying in her eyes. "I think that's pretty good for a day's work. Now come on. Let's open those doors."

THIRTY-FOUR

First Prize: A Giant!
Second Prize: Two Giants!

I DIDN'T think Mallory was as okay with killing the thralls as she let on.

When we failed to open the doors with Jack, brute force, or any amount of yelling *open sesame*, Mallory screamed in rage. She kicked one of the doors, broke her foot, then hopped off cursing and crying.

Samirah frowned. "Magnus, go talk to her."

"Why me?" I didn't like the way Mallory was slashing the air with her knives.

"Because you can heal her foot," Sam said, annoyingly sensible as usual. "And I need time to think about this door problem."

That didn't strike me as a good trade-off, but I went, Jack floating along next to me, saying, "Ah, Norway! Good memories! Ah, a pile of dead thralls! Good memories!"

I stopped just out of reach of Mallory's knives. "Hey, Mack, can I heal that foot for you?"

She glowered. "Fine. Seems to be Heal Mallory's Stupid Injuries day."

I knelt and put my hands on her boot. She cursed when I mended the bones, popping them back into place with a burst of summery magic.

I rose warily. "How you doing?"

"Well, you just healed me, didn't you?"

"I wasn't talking about the foot." I gestured toward the dead thralls.

She scowled. "I didn't see any other way. Did you?"

In truth, I didn't. I was pretty sure Mallory's solution was the way we'd been *meant* to use the whetstone. The gods, or our wyrd, or some twisted sense of Nornish humor had dictated that we would sail halfway across the world, undergo many hardships to win a gray rock, then use it to trick nine miserable thralls into killing one another.

"Sam and I couldn't have done it," I admitted. "You're the doer, just like Frigg said."

Jack floated over, his blade shuddering and warbling like a hand saw. "Frigg? Oh, man, I don't like Frigg. She's too quiet. Too devious. Too—"

"She's my ma," Mallory grumbled.

"Oh, *that* Frigg!" Jack said. "Yeah, she's great."

"I hate her," Mallory said.

"Gods, me too!" Jack commiserated.

"Jack," I said, "why don't you go check on Sam? Maybe you can advise her on getting through those doors. Or you could sing to her. I know she'd love that."

"Yeah? Cool!" Jack zoomed off to serenade Sam, which meant Sam would want to hit me later, except it was Ramadan, so she had to be nice to me. Wow, I was a bad person.

Mallory tested her weight on her foot. It seemed to work fine. I did good healing for a bad person.

"I'll be okay," she said, without much confidence. "Just been a lot for one day. Learning about Frigg, on top of . . . everything else."

I thought about Mallory and Halfborn's constant arguments on the ship. I did not understand their relationship, but I knew they needed each other as much as Hearthstone needed Blitzen or our Viking boat needed to be yellow. It didn't make much sense. It wasn't easy. But it was just the way things had to be.

"It's eating him up inside," I told her. "You two arguing."

"Well, he's a fool." She hesitated. "I mean . . . assuming you're talking about Gunderson."

"Smooth, Mack," I said.

"Shut up, Beantown." She marched off to check on Sam.

At the doors, Jack was trying to help by suggesting songs he could sing to inspire new ideas for getting inside: "Knockin' on Heaven's Door," "I Got the Keys," or "Break on Through (to the Other Side)."

"How about none of the above?" Sam said.

" 'None of the Above' . . ." Jack mused. "Is that by Stevie Wonder?"

"How's it going, guys?" I asked. I didn't know if it was physically possible to strangle a magic sword, but I didn't want to see Sam try.

"Not well," she admitted. "There's no lock. No hinges. No keyhole. Jack refuses to try cutting through the iron—"

"Hey," Jack said. "These doors are a *masterpiece*. Look at that craftsmanship! Besides, I'm pretty sure they're magic."

Sam rolled her eyes. "If we had a drill, maybe we could make a hole in the iron and I could slither through as a snake. But since we don't have a drill—"

From the other side of the doors, a woman's voice called, "Have you tried prying apart the seam?"

We all jumped back. The voice had sounded very close to the door, as if the woman had been listening with her ear pressed to the metal.

Jack quivered and glowed. "She speaks! Oh, beautiful door, speak again!"

"I'm not the door," said the voice. "I am Gunlod, daughter of Suttung."

"Oh," Jack said. "That's disappointing."

Mallory put her mouth to the door. "You're Suttung's daughter? Are you guarding the prisoner?"

"No," Gunlod said. "I *am* the prisoner. I've been locked in here all by myself for . . . Actually, I've lost track of time. Centuries? Years? Which is longer?"

I turned to my friends and used sign language, which was helpful even when there wasn't a Hearthstone around. *Trap?*

Mallory made a V and whacked the back of her hand against her forehead, meaning *stupid*. Or *duh*.

Not much choice, Sam signed. Then she called through the doors, "Miss Gunlod, I don't suppose there's a latch on the inside? Or a bolt you could turn?"

"Well, it wouldn't be a very good prison if my father put a latch or a bolt where I could reach it. He usually just yanks the doors open with my Uncle Baugi. It takes both of them with their super giant strength. You don't have two people out there with super giant strength, by chance?"

Sam sized me up. "I'm afraid not."

I stuck out my tongue at her. "Miss Gunlod, is Kvasir's Mead in there with you, by chance?"

"A little," she said. "Most of it was stolen by Odin a long

time ago." She sighed. "What a charmer he was! I let him get away, which of course is why my father locked me up. But there's still some left at the bottom of the last vat. It's my father's most prized possession. I suppose you want it?"

"That would be great," I admitted.

Mallory elbowed me in the ribs. "If you could help us, Miss Gunlod, we'd be happy to free you, too."

"How sweet!" said Gunlod. "But I'm afraid my freedom is impossible. My father and my uncle have bound my life force to this cave. That's part of my punishment. I would die if I tried to leave."

Sam winced. "That seems a bit harsh."

"Yes." Gunlod sighed. "Though I did give the most valuable elixir in the Nine Worlds to our greatest enemy, so . . . there's that. My son tried to undo the spell on the cave, but even he failed. And he's the god Bragi!"

Mallory's eyes widened. "Your son is Bragi, god of poetry?"

"That's him." Gunlod's voice filled with pride. "He was born here, nine months after Odin visited me. I may have mentioned, Odin was a charmer."

"Bragi," I said. "Is he braggy?"

Mallory signed, *Don't ruin things, idiot.* "Magnus is only kidding. Of course he knows that *brag* literally means to recite poetry. Which is why Bragi is a lovely name. Bragging is a fantastic skill."

I blinked. "Right, I knew that. So anyway, Miss Gunlod, you said something about prying the seam?"

"Yes, I think it might be possible," she said. "With two blades, you might be able to wedge the doors apart just enough for me to get a glimpse of your faces, have a breath of fresh air, maybe see sunlight again. That would be quite enough for me. Do you still have sunlight?"

"For now, yeah," I said, "though Ragnarok may be coming up soon. We're hoping to use the mead to stop it."

"I see," Gunlod said. "I think my son Bragi would approve of that."

"Then if we manage to pry the doors apart," I said, "do you think you could pass us the mead through the opening?"

"Hmm, yes. I have an old garden hose here. I could siphon the mead from the vat, as long as you have a container to put it in."

I wasn't sure why Gunlod would have an old garden hose lying around in her cave. Maybe she grew mushrooms in there, or maybe the hose was to activate her Slip 'N Slide.

Sam pulled a canteen from her belt. Of course the fasting girl was the only one who had remembered to bring water. "I've got a container, Gunlod."

"Wonderful!" Gunlod said. "Now you'll need two blades—thin and very strong. Otherwise they'll break."

"Don't look at me!" Jack said. "I'm one thick blade, and I'm too young to break!"

Mallory sighed. She unsheathed her knives. "Miss Gunlod, it so happens I have two thin, supposedly unbreakable daggers. You might want to step back from the doors now." Mallory jammed the points of her weapons into the seam. They were just narrow enough to wedge inside, almost up to the hilts. Then Mallory pushed the grips away from each other, prying the doors apart.

With a vast creaking sound, the doors parted, forming a

V-shaped crack no more than an inch wide where the knives crossed. Mallory's arms trembled. She must have been using all her einherji strength to keep the seam open. Beads of perspiration dotted her forehead.

"Hurry," she grunted.

On the other side of the doors, Gunlod's face appeared— pale but beautiful icy blue eyes framed by wisps of golden hair. She inhaled deeply. "Oh, fresh air! And sunlight! Thank you so much."

"No problem," I said. "So, about that old hose . . ."

"Yes! I've got it ready." Through the crack, she fed the end of an old black rubber hose. Sam fit it into the mouth of her canteen, and liquid began gurgling into the metal container. After so many challenges trying to win the Mead of Kvasir, I hadn't expected the sound of victory to make me want to find a urinal.

"Okay, that's it," Gunlod said. The hose retracted. Her face reappeared. "Good luck stopping Ragnarok. I hope you become wonderful braggers!"

"Thanks," I said. "Are you sure we can't try to free you? We've got a friend back at our ship who's good with magic."

"Oh, you'd never have time," Gunlod said. "Baugi and Suttung will be here any minute."

Sam squeaked, *"What?"*

"Didn't I mention the silent alarm?" Gunlod asked. "It triggers as soon as you start messing with the doors. I imagine you have two, maybe three minutes before my father and uncle swoop down on you. You should hurry. Nice meeting you!"

Mallory pulled her knives out of the seam. The doors clunked together once more.

"And that," she said, wiping her brow, "is why I don't trust nice people."

"Guys." I pointed north, toward the tops of the mountains. Gleaming in the Norwegian sunlight, growing larger by the second, were the forms of two massive eagles.

THIRTY-FIVE

I Get an Assist from the Murder Murder

"WELP," I SAID, which was usually how I started conversations about ways to save our butts from certain destruction. "Any ideas?"

"Drink the mead?" Mallory suggested.

Sam rattled her canteen. "Sounds like there's only one swig in here. If it doesn't work fast enough, or it wears off before Magnus faces Loki . . ."

A squadron of tiny T.J.s started bayoneting my gut. Now that we'd gotten the mead, my looming challenge with Loki felt too real, too imminent. I forced that fear to the back burner. I had more immediate problems.

"I don't think poetry is going to help with these guys," I said. "Jack, what are our odds in combat?"

"Hmmm," Jack said. "Baugi and Suttung. I know them by reputation. Strong. Bad. I can take down one of them, most likely, but both at once, before they manage to squash you all flat . . . ?"

"Can we outrun them?" I asked. "Outfly them? Get back to the ship for reinforcements?"

Sadly, I already knew the answer. Watching the eagles fly, seeing how big their forms had gotten in the past minute, I knew they'd be on us soon. These guys were fast.

Sam slung the canteen over her shoulder. "*I might be able to outfly them, at least as far as the ship, but carrying two people? Impossible. Carrying even one will slow me down.*"

"Then we divide and conquer," Mallory said. "Sam, take the mead. Fly back to the ship. Maybe one giant will follow you. If not, well, Magnus and I will do our best against both of them. At least you'll get the mead back to the others."

Somewhere off to my left, a little voice chirped: *The redhead is smart. We can help.*

In a nearby tree sat a murder of crows. (That's what you call a group of them. You learn useless facts like that in Valhalla.) "Uh, guys," I told my friends, "those crows claim they can help."

Claim? squawked another crow. *You don't trust us? Send your two friends back to the ship with the mead. We'll give you a hand here. All we ask for in return is something shiny. Anything will do.*

I related this to my friends.

Mallory glanced toward the horizon. The giant eagles were getting awfully close. "But if Sam tries to carry me, I'll slow her down."

"The walnut!" Sam said. "Maybe you can fit inside—"

"Oh, no."

"We're wasting time!" Sam said.

"Gah!" Mallory fished out the shell and opened the halves. "How do I—?"

Imagine a silk scarf getting sucked into the nozzle of a vacuum cleaner, disappearing with a rude *slurp*. That's pretty much what happened to Mallory. The walnut closed and dropped to the ground, a tiny voice inside yelling Gaelic curses.

Sam snatched up the nut. "Magnus, you sure about this?"

"I'm fine. I've got Jack."

"You've got Jack!" Jack sang.

Sam shot skyward, leaving me with just my sword and a flock of birds.

I looked at the crows. "Okay, guys, what's the plan?"

Plan? cawed the nearest crow. *We just said we'd help. We don't have a plan, per se.*

Stupid misleading crows. Also, what kind of bird uses the term *per se?*

Since I didn't have time to murder the entire murder, I contemplated my limited options. "Fine. When I give you guys the signal, fly in the nearest giant's face and try to distract him."

Sure, chirped a different crow. *What's the signal?*

Before I could think of one, a huge eagle plummeted down and landed in front of me.

The only good news, if you could call it that: the other eagle kept flying, pursuing Sam. We had divided. Now we needed to conquer.

I hoped the eagle in front of me would morph into a small, easy-to-defeat giant, preferably one who used Nerf weapons. Instead, he rose to thirty feet tall, his skin like chipped obsidian. He had Gunlod's blond hair and pale blue eyes, which looked very strange with the rocky volcanic skin. Ice and snow flecked his whiskers like he'd been face-diving in a box of Frosted Flakes. His armor was stitched from various hides, including some that looked like endangered species:

zebra, elephant, einherji. In the giant's hand glittered an onyx double-sided ax.

"WHO DARES STEAL FROM THE MIGHTY SUTTUNG?" he bellowed. "I JUST FLEW IN FROM NIFLHEIM, AND BOY, ARE MY ARMS TIRED!"

I couldn't think of any response that did not involve high-pitched screaming.

Jack floated right up to the giant. "I don't know, man," he volunteered. "Some dude just swiped your mead and took off that way. I think he said his name was Hrungnir." Jack pointed in the general direction of York, England.

I thought that was a pretty good fake-out, but Suttung only frowned.

"Nice try," he rumbled. "Hrungnir would never dare cross me. *You* are the thieves, and you have pulled me away from important work! We are about to launch the great ship *Naglfar*! I can't be flying home every time the alarm goes off!"

"So *Naglfar* is close, then?" I asked.

"Oh, not too far," Suttung admitted. "Once you cross into Jotunheim, you follow the coast to the border of Niflheim and . . ." He scowled. "Stop trying to trick me! You are thieves and you must die!"

He raised his ax.

"Wait!" I yelled.

"Why?" demanded the giant.

"Yeah, why?" demanded Jack.

I hated it when my sword sided with a giant. Jack was ready to fight, but I had bad memories of Hrungnir, the last stone giant we'd faced. He hadn't been an easy slice-and-dice. Also, he exploded on death. I wanted every advantage I could get against Suttung, including the use of my murder of unhelpful crows, for whom I had not yet thought of a signal.

"You claim we're thieves," I said, "but how'd *you* get that mead, thief?"

Suttung kept his ax suspended over his head, giving us an unfortunate view of his blond underarm hair in his obsidian armpits. "I am no thief! My parents were slain by two evil little dwarves, Fjalar and Gjalar."

"Ah, I hate those guys," I said.

"Right?" Suttung agreed. "I would have slaughtered them as payback, but they offered me Kvasir's Mead instead. It is mine by right of wergild!"

"Oh." That kind of took the wind out of my argument. "Still, that mead was created from the blood of Kvasir, a murdered god. It belongs to the gods!"

"So you would make things right," the giant summed up, "by stealing the mead yet again for yourself? And killing my brother's thralls in the process?"

I may have mentioned that I don't like giant logic.

"Maybe?" I said. Then, in a stroke of genius, I thought of a signal for my avian allies: "EAT CROW!"

Sadly, the crows were slow to recognize my brilliance.

Suttung yelled, "DIE!"

Jack tried to intercept the ax, but it had gravity, momentum, and the force of a giant behind it. Jack did not. I dove aside as the ax split the field where I'd been standing.

Meanwhile, the crows had a leisurely conversation.

Why did he say "eat crow"? one cawed.

It's an idiomatic expression, another explained. *It means:* to admit you were wrong.

Yes, but why did he say it? asked a third.

"RARRRR!" Suttung yanked his ax from the ground.

Jack flew into my hand. "We can take him together, señor!"

I really hoped those were not going to be the last words I ever heard.

Crows, one of the crows said. *Hey, wait a minute. We're crows. I bet that was the signal!*

"Yes!" I yelped. "Get him!"

"Okay!" Jack yelled happily. "We will!"

Suttung raised his ax over his head once more. Jack pulled me into battle as the murder of crows rose from their tree and swarmed Suttung's face, pecking at his eyes and nose and Frosted Flakes beard.

The giant roared, stumbling and blind.

"Ha, HA!" Jack yelled. "We have you now!"

He yanked me forward. Together, we plunged Jack into the giant's left foot.

Suttung howled. His ax slipped from his hands, the heavy blade impaling itself in the skull of its owner. And that, kids, is why you should never use a battle-ax without wearing your safety helmet.

The giant fell with a thunderous *THUD*, right on top of the pile of thralls.

The crows settled on the grass around me.

That wasn't very chivalrous, one remarked. *But you're a Viking, so I guess chivalry doesn't apply.*

You're right, Godfrey, another agreed. *Chivalry was more of a late-medieval concept.*

A third crow cawed: *You're both forgetting about the Normans—*

Bill, just stop, said Godfrey. *No one cares about your doctoral thesis on the Norman invasion.*

Shiny things? asked the second crow. *We get shiny things now?*

The entire murder peered at me with beady, greedy black eyes.

"Uh . . ." I only had one shiny thing—Jack, who was presently doing his victory dance around the giant's corpse, singing, "Who killed a giant? I killed a giant! Who's a giant killah? I'm a giant killah!"

As tempting as it was to leave him with the crows, I thought I might need my sword the next time a giant had to be stabbed in the foot.

Then I glanced at the pile of dead thralls.

"Right over there!" I told the crows. "Nine extremely shiny scythe blades! Will those do?"

Hmm, said Bill. *I'm not sure where we'd put them.*

We could rent a storage unit, suggested Godfrey.

Good idea! said Bill. *Very well, dead mortal boy. It was nice doing business with you.*

"Just be careful," I warned. "Those blades are sharp."

Oh, don't worry about us, squawked Godfrey. *You've got the most dangerous path ahead of you. You'll only find one friendly port between here and the Ship of the Dead—if you can even call the fortress of Skadi friendly.*

I shivered, remembering what Njord had told me about his estranged wife.

It's a wretched place, Bill cawed. *Cold, cold, cold. And no shiny things, like, at all. Now if you'll excuse us, we have to start picking our way through all this carrion to get at those shiny blades.*

I love our job, said Godfrey.

Agreed! squawked the other crows.

They fluttered over to the pile of bodies and went to work, which was not something I wanted to watch.

Before the murder could murder themselves on the scythe blades and blame me for it, Jack and I began our long hike back to the *Big Banana*.

THIRTY-SIX

The Ballad of Halfborn, Hovel-Hero

OUR CREW had taken care of the other giant.

I could tell because of the badly hacked-up, decapitated giant body sprawling on the beach next to our dock. His head was nowhere to be seen. A few fishermen made their way around the corpse, holding their noses. Maybe they thought the giant was a dead whale.

Samirah stood grinning on the dock. "Welcome back, Magnus! We were getting worried."

I tried to match her smile. "Nah. I'm fine."

I explained what had happened with the crows and Suttung.

The hike to the ship had actually been pleasant—just me and Jack enjoying the meadows and rural back roads of Norway. Along the way, goats and birds had made critical comments about my personal hygiene, but I couldn't blame them. I looked like I'd trekked through half the country and rolled down the other half.

"Kid!" Blitzen came running down the gangplank, Hearthstone right behind him. "I'm glad you're okay— Oh, yikes!" Blitz stepped back hastily. "You smell like that Dumpster on Park Street."

"Thanks," I said. "That's the smell I was going for."

I couldn't tell much about Blitz's condition since he wore his anti-sun netting, but he sounded cheerful enough.

Hearthstone looked much better, like a solid day of sleep had taken the edge off our experiences in Alfheim. The pink-and-green scarf from Alex looped jauntily across his black leather lapels.

Stone was useful? he signed.

I thought about the pile of dead bodies we'd left in the valley. *We got the mead,* I signed. *Couldn't have done it without the whetstone.*

Hearth nodded, apparently satisfied. *You do smell, though.*

"So I've been told." I gestured at the corpse of the giant. "What happened here?"

"That," Sam said, her eyes twinkling, "was all Halfborn Gunderson." She yelled toward the deck of the ship, "Halfborn!"

The berserker was having a heated conversation with T.J., Alex, and Mallory. He looked relieved to come to the railing.

"Ah, there he is!" Halfborn said. "Magnus, would you please explain to T.J. that those thralls had to die? He's giving Mack a hard time about it."

Three things struck me about this:

The nickname Mack had been officially adopted.

Halfborn was *defending* Mallory Keen.

And, oh, right. It figured that T.J., being the son of a freed slave, might have a wee bit of a problem with us slaughtering nine thralls.

"They were *slaves*," T.J. said, his voice heavy with anger. "I get what happened. I get the reasoning. But still . . . you guys killed them. You can't expect me to be okay with that."

"They were jotuns!" Halfborn said. "They weren't even human!"

Blitz cleared his throat. "A gentle reminder, berserker. Hearth and I aren't human, either."

"Ah, you know what I mean. I can't believe I'm saying this, but Mack did the right thing."

"Don't defend me," Mallory snapped. "That makes it so much worse." She faced Thomas Jefferson Jr. "I'm sorry it had to happen that way, T.J. I really am. It was a bloody mess."

T.J. hesitated. Mallory so rarely apologized that when she did, it carried a lot of force. T.J. gave her a grudging nod—not like everything was okay, but like he would at least consider her words. He glared at Halfborn, but Mallory put her hand on the infantryman's shoulder. I remembered what Sam had said about T.J. and Halfborn once being enemies. Now I could see just how much they needed Mallory to keep them on the same team.

"I'm going below." T.J. glanced over at the corpse of the giant. "The air is fresher down there." He marched off.

Alex puffed out her cheeks. "Honestly, I don't see that you guys had much choice. But you'll have to give T.J. some processing time. He was already pretty miffed since we spent our morning searching Fläm and found nothing but tourists and troll souvenirs."

Blitzen grunted. "At least we have the mead now. So this wasn't all for nothing."

I hoped he was right. Whether I could defeat Loki in a flyting . . . that remained to be seen, and I had the feeling that no matter how magical the mead was, my success would depend on *me*. Alas, *me* was my least favorite person to depend on.

"But what about this giant?" I asked, anxious to change the subject. "He's Baugi, right? How did you kill him?"

Everybody looked at Halfborn.

"Oh, come on!" Halfborn protested. "You guys helped a lot."

Hearthstone signed, *Blitz and I slept through it.*

"T.J. and I tried to fight him," Alex admitted. "But Baugi dropped a building on us." She pointed down the shoreline. I hadn't noticed it before, but one of the lovely blue cottages of Fläm had been scooped up from its spot on Main Street—which now had a gaping hole like a missing tooth—and slammed onto the beach, where the cottage had collapsed like a deflated bouncy house. What the locals made of this, I had no idea, but nobody seemed to be running around town in a panic.

"By the time I got back to the ship," Sam said, "the giant was only thirty seconds behind me. I had just enough energy left to explain what was happening. Halfborn took it from there."

The berserker glowered. "It wasn't so much."

"Not so much?" Sam turned to me. "Baugi landed in the middle of town, turned into giant form, and started stomping around and yelling threats."

"He called Fläm a dirty hovel," Halfborn grumbled. "Nobody says that about my hometown."

"Halfborn charged him," Sam continued. "Baugi was like forty feet tall—"

"Forty-*five*," Alex corrected.

"And he had this glamour cast over him, so he looked extra terrifying."

"Like Godzilla." Alex considered. "Or maybe my dad. I have trouble telling them apart."

"But Halfborn just charged right in," Sam continued, "yelling *'For Fläm!'*"

"Not the best war cry," Gunderson admitted. "Luckily for me, the giant wasn't as strong as he looked."

Alex snorted. "He was plenty strong. You just went . . . well, berserk." Alex cupped her hand like she was telling me a secret. "This guy is *scary* when he goes into full berserker mode. He literally hacked the giant's feet out from under him. Then, when Baugi fell to his knees, Halfborn went to work on the rest of him."

Gunderson harrumphed. "Ah, now, Fierro, you wired off his head. It went flying"—he gestured into the fjord—"somewhere out there."

"Baugi was almost dead by that point," Alex insisted. "He was in the process of falling over. That's the only reason the head flew so far."

"Well," Halfborn said, "he's dead. That's all that matters."

Mallory spat over the side of the boat. "And I missed the whole thing, because I was stuck inside the walnut."

"Yes," Halfborn muttered. "Yes, you did."

Was it my imagination, or did Halfborn sound disappointed that Mallory had missed his moment of glory?

"Once you're in the walnut," Mallory said, "you can't get out until somebody *lets* you out. Sam didn't remember I was in there for, like, twenty minutes—"

"Oh, come on," Sam said. "It was more like five."

"Felt longer."

"Mmm." Halfborn nodded. "I imagine time goes slower when you're inside a nut."

"Shut up, oaf," Mallory growled.

Halfborn grinned. "So are we making sail, or what? Time's a-wasting!"

The temperature dropped as we sailed into the sunset. Amidships, Sam did her evening prayer. Hearthstone and Blitzen sat at the prow, gazing in quiet awe at the fjord walls. Mallory went below to check on T.J. and cook up some dinner.

I stood at the rudder next to Halfborn Gunderson, listening to the sail ripple in the wind and the magical oars swish through the water in perfect time.

"I'm fine," Halfborn said.

"Hmm?" I glanced over. His face was blue in the evening shadows, like he'd painted it for combat (as he sometimes did).

"You were going to ask if I was okay," he said. "That's why you're standing here, right? I'm fine."

"Ah. Good."

"I'll admit it was strange walking through the streets of Fläm, thinking about how I grew up there in a little hut with just my mom. Prettier place than I remembered. And I may have wondered what would've happened if I'd stayed there, gotten married, had a life."

"Right."

"And when Baugi insulted the place, I lost it. I wasn't expecting to have any . . . you know, *feelings* about being home."

"Sure."

"It's not like I expect anybody to write a ballad about me saving my hometown." He tilted his head as if he could almost hear the melody. "I'm glad to be out of that place again. I don't regret my choices when I was alive, even if I did leave my mom behind and never saw her again."

"Okay."

"And Mallory meeting her own mother . . . that didn't raise any particular emotions in me. I'm just glad Mack found out the truth, even if she did run off on a wild train ride without telling us, and could've gotten herself killed, and I never would've known what happened to her. Oh, and you and Sam, too, of course."

"Of course."

Halfborn hit the rudder handle. "But *curse* that vixen! What was she *thinking*?"

"Uh—"

"The daughter of *Frigg*?" Halfborn's laugh sounded a little hysterical. "No wonder she's so . . ." He waved his hand, making signs that could've meant almost anything: *Exasperating? Fantastic? Angry? Food processor?*

"Mmm," I said.

Halfborn patted my shoulder. "Thanks, Magnus. I'm glad we had this talk. You're all right, for a healer."

"Appreciate it."

"Take the rudder, will you? Just stay in the middle of the fjord and watch out for krakens."

"Krakens?" I protested.

Halfborn nodded absently and went below, maybe to check on dinner, or Mallory and T.J., or simply because I smelled bad.

By full dark, we'd reached the open sea. I didn't crash the ship or release any krakens, which was good. I did not want to be *that* guy.

Samirah came aft and took over rudder duty from me. She was chewing Medjool dates with her usual expression of post-fast ecstasy. "How are you holding up?"

I shrugged. "Considering the kind of day we've had? Good, I guess."

She raised her canteen and sloshed around Kvasir's Mead. "You want to take charge of this? Smell it or sip it or something, just to test it?"

The idea made me nauseous. "Keep it for now, please. I'll wait until I absolutely have to drink it."

"Sensible. The effect might not be permanent."

"It's not just that," I said. "I'm afraid I'll drink it and—and it won't be enough. That I *still* won't be able to beat Loki."

Sam looked like she wanted to give me a hug, though hugging a boy wasn't something a good Muslima would ever do. "I wonder the same thing, Magnus. Not about you, but about me. Who knows if I'll have the strength to face my father again? Who knows if any of us will?"

"Is that supposed to boost my morale?"

Sam laughed. "All we can do is try, Magnus. I choose to believe that our hardships make us stronger. Everything we've been through on this voyage—it *matters*. It increases our chances of victory."

I glanced toward the prow. Blitzen and Hearthstone had fallen asleep side by side in their sleeping bags at the base of the dragon figurehead. It seemed a strange place to sleep, given our adventure in Alfheim, but they both seemed at peace.

"I hope you're right, Sam," I said. "Because some of it's been pretty rough."

Sam sighed as if letting go of all the hunger, thirst, and curse words she'd kept inside while fasting. "I know. I think the hardest thing we can ever do is see someone for who they really are. Our parents. Our friends. Ourselves."

I wondered if she was thinking about Loki, or maybe herself. She could have been talking about any of us on the ship. None of us were free of our pasts. During the voyage, we'd looked into some pretty harsh mirrors.

My moment at the mirror was yet to come. When I faced Loki, I was sure he'd delight in magnifying my every fault, stripping bare my every fear and weakness. If he could, he would reduce me to a sniveling grease spot.

We had until tomorrow to reach *Naglfar*, Frigg had said . . . or the next day at the latest. I found myself wavering, almost wishing we would miss the deadline so I wouldn't have to face Loki one-on-one. But no. My friends were counting on me. For the sake of everybody I knew, everybody I *didn't* know . . . I had to delay Ragnarok as long as possible. I had to give Sam and Amir a chance at a normal life, and Annabeth and Percy, and Percy's baby sister, Estelle. They all deserved better than planetary destruction.

I said good night to Sam, then spread my own sleeping bag out on the deck.

I slept fitfully, dreaming of dragons and thralls, of falling down mountains and battling clay giants. Loki's laughter echoed in my ears. Over and over, the deck turned to a gruesome patchwork of dead men's keratin, enfolding me in a disgusting toenail cocoon.

"Good morning," said Blitzen, jolting me awake.

The morning was bitter cold and steel gray. I sat up, breaking a sheet of ice that had formed on my sleeping bag. Off our starboard side, snowcapped mountains loomed even taller than the fjords of Norway. All around us, the sea was a broken-up puzzle of ice blocks. The deck was completely glazed in frost, turning our bright yellow warship the color of weak lemonade.

Blitzen was the only other person on deck. He was bundled up, but he wasn't wearing any sun protection, despite the fact that it was clearly daytime. That could only mean one thing.

"We're not in Midgard anymore," I guessed.

Blitzen smiled wearily, no humor in his eyes. "We've been in Jotunheim for hours now, kid. The others are below, trying to stay warm. You . . . well, being the son of the summer god, you're more resistant to cold, but even *you* are going to start having trouble soon. Judging from how fast the temperature is dropping, we're getting close to the borders of Niflheim."

I shivered instinctively. Niflheim, the primordial realm of ice: one of the few worlds I hadn't yet visited, and one I wasn't anxious to explore.

"How will we know when we're there?" I asked.

The ship lurched with a juddering noise that loosened my joints. I staggered to my feet. The *Big Banana* was dead in the water. The surface of the sea had turned to solid ice in every direction.

"I'd say we're here." Blitz sighed. "Let's hope Hearthstone can summon some magical fire. Otherwise we're all going to freeze to death within the hour."

THIRTY-SEVEN

Alex Bites My Face Off

I HAVE DIED many painful deaths. I've been impaled, decapitated, burned, drowned, crushed, and thrown off the terrace of floor 103.

I prefer all of those to hypothermia.

After only a few minutes, my lungs felt like I was breathing glass dust. We got all hands on deck—another nautical term I finally understood—to deal with the ice problem, but we had little success. I sent Jack out to break up the floe in front of us, while Halfborn and T.J. used poleaxes to chip away at the port and starboard sides. Sam flew ahead with a rope and tried to tug us along. Alex turned into a walrus and pushed from behind. I was too cold to make any jokes about how nice she looked with tusks, whiskers, and flippers.

Hearthstone summoned a new rune:

$$\langle$$

He explained this was *kenaz*: the torch, the fire of life. Instead of disappearing in a flash, like most runes did, kenaz continued to burn above the foredeck—a floating bend of fire five feet high, melting the frost on the deck and rigging. Kenaz kept us warm enough to avoid instant death, but Blitz fretted that sustaining the rune for an extended period would also burn up Hearth's energy. A few months ago, expending so much energy would have killed him. Now he was stronger. Still, I worried, too.

I found a pair of binoculars in the supplies and scanned the mountains for any promise of shelter or harbor. I saw nothing but sheer rock.

I didn't realize my fingers were turning blue until Blitz pointed it out. I summoned a little Frey-warmth into my hands, but the effort made me dizzy. Using the power of summer here was like trying to remember everything that had happened on my first day of elementary school. I knew summer still existed, somewhere, but it was so distant, so vague, I could barely conjure a memory of it.

"B-blitz, y-you don't look affected," I noted.

He scratched the ice from his beard. "Dwarves do well in the cold. You and I will be the last ones to freeze to death. But that's not much comfort."

Mallory, Blitz, and I tried using oars to push away the ice as Halfborn and T.J. broke it up. We alternated duties, going belowdecks two or three at a time to warm up, though below wasn't much warmer. We would have made faster time just getting out and walking, but Walrus Alex reported that the ice had some nasty thin spots. Also, we had nowhere to shelter. At least the ship offered supplies and some cover from the wind.

My arms started to go numb. I got so used to shivering I couldn't tell whether it had started to snow or whether my vision was blurred. The fiery rune was the only thing keeping us alive, but its light and heat slowly faded. Hearthstone sat cross-legged beneath the kenaz, his eyes closed in intense concentration. Beads of sweat dripped from his brow and froze as soon as they splattered on the deck.

After a while, even Jack started to act glum. He no longer seemed interested in serenading us or joking about doing ice-breaker activities.

"And this is the *nicest* part of Niflheim," Jack grumbled. "You should see the cold regions!"

I'm not sure how much time passed. It seemed impossible that there had been any life before this one: breaking ice, pushing ice, shivering, dying.

Then, at the prow, Mallory croaked, "Hey! Look!"

In front of us, the swirling snow thinned. Only a few hundred yards ahead, jutting from the main line of cliffs, was a jagged peninsula like the blade of a corroded ax. A thin line of black-gravel beach hugged the base. And toward the top of the cliff . . . were those fires flickering?

We turned the ship in that direction, but we didn't make it far. The ice thickened, cementing our hull in place. Above Hearth's head, the kenaz rune guttered weakly. We all gathered on the deck, solemn and silent. Every blanket and extra piece of clothing in the hold had been wrapped around us.

"W-walk for it," Blitz suggested. Even he was starting to stutter. "We pair up for warmth. G-get across the ice to the shore. Maybe we find shelter."

It wasn't so much a "survival plan" as a plan for dying in a different place, but we grimly went to work. We shouldered all the supplies we couldn't live without—some food, water, the canteen of Kvasir's Mead, our weapons. Then we climbed onto the ice and I folded the *Big Banana* into a handkerchief, because dragging the ship along behind us would've been, well, a drag.

Jack volunteered to float in front of us and test the ice with his blade. I wasn't sure whether that would make things more or less dangerous for us, but he refused to go back into pendant form, because the aftereffects of his extra exertion would've killed me. (He's thoughtful that way.)

As we paired up, somebody's arm curled around my waist. Alex Fierro wedged herself next to me, wrapping a blanket around our heads and shoulders. I looked at her in amazement. A pink wool scarf covered her head and mouth, so all I could see were her two-toned eyes and some wisps of green hair.

"Sh-shut up," she stammered. "You're w-warm and s-summery."

Jack led the way across the ice. Behind him, Blitzen did his best to prop up Hearthstone, who stumbled along with the rune of kenaz above him, though its heat was now more like a candle's than a bonfire's.

Sam and Mallory followed, then T.J. and Halfborn, and finally Alex and me. We trudged across the frozen sea, making our way toward that outcropping of rock, but our destination seemed to get farther away with every step. Could the cliff be a mirage? Maybe distance was fluid on the borders of Niflheim and Jotunheim. Once, in the hall of Utgard-Loki, Alex and I had rolled a bowling ball all the way to the White Mountains in New Hampshire, so I supposed anything was possible.

I couldn't feel my face anymore. My feet had turned to one-gallon boxes of squishy ice cream. I thought how sad it would be to come as far as we had, facing so many gods, giants, and monsters, only to keel over and freeze to death in the middle of nowhere.

I clung to Alex. She clung to me. Her breath rattled. I wished she still had her walrus blubber, because she was all skin and bone, as wiry as her garrote. I wanted to chide her, *Eat, eat! You're wasting away.*

I appreciated her warmth, though. Under any other circumstances, she would've killed me for getting this close. Also, I would've freaked out from so much physical contact. I considered it a personal triumph that I'd learned to hug my friends once in a while, but I wasn't usually good with closeness. The need for warmth, and maybe the fact that this was Alex, made it okay somehow. I concentrated on her scent, a sort of citrusy fragrance that made me think of orange groves in a sunny valley in Mexico—not that I'd ever been to a place like that, but it smelled nice.

"Guava juice," Alex croaked.

"Wh-what?" I asked.

"Roof d-deck. B-back B-bay. That was nice."

She's clinging to good memories, I realized. *Trying to stay alive.*

"Y-yeah," I agreed.

"York," she said. "Mr. Ch-chippy. You d-didn't know what *t-takeaway* meant."

"I hate you," I said. "Keep t-talking."

Her laugh sounded more like a smoker's cough. "Wh-when you returned from Alfheim. The look—the look on your f-face when I t-took b-back m-my pink glasses."

"B-but you *were* glad to see me?"

"Eh. Y-you have some entertainment v-value."

Struggling to walk on the ice, our heads so close together,

I could almost imagine Alex and I were a clay warrior with two faces, a twin being. The thought was comforting.

Maybe fifty yards from the cliff, the kenaz rune sputtered out. Hearth stumbled against Blitz. The temperature plummeted further, which I didn't think was possible. My lungs expelled their last bit of warmth. They screamed when I tried to inhale.

"Keep going!" Blitz yelled back to us hoarsely. "I am *not* dying in this outfit!"

We obliged, marching step by step toward the narrow gravel beach, where at least we could die on solid ground.

Blitz and Hearth were almost to the shore when Alex stopped abruptly.

I didn't have any energy left either, but I thought I should try to sound encouraging. "We—we have to k-keep going." I looked over. We were nose-to-nose under the blankets. Her eyes glinted, amber and brown. Her scarf had dipped below her chin. Her breath was like limes.

Then, before I even knew what was happening, she kissed me. She could have bitten off my mouth and I would have been less surprised. Her lips were cracked and rough from the cold. Her nose fit perfectly next to mine. Our faces aligned, our breath mixed. Then she pulled away.

"I wasn't going to die without doing that," she said.

The world of primordial ice must not have frozen me completely, because my chest burned like a coal furnace.

"*Well?*" She frowned. "Stop gaping and let's move."

We trudged toward the shore. My mind wasn't working properly. I wondered if Alex had kissed me just to inspire me to keep going, or to distract me from our imminent deaths. It didn't seem possible she'd actually *wanted* to kiss me. Whatever the case, that kiss was the only reason I made it to shore.

Our friends were already there, huddled against the rocks. They hadn't seemed to notice the kiss between Alex and me. Why would they? Everyone was too busy freezing to death.

"I—I have g-gunpowder," T.J. stuttered. "C-could make a f-fire?"

Unfortunately, we had nothing to burn except our clothes, and we needed those.

Blitz looked miserably at the cliff face, which was sheer and unforgiving.

"I—I'll try to shape the rock," he said. "Maybe I can dig us a cave."

I'd seen Blitz mold solid rock before, but it took a lot of energy and concentration. Even then, he'd only been making simple handholds. I didn't see how he'd have the strength to dig an entire cave. Nor was that going to save us. But I appreciated his stubborn optimism.

He'd just dug his fingers into the stone when the entire cliff rumbled. A line of blazing light etched the shape of a door, twenty feet square, that swung inward with a deep grinding noise.

In the opening stood a giantess as terrible and beautiful as the Niflheim landscape. She was ten feet tall, dressed in white and gray furs, her brown eyes cold and angry, her dark hair braided in multiple strands like a cat-o'-nine-tails whip.

"Who *dares* rock-shape my front door?" she asked.

Blitz gulped. "Uh, I—"

"Why should I not kill you all?" the giantess demanded. "Or perhaps, since you look half-dead already, I'll just close my door and let you freeze!"

"W-wait!" I croaked. "Sk-skadi . . . You're Skadi, right?"

Gods of Asgard, I thought, *please let this be Skadi and not some random giantess named Gertrude the Unfriendly.*

"I—I'm M-magnus Chase," I continued. "Njord is my grandfather. H-he sent me to f-find you."

A variety of emotions rippled across Skadi's face: irritation, resentment, and maybe just a hint of curiosity.

"All right, frozen boy," she growled. "That gets you in the door. Once you've all thawed out and explained yourselves, I'll decide whether or not to use you for archery targets."

THIRTY-EIGHT

Skadi Knows All, Shoots All

I DIDN'T WANT to let go of Alex. Or maybe I just physically couldn't.

Two of Skadi's jotun servants literally had to pull us apart. One of them carried me up a winding set of stairs into the fortress, my body still hunched in hobbling-old-man position.

Compared to outside, Skadi's hall felt like a sauna, though the thermostat probably wasn't set much higher than freezing. I was carried through high stone corridors with vaulted ceilings that reminded me of the big old churches in Back Bay (great places to warm up in when you're homeless in winter). Occasionally a booming sound echoed through the fortress, like someone was shooting cannons in the distance. Skadi barked orders to her servants, and we were all taken to separate rooms to get cleaned up.

A jotun manservant (giantservant?) lowered me into a bath so hot I hit a high note I hadn't been able to sing since fourth grade. While I soaked, he gave me something to drink—a vile herbal concoction that burned my throat and made my fingers and toes spasm. He hauled me out of the bath, and by the time he got me dressed in a white wool tunic and breeches, I had to admit I felt almost okay again, even with Jack now hanging back on my neck chain as a runestone. The color of my toes and fingers had returned to pink. I could feel my face. My nose had not fallen off from frostbite, and my lips were right where Alex had left them.

"You'll live," the jotun grumbled, like this was a personal failure on his part. He gave me comfortable fur shoes and a thick warm cloak, then led me out to the main hall, where my friends were waiting.

The hall was standard Viking for the most part: a rough-hewn stone floor covered with straw, a ceiling made from spears and shields, three tables in a U shape around a central fire, though Skadi's flames burned white and blue and seemed to give off no heat.

Along one side of the hall, a row of cathedral-size windows opened onto a blizzard-blurred vista. I saw no glass on the windows, but the wind and snow didn't trespass inside.

At the center table, Skadi sat on a throne carved from yew wood and overlain with furs. Her servants bustled around, putting out platters of fresh bread and roasted meat, along with steaming mugs that smelled like . . . hot chocolate? Suddenly I liked Skadi a lot more.

My friends were all dressed like me, in white wool, so we looked like a secret society of very clean monks—the Fellowship of the Bleach. I'll admit I scanned for Alex first, hoping to sit next to her, but she was on the far bench, wedged between Mallory and Halfborn with T.J. at the end.

Alex caught me. She mimicked my gawping face like *What are* you *looking at?*

So, it was back to normal, then. One life-and-death kiss, and we returned to our regularly scheduled snark. Great.

I sat next to Blitzen, Hearthstone, and Sam, which was just fine.

We all dug into our dinner, except for Sam. She hadn't bathed—since that was also against Ramadan rules—but she'd changed clothes. Her hijab had shifted color to match her white outfit. Somehow, she managed not to stare longingly at everyone else's food, which convinced me beyond a doubt that she had superhuman endurance.

Skadi lounged on her throne, her cat-o'-nine-tails hair draped over her shoulders, her fur cloak making her look even larger than she was. She spun an arrow on top of her knee. Behind her, the wall was lined with racks of equipment: skis, bows, quivers of arrows. I guessed she was a fan of cross-country archery.

"Welcome, travelers," said our host, "to *Thrymheimr*—in your language, Thunder Home."

As if on cue, a rumble shook the room—the same *boom* I'd heard when deeper in the fortress. Now I knew what it was: snow thunder. You heard it in Boston sometimes when a snowstorm mixed with a thunderstorm. It sounded like firecrackers going off inside a cotton pillow, if you magnified that sound by a million.

"Thunder Home." Halfborn nodded gravely. "A good name, considering, you know, the constant—"

Thunder boomed again, rattling the plates on the table.

Mallory leaned over to Alex. "I can't reach Gunderson. Hit him for me, will you?"

Despite the huge size of the hall, the acoustics were perfect. I could hear every whisper. I wondered if Skadi had designed the place with that in mind.

The giantess wasn't eating from the plate in front of her. Best-case scenario: she was fasting for Ramadan. Worst-case scenario: she was waiting until we were sufficiently fattened up so she could enjoy us as her main course.

She tapped her arrow on her knee while studying me intently.

"So, you're one of Njord's, eh?" she mused. "Child of Frey, I suppose."

"Yes, uh, ma'am." I wasn't sure if *Lady* or *Miss* or *Huge Scary Person* was the appropriate title, but Skadi didn't kill me, so I figured I hadn't offended her. Yet.

"I can see the resemblance." She wrinkled her nose, as if the similarity was not a point in my favor. "Njord wasn't the worst husband. He was kind. He had beautiful feet."

"Outstanding feet," Blitz agreed, wagging a pork rib for emphasis.

"But we just couldn't get along," Skadi continued. "Irreconcilable differences. He didn't like my hall. Can you believe it?"

Hearthstone signed, *You have a beautiful hall.*

The gesture for *beautiful* was circling your hand in front of your face, then spreading your fingertips apart like *poof!* The first few times I saw it, I thought Hearth was saying *This thing makes my face explode.*

"Thank you, elf," said Skadi (because all the best jotuns understand ASL). "Certainly, Thunder Home is better than Njord's seaside palace. All those gulls constantly screeching—I couldn't stand the noise!"

Snow thunder shook the room again.

"Yes," Alex said, "no peace and quiet, like here."

"Exactly," said Skadi. "My father built this fortress, may his soul rest with Ymir, the first giant. Now Thrymheimr is mine, and I don't intend to leave it. I've had my fill of the Aesir!" She leaned forward, still holding that wicked barbed arrow. "Now tell me, Magnus Chase, why did Njord send you to me? *Please* tell me he doesn't still harbor illusions about us getting back together."

Why me? I thought.

Skadi seemed okay. I'd met enough giants to know they weren't all bad, any more than all gods were good. But if Skadi was done with the Aesir, I wasn't sure she'd welcome us going after Loki, who was, of course, the Aesir's main enemy. I definitely didn't want to tell her that my grandfather, the god of seaside pedicures, still pined for her.

On the other hand, some gut instinct told me Skadi would see through any lies or omissions as easily as she heard every whisper in this hall. Thrymheimr was not a place for hiding secrets.

"Njord wanted me to see how you felt about him," I admitted.

She sighed. "I don't believe this. He didn't send you with flowers, did he? I told him to *stop* it with the bouquets."

"No flowers," I promised, suddenly sympathizing with all the innocent Niflheim delivery persons she had probably shot dead. "And Njord's feelings aren't the main reason we're here. We've come to stop Loki."

The servants all stopped what they were doing. They glanced at me, then at their mistress, as if thinking *Well, this should be interesting.* My friends watched me with expressions that ranged from *You got this!* (Blitzen) to *Please don't screw up as much as usual* (Alex).

Skadi's dark eyes glittered. "Go on."

"Loki is getting his ship *Naglfar* ready to sail," I said. "We're here to stop him, recapture him, and bring him back to the Aesir so we'd don't have to fight Ragnarok, like, tomorrow."

Another peal of thunder shook the mountain.

The giantess's face was impossible to read. I imagined her sending her arrow across the room and embedding it in my chest like a mistletoe dart.

Instead, she threw back her head and laughed. "Is *that* why you're carrying Kvasir's Mead? You intend to challenge Loki to a flyting?"

I gulped. "Uh . . . yeah. How do you know we have Kvasir's Mead?"

My second, unspoken, question was: *And are you going to take it away from us?*

The giantess leaned forward. "I am fully aware of everything that happens in my hall, Magnus Chase, and everyone who passes through it. I have taken inventory of your weapons, your supplies, your powers, your scars." She scanned the room, her eyes resting on each of us—not with sympathy, more like she was picking targets. "I also would have known if you'd lied to me. Be glad you did not. So, tell me: Why should I let you continue your quest? Persuade me not to kill you."

Halfborn Gunderson wiped his beard. "Well, for one thing, Lady Skadi, killing us would be a lot of trouble. If you know our abilities, you know we're excellent fighters. We'd give you quite a challenge—"

An arrow thudded into the table an inch from Halfborn's hand. I didn't even see how it happened. I looked back at

Skadi—she suddenly had a bow in her hand, a second arrow already nocked and ready to fly.

Halfborn didn't flinch. He set down his hot chocolate and belched. "Lucky shot."

"Ha!" Skadi lowered her bow, and my heart started pumping blood again. "So you have bravery. Or foolhardiness, at least. What else can you tell me?"

"That we're no friends of Loki's," Samirah volunteered. "And neither are you."

Skadi raised an eyebrow. "What makes you say so?"

"If you were a friend of Loki's, we would already be dead." Sam gestured toward the windows. "The Harbor of *Naglfar* is close, isn't it? I can sense my father nearby. You don't like Loki gathering his army right on your doorstep. Let us continue our quest, and we can take my father off the board."

Alex nodded. "Yes, we can."

"Interesting," Skadi mused. "*Two* children of Loki sit at my dinner table, and you both seem to hate Loki even more than I do. Ragnarok makes strange allies."

T.J. clapped once, so loudly we all flinched (except for Hearth). "I knew it!" He grinned and pointed at Skadi. "I *knew* this lady had good taste. Hot chocolate this tasty? A hall this awesome? And her servants don't wear thrall collars!"

Skadi curled her lip. "No, einherji. I detest the keeping of slaves."

"*See?*" T.J. gave Halfborn a *told-you-so* look. More thunder rattled the plates and cups, as if agreeing with T.J. The berserker just rolled his eyes.

"I *knew* this lady hated Loki," T.J. summed up. "She's a natural Union supporter!"

The giantess frowned. "I am not sure what that means, my very enthusiastic guest, but you are right: I am no friend of Loki's. There was a time when he didn't seem so bad. He could make me laugh. He was charming. Then, during the flyting in Aegir's hall . . . Loki insinuated that—that he had shared my bed."

Skadi shuddered at the memory. "In front of all the other gods, he slighted my honor. He said *horrible* things. And so, when the gods bound him in that cave, I was the one who found the serpent and set it over Loki's head." She smiled coldly. "The Aesir and Vanir were satisfied just to bind him for eternity, but that wasn't enough for me. I wanted him to experience the drip, drip, drip of poison in his face for the rest of time, just the way his words had made *me* feel."

I decided I would not be slighting Skadi's honor anytime soon.

"Well, ma'am . . ." Blitz tugged at his wool tunic. He was the only one of us who didn't look comfortable in his new threads, probably because the outfit did not allow him to wear an ascot. "Sounds like you gave the villain just what he deserved. Will you help us, then?"

Skadi set her bow across the table. "Let me understand this: you, Magnus Chase, plan to defeat Loki, the silver-tongued master of insults, in a verbal duel."

"Right."

She looked like she was waiting for me to wax poetic about my prowess with verbs and adjectives and whatnot. Honestly, that one-word answer was all I could manage.

"Well, then," Skadi said, "it's a very good thing you have Kvasir's Mead."

My friends all nodded. Thanks a lot, friends.

"You were also wise not to drink it yet," Skadi continued. "You have such a small amount, there is no telling how long its effect will last. You should drink it in the morning, just before you leave. That should allow enough time for the mead to take effect before you face Loki."

"Then you know where he is?" I asked. "He's *that* close?" I wasn't sure whether to be relieved or petrified.

Skadi nodded. "Beyond my mountain there lies a frozen bay where *Naglfar* sits at its moorings. In giant terms, it is only a few good strides away."

"What is that in human terms?" asked Mallory.

"It won't matter," Skadi assured her. "I will give you skis to speed you on your way."

Hearth signed, *Skis?*

"I'm not so good on skis," Blitz muttered.

Skadi smiled. "Fear not, Blitzen, son of Freya. My skis will look good on *you*. You will have to reach the ship before midday tomorrow. By then, the ice blocking the bay will be sufficiently melted for Loki to sail into open waters. If that happens, nothing will be able to stop Ragnarok."

I met Mallory's eyes across the hearth fire. Her mom, Frigg, had been right. By the time we set foot on *Naglfar*, *if* we reached it, forty-eight hours would have passed since Fläm.

"If you manage to board the ship," Skadi said, "you will somehow have to make your way through legions of giants and undead. They will, of course, try to kill you. But if you succeed in getting face-to-face with Loki and issuing your challenge, he will be honor-bound to accept. The fighting will stop long enough for the flyting."

"So," Alex said, "it'll be cake, then."

Skadi's cat-o'-nine-tails hair slithered across her shoulders as she regarded Alex. "You have an interesting definition of *cake*. Assuming Magnus somehow defeats Loki in a flyting, and weakens him enough to capture . . . how will you imprison him?"

"Um," Mallory said. "We have a walnut shell."

Skadi nodded. "That is good. A walnut shell might do it."

"So, if I defeat Loki in the flyting," I said, "and we do the walnut shell, et cetera . . . then we shake hands with Loki's crew, everybody says 'good game,' and they let us go, right?"

Skadi snorted. "Hardly. The cease-fire will end as soon as the contest is over. Then, one way or another, the crew will kill you."

"Well, then," Halfborn said. "Why don't you come with us, Skadi? We could use an archer in our group."

Skadi laughed. "This one amuses me."

"Yeah, that feeling wears off quickly," Mallory muttered.

The giantess rose. "Tonight you will stay in my hall, little mortals. You can sleep peacefully knowing that there is nothing to fear in Thunder Home. But in the morning"—she pointed to the white abyss beyond her windows—"out you go. The last thing I want is to get Njord's hopes up by pampering his grandson."

THIRTY-NINE

I Become as Poetic as . . .
Like, a Poetic Person

DESPITE SKADI'S PROMISE, I didn't sleep peacefully.

The coldness of the chamber and the constant booming didn't help. Nor did the knowledge that in the morning Skadi was apparently going to fit us with skis and throw us out a window.

Also, I kept thinking about Alex Fierro. You know, maybe just a little. Alex was a force of nature, like the snow thunder. She struck when she felt like it, depending on temperature differentials and storm patterns I couldn't possibly predict. She shook my foundations in a way that was powerful but also weirdly soft and constrained, veiled in blizzard. I couldn't assign any motives to her. She just did what she wanted. At least, that's how it felt to me.

I stared at the ceiling for a long time. Finally, I got out of bed, used the washbasin, and changed into new wool clothes—white and gray, the colors of snow and ice. My runestone pendant hung cold and heavy on my neck, like Jack was catching some winks. I gathered my few supplies, then wandered into the corridors of Thunder Home, hoping I didn't get killed by a startled servant or a random arrow.

In the great hall, I found Sam at prayer. Jack hummed

against my collarbone, informing me in a sleepy, irritated tone
that it was four in the morning, Niflheim Standard Time.

Sam had faced her prayer rug toward the huge open windows. I guessed the blur of white outside made a good blank
screen to stare at while you meditated on God or whatever. I
waited until she finished. I'd come to recognize her routine by
now. A moment of silence at the end—a sort of peaceful set-
tling that even the thunder couldn't disturb—then she turned
and smiled.

"Good morning," she said.

"Hey. You're up early."

I realized that was a stupid thing to say to a Muslim. If
you're observant, you never sleep late, because you have to be
up for prayers before first light. Being around Sam, I'd started
to pay more attention to the timing of dawn and dusk, even
when we were in other worlds.

"I didn't sleep much," she said. "I figured I would get in a
good meal or two." She patted her stomach.

"How do you know prayer times in Jotunheim?" I asked.
"Or where Mecca is?"

"Heh. I take my best guess. That's allowed. It's the intention that counts."

I wondered if the same would be true of my coming challenge. Maybe Loki would say, *Well, Magnus, you really sucked at
flyting, but you did your best and it's the intention that counts, so
you win!*

"Hey." Sam's voice jarred me out of my thoughts. "You'll
do fine."

"You're awfully calm," I noted. "Considering . . . you know,
today's the day."

Sam adjusted her hijab, which was still white to match her outfit. "Last night was the twenty-seventh night of Ramadan. Traditionally, that's the Night of Power."

I waited. "Is that when you get supercharged?"

She laughed. "Sort of. It commemorates when Muhammad received his first revelation from the angel Gabriel. Nobody knows exactly which night it is, but it's the holiest of the year—"

"Wait, it's your holiest night, and you don't know when it is?"

Sam shrugged. "Most people go with the twenty-seventh, but yeah. It's one of the nights of the last ten days of Ramadan. Not knowing keeps you on your toes. Anyway, last night it just *felt* right. I stayed up praying and thinking, and I just felt . . . confirmed. Like there *is* something bigger than all this: Loki, Ragnarok, the Ship of the Dead. My dad may have power over me because he's my dad. But he's not the biggest power. *Allahu akbar.*"

I knew that term, but I'd never heard Sam use it before. I'll admit it gave me an instinctive jolt in the gut. The news media loved to talk about how terrorists would say that right before they did something horrible and blew people up.

I wasn't going to mention that to Sam. I imagined she was painfully aware. She couldn't walk the streets of Boston in her hijab most days without somebody screaming at her to go home, and (if she was in a bad mood) she'd scream back, "I'm from Dorchester!"

"Yeah," I said. "That means *God is great,* right?"

Sam shook her head. "That's a slightly inaccurate translation. It means God is *greater.*"

"Than what?"

"Everything. The whole point of saying it is to remind your-self that God is greater than whatever you are facing—your fears, your problems, your thirst, your hunger, your anger. Even your issues with a parent like Loki." She shook her head. "Sorry, that must sound really hokey to an atheist."

I shrugged, feeling awkward. I wished I could have Sam's level of faith. I didn't, but it clearly worked for her, and I needed her to be confident, especially today. "Well, you sound super-charged. That's what counts. Ready to kick some undead butt?"

"Yep." She smirked. "What about you? Are you ready to face *Alex*?"

I wondered if God was greater than the punch in the stom-ach Sam had just given me. "Um, what do you mean?"

"Oh, Magnus," she said. "You are so emotionally near-sighted it's almost cute."

Before I could think of some clever way not to respond to that—perhaps by shouting *Look over there!* and running away—Skadi's voice boomed through the hall. "There are my early risers!"

The giantess was dressed in enough white fur to outfit a family of polar bears. Behind her, a line of servants trudged in carrying an assortment of wooden skis. "Let's rouse your friends and get you on your way!"

Our friends were not thrilled about getting up.

I had to pour ice water on Halfborn Gunderson's head *twice*. Blitz grumbled something about ducks and told me to go away. When I tried to shake Hearth awake, he stuck one hand above the covers and signed, *I am not here.* T.J. bolted out of bed screaming, "CHARGE!" Fortunately he wasn't armed, or he would've run me through.

Finally, everybody assembled in the main hall, where Skadi's servants set out our last meal—sorry, our *breakfast*—of bread, cheese, and apple cider.

"This cider was made from the apples of immortality," Skadi said. "Centuries ago, when my father kidnapped the goddess Idun, we fermented some of her apples into cider. It's quite diluted. It won't make you immortal, but it will give you a boost of endurance, at least long enough to get through the wilds of Niflheim."

I drained the cup. The cider didn't make me feel particularly boosted, but it did tingle a little. It settled the crackling and popping in my stomach.

After eating, we tried on our skis with varying degrees of success. Hearthstone waddled around gracefully in his (who knew elves could waddle gracefully?), while Blitz tried in vain to find a pair that matched his shoes. "Do you have anything smaller?" he asked. "Also, maybe in a dark brown? Like a mahogany?"

Skadi patted him on the head, which wasn't something dwarves appreciated.

Mallory and Halfborn shuffled around with ease, but both of them had to help T.J. stay on his feet.

"Jefferson, I thought you grew up in New England," Halfborn said. "You never skied?"

"I lived in a city," T.J. grumbled. "Also, I'm Black. There weren't a lot of Black guys skiing down the Boston waterfront in 1861."

Sam looked a little awkward on her skis, but since she could fly, I wasn't too worried about her.

As for Alex, she sat by an open window putting on a pair of hot-pink ski boots. Had she brought them with her? Had she tipped a servant a few kroner to find her a pair in Skadi's supply closet? I had no idea, but she wouldn't be skiing off to her death in bland white and gray. She wore a green fur cloak— Skadi must have skinned a few Grinches to make it—over her mauve jeans and green-and-pink sweater vest. To top off the look, she wore an Amelia Earhart–style aviator's cap with her pink sunglasses. Just when I thought I'd seen all the outfits nobody but Alex could pull off, she pulled off a new one.

As she adjusted her skis, she paid no attention to the rest of us. (And by *the rest of us*, I mean me.) She seemed lost in her thoughts, maybe considering what she would say to her mother, Loki, before she attempted to garrote his head off.

At last we were all in skis, standing in pairs next to the open windows like a group of Olympic jumpers.

"Well, Magnus Chase," Skadi said, "all that remains is the drinking of the mead."

Sam, standing on my left, offered me the canteen.

"Oh." I wondered if it was safe to drink mead before operating skis. Maybe the laws were more lax out here in the hinterlands. "You mean now?"

"Yes," Skadi said. "Now."

I uncapped the canteen. This was the moment of truth. We'd ventured across worlds and nearly died countless times. We'd feasted with Aegir, battled pottery with pottery, slain a dragon, and siphoned mead with an old rubber hose just so I could drink this honeyed blood beverage, which would hopefully make me poetic enough to talk smack about Loki.

I saw no point in doing a taste test. I chugged down the mead in three big gulps. I was expecting the taste of blood, but Kvasir's Mead tasted more like . . . well, mead. It certainly didn't burn like dragon's blood, or even tingle like Skadi's cider of not-quite-immortality.

"How do you feel?" Blitz asked hopefully. "Poetic?"

I burped. "I feel okay."

"That's it?" Alex demanded. "Say something impressive. Describe the storm."

I gazed out the windows into the blizzard. "The storm looks . . . white. Also cold."

Halfborn sighed. "We're all dead."

"Good luck, heroes!" Skadi called.

Then her servants pushed us out the windows into the void.

FORTY

I Get a Collect Call from Hel

WE HURTLED through the sky like things that hurtle through the sky.

The wind whipped my face. The snow blinded me. The cold was so bad it made me cold.

Okay, yeah, the mead of poetry *definitely* wasn't working.

Then gravity took hold. I hated gravity.

My skis scraped and hissed against packed snow. I hadn't been skiing in a *long* time. I'd never done it careening down a forty-five-degree slope in subzero temperatures and blizzard conditions.

My eyeballs froze. The cold seared my cheeks. Somehow, I avoided a wipeout. Each time I started to wobble, my skis autocorrected, keeping me upright.

Off to my right, I caught a glimpse of Sam flying along, her skis six feet above the ground. Cheater. Hearthstone zipped past on my left, signing, *On your left*, which was not very helpful.

In front of me, Blitzen fell out of the sky, screaming at the top of his lungs. He hit the snow and immediately executed a series of dazzling slaloms, figure eights, and triple flips. Either he was a *much* better skier than he'd let on, or his magical skis had an evil sense of humor.

My knees and ankles burned with strain. The wind ripped straight through my superheavy giant-weave clothes. I figured any minute I would stumble more than my magical skis could compensate for. I'd hit a boulder, break my neck, and end up sprawled across the snow like . . . Forget it. I'm not even trying that one.

Suddenly the slope evened out. The blizzard abated. Our speed decreased, and all eight of us slid to a gentle stop like we'd just finished the bunny slope at Mount Easy McWeakSauce.

(Hey, that was a simile! Maybe my usual just-average skill with description was coming back!)

Our skis popped off of their own accord. Alex was the first one back in motion. She ran ahead and took cover behind a low stone ridge that cut across the snow. I suppose that made sense, since she was the most colorful target within five square miles. The rest of us joined her. Our riderless skis turned around and zipped back up the mountain.

"So much for an exit strategy." Alex looked at me for the first time since last night. "You'd better start feeling poetic soon, Chase. 'Cause you're out of time."

I peeked over the ridge and saw what she meant. A few hundred yards away, through a thin veil of sleet, aluminum-gray water stretched to the horizon. At the near shore, rising from the icy bay, was the dark shape of *Naglfar*, the Ship of the Dead. It was so huge that if I hadn't known it was a sailing vessel, I might have thought it was another promontory like Skadi's mountain fortress. Its mainsail would've taken several days to climb. Its massive hull must have displaced enough water to fill the Grand Canyon. The deck and gangplanks swarmed with what looked like angry ants, though I had a feeling that if we were closer, those shapes would have resolved into giants and zombies—thousands upon thousands of them.

Before, I'd only seen the ship in dreams. Now, I realized how desperate our situation was: eight people facing an army designed to destroy worlds, and our hopes hinged on me finding Loki and calling him some bad names.

The absurdity of it might have made me feel hopeless. Instead, it made me angry.

I didn't feel poetic, exactly, but I *did* feel a burning in my throat—the desire to tell Loki exactly what I thought of him. Some choice colorful metaphors sprang to mind.

"I'm ready," I said, hoping I was right. "How do we find Loki without getting killed?"

"Frontal charge?" T.J. suggested.

"Uh—"

"I'm *kidding*," T.J. said. "Clearly, this calls for diversionary tactics. Most of us should find a way to the front of the vessel and attack. We cause a disturbance, draw as many of those baddies as we can away from the gangplanks, give Magnus a chance to get aboard and challenge Loki."

"Wait a second—"

"I agree with Union Boy," said Mallory.

"Yep." Halfborn hefted his battle-ax. "Battle-Ax is thirsty for jotun blood!"

"Hold on!" I said. "That's suicide."

"Nah," Blitz said. "Kid, we've been talking about this, and we've got a plan. I brought some dwarven ropes. Mallory's got grappling hooks. Hearth's got his runestones. With luck, we can scale the prow of that ship and start making chaos."

He patted one of the supply bags he'd carried from the *Big Banana*. "Don't worry, I've got some surprises in store for those undead warriors. You sneak up the aft gangway, find Loki, and demand a duel. Then the fighting should stop. We'll be fine."

"Yeah," Halfborn said. "Then we'll come watch you beat that meinfretr at insults."

"And I'll throw a walnut at him," Mallory finished. "Give us thirty minutes or so to get in position. Sam, Alex—take good care of our boy."

"We will," Sam said.

Even Alex did not complain. I realized I'd been completely outmaneuvered. My friends had united on a plan to maximize my chances, regardless of how dangerous it might be for them.

"Guys—"

Hearth signed, *Time is wasting. Here. For you.*

From his pouch, he handed me othala—the same runestone we'd taken from Andiron's cairn. Lying in my palm, it brought back the smell of rotting reptile flesh and burnt brownies.

"Thanks," I said, "but . . . why this particular rune?"

Does not just mean inheritance, Hearth signed. *Othala symbolizes aid on a journey. Use it once we are gone. It should protect you.*

"How?"

He shrugged. *Don't ask me. I'm just the sorcerer.*

"All right, then," T.J. said. "Alex, Sam, Magnus—we'll see you on that ship."

Before I could object, or even thank them, the rest of the group trundled off through the snow. In their jotunish white clothes, they quickly disappeared into the terrain.

I turned to Alex and Sam. "How long have you all been planning this?"

Despite her cracked and bleeding lips, Alex grinned. "About as long as you've been clueless. So, a while."

"We should get going," Sam said. "Shall we try your rune?"

I looked down at othala. I wondered if there was some connection between inheritance and aid on a journey. I couldn't think of any. I didn't like where this rune came from or what it stood for, but I supposed it made sense that I'd have to use it. We'd earned it with a lot of pain and suffering, the same way we'd earned the mead.

"Do I just throw it in the air?" I wondered.

"I imagine Hearth would say . . ." Alex continued in sign language: *Yes, you idiot.*

I was pretty sure that wasn't what Hearth would say.

I tossed the rune. The othala dissolved in a wisp of snow. I hoped it would reappear in Hearth's rune bag after a day or two, the way runes usually did after he used them. I definitely didn't want to buy him a replacement.

"Nothing happened," I noted. Then I glanced to either side of me. Alex and Sam had disappeared. "Oh, gods, I vaporized you!" I tried to stand up, but unseen hands grabbed me from either side and dragged me back down.

"I'm right here," Alex said. "Sam?"

"Here," Sam confirmed. "It seems the rune made us invisible. I can see myself, but not you guys."

I glanced down. Sam was right. I could see myself just fine, but the only sign of my two friends was their impressions where they sat in the snow.

I wondered why othala had chosen invisibility. Was it drawing on my personal experience, feeling invisible when I was homeless? Or maybe the magic was shaped by Hearthstone's family experience. I imagined he'd wished he were invisible to his father for most of his childhood. Whatever the case, I didn't intend to waste this chance.

"Let's get moving," I said.

"Hold hands," Alex ordered.

She took my left hand with no particular affection, as if I were a walking stick. Sam did not take my other hand, but I suspected it wasn't for religious reasons. She just liked the idea of Alex and me holding hands. I could almost *hear* Sam smiling.

"Okay," she said, "let's go."

We trudged along the stone ridge, heading for the shore. I worried about leaving a trail of footprints, but the snow and wind quickly blew away all traces of our passage.

The temperature and wind were as bitter as the day before, but Skadi's apple cider must have been working. My breathing didn't feel like I was inhaling glass. I didn't have the need to check my face every few seconds to make sure my nose hadn't fallen off.

Over the howl of the wind and the boom of glaciers calving into the bay, other sounds reached us from the deck of *Naglfar*—chains clanking, beams creaking, giants barking orders, and the boots of last-minute arrivals tromping across the fingernail deck. The ship must have been very close to sailing.

We were about a hundred yards from the dock when Alex yanked on my hand. "Down, you idiot!"

I dropped in place, though I didn't see how we could hide much better than being invisible.

Emerging from the wind and snow, passing within ten feet

of us, a troop of ghoulish soldiers marched toward *Naglfar*. I hadn't seen them coming, and Alex was right: I didn't want to trust that invisibility would keep me hidden from these guys.

Their tattered leather armor was glazed with ice. Their bodies were nothing but desiccated bits of flesh clinging to bones. Blue spectral light flickered inside their rib cages and skulls, making me think of birthday candles parading across the worst birthday cake ever.

As the undead tromped past, I noticed that the soles of their boots were studded with nails, like cleats. I remembered something Halfborn Gunderson had once told me: because the road to Helheim was icy, the dishonored dead were buried with nailed shoes to keep them from slipping along the way. Now those boots were marching their owners back to the world of the living.

Alex's hand shivered in mine. Or maybe I was the one shivering. At last the dead passed us, heading for the docks and the Ship of the Dead.

I got unsteadily to my feet.

"Allah defend us," Sam muttered.

I desperately hoped that if the Big Guy was real, Sam had some pull with him. We were going to need defending.

"Our friends are facing *that*," Alex said. "We've got to hurry."

She was right again. The only thing that would make me want to go aboard a ship filled with thousands of those zombies was knowing that if we didn't, our friends would fight them alone. That wasn't going to happen.

I stepped into the tracks left by the dead army, and immediately, whispering voices filled my head: *Magnus. Magnus.*

Pain spiked my eyes. My knees buckled. I *knew* these voices. Some were harsh and angry, others kind and gentle. All of them echoed in my mind, demanding attention. One of them . . . One voice was my mother's.

I staggered.

"Hey," Alex hissed. "What are you—? Wait, what *is* that?"

Did she hear the voices, too? I turned, trying to pinpoint their source. I hadn't seen it before, but about fifty feet away, in the direction from which the zombies had come, a dark square hole had appeared in the snow—a ramp leading down into nothingness.

Magnus, whispered Uncle Randolph's voice. *I'm so sorry, my boy. Can you ever forgive me? Come down. Let me see you once more.*

Magnus, said a voice I'd only heard in dreams: Caroline, Randolph's wife. *Please forgive him. His heart was in the right place. Come, darling. I want to meet you.*

Are you our cousin? said the voice of a little girl—Emma, Randolph's older daughter. *My daddy gave me an othala rune, too. Would you like to see it?*

Most painful of all, my mom called *Come on, Magnus!* in the cheerful tone she used to use when she was encouraging me to hurry up the trail so she could share an amazing vista with me. Except now there was a coldness to her voice, as if her lungs were filled with Freon. *Hurry!*

The voices tore at me, taking little pieces of my mind. Was I sixteen? Was I twelve or ten? Was I in Niflheim or the Blue Hills or on Uncle Randolph's boat?

Alex's hand dropped from mine. I didn't care.

I stepped toward the cave.

Somewhere behind me, Sam said, "Guys?"

She sounded concerned, on the edge of panic, but her voice didn't seem any more real to me than the whispering spirits. She couldn't stop me. She couldn't see my footprints on the trampled path left by the zombie soldiers. If I ran, I could make it down that icy road and plunge into Helheim before my friends knew what had happened. The thought thrilled me.

My family was down there. Hel, the goddess of the dishonored dead, had told me as much when I'd met her on Bunker Hill. She'd promised I could join them. Maybe they needed my help.

Jack pulsed warmly against my throat. Why was he doing that?

Off to my left, Alex muttered, "No. No, I won't listen."

"Alex!" Sam said. "Thank God. Where's Magnus?"

Why did Sam sound so concerned? I had a vague recollection that we were in Niflheim for a reason. I—I probably shouldn't be diving into Helheim right now. That would probably kill me.

The whispering voices got louder, more insistent.

My mind fought against them. I resisted the urge to run toward that dark ramp.

I was invisible because of the othala rune—the rune of inheritance. What if this was the downside of its magic? It was allowing me to hear the voices of my dead, pulling me into their realm.

Alex found my hand again. "Got him."

I fought down a surge of irritation. "Why?" I croaked.

"I know," Alex said, her voice surprisingly gentle. "I hear them, too. But you can't follow them."

Slowly the dark ramp closed. The voices stopped. The wind and snow began to erase the tracks of the zombies.

"You guys okay?" Sam called, her voice an octave higher than usual.

"Yeah," I said, not feeling very okay. "I—I'm sorry about that."

"Don't be." Alex squeezed my fingers. "I heard my grandfather. I'd almost forgotten what he sounded like. And other voices. Adrian . . ." She choked on the name.

I almost didn't dare ask. "Who?"

"A friend," she said, loading the word with all sorts of possible meanings. "Committed suicide."

Her hand went limp in mine, but I didn't let her go. I was tempted to reach out with my power, to try to heal her, to share the backwash of pain and memories that would flood my head from Alex's past. But I didn't. I hadn't been invited there.

Sam was silent for a count of ten. "Alex, I'm so sorry. I—I didn't hear anything."

"Be glad," I said.

"Yeah," Alex agreed.

Part of me was still resisting the urge to run across the snow, fling myself down, and claw at the ground until the tunnel reopened. I'd heard my mother. Even if it was just a cold echo. Or a trick. A cruel joke from Hel.

I turned toward the sea. Suddenly I was more afraid of staying on solid ground than I was of boarding the Ship of the Dead.

"Let's go," I said. "Our friends are counting on us."

FORTY-ONE

I Call a Time-Out

THE GANGPLANK was made of toenails.

If that isn't enough to gross you out, then no amount of Kvasir's Mead will help me give you a sufficiently disgusting description. Though the ramp was fifty feet wide, it got so much traffic we had trouble finding an opening. We timed our ascent to follow a troop of zombies aboard, but I almost got stepped on by a giant carrying a stack of spears.

Once at the top, we ducked to one side, pressing ourselves against the railing.

In person, the ship was even more horrible than in my dreams. The deck seemed to stretch out forever—a glistening patchwork of yellow, black, and gray nail plates, like the hide of some armored prehistoric creature. Hundreds of giants bustled about, looking almost human-size in comparison with the vessel: stone giants, mountain giants, frost giants, hill giants, and a few nattily dressed fellows who might have been metropolitan giants, all coiling ropes, stacking weapons, and shouting at each other in a variety of jotun dialects.

The undead were not so industrious. Taking up most of the vast deck, they stood at attention in ranks of ghostly white and blue, tens of thousands, like they were waiting for a parade review. Some were mounted on zombie horses. Others had zombie dogs or wolves at their side. A few even had zombie birds of prey perched on their skeletal arms. They all seemed perfectly content to stand in silence until further orders. Many of them had waited centuries for this final battle. I supposed they figured a little longer wouldn't hurt.

The giants did their best to avoid the undead. They stepped gingerly around the legions, cursing them for being in the way, but didn't touch them or threaten them directly. I imagined I might feel the same way if I found myself sharing a ship with a horde of strangely well-behaved, heavily armed rodents.

I scanned the deck for Loki. I spotted nobody in a bright white admiral's uniform, but that meant nothing. In those vast crowds, he could have been anywhere, disguised as anyone. Or he could have been belowdecks, having a leisurely pre-Ragnarok breakfast. So much for my plan of walking right up to him unopposed and saying *Hi. I challenge you to a duel of name-calling, Stupid Head.*

On the foredeck, maybe half a mile away, a giant paced back and forth, waving an ax and shouting orders. He was too far off for me to make out many details, but from my dreams I recognized his hunched, gaunt form and his elaborate rib-cage shield. He was Hrym, captain of the vessel. His voice carried over the din of crashing waves and growling jotuns:

"MAKE READY, YOU COW-FOOTED COWARDS! THE PASSAGE IS CLEAR! IF YOU DON'T MOVE FASTER, I'LL FEED YOU TO GARM!"

Then, somewhere behind the captain, toward the prow, an explosion shook the boat. Screaming, smoking giants tumbled through the air like acrobats shot from cannons.

"WE'RE UNDER ATTACK!" someone yelled. "GET THEM!"

Our friends had arrived.

I couldn't see them, but over the din of confusion, I heard the brassy tones of a reveille from a bugle. I could only assume T.J. had found the instrument under his firing caps, marksman's glasses, and hardtack.

Above Captain Hrym, a golden rune blazed in the sky:

$$\triangleright$$

Thurisaz, the sign for destruction, but also the symbol of the god Thor. Hearthstone couldn't have picked a better rune to strike fear and confusion into a bunch of giants. Lightning bolts blasted from the rune in every direction, frying giants and undead alike.

More giants swarmed the upper deck. Not that they had much choice. The ship was so packed with troops that the crowds pushed the front lines forward whether they wanted to go or not. An avalanche of bodies choked ramps and stairways. A mob overtook Captain Hrym and carried him along as he waved his ax above his head and yelled to no effect.

The undead legions mostly stayed in their ranks, but even they turned their heads toward the chaos, as if mildly curious.

Next to me, Sam muttered, "Now or never."

Alex let go of my hand. I heard the hissing sound of her garrote being pulled from her belt loops.

We started forward, occasionally touching each other's shoulders to keep our bearings. I ducked as a giant strode over me. We wove our way through a legion of zombie cavalry, their spears bristling with frosty light, their horses' dead white eyes staring at nothing.

I heard a war cry that sounded as if it had come from Halfborn Gunderson. I hoped he hadn't taken his shirt off like he normally did in combat. Otherwise he might catch cold while he fought to the death.

Another rune exploded over the prow:

$$|$$

Isa, ice, which must have been easy to cast in Niflheim. A wave of frost surged across *Naglfar's* port side, turning a whole swath of giants into ice sculptures.

In the gray morning light, I caught the glint of a small bronze object flying toward Captain Hrym, and I thought one of my friends had lobbed a grenade. But instead of exploding, the "grenade" enlarged as it fell, expanding to an impossibly large size, until the captain and a dozen of his nearest jotun friends disappeared under a metal duck the size of a Starbucks store.

Near the starboard rail, another bronze mallard ballooned into being, pushing a battalion of zombies into the sea. Giants screamed and fell back in chaos, as one does when large metal ducks rain from the sky.

"Expand-o-ducks," I said. "Blitz outdid himself."

"Keep going," Alex said. "We're close now."

Perhaps we shouldn't have spoken. In the nearest line of zombie warriors, a thane with golden armbands turned his wolf-faced helmet in our direction. A snarl rattled in his rib cage.

He said something in a language I didn't know—his voice wet and hollow like water dripping in a coffin. His men drew rusted swords from moldy sheaths and turned to face us.

I glanced at Sam and Alex. They were visible, so I assumed I was, too. Like some sort of bad joke—the kind of magical protection you'd expect from Mr. Alderman—our othala cover had broken in the exact center of the ship's main deck in front of a legion of undead.

Zombies encircled us. Most of the giants were still running forward to deal with our friends, but a few jotuns noticed us, yelled in outrage, and came to join the killing party.

"Well, Sam," Alex said. "It's been nice knowing you."

"What about me?" I asked.

"Jury's still out." She turned into a mountain lion and lunged at the draugr thane, biting his head clean off, then moved through the ranks, changing form effortlessly from wolf to human to eagle, each one deadlier than the last.

Sam pulled out her Valkyrie spear. With searing light, she blasted through the undead, burning dozens at a time, but hundreds more pressed forward, their swords and spears bristling.

I drew Jack and yelled, "Fight!"

"OKAY!" he yelled back, sounding just as panicked as I was. He whirled around me, doing his best to keep me safe, but I found myself with a problem particular to children of Frey.

Einherjar have a saying: *Kill the healer first.*

This military philosophy was perfected by seasoned Viking warriors who, once in Valhalla, learned to play video games.

The idea is simple: you target any guy in the enemy's ranks who can heal your opponents' wounds and send them back into combat. Kill the healer, and the rest die sooner. Besides, the healer is probably soft and squishy and easy to eliminate.

Evidently giants and zombies also knew this pro tip. Maybe they played the same video games einherjar did while waiting for Doomsday. Somehow, they pegged me for a healer, ignored Alex and Sam, and crowded toward me. Arrows flew past my ears. Spears jabbed at my belly. Axes hurtled between my legs. The quarters were much too close for so many combatants. Most of the draugr weapons found draugr targets, but I supposed zombies didn't worry too much about friendly fire.

I did what I could to look fighterly. With my einherji strength, I punched straight through the nearest zombie's chest cavity, which was like punching through a vat of dry ice. Then, as he fell, I grabbed his sword and impaled his nearest comrade.

"Who needs a healer *now?*" I yelled.

For about ten seconds, we seemed to be doing okay. Another rune exploded. Another expand-o-duck visited mallard-shaped destruction upon our enemies. From the prow came the sharp report of T.J.'s 1861 Springfield. I heard Mallory cursing in Gaelic.

Halfborn Gunderson yelled, "I AM HALFBORN OF FLÄM!"

To which a dim-witted giant replied, "Fläm? What a dump!"

"RARRRRGGGHH!" Halfborn's howl of anger shook the boat, followed by the sound of his battle-ax plowing through rows of bodies.

Alex and Sam fought like twin demons—Sam's blazing

spear and Alex's razor-sharp garrote scything through the undead with equal speed.

But with so many enemies surrounding us, it was only a matter of time before a hit connected. The butt of a spear caught me in the side of my head and I crumpled to my knees.

"Señor!" Jack shouted.

I saw a zombie's ax blade hurtling toward my face. I knew Jack wouldn't have time to stop it. With all the poetic prowess of a Kvasir's Mead drinker, I thought, *Well, this sucks.*

Then something happened that was *not* my death.

Angry pressure built in my stomach—a certainty that all this fighting had to stop, *must* stop if we were going to complete our mission. I roared even louder than Halfborn Gunderson.

Golden light exploded outward in all directions, blasting across the deck of the ship, ripping swords from their owners' hands, turning projectiles in midair and sending them hurtling into the sea, stripping entire battalions of their spears and shields and axes.

I staggered to my feet.

The fighting had stopped. Every weapon within the sound of my voice had been violently blasted from its owner's reach. Even Jack had gone flying somewhere off the starboard side, which I imagined I'd be hearing about later if I survived. Everyone on the ship, friend and enemy, had been disarmed by the Peace of Frey, a power I'd only managed to invoke once before.

Wary giants and confused zombies backed away from me. Alex and Sam ran to my side.

My head throbbed. My vision swam. One of my molars was missing, and my mouth was full of blood.

The Peace of Frey was a pretty good party trick. It definitely got everyone's attention. But it wasn't a permanent fix. Nothing would stop our enemies from simply retrieving their weapons and returning to the business of healer-slaughter.

But before the moment of empty-handed awe wore off, a familiar voice spoke somewhere to my left: "Well, now, Magnus. That was dramatic!"

The draugr parted to reveal Loki in his crisp white admiral's uniform, his hair the color of autumn leaves, his scarred lips twisted in a grin, his eyes bright with malicious humor.

Behind him stood Sigyn, his long-suffering wife, who had spent centuries collecting serpent venom in a cup to keep it from dripping into Loki's face—a duty which was *totally* not covered in your typical marriage vows. Her pale, emaciated face was impossible to read, though bloodred tears still streamed from her eyes. I thought I detected a slight tightness in her lips, as if she were disappointed to see me again.

"Loki . . ." I spat blood. I could barely make my mouth work. "I challenge you to a flyting."

He stared at me as if waiting for me to complete the sentence. Maybe he expected me to add: *a flyting . . . with this other guy who's good at insults and way more intimidating than I am.*

Around us, the endless ranks of warriors seemed to be holding their breath, even though the zombies had no breath to hold.

Njord, Frigg, Skadi—all of them had assured me that Loki would *have* to accept my challenge. That was tradition. Honor demanded it. I might have a busted mouth, a ringing head, and no guarantee that the Mead of Kvasir would weave poetry with my vocal cords, but at least I would now get my shot to defeat the trickster in a war of words.

Loki lifted his face to the cold gray sky and laughed.

"Thanks anyway, Magnus Chase," he said. "But I think I'll just kill you."

FORTY-TWO

I Start Small

SAM LUNGED. I guess she was the *least* surprised that Loki would pull a sleazeball move like refusing my challenge.

Before her spear could hit her father's chest, a loud voice roared, "STOP!"

Sam stopped.

My mind was still fuzzy. For a second, I thought Loki had shouted the order, and Sam had been forced to obey. All Sam's training and practice, her fasting and confidence, had been for nothing.

Then I realized Loki hadn't given the order at all. In fact, he looked quite annoyed. Sam had stopped of her own free will. Crowds of draugr and giants parted as Captain Hrym limped toward us. His ax was missing. His fancy rib-cage shield was dented with an impression that might have been made by a very large duck's bill.

His ancient face wasn't any prettier up close. Wisps of icicle-white beard clung to his chin. His pale blue eyes gleamed deep in their sockets like they were melting their way into his brain. His leathery mouth made it difficult to tell if he was glowering at us or about to spit out a watermelon seed.

And the captain's smell: *yeesh.* Hrym's moldy white furs

made me nostalgic for the regular "old man" odors of Uncle Randolph's closet.

"Who called for a challenge?" Hrym boomed.

"I did," I said. "A flyting against Loki, unless he is too scared to face me."

The crowd murmured, "Ooooohhhhh."

Loki snarled. "Oh, please. You can't bait me, Magnus Chase. Hrym, we don't have time for this. The ice has melted. The way is clear. Smash these trespassers and let's sail!"

"Now wait a minute!" Hrym said. "This is my ship! I am captain!"

Loki sighed. He took off his admiral's hat and punched the inside, obviously trying to control his temper.

"My dear friend." He smiled up at the captain. "We've been through this. We *share* command of *Naglfar*."

"Your troops," Hrym said. "My ship. And when we are in disagreement, all ties must be broken by Surt."

"*Surt?*" I gulped down another mouthful of blood. I wasn't thrilled to hear the name of my least favorite fire giant—the dude who'd blasted a hole in my chest and knocked my flaming corpse off the Longfellow Bridge. "Is, uh, Surt here, too?"

Loki snorted. "A fire giant in Niflheim? Not likely. You see, my dense young einherji, Surt technically owns this ship—but that's just because *Naglfar* is registered in Muspellheim. More favorable tax laws."

"That's not the point!" yelled Hrym. "Since Surt is not here, final command is mine!"

"No," Loki said with strained patience. "Final command is *ours*. And I say our troops need to get moving!"

"And I say a properly issued challenge must be accepted! Those are standard rules of engagement. Unless you *are* too cowardly, as the boy claims."

Loki laughed. "Cowardly? Of facing a child like this? Oh, please! He's nothing."

"Well, then," I said. "Show us your silver tongue—unless that got burned along with the rest of your face."

"Ooooohhhhh!" said the crowd.

Alex raised an eyebrow at me. Her expression seemed to say *That was not as lame as I might have expected.*

Loki gazed at the heavens. "Father Farbauti, Mother Laufey, why me? My talents are wasted on this audience!"

Hrym turned to me. "Will you and your allies abide by a cease-fire until the flyting is done?"

Alex responded, "Magnus is our flyter, not our leader. But, yes, we will hold off our attacks."

"Even the ducks?" Hrym asked gravely.

Alex frowned, as if this was a serious request indeed. "Very well. Even the ducks."

"Then it is agreed!" Hrym bellowed. "Loki, you have been challenged! By ancient custom, you must accept!"

Loki bit back whatever insult he was going to fling at the captain, probably because Hrym was twice as tall as he was. "Very well. I will insult Magnus Chase into the deck boards and smear his remains under my shoe. *Then* we will sail! Samirah, dear, hold my hat."

He tossed his admiral's cap. Samirah let it fall at her feet.

She smiled at him coldly. "Hold your own hat, *Father.*"

"Ooooohhhhh!" said the crowd.

Anger rippled across Loki's face. I could almost see the ideas churning in his head—all the wonderful ways he could torture us to death—but he said nothing.

"A FLYTING!" Hrym announced. "Until it is over, let no more blows be struck! Let no more ducks be thrown! Allow those enemy warriors forward to see the contest!"

With some jostling and cursing, our friends made their way through the crowd. Considering what they'd been through, they looked all right. Halfborn had indeed taken off his shirt. Written across his chest in what looked like giant's blood was FLÄM with a big heart around it.

T.J.'s rifle muzzle steamed in the cold from so many discharges. His bayonet dripped zombie slime, and his bugle had been twisted into a brass pretzel. (I couldn't really blame our enemies for doing that.)

Hearthstone looked unharmed but drained, which was understandable after destroying so many enemies with ice and lightning. At his side strode Blitzen, and giants ten times the dwarf's size scrambled to get out of his way. Some muttered fearfully, calling him *duck master*. Others clawed at their necks, which Blitzen had somehow collared with tight-fitting chain mail neckties. Giants live in fear of neckties.

Mallory Keen was hopping, apparently having re-broken the same foot she'd broken in Norway. But she hopped fiercely, like a true warrior and daughter of Frigg. She sheathed her knives and signed to me, *I have the walnut.*

That would have made a great code phrase if we were spies talking about a nuclear weapon or something. Unfortunately, she just meant that she had the walnut. Now it was up to me to get Loki into it. I wondered if Mallory could open it and suck him inside without me first beating him in insult combat. Probably not. Nothing so far had been that simple. I doubted easy mode would start now.

Finally, Jack came floating back to me, grumbling, "Peace-of-Freying me? Not cool, señor." Then he settled next to Samirah to watch the action.

The crowd made a rough circle maybe thirty feet in diameter around Loki and me. Surrounded by giants, I felt like I was at the bottom of a well. In the sudden quiet, I could hear the rumble of snow thunder in the distance, the crackle of melting glacial ice, the quiver and whine of *Naglfar's* iron mooring cables straining to break free.

My head throbbed. My busted mouth oozed blood. My hole where the tooth used to be had started to hurt, and I did not feel poetic.

Loki grinned. He spread his arms as if to welcome me with an embrace.

"Well, Magnus, look at you—flyting in the big leagues like a grown-up! Or whatever you call an einherji who can't age but is learning to be not *quite* so much of a whiny brat. If you weren't such a useless piece of fluff, I might be impressed!"

The words stung. I mean they *literally* stung. They seemed to splash into my ear canals like acid, trickling down my eustachian tubes and into my throat. I tried to reply, but Loki thrust his scarred face into mine.

"Little son of Frey," he said. "Walking into a battle he can't win, with no clue, no planning—just a little mead in his stomach! Did you really think that would compensate for your complete lack of skill? I suppose it makes sense. You're so used to relying on your friends to do all your fighting. Now it's your turn! Sad! A no-talent loser! Do you even know what you *are*, Magnus Chase? Should I tell you?"

The crowd laughed and jostled each other. I didn't dare look at my friends. Shame washed through me.

"Y-you're one to talk," I managed. "Are you a giant masquerading as a god, or a god masquerading as a giant? Are you on anybody's side but your own?"

"Of course not!" Loki laughed. "We're all free agents on this ship, aren't we, gang? We look out for ourselves!"

The giants roared. The zombies shifted and hissed, their icy blue auras crackling in their skulls.

"Loki looks out for Loki." He drummed his fingers on his admiralty medals. "I can't trust anyone else, can I?"

His wife, Sigyn, tilted her head ever so slightly, but Loki didn't seem to notice.

"At least I'm honest about it!" Loki continued. "And to answer your question, I'm a giant! But here's the thing, Magnus. The Aesir are just a different generation of giants. So they're giants, too! This whole gods-versus-giants thing is ridiculous. We're one big unhappy family. That's something you should understand, you dysfunctional little human. You say you choose your family. You say you've got a new group of brothers and sisters in Valhalla, and isn't that sweet? Stop lying to yourself. You're *never* free of your blood. You are just like your real family. As weak and love-besotted as Frey. As desperate and spineless as old Uncle Randolph. And as stupidly optimistic and as *dead* as your mother. Poor kid. You've got the worst of both sides, Frey and Chase. You're a mess!"

The crowd laughed. They seemed to grow larger, drowning me in their shadows.

Loki loomed over me. "Stop lying to yourself, Magnus. You're *nobody*. You're a *mistake*, one of Frey's many bastards. He left your mom, forgot you completely until you recovered his sword."

"That's not true."

"But it is! You know it! At least I *claim* my children. Sam and Alex here—they've known me since they were little kids! But you? You're not even worth Frey sending a birthday card. And who does your hair?"

He howled. "Oh, right. Alex cut it, didn't she? You didn't think that *meant* anything, did you? She doesn't care about Magnus Chase. She just needed to use you. She's her mother's child. I'm so proud."

Alex's face was livid, but she didn't speak. None of my friends moved or made a sound. This was my fight. They couldn't interfere.

Where was the magic of Kvasir's Mead? Why couldn't I come up with a decent zinger? Did I really think the mead could compensate for my complete lack of skill?

Wait . . . those were Loki's words, burrowing into my brain. I couldn't let him define me.

"You're evil," I said. Even that sounded halfhearted.

"Oh, come on!" Loki grinned. "Don't throw that good-and-evil stuff at me. That's not even a Norse concept. Are you *good* because you kill your enemies, but your enemies are *bad* because they kill you? What sort of logic is that?"

He leaned in close. He was definitely taller than I was now. The top of my head barely reached his shoulders. "A little secret, Magnus. There is no good and evil. There's only capable and incapable. I am *capable*. You . . . are not."

He didn't push me, not physically, but I stumbled back. I was literally withering under the laughter of the crowd. Even Blitzen was taller than me now. Behind Loki, Sigyn watched me with interest, her red tears glistening down her cheeks.

"Aww." Loki pouted with fake sympathy. "What are you going to do now, Magnus? Complain that I'm mean? Criticize me for murder and deceit? Go right ahead! Sing my greatest hits! You just wish you were so capable. You can't fight. You can't think on your feet. You can't even express yourself in front of your so-called friends! What chance do you have against me?"

I continued to shrink. A few more lines from Loki and I would be two feet tall. Around my boots, the decking began to scritch and shift, finger- and toenails curling upward like hungry plant shoots.

"Give it your best shot!" Loki challenged. "No? Still tongue-tied? Then I guess I'll tell you what I *really* think of you!"

I looked at the leering faces of giants, and the grim faces of my friends, all forming a ring around me, and I knew this was a well I would never climb out of.

FORTY-THREE

I Have a Big Finish

I DESPERATELY tried to think of my best insults: *You're a meinfretr. You're dumb. You're ugly.*

Yeah . . . my best really wasn't that impressive, especially coming from a guy who was literally shrinking under Loki's onslaught.

Hoping for inspiration, I glanced again at my friends. Sam looked stern and determined, somehow still believing in me. Alex Fierro looked angry and defiant, somehow still believing that if I messed this up, she would kill me. Blitz had developed a tic in his eye like he was watching me ruin a beautiful tailoring job. Hearthstone seemed sad and weary, scrutinizing my face as if searching for a lost rune. T.J., Mallory, and Halfborn were all tense, scanning the giants around them, probably trying to formulate a Plan B in which the *B* stood for *Bad Magnus*.

Then my gaze rested on Sigyn, standing discreetly behind her husband, her hands laced, her strange red eyes fixed on me as if she were waiting.

Waiting for what? She had stood by her husband's side when everyone else abandoned him. For centuries, she had tended to him, keeping the snake's venom from his face as much as she could, despite the fact that Loki had cheated on her, verbally abused her, ignored her. Even now, he barely looked at her.

Sigyn was loyal beyond belief. Yet back in Loki's cave, during the giant's wedding ceremony, I was almost positive she had helped us, distracting her husband at a critical time to keep him from killing me and my friends.

Why would she resist her husband like that? What did she want? It was almost as if she was subtly working to undermine him, as if she *wanted* to delay Ragnarok and see her husband back in his cave, lashed to the rocks and suffering.

Maybe Loki was right. Maybe he couldn't trust anyone, not even Sigyn.

Then I thought about what Percy Jackson had told me back on the deck of the USS *Constitution*: that my biggest strength wasn't my training. It was the team around me.

A flyting was supposed to cut people down to size, to insult them into nothingness. But I was a healer. I didn't cut people. I put them back together. I couldn't play by Loki's rules and hope to win. I had to play by *my* rules.

I took a deep breath. "Let me tell you about Mallory Keen."

Loki's smile wavered. "Who is that and why should I care?"

"I'm so glad you asked." I projected my voice into the crowd with as much volume and confidence as my tiny little lungs would allow. "Mallory Keen sacrificed her life to correct her own mistake and saved the lives of a bunch of schoolkids! Now she is the fiercest fighter and the best curser in Valhalla. She holds floor nineteen together as a team, even when we want to kill each other! Can any of you claim the same level of camaraderie?"

The giants shifted uncomfortably. The draugr eyed each other like *I've been wanting to kill this guy forever, but he's already dead.*

"Mallory opened the doors of Suttung's cave with just two daggers!" I continued. "She defeated the nine thralls of Baugi with nothing but trickery and a rock! And when she found out she was the daughter of Frigg, she refrained from attacking the goddess!"

"Ooh." The giants nodded appreciatively.

Loki waved aside my words. "I don't think you understand how a flyting works, little man. Those aren't even *insults—*"

"Let me tell you about Halfborn Gunderson!" I shouted over him. "Berserker extraordinaire, the glory of Fläm! He conquered kingdoms with Ivar the Boneless. He singlehand-edly slew the giant Baugi, saving his hometown and making his mother proud! He has steered our boat straight and true across the Nine Worlds, his battle-ax doing more damage than most battalions, and he's done all this while wearing no shirt!"

"He pulls it off pretty well, too," muttered another giant, poking the berserker's abs. Halfborn slapped his hand away.

"And the deeds of Thomas Jefferson Junior!" I yelled. "Those are worthy of any Viking hall! He charged into enemy gunfire to meet his nemesis, Jeffrey Toussaint, face-to-face. He died taking up an impossible challenge, like a worthy son of Tyr! He is the heart and soul of our fellowship, a driving force that never fails. He defeated the giant Hrungnir with his trusty Springfield 1861, and wears the flint shard from the giant's heart above his eye as a badge of honor. It can also light matches!"

"Mmmm." The giants nodded, no doubt thinking how handy this would be for lighting their pipes in the cold winds of Niflheim.

"And Blitzen, son of Freya!" I smiled at my dwarf friend, whose eyes were getting dewy. "He bested Eitri Junior, at the forges of Nidavellir. He makes the best cutting-edge fashions in the Nine Worlds. He sewed the magical bowling bag of Tiny! He stood face-to-face, empty-handed against the dragon Alderman and forced the monster to back down. His patented stainless-steel neckties and expand-o-ducks are the stuff of jotun nightmares!"

Several giants wailed in terrified agreement.

"Stop this!" Loki spat. "This is ridiculous! What's all this— this *positivity*? Magnus Chase, your hair is still horrible and your clothes—"

"Hearthstone!" I roared. Was it my imagination, or was I getting taller again? It seemed I could look my opponent in the eyes now without straining my neck. "The greatest rune magician in the Nine Worlds! His bravery is legendary! He is willing to sacrifice anything for his friends. He has overcome the most horrible challenges—the death of his brother, the scorn of his family . . ." My voice cracked with emotion, but Loki did not speak into the void. The crowd stared at me expectantly, some with tears in their eyes.

"His own father turned into a dragon," I said. "Yet *Hearthstone* faced him, faced his worst nightmares and emerged victorious, breaking a curse, destroying hatred with compassion. Without him, we would not be here. He is the mightiest and most beloved elf I know. He is my brother."

Hearthstone placed his hand on his heart. His face was as pink as the scarf Alex had given him.

Captain Hrym sniffled. It seemed like he wanted to give Hearthstone a hug but was afraid that might not look good in front of his crew.

"Samirah al-Abbas," I said. "Daughter of Loki, but better than Loki!"

Loki laughed. "I *beg* your pardon? This girl is not even—"

"A Valkyrie, sworn to Odin's most important tasks!" My words were coming easily now. I could feel a rhythm to them, an unstoppable cadence and certainty. Maybe that was because of Kvasir's Mead. Or maybe it was because I was speaking the truest things I knew. "You have felt her spear of light scorch your forces in combat! Her stamina is steel. Her faith is unwavering. She has overcome her father's sway! She saved our ship from the dreaded vatnavaettir! She outflew the great Baugi in his eagle form, delivering Kvasir's Mead to our crew! And she has done all of this while *fasting for Ramadan*."

Several giants gasped. Some put their hands to their throats as if just realizing how thirsty they were.

"Samirah," Loki growled, "turn into a lizard and scuttle away, my dear."

Sam frowned at him. "No, Father, I don't think I will. Why don't you?"

"Oooh!" Some of the giants even clapped.

I was definitely taller than usual now. Or wait . . . Loki was getting shorter.

But I needed more. I turned to Alex. "Let me tell you all about Alex Fierro!"

"Saving the best for last?" Alex asked, a hint of challenge in her voice.

"She is our secret weapon!" I said. "The Terror of Jorvik! The creator of Pottery Barn, ceramic warrior!"

"I got some lovely place mats at Pottery Barn," one of the giants muttered to a friend.

"At the House of Chase, he decapitated a wolf with nothing more than a wire, then drank guava juice from the horn of my ancestors!"

"He?" asked a giant.

"Just go with it," said another.

"She once decapitated Grimwolf the elder lindworm!" I continued. "She defeated the sorcery of Utgard-Loki in a bowling tournament of horrors! She won the trust and affection of the goddess Sif! She kept me alive across the frozen sea of Niflheim, and when she kissed me under that blanket yesterday . . ." I met Alex's two-color eyes. "Well, that was just about the best thing that ever happened to me."

I turned toward Loki. My face was burning. I'd spoken maybe just a wee bit more truth than I'd intended, but I couldn't let that break my momentum.

"Loki, you asked me who I am? I'm part of this team. I'm Magnus Chase from floor nineteen, Hotel Valhalla. I'm the son of Frey, son of Natalie, friend of Mallory, Halfborn, T.J., Blitzen, Hearthstone, Samirah, and Alex. This is my family! This is my othala. I know they will always support me, which is why I'm standing here, triumphant, on *your* ship, surrounded by my family, and you . . . even in the midst of thousands, you. Are. Still. Alone."

Loki hissed. He backed into a wall of scowling draugr. "I am not alone! Sigyn! Dear wife!"

Sigyn had vanished. At some point during the flyting, she must have retreated into the crowd. That silent act spoke louder than centuries of verbal abuse.

"Alex! Samirah!" Loki tried for a confident smile. "Come on, my dears. You *know* I love you! Don't be difficult. Kill your friends for me and all will be forgiven."

Alex adjusted her shaggy green fur cloak over her sweater vest. "Sorry, Mom. I'm afraid I gotta say no."

Loki dashed toward Samirah, who pushed him back at spear point. The trickster was about three feet tall now. He tried changing form. Fur sprouted across his brow. Fishy scales appeared on the backs of his hands. Nothing seemed to stick.

"You can't hide from yourself, Loki," I said. "No matter what form you take, you're still you—alone, scorned, bitter, faithless. Your insults are hollow and desperate. You don't stand a chance against us, because you don't have an *us*. You are Loki, always alone."

"I *hate* you all!" the god screamed, spittle flying. Acid oozed from his pores, hissing against the deck. "None of you are worthy of my company, much less my leadership!"

As Loki shrank, his scarred face rippled, contorting with rage. Acid steamed in puddles all around him. I wondered if this was all the venom that Skadi's viper had dripped on him over the centuries, or if it was simply part of Loki's essence. Perhaps Sigyn had tried to shield Loki from the snake because she knew her husband was already full of poison. He could barely keep his human form from liquefying into the stuff.

"You think your happy friendship speech means anything?" he snarled. "Is it time for a group hug now? You make me sick!"

"You'll have to speak up," I said. "It's hard to hear you from way down there."

Loki paced and ranted, no more than a few inches tall now, wading through puddles of his own venom. "I will kill you slowly! I will have Hel torture the spirits of everyone you love! I will—"

"Escape?" Samirah asked, blocking Loki with her spear point as he darted left. He ran to the right, but Alex put down her pink ski boot to stop him.

"I don't think so, Mom," said Alex. "I like you down there. And now, Mallory Keen has a lovely parting gift for you."

Mallory hopped forward and brought out the walnut.

"No!" Loki squeaked. "No, you wouldn't dare! I will never—"

Mallory tossed the nut toward the miniature god. The shell opened, inhaling Loki with a vicious sucking noise, then snapped shut again. The walnut rattled and quivered on the deck. A little voice was shouting obscenities from inside, but the shell remained sealed.

The giants frowned down at the walnut.

Captain Hrym cleared his throat. "Well, that was interesting." He turned to me. "Congratulations, Magnus Chase! You won that flyting fair and square. I am impressed! I hope you'll accept my apology for having to kill you all now."

FORTY-FOUR

Why Do They Get Cannons?
I Want Cannons

I DID NOT accept his apology.

Neither did my friends. They formed a protective ring around me and began slashing through the enemy ranks, slowly shuffling toward the starboard side of the ship.

Still hopping on one leg, Mallory Keen scooped up her evil walnut and dropped it in her pocket, then demonstrated her dual-knife-wielding prowess by stabbing her blades into Captain Hrym's crotch.

Halfborn and T.J. fought like killing machines. I didn't want to give myself credit for their gusto, but the way they plowed through troops of draugr was awe-inspiring, almost as if they were determined to be as good as I'd described them—as if my words had made them larger while making Loki smaller.

"Follow me!" Sam yelled, her spear of light blasting a path to starboard. Alex swung her garrote like a whip, lopping off the heads of any giants who came too close.

I was afraid Blitzen might get trampled in the crush, but Hearthstone knelt and let the dwarf climb onto his shoulders. Okay, that was a new one. I didn't think Hearth had the physical strength to carry Blitz, who was short but stout and hardly a little kid. Yet Hearth managed, and from the unquestioning way Blitz accepted the ride, I got the feeling they'd done this before.

Blitz threw neckties and expand-o-ducks like Mardi Gras beads, sowing terror in the enemy's ranks. Meanwhile Hearth lobbed a familiar rune toward the foredeck:

M

Ehwaz, the rune of the steed, exploded with golden light. Suddenly, floating in the air above us, was our old friend Stanley the eight-legged horse.

Stanley surveyed the chaos, whinnied as if to say *Fight scene cameo? Okay.* Then he leaped into the fray, fly-galloping on the skulls of jotuns and generally causing havoc.

Jack, buzzing angrily, flew to my side. "I have a blade to grind with you, señor."

"What?" I ducked as a spear flew over my head.

"You give this beautiful speech," Jack said. "And who do you leave out? *Really?*"

Jack hilt-punched a giant so hard the poor guy flew backward, domino-toppling a line of zombie cavalry.

I gulped down my mortification. How could I have forgotten my sword? Jack *hated* being forgotten.

"Jack, you were my secret weapon!" I said.

"You said that about Alex!"

"Uh, I mean you were my ace in the hole! I was saving the best for, you know, emergency poetry!"

"A likely story!" He chopped through the nearest clump of draugr like a Vitamix.

"I—I'll get Bragi the god of poetry to *personally* write an epic about you!" I blurted out, regretting the promise as soon as I made it. "You're the best sword ever! Honestly!"

"An epic, huh?" He glowed a brighter shade of red, or maybe that was all the gore dripping from his blade. "By Bragi, huh?"

"Absolutely!" I said. "Now let's get out of here. Show me your best stuff so, you know, I can describe it to Bragi later."

"Hmph." Jack whirled toward a metropolitan giant, snicker-snacking him into natty pieces. "I suppose I can do that."

He went to work, slashing our enemies like a frantic Black Friday shopper rifling through clothes racks. "No, no, no!" Jack yelled. "I don't like you! Get out of my way! You're ugly!"

Soon our little cluster of heroes reached the starboard rail. Unfortunately, the drop over the side was four hundred feet at least, straight into the icy gray waters. My stomach twisted. This was *twice* as long a fall as the one I'd flubbed from the mainmast of Old Ironsides.

"We'll die if we jump," Mallory noted.

The enemy horde pressed us against the rail. No matter how well we fought, our enemies wouldn't even have to *hit* us to kill us now. Their sheer numbers would flatten us or push us overboard.

I pulled out my yellow handkerchief. "I can summon *Mikillgulr*, the way we did in Aegir's hall."

"Except we're falling *down* now," Alex said. "Not floating up. And there's no Njord to protect us."

"She's right," Blitz yelled, throwing a generous handful of neckties to his admirers. "Even if the ship doesn't break apart on impact, all our bones will."

Sam peered over the side. "And even if we survived, those guns would blow our ship out of the water."

"Guns?" I followed her gaze. I hadn't noticed them before, probably because the ports had been closed, but now the side of *Naglfar*'s hull bristled with rows of cannon muzzles.

"That's not fair," I said. "Vikings didn't have cannons. How come *Naglfar* gets cannons?"

T.J. jabbed a zombie with his bayonet. "I'll be sure to lodge a complaint with the Ragnarok Rules Committee. But right now, whatever we're going to do, we need to do it!"

"Agreed!" Halfborn shouted, his ax slicing through a pack of skeletal wolves.

"I've got a plan," Sam announced. "You're not going to like it."

"I love it!" Blitz cried. "What is it?"

"Jump," Sam said.

Alex ducked a javelin. "But the whole breaking-every-bone-in-our-bodies thing . . . ?"

"No time to explain," Sam said. "Jump!"

When your Valkyrie tells you to jump, you jump. I was the first one over the side. I tried to remember what Percy had told me—skydiver, eagle, arrow, butt—though I knew that falling from this height, none of it would matter.

I hit the water with a mighty *floom*. I had died enough times to know what to expect—a sudden overwhelming surge of pain followed by complete darkness. But that didn't happen. Instead, I bobbed to the surface, gasping and shivering but completely unharmed. I realized something was buoying me up.

The water churned and bubbled around me like I'd fallen into a Jacuzzi. Between my legs, the current felt almost solid, as if I was sitting astride a creature sculptured from the sea. Directly in front of me, a head rose from the waves—a strong neck of gray water, a mane of frost, a majestic snout spewing plumes of icy mist from its nostrils. I was riding a vatnavaettir—a water horse.

My friends plunged into the water, too, each dropping right onto the back of a waiting horse spirit. The vatnavaettir whinnied and bucked as spears rained down around us.

"Let's move!" Sam swooped down with her blazing spear and settled onto the back of the lead water horse. "Toward the mouth of the bay!"

The horses raced away from the Ship of the Dead. Giants and draugr screamed in outrage. Spears and arrows splashed in the water. Cannons boomed. Shells exploded near enough to spray us with water, but the vatnavaettir were faster and more maneuverable than any ship. They zigged and zagged, rocketing across the bay with incredible speed.

Jack flew up beside me. "Hey, señor, did you see that one disembowelment I did?"

"Yeah," I said. "It was amazing!"

"And the way I cut off that jotun's limbs?"

"Right!"

"I hope you were taking notes for Bragi's epic."

"Absolutely!" I made a mental note to start taking more mental notes.

A different equine figure zoomed above us—Stanley the eight-legged horse, checking that we were okay. He whinnied like *Okay, guess we're done here? Have a nice day!*

Then he shot toward the steel gray clouds.

The water horse was surprisingly warm, like a living animal, which kept my legs and crotch from freezing completely in the frigid water. Still, I remembered Mallory's and Halfborn's stories about vatnavaettir dragging their victims to the bottom of the sea. How was Samirah controlling them? If the herd decided to take a dive, we were all dead.

Yet we kept racing forward, toward the gap in the glaciers at the mouth of the bay. Already I could see the water beginning to refreeze, the ice floes thickening and hardening. Summer in Niflheim, which lasted about twelve minutes, was now over.

Behind us, the boom of cannons carried over the water, but the ship *Naglfar* remained at its moorings. I could only hope, since we had their admiral in a walnut, the ship would be forced to stay there.

We shot out of the bay into the frosty sea, our water horses picking us a path through the broken ice floes. Then we turned south toward the much safer, monster-infested open waters of Jotunheim.

FORTY-FIVE

If You Understand What Happens in This Chapter, Please Tell Me, Because I Have No Clue

THREE DAYS is a long time to sail with an evil walnut.

After the water horses dumped us—"They got bored," Sam explained, which was far better than them drowning us—I summoned the *Big Banana* and we all climbed aboard. Hearthstone managed to invoke the fire rune kenaz, which saved us from freezing to death. We sailed west, trusting our magic ship to take us where we needed to go.

The first twelve hours or so, we were all running on pure adrenaline and terror. We got into dry clothes. I healed Mallory's foot. We ate. We didn't talk much. We grunted and pointed at things we needed. No one slept. Sam chanted her prayers, which was amazing, since the rest of us probably couldn't have formed simple sentences.

Finally, when the gray sun sank and the world still hadn't ended, we started to believe that *Naglfar* really wasn't sailing after us. Loki would not be busting out of his tiny prison. Ragnarok wouldn't be starting this summer, at least. We had survived.

Mallory clutched the walnut. She refused to let go of it. She huddled against the prow, examining the sea with narrowed eyes, her red hair whipping in the wind. After about an hour of this, Halfborn Gunderson sat down next her. She didn't kill him. He muttered to her for a long time, words I didn't try to hear. She started to cry, expelling something from herself that sounded almost as bitter as Loki's venom. Halfborn put his arm around her, looking not happy exactly, but content.

The next day, Blitzen and Hearthstone went into nurturing mode, making sure everybody had food, everybody was warm enough, nobody was alone if they didn't want to be. Hearth spent a lot of time listening to T.J. talk about war and slavery and what constituted an honorable challenge. Hearth was an excellent listener.

Blitz sat with Alex Fierro all afternoon, showing her how to make a sweater vest out of chain mail. I wasn't sure Alex needed a chain mail sweater vest, but the work seemed to calm them both.

After her evening prayers, Samirah came up to me and offered me a date. (The kind you eat, of course.) We chewed our fruit and watched the strange constellations of Jotunheim blink above us.

"You were amazing," Sam said.

I let that sink in. Samirah wasn't big on doling out praise, any more than Mallory was big on doling out apologies.

"Well, it wasn't poetry," I said at last. "More like pure panic."

"Maybe there's not much difference," Sam said. "Besides, just take the compliment, Chase."

"Okay. Thank you." I stood next to her, watching the horizon. It felt nice just to be with a friend, enjoying the stars, not worrying about dying in the next five minutes.

"You did great, too," I said. "You stood up to Loki and defeated him."

Sam smiled. "Yeah. I had a lot of thanks to give in my prayers tonight."

I nodded. I wondered if I should be thanking someone, too—I mean, apart from my friends on the boat, of course. Sigyn, maybe, for her silent support, her passive resistance against her husband. If the gods put Loki back in his cave, I wondered if Sigyn would be going with him.

Maybe Uncle Randolph deserved a thank-you, too, for leaving me those notes about Kvasir's Mead. He'd tried to do something right at the end, no matter how spectacularly he'd betrayed me.

Thinking about Randolph reminded me of the voices from Helheim, tempting me to join them in the darkness. I locked that memory away. I wasn't feeling strong enough to face it just yet.

Sam pointed toward Alex, who was trying on her new sweater vest. "You should go talk to her, Magnus. That was kind of a bombshell you dropped during the flyting."

"You mean . . . oh." My stomach curled with embarrassment, like it was trying to hide behind my right lung. In front of my eight closest friends and several thousand enemies, I'd announced how much I'd enjoyed a private kiss from Alex.

Sam chuckled. "She probably won't be _too_ mad. Go. Get it over with."

Easy for Sam to say. She knew exactly where she stood in her relationship with Amir. She was happily engaged and never had to worry about secret kisses under blankets because she was a good Muslim girl and would never do such a thing. I, alas, was not a good Muslim girl.

I walked over to Alex. Blitzen saw me coming, nodded to me nervously, and fled.

"What do you think, Magnus?" Alex spread her arms, showing off her glittering new fashion statement.

"Yeah," I said. "I mean, not many people can pull off the plaid chain mail sweater vest, but yeah."

"It's not plaid," Alex said. "It's more *a cuadros*, like diamonds. Checkered."

"Okay."

"So . . ." She crossed her arms and sighed, examining me like *What are we going to do with you?* It was a look I'd gotten from teachers, coaches, social workers, police, and a few of my closest relatives. "That declaration of yours back on *Naglfar*—that was all very sudden, Magnus."

"I . . . uh. Yeah. I wasn't really thinking."

"Clearly. Where did that even come from?"

"Well, you did kiss me."

"I mean, you can't surprise somebody like that. Suddenly I'm the greatest thing that ever happened to you?"

"I—I didn't exactly say—" I stopped myself. "Look, if you want me to take it back . . ."

I couldn't form a complete thought. And I couldn't see any way to extract myself from this conversation with my dignity intact. I wondered if I was suffering withdrawal symptoms from Kvasir's Mead, paying the price for my successful performance on *Naglfar*.

"I'm going to need some time," Alex said. "I mean, I'm flattered, but this is all so out of the blue. . . ."

"Uh."

"I don't just date any einherji with a pretty face and a nice haircut."

"No. Yeah. Pretty face?"

"I appreciate the offer. Really. But let's put this on hold and I'll get back to you." She held up her hands. "A little space, Chase."

She strode off, glancing back once with a smirk that made my toes curl up in my woolen socks.

Hearthstone appeared at my side, his expression inscrutable as always. His scarf, for reasons unknown, had changed to *a cuadros*, red and white checkers. We watched Alex walking away.

"What just happened?" I asked him.

There are no words for it in sign language, he said.

On our third morning at sea, T.J. called from the halyard, "Hey! Land!"

I thought the expression was *land, ho!* But maybe they did things differently in the Civil War. We all jostled to the prow of the *Big Banana*. A vast flat landscape of red and gold spread across the horizon, as if we were sailing straight toward the Saharan desert.

"That's not Boston," I noted.

"That's not even Midgard." Halfborn frowned. "If our ship followed the currents *Naglfar* would have taken, that means—"

"We're landing at Vigridr," Mallory offered. "The Last Battlefield. This is the place where we'll all die someday."

Strangely, nobody screamed *Turn this boat around!*

We stood transfixed as the *Big Banana* took us in, aiming

for one of a jillion docks that jutted into the surf. At the end of the pier, a group of figures stood waiting—men and women, all resplendent in glittering armor and colorful cloaks. The gods had turned out to welcome us.

FORTY-SIX

I Win a Fluffy Bathrobe

ALONG THE abandoned shore, which was built up with the universe's longest boardwalk, stretched thousands of empty kiosks and miles of stanchions for queuing, with signs pointing this way and that:

JOTUNS →

← AESIR

WILL CALL →

← SCHOOL GROUPS

Our dock featured a large red sign with a stylized bird and a big number five. Underneath, in English and in runes, the sign read: REMEMBER, YOU PARKED AT RAVEN FIVE! HAVE A NICE RAGNAROK! I supposed our parking situation could have been worse. We could've docked at Bunny Rabbit Twelve or Ferret One.

I recognized many of the gods in our greeting party. Frigg stood in her cloud-white dress and glowing war helm, her bag of knitting supplies under one arm. She smiled kindly at Mallory. "My daughter, I knew you would succeed!"

I wasn't sure if she meant that in an I-could-tell-your-future way or an I-had-faith-in-you way, but I thought it was nice of her to say regardless.

Heimdall, the guardian of the Rainbow Bridge, grinned at me, his stark white eyes like frozen milk. "I saw you coming from five miles away, Magnus! That yellow boat. *WOW*."

Thor looked like he'd just woken up. His red hair was flat on one side, his face creased with pillow marks. His hammer, Mjolnir, hung at his belt, attached to his breeches with a bike chain. He scratched his hairy abs under his Metallica T-shirt and farted amiably. "I hear you insulted Loki into a little two-inch-tall man? Good work!"

His wife, Sif, with the flowing golden hair, rushed to embrace Alex Fierro. "My dear, you look *lovely*. Is that a new sweater vest?"

A big man I'd never seen before, with dark skin, a glistening bald scalp, and black leather armor, offered his left hand to Thomas Jefferson Jr. The god's right hand was missing, the wrist covered in a gold cap. "My son. You've done well."

T.J.'s mouth fell open. "Dad?"

"Take my hand."

"I—"

"I challenge you to take my hand," the god Tyr amended.

"I accept!" T.J. said, and let himself be hauled onto the dock.

Odin was wearing a three-piece suit in charcoal gray chain mail that I guessed was custom-made by Blitzen himself. The All-Father's beard was neatly trimmed. His eye patch gleamed like stainless steel. His ravens, Thought and Memory, perched on his shoulders, their black feathers complementing his jacket beautifully.

"Hearthstone," he said. "Well done with the rune magic,

lad. Those visualization tricks I taught you must have really paid off!"

Hearth smiled weakly.

From the back of the crowd, two other gods pushed forward. I'd never seen them together before, but now it was obvious how alike the twin brother and sister were. Freya, goddess of love and wealth, shone in her golden gown, the scent of roses wafting around her. "Oh, Blitzen, my beautiful boy!"

She cried red-gold tears, shedding about forty thousand dollars' worth all over the dock as she embraced her son.

Next to her stood my dad, Frey, god of summer. In his battered jeans, flannel shirt, and boots, his blond hair and beard wild and unkempt, he looked like he'd just come back from a three-day hike.

"Magnus," he said, as if we'd just seen each other five minutes ago.

"Hey, Dad."

He reached over hesitantly and patted my arm. "Good job. Really."

In runestone form, Jack buzzed and tugged until I let him off my neck chain. He expanded into sword form, glowing purple with irritation. "Hi, Jack," he said, mimicking Frey's deep voice. "How you doing, Jack, old buddy?"

Frey winced. "Hello, Sumarbrander. I didn't mean to ignore you."

"Yeah, yeah. Well, *Magnus* here is going to get *Bragi* to write an epic poem about me!"

Frey raised an eyebrow. "You are?"

"Uh—"

"That's right!" Jack huffed. *"Frey* never got Bragi to write an epic poem about me! The only thing *he* ever gave me was a stupid Hallmark Sword's Day card."

Added to my mental notes: there was such a thing as Sword's Day. I silently cursed the greeting-card industry.

My father smiled, a little sadly. "You're right, Jack. A good sword deserves a good friend." Frey squeezed my shoulder. "And it looks like you've found one."

I appreciated the heartwarming sentiment. On the other hand, I was afraid my dad had just turned my rash promise about finding Bragi into a divinely ordained decree.

"Friends!" Odin called. "Let us retire to our feasting tent on the field of Vigridr! I have reserved tent Lindworm Seven! That's Lindworm Seven. If you get lost, follow the mauve arrows. Once there"—his expression turned brooding—"we will discuss the fate of all living things."

I'm telling you, you can't even get a meal with these gods without discussing the fate of all living things.

The feast tent was set up in the middle of the field of Vigridr, which was a long way from the docks, since (according to Samirah) Vigridr stretched three hundred miles in every direction. Fortunately, Odin had arranged for a small fleet of golf carts.

The landscape was mostly grasslands of red and gold, with the occasional river, hill, and stand of trees, just for variety. The pavilion itself was made of cured leather, the sides open, the main hearth blazing, and the tables laden with food. It made me think of pictures I'd seen from old travel magazines, of people having luxury safari banquets on the African savannah. My mom used to love travel magazines.

The gods sat at the thanes' table, as one might expect. Valkyries hurried around serving everyone, though they got distracted when they saw Samirah and came over to give her hugs and gossip.

Once everyone was settled and the mead was poured, Odin pronounced in a grave voice: "Bring forth the walnut!"

Mallory rose. With a quick glance at Frigg, who nodded encouragement, Mallory walked to a freestanding stone pedestal in front of the hearth. She set down the walnut then returned to her seat.

The gods all leaned forward. Thor glowered. Tyr laced his left-hand fingers with the nonexistent digits on his right hand. Frey stroked his blond beard.

Freya pouted. "I don't like walnuts, even if they *are* a great source of omega-three fatty acids."

"This walnut has no nutritional value, sister," Frey said. "It holds Loki."

"Yes, I know." She frowned. "I was just saying, in general . . ."

"Is Loki quite secure?" Tyr asked. "He won't pop out and challenge me to personal combat?"

The god sounded wistful, as if he'd been dreaming about that possibility.

"The walnut will hold him," Frigg said. "At least until we return him to his chains."

"Bah!" Thor raised his hammer. "I say I should just smash him right now! Save us all a lot of trouble."

"Honey," said Sif, "we've talked about this."

"Indeed," said Odin, his ravens squawking on the high back of his throne. "My noble son Thor, we've been over this approximately eight thousand six hundred and thirty times. I'm not sure you're using strategies for active listening. We cannot change our foretold destinies."

Thor huffed. "Well, what's the use of being a god, then? I've got a perfectly good hammer and this nut is just begging to be cracked! Why not CRACK it?"

That sounded like a pretty reasonable plan to me, but I didn't say so. I was not in the habit of disagreeing with Odin the All-Father, who controlled my afterlife and my minibar privileges at the Hotel Valhalla.

"Maybe . . ." I said, self-conscious as all eyes turned toward me. "I dunno. . . . We could come up with a more secure place to keep him, at least? Like—I'm just thinking aloud here—a maximum-security prison with actual guards? And chains that aren't made from the intestines of his sons? Or, you know, we could just avoid the intestine thing altogether. . . ."

Odin chuckled, like I was a puppy that had learned a new trick. "Magnus Chase, you and your friends have acted bravely and nobly. Now you must leave matters to the gods. We cannot change Loki's punishment in any meaningful way. We can only restore it to what it was, so that the great sequence of events leading to Ragnarok will be held in check. At least for now."

"Hmph." Thor quaffed his mead. "We keep delaying Ragnarok. Why not just get it over with? I could use a good fight!"

"Well, my son," said Frigg, "we are delaying Ragnarok

because it will destroy the cosmos as we know it, and because most of us will die. You included."

"Besides," Heimdall added, "we *just* now got the ability to take quality selfies on our cell phones. Can you imagine how much better the tech will be in a few more centuries? I can't wait to VR-stream the apocalypse to my millions of followers on the cyber-cloud!"

With a pensive expression, Tyr pointed to a nearby copse of golden trees. "I will die right over there . . . killed by Garm, the guard dog of Hel, but not before I smite his head in. I can't wait for that day. I dream of Garm's fangs ripping into my stomach."

Thor nodded sympathetically, like *Yes, good times!*

I scanned the horizon. I, too, was destined to die here at Ragnarok, assuming I didn't get killed in some danger-ous quest before then. I didn't know the exact location, but we might be having lunch in the very spot where I would be impaled, or Halfborn would fall with a sword in his gut, or Alex . . . I couldn't think about it. Suddenly I wanted to be anywhere but here.

Samirah coughed for attention. "Lord Odin," she said, "what *are* your plans for Loki, then, since his original bonds were cut?"

Odin smiled. "Not to worry, my brave Valkyrie. Loki will be returned to the cave of punishment. We will put new enchantments upon the place to hide its location and prevent further breaches. We will reforge his bonds, making sure they are stronger than ever. The best dwarven smiths have agreed to undertake this task."

"The *best* dwarven smiths?" Blitz asked.

Heimdall nodded enthusiastically. "We got a package deal on all four bindings from Eitri Junior!"

Blitz started to curse, but Hearthstone clamped a hand over his friend's mouth. I thought for sure Blitzen would get up and start throwing expand-o-ducks in a fit of rage.

"I see . . ." said Samirah, clearly not excited about Odin's plan.

"What about Sigyn?" I asked. "Will you let her stay by Loki's side again, if she wants?"

Odin frowned. "I had not considered this."

"It wouldn't do any harm," I said quickly. "She . . . she means well, I think. I'm pretty sure she didn't want him to escape in the first place."

The gods muttered among themselves.

Alex gave me a questioning look, no doubt wondering why I cared so much about the wife of Loki. I wasn't sure myself why I felt it was important. If Sigyn wanted to be by Loki's side, whether it was for compassion or some other reason, I figured it was the least the gods could do for her. Especially considering they'd murdered her kids and used the guts as chains for their dad.

I remembered what Loki had told me about good and evil, gods and giants. He had a point. I wasn't necessarily sitting with the good guys. I was just sitting with one side of the final war.

"Very well," Odin decided. "Sigyn may stay with Loki if she wishes. Any other questions about Loki's punishment?"

I could tell that a lot of my friends wanted to stand up and say *Yes. ARE YOU CRAZY?*

But no one did. None of the gods raised objections or pulled out weapons.

"I must say," Freya noted, "this is the best godly meeting we've had in centuries." She smiled at me. "We try to avoid having too many of us together in one place. It usually leads to trouble."

"The last time was the flyting with Loki," Thor grumbled. "In Aegir's hall."

I didn't like being reminded of Aegir, but it made me remember a promise. "Lord Odin, I—I was supposed to bring Aegir a sample of Kvasir's Mead, as payment for him sort of not killing us and sort of letting us go, but—"

"Never fear, Magnus Chase. I will speak with Aegir on your behalf. I may even grant him a small sample of Kvasir's Mead from my special reserve supply, assuming he'll put me on the list for his Pumpkin Spice."

"And me," Thor said.

"And me," said the other gods, raising their hands.

I blinked. "You . . . have a special reserve supply of Kvasir's Mead?"

"Of course!" said Odin.

This raised some interesting questions, such as why had the gods made us run all around creation risking our lives to get that mead from the giants when Odin could have just handed me some? That simple solution probably hadn't even occurred to Odin. He was a leader, not a sharer.

My father caught my eye. He shook his head like *Don't ask. Aesir are weird.*

"Well, then!" Odin pounded his fist on the table. "I agree with Freya. This meeting has gone surprisingly well. We will take the walnut. We will send you heroes back to Valhalla to enjoy a great feast in your honor. Any other business before we adjourn?"

"Lord Odin," Frey said. "My son and his friends have done us a great service. Shouldn't we . . . reward them? Isn't that customary?"

"Hmm." Odin nodded. "I suppose you're right. I could make them all einherjar in Valhalla! But, ah, most of them already are."

"And the rest of us," Sam added quickly, "would like to stay alive a little longer, Lord Odin, if you don't mind."

"Well, there you are!" Odin said. "As a reward, our living heroes will get to stay alive! I'll also give you each five auto-graphed copies of my new book, *Motivational Heroism.* As for the einherjar, in addition to the celebratory feast and the books, I'll throw in a complimentary Hotel Valhalla Turkish bathrobe for each of you! Eh?"

Odin seemed so pleased with himself, none of us had the heart to complain. We just nodded and smiled halfheartedly.

"Hmm, Turkish bathrobe," T.J. said.

"Hmm, staying alive," Blitz said.

Nobody mentioned the autographed motivational books.

"Finally, Magnus Chase," said the All-Father, "I understand *you* were the one who stood toe-to-toe with Loki and took the brunt of his withering insults. Would you ask any special boon of the gods?"

I gulped. I looked around at my friends, trying to let them know that I didn't find it fair for me to get special treat-ment. Defeating Loki had been a group effort. That was the whole point. Waxing poetic about our *team* was what got Loki trapped, not my skill itself.

Besides, I didn't keep a list of boons in my back pocket. I was a man of few needs. I was happy being boonless.

Then I recalled my Uncle Randolph's last act of atonement, trying to steer me toward Kvasir's Mead. I thought about how sad and lonely his house seemed now, and how happy and peaceful I'd felt on the roof deck with Alex Fierro. I even remembered a bit of advice Andvari's ring had whispered in my mind, right before I'd given the golden treasure back to the fish.

Othala. Inheritance. The hardest rune of all to make sense of.

"Actually, Lord Odin," I said, "there *is* one favor I would ask."

FORTY-SEVEN

Surprises All Around, Some of Them Even Good

YOUR TYPICAL trip back home.

Golf-cart rides, trying to remember where we parked our warship, sailing into the treacherous mouth of an unknown river, getting sucked into rapids that shot us into the tunnels underneath Valhalla, jumping off a moving ship and watching the *Big Banana* disappear into the darkness, no doubt on its way to pick up the next lucky group of adventurers bound for glory, death, and Ragnarok-postponing shenanigans.

The other einherjar welcomed us as heroes and carried us to the feast hall for a big celebration. There we found that Helgi had arranged a special surprise for Samirah, thanks to a tip-off from Odin himself. Standing by our regular table, looking very confused, wearing a name tag around his neck that proclaimed VISITOR. MORTAL! DO NOT KILL! was Amir Fadlan.

He blinked several times when he saw Sam. "I—I am so confused. Are you real?"

Samirah tented her hands over her face. Her eyes teared up. "Oh. I'm real. I so want to hug you right now."

Alex gestured at the crowds pouring in for dinner. "You'd better not. Since we're all your extended family here, you've got several thousand heavily armed male chaperones present."

I realized Alex was including himself in that group. At

some point during the voyage home, he had shifted to male.

"This is . . ." Amir looked around in wonder. "Sam, this is where you *work*?"

Samirah made a sound somewhere between a laugh and a joyful sob. "Yes, my love. Yes, it is. And it's Eid al-Fitr, isn't it?"

Amir nodded. "Our families are planning dinner together tonight. Right now. I didn't know if you would be free to—"

"Yes!" Samirah turned to me. "Would you give my apologies to the thanes?"

"No apologies necessary," I assured her. "Does this mean Ramadan is over?"

"Yes!"

I grinned. "Sometime this week, I am taking you out for lunch. We're going to eat in the sunlight and laugh and laugh."

"Deal!" She spread her arms. "Air hug."

"Air hug," I agreed.

Alex smirked. "Looks like they'll need me for chaperone duty, if you all will excuse me."

I didn't want to excuse him, but I didn't have much choice. Sam, Amir, and Alex rushed off to celebrate Eid and eat massive quantities of tasty food.

For the rest of us, the evening was all about drinking mead, getting patted on the back a few thousand times, and hearing the thanes give speeches about how great we were, even if the quality of heroes was *much* better back in their day. Above, in the branches of the Tree of Laeradr, squirrels and wombats and tiny deer ran around as usual. Valkyries zipped here and there serving food and mead.

Toward the end of the feast, Thomas Jefferson Jr. tried to teach us some of his old marching songs from the Fifty-Fourth

Massachusetts. Halfborn Gunderson and Mallory Keen alternately threw plates at each other and rolled around in the aisles, kissing, while the other Vikings laughed at them. It made my heart glad to see them together again . . . though it also made me feel a little empty.

Blitzen and Hearthstone had become such fixtures in Valhalla that Helgi announced they were being made honorary hotel guests, free to come and go as they pleased, though he made a point to say they did not have rooms, or minibar keys, or any sort of immortality, so they should act accordingly and avoid flying projectiles. Blitz and Hearth were given large helmets that said HONORARY EINHERJI, which they didn't look too happy about.

As the party was breaking up, Blitzen clapped me on the back, which was sore from all the other clapping that my back had received that night. "We're heading out, kid. Gotta get some sleep."

"You guys sure?" I asked. "Everybody is heading to the after-party. We're doing a tug-of-war over a lake of chocolate."

Sounds fun, Hearthstone signed. *But we will see you tomorrow. Yes?*

I knew what he was asking: Was I really serious about following through with my plan—the favor I'd asked Odin?

"Yeah," I promised. "Tomorrow it is."

Blitz grinned. "You're a good man, Magnus. This is going to be awesome!"

The tug-of-war was fun, though our side lost. I think that's because Hunding was our anchor and he wanted to bathe in chocolate.

At the end of the night, exhausted, happy, and doused

in Hershey's syrup, I staggered back to my room. As I passed Alex Fierro's door, I stopped for a moment and listened, but I heard nothing. He was probably still out enjoying Eid al-Fitr with Sam and Amir. I hoped they were having a great celebration. They'd earned it.

I stumbled into my room. I stood in the foyer, dripping chocolate all over the carpet. Luckily, the hotel had great magical clean-up service. I remembered the first time I'd entered this room, the day I died falling off the Longfellow Bridge. I had stared in wonder at all the amenities—the kitchen, the library, the couch and big-screen TV, the big atrium with the starry night sky twinkling through the tree branches.

Now there were more photos on the mantel. One or two magically appeared every week. Some were old pictures of my family: my mom, Annabeth, even Uncle Randolph and his kids and wife during happier times. But there were also newer pictures—me with my friends from floor nineteen, a photo I'd taken with Blitz and Hearth when we were still homeless. We'd borrowed somebody's camera to do a group selfie. How the Hotel Valhalla had retrieved that shot from the ether, I didn't know. Maybe Heimdall kept a cloud library of all selfies ever taken.

For the first time, I realized that walking into this room felt like coming home. I might not live at the hotel forever. In fact, I'd just had lunch that afternoon at the place where I would probably die someday. Still . . . this felt like a good place to hang my sword.

Speaking of which . . . I took off my neck chain, careful not to wake up Jack, and set his runestone pendant on the coffee table. He hummed contentedly in his sleep, probably dreaming of Percy's sword Riptide and all the other weapons he had loved. I wasn't sure how I was going to locate the god Bragi and get him to write an epic about Jack, but that was a problem for another day.

I'd just pulled off my sticky chocolate-soaked shirt when a voice behind me said, "You might want to close the door before you start changing."

I turned.

Alex leaned against the door frame, his arms crossed over his chain mail sweater vest, his pink glasses low on his nose. He shook his head in disbelief. "Did you lose a mud-wrestling contest?"

"Uh." I looked down. "It's chocolate."

"Okay. I'm not going to ask."

"How was Eid?"

Alex shrugged. "Fine, I guess. A lot of happy people partying. Lots of food and music. Relatives hugging each other. Not really my scene."

"Right."

"I left Sam and Amir in good company with their whole families. They looked . . . Happy doesn't cover it. Delighted? Ecstatic?"

"Head over heels?" I suggested. "Over the moon?"

Alex met my eyes. "Yeah. That works."

Drip. Drip. Chocolate dribbled from my fingertips in a completely suave and attractive way.

"So, anyway," Alex said. "I was thinking about your proposal."

My throat constricted. I wondered if I had a chocolate

allergy I didn't know about, and I was dying in a new and interesting manner.

"My what?" I squeaked.

"About the mansion," he clarified. "What did you *think* I meant?"

"No, of course. The proposal about the mansion. Absolutely."

"I guess I'm in," he said. "When do we start?"

"Uh, great! Tomorrow we can do the initial walk-through. I'll get the keys. Then we wait for the lawyers to do their thing. Maybe a couple of weeks?"

"Perfect. Now go take a shower. You're disgusting. I'll see you at breakfast."

"Okay."

He turned to leave, then hesitated. "One more thing."

He walked up to me. "I've also been thinking about your declaration of undying love or whatever."

"I didn't—it wasn't—"

He clamped his hands on the sides of my gooey face and kissed me.

I had to wonder: Was it possible to dissolve into chocolate on a molecular level and melt into a puddle on the carpet? Because that's how I felt. I'm pretty sure Valhalla had to resurrect me several times during the course of that kiss. Otherwise, I don't know how I was still in one piece when Alex finally pulled away.

He studied me critically, his brown and amber eyes taking me in. He had a chocolate mustache and goatee now, and chocolate down the front of his sweater vest.

I'll be honest. A small part of my brain thought, *Alex is male right now. I have just been kissed by a dude. How do I feel about that?*

The rest of my brain answered: *I have just been kissed by Alex Fierro. I am absolutely great with that.*

In fact, I might have done something typically embarrassing and stupid, like making the aforementioned declaration of undying love, but Alex spared me.

"Eh." He shrugged. "I'll keep thinking about it. I'll get back to you. In the meantime, definitely take that shower."

He left, whistling a tune that might have been a Frank Sinatra song from the elevator, "Fly Me to the Moon."

I'm great at following orders. I went to take a shower.

FORTY-EIGHT

The Chase Space Becomes a Place

ODIN'S LAWYERS were good.

In two weeks, all the paperwork was done. Odin had to wrangle with various Boston zoning commissions, the mayor's office, and several neighborhood associations, but he'd cleared those hurdles in record time, as only a god with infinite money and a background in motivational speaking could. Uncle Randolph's will had been fully executed. Annabeth had cheerfully signed off.

"I think this is *awesome*, Magnus," she said on the phone from California. "You are amazing. I—I kind of needed some good news right now."

That set my ears buzzing. Why did Annabeth sound like she'd been crying?

"You okay, cuz?"

She paused for a long time. "I will be. We . . . we got some bad news when we got out here."

I waited. She didn't elaborate. I didn't push. She would tell me if and when she wanted to. Still, I wished I could pull her through the phone and give her a hug. Now that she was on the other coast, I wondered when I would see her again. Did einherjar ever make it out to the West Coast? I'd have to ask Samirah.

"Percy okay?" I asked.

"Yeah, he's fine," she said. "Well . . . as fine as can be expected."

I heard his muffled voice in the background.

"He wants to know if any of his advice helped you on the sea voyage," Annabeth relayed.

"Absolutely," I said. "Tell him I kept my butt clenched the entire trip, just like he said."

That got a broken laugh. "I'll tell him."

"Take care of yourself."

She drew a shaky breath. "I will. You, too. We'll talk more next time I see you."

That gave me hope. There would be a next time. Whatever was going on in my cousin's life, whatever bad news she was dealing with, at least my friends and I had won her and Percy a reprieve from Ragnarok. I hoped they would have a chance at happiness.

I said my good-byes and got back to work.

In two more weeks, the Chase Mansion was open for business.

Our first guests moved in on July Fourth, Independence Day. It had taken Alex and me several days to convince them that our offer was serious and not some sort of scam.

We know where you're at, Alex told these kids. *We've been homeless, too. You can stay for as long or as little time as you want. No judgment. No expectations. Just mutual respect, okay?*

They came in, wide-eyed and shaking with hunger, and they stayed. We didn't advertise our presence in the neighborhood. We didn't make a big deal out of it. We certainly didn't rub it in the neighbors' faces. But in the legal documents, the mansion was called the Chase Space, a residence for homeless youth.

Blitzen and Hearthstone moved in. They served as cooks, tailors, and life advisors for the kids. Hearth taught them sign language. Blitz let the kids work in his shop, Blitzen's Best, which was right down the street and had reopened just in time for the high shopping season.

Alex and I went back and forth between Valhalla and the mansion, helping out, recruiting new kids. Some stayed a long time. Some didn't. Some only wanted a sandwich or pocket money or a bed for the night. They disappeared the next morning. That was okay. No judgment.

Occasionally, I'd pass one of the bedrooms and find Alex with her arm around some new kid who was crying his or her eyes out for the first time in years; Alex just being there, listening, understanding.

She'd look up, then motion with her head for me to keep moving, like *Give me some space, Chase.*

That first day we were open, the Fourth of July, we had a party for our guests on the roof deck. Blitzen and Hearthstone grilled hamburgers and hot dogs. The kids hung out with us, watching the fireworks explode over the Hatch Shell on the Esplanade, lights crackling through the low clouds and washing the Back Bay brownstones in red and blue.

Alex and I reclined next to each other in the lounge chairs, where we'd sat after killing the wolf in Randolph's library weeks before.

She reached over and took my hand.

She hadn't done that since we were marching invisibly toward the Ship of the Dead. I didn't question the gesture. I didn't take it for granted. I decided just to enjoy it. You have to do that with Alex. She is all about change. Moments don't last. You've got to enjoy each one for what it is.

"This is good," she said.

I didn't know if she meant what we'd accomplished with Chase Space, or the fireworks, or holding hands, but I agreed. "Yeah. It is."

I thought about what might come next. Our jobs as einherjar were never over. Until Ragnarok, we would always have more quests to undertake, more battles to fight. And I still had to find the god Bragi and convince him to write Jack his epic.

Also, I'd learned enough about othala to know that your inheritance never leaves you alone. Just as Hearthstone had had to revisit Alfheim, I had difficult things still to deal with. Chief among them: that dark road to Helheim, the voices of my dead relatives, my mom calling to me. Hel had promised that I would see my mom again someday. Loki had threatened that the spirits of my family would suffer for what I had done to him. Eventually, I would have to seek out the frozen land of the dead and see for myself.

But for now, we had fireworks. We had our friends, new and old. I had Alex Fierro next to me, holding my hand.

It might stop at any moment. We einherjar know we are destined to die. The world *will* end. The big picture cannot be changed. But in the meantime, as Loki once said, we can choose to alter the details. That's how we take control of our destiny.

Sometimes, even Loki can be right.

GLOSSARY

AEGIR—lord of the waves

AESIR—gods of war, close to humans

ALLAHU AKBAR—God is greater

ARGR—Norse for *unmanly*

BALDER—an Aesir god, son of Odin and Frigg, brother of many, including Thor; he was so handsome, gracious, and cheerful that he gave off light

BERSERKER—a Norse warrior frenzied in battle and considered invulnerable

BIFROST—the rainbow bridge leading from Asgard to Midgard

BOLVERK—an alias used by Odin

BRAGI—god of poetry

BRUNNMIGI—a being who urinates into wells

CAILLEACH—Gaelic for *witch* or *hag*

DRAUGR—Norse zombies

EID AL-FITR—a holiday celebrated by Muslims to mark the end of Ramadan

EINHERJAR (EINHERJI, sing.)—great heroes who have died with bravery on Earth; soldiers in Odin's eternal army; they train in Valhalla for Ragnarok, when the bravest of them will join Odin against Loki and the giants in the battle at the end of the world

EINVIGI—Norse for *single combat*

ELDHUSFIFL—Norse for *village idiot*

FARBAUTI—the jotun husband of Laufey and father of Loki

FENRIS WOLF—an invulnerable wolf born of Loki's affair with a giantess; his mighty strength strikes fear even in the gods, who keep him tied to a rock on an island. He is destined to break free on the day of Ragnarok.

FLYTING—a verbal duel of insults, in which the contestants must display prestige, power, and confidence

FREY—the god of spring and summer; the sun, the rain, and the harvest; abundance and fertility; growth and vitality. Frey is the twin brother of Freya and, like his sister, is associated with great beauty. He is lord of Alfheim.

FREYA—the goddess of love; twin sister of Frey

FRIGG—goddess of marriage and motherhood; Odin's wife and the queen of Asgard; mother of Balder and Hod

GARM—the guard dog of Hel

GINNUNGAGAP—the primordial void; a mist that obscures appearances

GJALLAR—Heimdall's horn

GLAMOUR—illusion magic

GROVE OF GLASIR—trees in the realm of Asgard, outside the doors of Valhalla, with golden red leaves. *Glasir* means *gleaming.*

HALAL—meat prepared as required by Muslim law

HEIMDALL—god of vigilance and the guardian of Bifrost, the gateway to Asgard

HEL—goddess of the dishonorable dead; born of Loki's affair with a giantess

HELHEIM—the underworld, ruled by Hel and inhabited by those who died in wickedness, old age, or illness

HRUNGNIR—brawler

HUGINN AND MUNINN—Odin's ravens, whose names mean *thought* and *memory*, respectively

HULDER—a domesticated forest sprite

IDUN—a beautiful goddess of youth, who supplies the other gods and goddesses with apples of immortality

INSHALLAH—God willing

JORMUNGAND—the World Serpent, born of Loki's affair with a giantess; his body is so long it wraps around the earth

JOTUN—giant

KENAZ—the torch, the fire of life

KONUNGSGURTHA—Norse for *king's court*

KVASIR—a man created from the spit of the Aesir and Vanir gods, to represent the peace treaty between them after their war

KVASIR'S MEAD—a drink that grants the gift of oration, created from a combination of Kvasir's blood and honey

LAUFEY—the jotun wife of Farbauti and mother of Loki

LINDWORM—a fearsome dragon the size and length of an eighteen-wheeler, with just two front legs and leathery brown bat-type wings too small for effective flight

LOKI—god of mischief, magic, and artifice; the son of two giants, Farbauti and Laufey; adept with magic and shape-shifting. He is alternatively malicious and heroic to the Asgardian gods and to humankind. Because of his role in the death of Balder, Loki was chained by Odin to three giant boulders with a poisonous serpent coiled over his head. The venom of the snake occasionally irritates Loki's face, and his writhing can cause earthquakes.

MAGHRIB PRAYER—the fourth of five formal daily prayers performed by practicing Muslims, prayed just after sunset

MEINFRETR—stinkfart

MIKILLGULR—Norse for *big yellow*

MIMIR—an Aesir god who, along with Honir, traded places with Vanir gods Frey and Njord at the end of the war between the Aesir and the Vanir. When the Vanir didn't like his counsel, they cut off his head and sent it to Odin. Odin placed the head in a magical well, where the water brought it back to life, and Mimir soaked up all the knowledge of the World Tree.

MINIÉ BALL—a type of bullet used in muzzle-loading rifles during the Civil War

MJÖÐ—Norse for *mead*

MJOLNIR—Thor's hammer

NAGLFAR—the Ship of Nails

NJORD—Vanir god of the sea, father of Frey and Freya

NØKK—a nixie, or water spirit

NORNS—three sisters who control the destinies of both gods and humans.

ODIN—the "All-Father" and king of the gods; the god of war and death, but also poetry and wisdom. By trading one eye for a drink from the Well of Wisdom, Odin gained unparalleled knowledge. He has the ability to observe all the Nine Worlds from his throne in Asgard; in addition to his great hall, he also resides in Valhalla with the bravest of those slain in battle.

OTHALA—inheritance

QURANIC—something relating or belonging to the Quran, the central religious text of Islam

RAGNAROK—the Day of Doom or Judgment, when the bravest

of the einherjar will join Odin against Loki and the giants in the battle at the end of the world

RAMADAN—a time for spiritual purification achieved through fasting, self-sacrifice, and prayers, celebrated in the ninth month of the Islamic calendar

RAN—goddess of the sea; wife of Aegir

RED GOLD—the currency of Asgard and Valhalla

SIF—goddess of the earth; mother of Uller by her first husband; Thor is her second husband; the rowan is her sacred tree

SIGYN—Loki's wife

SKADI—an ice giantess once married to Njord

SKALDS—poets who composed at the courts of leaders during the Viking Age

SLEIPNIR—Odin's eight-legged steed; only Odin can summon him; one of Loki's children

SUHUR—the pre-dawn meal eaten by practicing Muslims during Ramadan

SUMARBRANDER—the Sword of Summer

THANE—a lord of Valhalla

THOR—god of thunder; son of Odin. Thunderstorms are the earthly effects of Thor's mighty chariot rides across the sky, and lightning is caused by hurling his great hammer, Mjolnir.

THRALL—a slave, servant, or captive

THRYM—king of the jotun

THRYMHEIMR—Thunder Home

TREE OF LAERADR—a tree in the center of the Feast Hall of the Slain in Valhalla containing immortal animals that have particular jobs

TVEIRVIGI—double combat

TYR—god of courage, law, and trial by combat; he lost a hand to Fenris's bite when the Wolf was restrained by the gods

UTGARD-LOKI—the most powerful sorcerer of Jotunheim; king of the mountain giants

VALHALLA—paradise for warriors in the service of Odin

VALKYRIE—Odin's handmaidens who choose slain heroes to bring to Valhalla

VANIR—gods of nature; close to elves

VATNAVAETTIR (*each-uisce* in Ireland)—water horses

VIGRIDR—a plain that will be the site of the battle between the gods and Surt's forces during Ragnarok

VILI AND VE—the two younger brothers of Odin, who, together with him, shared a role in the shaping of the cosmos and are the first of the Aesir. When Odin was abroad for a long time, Vili and Ve ruled in his stead, alongside Frigg.

WERGILD—blood debt

WYRD—fate

YMIR—the ancestor of all gods and jotun

PRONUNCIATION GUIDE

AEGIR	*AY-gear*
AESIR	*AY-ser*
ALF SEIDR	*ALF SAY-der*
ALFHEIM	*ALF-haym*
ARGR	*ARR-ger*
ASGARD	*AZ-gahrrd*
BALDER	*BALL-der*
BAUGI	*BAW-ghee*
BIFROST	*BEE-frrohst*
BLODUGHADDA	*BLODE-oug-hadda*
BOLVERK	*BOLE-verrk*
BRAGI	*BRRAG-ee*
BYLGYA	*BOOL-ghooa*
CAILLEACH	*KAL-ee-yucck*
DAGAZ	*DAH-gahz*
DRAUGR	*DRRAW-ger*
DUFA	*DOO-vah*
EHWAZ	*AY-wahz*
EINHERJAR/EINHERJI	*in-HAIRR-yar/in-HAIRR-yee*
EINVIGI	*AYN-vee-gee*
ELDHUSFIFL	*EL-doos-feef-full*
ELDIR	*el-DEER*
FARBAUTI	*fahrr-BAW-tee*
FEHU	*FAY-hoo*
FENRIS	*FEHN-rrihss*
FIMAFENG	*FEE-ma-vehng*
FJALAR	*fee-YALL-ar*
FLÄM	*FLAHM*
FREY	*FRRAY*

FREYA	*FRRAY-uh*
FRIGG	*FRRIHG*
GARM	*GAHRRM*
GINNUNGAGAP	*GEEN-un-guh-gahp*
GJALAR	*gee-YALL-ar*
GJALLAR	*gee-YALL-ar*
GLASIR	*gla-SEER*
GUNLOD	*GOON-lode*
HAGALAZ	*HA-ga-lahts*
HEFRING	*HEV-rring*
HEIMDALL	*HAME-doll*
HEL	*HEHL*
HELGI	*HEL-ghee*
HELHEIM	*HEHL-haym*
HIMMINGLAEVA	*HEEM-meen-glah-vah*
HRÖNN	*HRRONE*
HRYM	*HRRIM*
HUGINN	*HOO-gihn*
HULDER	*HOOL-dihr*
HUNDING	*HOON-deeng*
HRUNGNIR	*HRROONG-neer*
HUSVAETTR	*HOOS-veht-tr*
IDUN	*ee-DOON*
ISA	*EES-ah*
JORMUNGAND	*YOHRR-mun-gand*
JORVIK	*YOHRR-vick*
JOTUN	*YOH-toon*
JOTUNHEIM	*YOH-tuhn-haym*
KENAZ	*KEH-nahtz*
KOLGA	*KOLE-gah*
KONUNGSGURTHA	*KO-noongs-goorr-tha*
KVASIR	*ki-VAH-seer*

LAERADR	*LAY-rrah-dur*
LAUFEY	*LAW-fay*
LAGAZ	*lah-GAHTS*
LINDWORM	*LIHND-wohrrm*
LOKI	*LOH-kee*
MEINFRETR	*MAYN-frih-ter*
MIDGARD	*MIHD-gahrrd*
MIKILLGULR	*MEE-keel-goo-ler*
MIMIR	*MEE-meer*
MJÖÐ	*mee-YOTH*
MJOLNIR	*MEE'OHL-neer*
MOKKERKALFE	*MOKE-kerr-kal-feh*
MUNDR	*MOON-der*
MUNINN	*MOON-in*
MUSPELL	*MOO-spel*
MUSPELLHEIM	*MOOS-pehl-haym*
NAGLFAR	*NAHG'L-fahr*
NIDAVELLIR	*Nee-duh-vehl-EER*
NIDHOGG	*NEED-hawg*
NIFLHEIM	*NIHF-uh-haym*
NJORD	*nee-YORD*
NØKK	*NAWK*
NORNS	*NOHRRNZ*
ODIN	*OH-dihn*
OTHALA	*OH-thal-ah*
RAGNAROK	*RAG-nuh-rrawk*
RAN	*RAN*
SAMIRAH AL-ABBAS	*sah-MEER-ah ahl-AH-bahss*
SIF	*SEEV*
SIGYN	*SEE-goon*
SKADI	*SKAH-dee*
SKALD	*SKAHLD*

SLEIPNIR	*SLAYP-neer*
SUMARBRANDER	*SOO-marr-brrand-der*
SUTTUNG	*SOOT-toong*
THIJASSI	*thee-YAH-see*
THOR	*THORE*
THRALL	*THRAWL*
THRYM	*THRRIMM*
THRYMHEIMR	*THRIM-haym-eer*
THRYNGA	*THRRIN-gah*
THURISAZ	*THOORR-ee-sahts*
TIWAZ	*TEE-vahz*
TVEIRVIGI	*tih-VAIR-vee-gee*
TYR	*TEER*
ULLER	*OO-lir*
UNN	*OON*
URNES	*OORR-nis*
URUZ	*OOR-oots*
UTGARD-LOKI	*OOT-gahrrd-LOH-kee*
VALHALLA	*Val-HAHL-uh*
VALKYRIE	*VAL-kerr-ee*
VANAHEIM	*VAN-uh-haym*
VANIR	*Vah-NEER*
VATNAVAETTIR	*vat-na-VAHT-teer*
VE	*VEH*
VIDAR	*VEE-dar*
VIGRIDR	*VEE-gree-der*
VILI	*VEE-lee*
WERGILD	*WIRR-gild*
WIGHT	*WHITE*
WYRD	*WOORD*
YGGDRASIL	*IHG-drruh-sihl*
YMIR	*EE-meer*

THE NINE WORLDS

ASGARD—the home of the Aesir

VANAHEIM—the home of the Vanir

ALFHEIM—the home of the light elves

MIDGARD—the home of humans

JOTUNHEIM—the home of the giants

NIDAVELLIR—the home of the dwarfs

NIFLHEIM—the world of ice, fog, and mist

MUSPELLHEIM—the home of the fire giants and demons

HELHEIM—the home of Hel and the dishonorable dead

RUNES (IN ORDER OF MENTION)

LAGAZ—water, liquefy

ᛚ

FEHU—the rune of Frey

ᚠ

OTHALA—inheritance

ᛟ

GEBO—gift

ᚷ

RAIDHO—traveling

ᚱ

KENAZ—the torch

ᚲ

ISA—ice

ᛁ

EHWAZ—horse, transportation

ᛗ

THURISAZ—the rune of Thor

ᚦ

COMING IN MAY 2018
FROM RICK RIORDAN

THE TRIALS OF APOLLO

◄ 3 ►

THE BURNING MAZE